LEGACY

WARRIORS OF THE DREXIAN ACADEMY

BOOK ONE

xoxo
Tana Stone

USA TODAY BESTSELLING AUTHOR
TANA STONE

LEGACY

THE
ASSASSINS

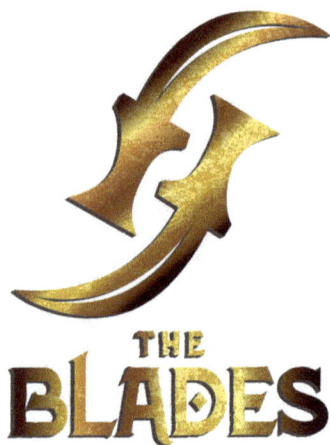

THE
BLADES

THE
IRONS

THE
WINGS

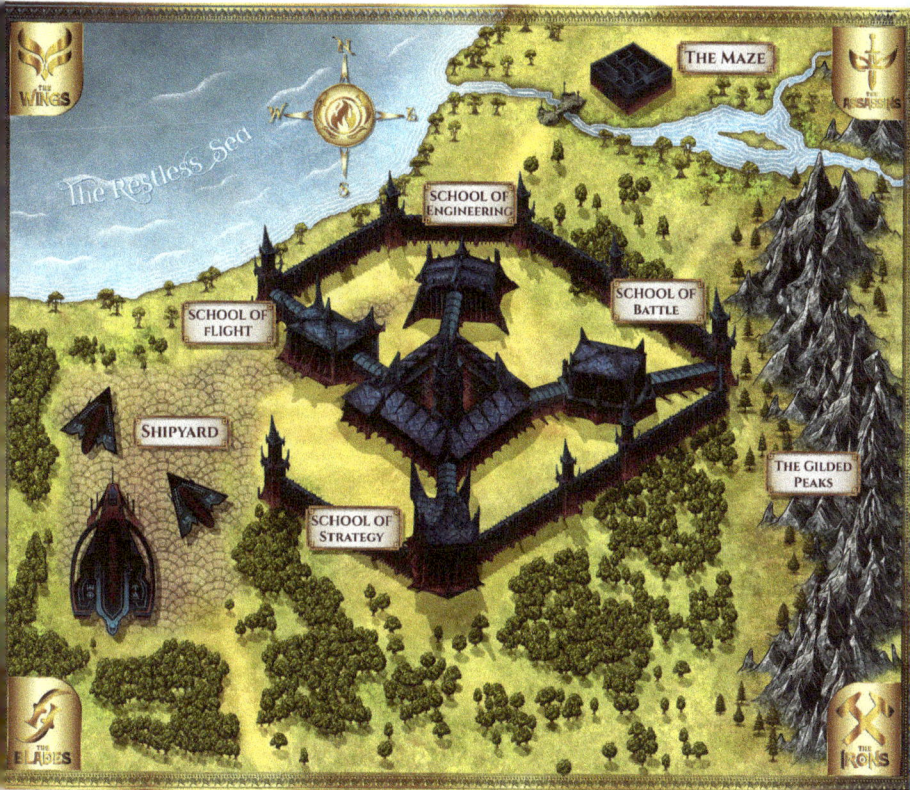

Between Gilded Peaks and the Restless Sea,
Where Assassins prowl and Blades roam,
The Irons hold fast while the Wings take flight,
And heroes are forged from stone.

—taken from *The Verse of the Drex*

THE ASSASSINS

CHAPTER 1

ARIANA

BEWARE OF THE ASSASSINS.

That should have been warning enough. That should have kept me away. That should have made any sane person change their mind.

But I wasn't just anyone, and considering what I was about to do, it was debatable if I was sane.

My stomach lurched again as we completed the final jump through space, the air rippling around me as the sleek black interior of the transport vessel came back into focus. I sucked in a lungful of air to quell my roiling gut and tried to ignore the scent of fuel from firing the jump drive over and over. It was the only way to get us to the Drexian home world without losing several decades, but even the advanced alien technology wasn't without side effects—one of them being making me want to puke all over the ebony floor.

You won't have to worry about the assassins if you don't survive the journey, I told myself with a healthy amount of disdain. A journey I wouldn't be taking if I had any sense.

I closed my eyes, remembering how I'd gotten myself into this mess. I'd been ready for a new assignment. I'd been willing to fly again. But I hadn't expected this.

As I breathed in the cool air of the ship I could almost detect traces of cigarette smoke and dust, my mind playing tricks on me as I remembered standing across from the commander of the Earth Planetary Force.

He'd glanced at me as the ceiling fan had lazily moved the hot, Texas air. "I read the reports of your last mission with the Drexian forces to protect their planet and academy, Lieutenant. Nice flying."

"Thank you, sir."

What wasn't in the report was how close I'd come to being blasted from the sky under the onslaught of the enemy's massive battleships and agile fighters. But I'd taken out more Kronock ships than anyone else, proving that I was still the best pilot in the fleet.

"I've also read the reports from your flight instructors and commanding officers." He'd flipped through a file of papers on his desk, a reminder that he was an old-school guy who despised tablets and digital records. "They all say the last pilot as good as you was…"

My sister, I'd finished the sentence for him, as his voice drifted off and he flipped the file shut. I'd been chasing my older sister since we were girls vying for our father's attention. She was the one person I could never quite catch, never quite beat.

"How would you like to train the next generation of pilots?"

Thoughts of my sister had evaporated as I'd snapped my head to his. "Teach?" I'd thought of my flight instructors and tried to imagine myself as one of them. It would be hard to get a safer posting than the front of a classroom.

"I would like that, sir."

He'd given a gruff nod as if he'd expected that answer. "I can't promise it will be easy. You'll be one of the first female instructors."

One of the first? At least two of my past instructors had been women.

"And there's a lot we don't know about their military training. They've never allowed us in before, and they're secretive about how they operate." He'd grunted. "No surprise there."

My pulse had fluttered. "Where would I be teaching, Commander?"

Not there.

Unease had fluttered in my chest as I thought of the ravaged, craggy planet and the ominous, black castle that was its military academy. I'd hoped to be posted to a base some place warm and sunny, not the harsh alien world.

The commander had leaned back in his chair, and the wheels squeaked in protest. "Your universal translator implant is still functioning?"

I'd moved my head up and down mutely, as my suspicion became dread.

"Good. You'll need it, if you're going to be one of the first females to integrate the Drexian Academy, Lieutenant. The Drexian admiral running the academy has requested our best pilot. I haven't told him that our best is a woman."

I'd kept my shoulders back. It had been tough enough rising to the top as a woman on Earth. As far as I knew, the mostly male Drexian society didn't have *any* females in its military.

Before I could voice my concerns, the commander had cleared his throat loudly. "It won't be easy, but if you can pull this off and pave the way for other women officers to serve in the Drexian forces, I'll make sure you get promoted to commander in charge of your own aviation fleet back here on Earth."

I would outrank my sister. "And if I don't succeed?"

"The Drexians insist on parity in our military exchanges, and the Drexian are tough bastards. Any Drexian who fails here is expelled from their military ranks. If they discharge you from your post at the academy, you will receive a discharge from our military, as well."

A discharge? Trepidation had iced my skin. I could be the first woman to break the barriers in the Drexian Academy—a living legend—or I could be a disgrace. That should have been when I'd declined. That should have been my cue to say no.

The commander eyed me, as if daring me to agree to something so crazy. For the first time, I'd wondered if he was sending me because he believed I was the best or if he was willing to risk me, a woman who'd pushed too many boundaries on Earth for his comfort.

"Do you accept the assignment?"

I'd thought of saying no and asking for another posting, any other posting. But I'd never backed down from a challenge before.

I'd thought of my sister. Sasha wouldn't have turned it down. She would have taken it simply to get the best of me. Not that she could do that now. Not when they'd offered the chance to me.

I'd pushed aside the last remnants of doubt as steely resolve consumed me. "I accept."

There had been no going back then, and there was no turning back now. Not when I was almost at the planet.

I opened my eyes, instantly transported from the hot, stuffy office on Earth to the interior of the transport ship. I snuck a sideways glance at the dark-haired Drexian pilots in the cockpit, hoping they couldn't sense my trepidation. Not that I cared what a couple of Drexians thought about me.

When the alien warrior race had revealed themselves to humans, I hadn't been one of the women swooning over the fact that they seemed to be a taller, harder, jacked-up version of human men. While other women had been signing up to volunteer as one of the tribute brides who would marry the aliens whose species was running short of women of their own, I'd ignored the Drexians.

Until I couldn't. Until I'd been called up to fight with them.

I pulled a folded piece of paper from my jacket pocket, the creases soft and feathered from being refolded so often. My hands trembled as I read the words in my sister's familiar handwriting.

Good luck, little sister. Don't let them push you around, and don't fuck up.

S

Sasha hadn't signed her name. A big, swishy *S* was all she ever signed. She also hadn't bothered with any pep talks or thoughtful advice. I choked on a laugh. 'Don't fuck up' wasn't bad. It was more than I'd ever gotten from my dad. No one in my family was overly sentimental, but for us, this note was gushing.

I refolded the limp paper and tucked it into my pocket, giving it a pat before dropping my hands to my lap. Even though she'd always been my fiercest competitor, I wished Sasha was going with me. I wished I could tell her about my doubts, even though this might have been the least dangerous mission I'd ever been assigned.

It only seems like it isn't dangerous, I reminded myself. And I suspected that when it came to this mission, appearances were deceiving.

Don't cross the Blades.

I curled my hands around my knees and dug my nails into the fabric of my uniform pants as I leaned my head back in the seat and closed my eyes, trying to override the warnings in my head. If my jump count was right, we should be at the Drexian planet soon, not that the prospect of arrival made my stomach any less twitchy.

It was one thing to join a battle in the skies. Flying was what I loved and what I did best. It was another to join the Drexian military academy as part of a human-alien integration decided on by politicians.

"Because forced integration always goes so well," I whispered, before a low, dark laugh escaped my lips and echoed off the ship's walls.

Although humans and Drexians were allies and had been co-mingling and mating for a while, the species had been less than enthusiastic about welcoming us to their planet. I'd learned since accepting the posting that the prospect of us joining their warrior training school had been an even tougher sell, which begged the question why I was currently on route there.

"Because you've never been able to back down from a challenge, you idiot."

I didn't worry about anyone hearing me. Besides the fact that the engine's husky rumble masked most other sounds, I was the only passenger in the rows of seats facing each other behind the pilots. The only one foolish enough to say yes.

That wasn't entirely true. More humans would be joining me, but I was the first military officer from Earth who'd accepted a posting.

Being the first should have made my chest swell. I'd spent my entire life chasing first place and usually getting it. I was valedictorian of my high school. I was first in my flight class. I was first to lead my squadron into battle. Now I would be the first human instructor in their academy. Even my father couldn't deny my achievements after this.

Trust the Irons.

Huffing out a breath as if purging myself of the treacherous thoughts gathering restlessly in the recesses of my mind, I did what I always did to distract myself. I repeated facts, just like I'd repeated instrument functions to myself over and over when I'd first learned to fly.

"The Drexian Warrior Academy was established millennia ago to train cadets in engineering, strategy, battle, and eventually flight." Despite the reputation of the alien school, I'd been able to find little about it, and what I had found had only made me more curious. "Four schools. Four rules."

The ship's engines shifted, and I opened my eyes. We were in our descent. There were no windows or view screens in the compact seating area, but I didn't need to look out to know what the Drexian world looked like upon approach. I'd seen plenty of it when I'd been defending it from the air.

Everything on the world seemed as hard and tough as the aliens who emerged from it—the jagged peaks topped with ice, the rough sea battering the cliffs, the sprawling academy forged from obsidian stone that sent tall spires into the granite sky. I couldn't imagine a time when the menacing castle hadn't made entering cadets quake in their boots.

My right leg jiggled as I repeated the scant information I'd been able to find on the academy that would be my new home. I didn't know what it meant, but I would soon.

"Beware the Assassins. Don't cross the Blades. Trust the Irons."

The hard jolt of the ship stopped me, and then a tall Drexian appeared in the arched opening leading to the cockpit. The only color on his dark uniform was the bronze academy emblem over his heart—curved blades arching around a flame. The co-pilot tilted his head at me before he finished the final line of my recitation for me.

"The Wings go as one."

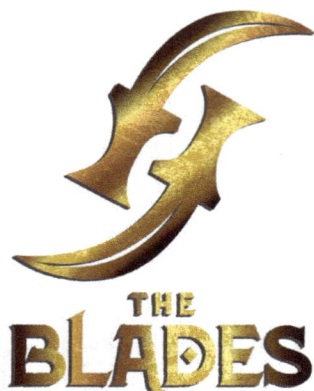

THE BLADES

CHAPTER 2

ARIANA

THE *WINGS GO AS ONE*.

I followed the Drexian down the ramp of the transport. At least I now knew that the four rules I'd found were legit. I still had no clue what they meant, but at least I knew that the paltry information I'd been able to scrounge up was accurate.

Four schools. Four rules.

Beware the Assassins.

Don't cross the Blades.

Trust the Irons.

The Wings go as one.

Part of me wanted to ask the Drexian in front of me what it meant and if it was something I needed to know, but the co-pilot had been less than chatty during our journey and now he was lengthening the distance between us as he strode across the damaged shipyard toward the ominous school.

The *four schools* part I knew. The academy had four divisions within it: the School of Flight, the School of Engineering, the School of Military Strategy, and the School of Battle. It made sense that the four rules matched up with the four schools, but that still gave me little idea what the warnings meant. Were they intended to scare the cadets, or were they crucial clues on navigating the school?

I tipped my head up to take in the gleaming exterior of the towers and spires that were pockmarked from weapons fire. The cracks and holes in the ebony stone only made the structure look more imposing, if that was possible. Gray clouds were feathered across the sky, with only occasional shards of pale light piercing the thick haze.

I'd done a lot of bold and arguably boneheaded things in my life—jumping off the two-story roof of my house in an early attempt to fly, volunteering in the battle to defend Earth—but this might be my most reckless. What did I know about the Drexian home world and their secrets-shrouded academy? Not much, aside from four inscrutable rules that told me jack shit about how to survive the place that wasn't already obvious.

Who doesn't avoid Assassins? Don't cross Blades? Weird, but I can avoid crossing knives. I'd be happy to trust the Irons if I knew what they were. And the Wings?

I paused to take in the fighter jets with polished, black hulls lined up on the shipyard that extended from the towering castle. These were the only wings I knew, and my fingers tingled with familiarity as I approached one and ran a hand across the cool metal.

It didn't matter that I didn't understand this strange place and its baffling rules. It didn't matter that I was walking into a place filled with huge, badass aliens who were not accustomed to working alongside women.

All that mattered was flying. Flying, I knew.

I strode up the short ramp of a ship, my confidence growing with every step. I paused at the top, stopping behind a Drexian with tattoos peaking from beneath the sleeves of a black tee.

"Not that I blame him," the Drexian muttered, clearly thinking he was alone. "If I had a female like that—"

"You'd what?" I couldn't help myself from interrupting him and making him jump.

He jerked and spun around. "Who are you, and what are you doing on my ship?"

I crossed my arms over my chest, noting his ice-blue eyes that were in sharp contrast to his dark hair and bronze skin. "Your ship? I thought this fighter was the property of the Drexian Academy."

He mirrored my stance. "It is, but I'm a flight instructor, which makes this ship my domain."

I gave him a hint of a grin. "Then I guess that makes it my domain, too."

He didn't return my smile, his lips pulling down in a scowl. "Before I summon security, I'll ask you again. Who are you, and what are you doing here?"

I held his eyes for a moment. It was kind of fun to unsettle the tough aliens and not as hard as I would have thought. But probably not the best way to make friends. I relaxed my stance and slapped him on the shoulder. "Chill out, Drexian. I'm not here to hijack your ship if that's what's got your panties in a wad."

He glanced down at his pants, confusion etched on his face.

"I was part of the mission to aid Drex and its academy during the Kronock invasion. I'm sure you're aware that humans are working on the Drexian space stations now, and that Earth Planetary Force has joined your military. When the call for help reached Earth, I was one of the ones to respond."

He cleared his throat and uncrossed his arms. "Thank you for your assistance."

I winked at him. "Don't mention it, flyboy."

I edged around him and headed toward the cockpit with the Drexian close at my heels. "You've told me why you came to the academy. It's been many days since the attack. Why are you still here?"

When I reached the cockpit, I pivoted on my heel so quickly he almost bumped into me "I didn't stay. I returned." Not entirely my idea, but he didn't need to know that. "The powers that be thought it might be a good idea to start integrating humans into the academy."

"Humans? At the Drexian Academy?"

I gave him what I hoped was a disarming smile. "If we're going to be fighting and working together, we might as well be trained together."

He looked at me like I'd sprouted a second head. "And you're part of this new integration?"

I tapped a finger on his chest. "You're smarter than you look, Drexian."

"Lieutenant Volten." He squared his shoulders. "If you're going to be a cadet at the Drexian Academy, you should learn how to address your instructors."

I eyed him. This guy was far from the first guy who'd assumed he outranked me, and I doubted he'd be the last. "Well, Lieutenant Volten, I'm not a cadet. I'm the new flight instructor. It looks like we're going to be working together." I slapped a hand on his chest as I slipped around him and flopped into the pilot's seat. "And when you stop looking like you've been hit with a stun gun, you can call me Ariana."

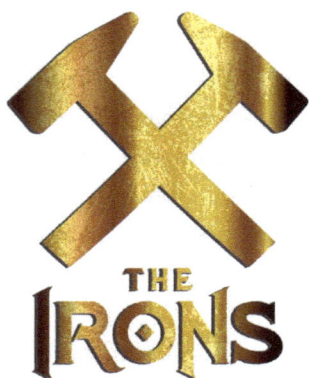

THE IRONS

CHAPTER 3

VOLTEN

"NICE TO MEET YOU, FLYBOY." THE HUMAN FEMALE THUMPED me on the shoulder as she strode down the ship's ramp, pausing at the bottom to turn back to me, flick her sideswept, brown bangs from her eyes, and give me a wink. "I'll see you around."

I was unable to respond, the words lodged somewhere in my throat. Who was I kidding? I had no words. The human female had not only waltzed onto my ship and proven that she knew her way around the cockpit, but she'd also rendered me utterly speechless, which had never happened to me with a female before that moment.

I cleared my throat, wondering if I should call out something to her retreating back. Since the sight of her shapely ass in form-fitting uniform pants meant I still couldn't manage to form an intelligible thought in my brain, I decided against it.

"Smooth," I told myself finally, scraping a hand through my hair and blowing out a breath.

I had no reason to believe that the woman who'd introduced

herself to me as Ariana was lying when she'd said she was one of the new humans brought to integrate the Drexian Academy. It made sense that if humans and Drexians were working together to create planetary defenses and space stations, then they would also train warriors together. Since my species had been sourcing mates from Earth for decades—a fact recently revealed to Earthlings—our peoples were even more linked than humans had known. What I hadn't expected was for her to tell me that she wasn't a cadet, she was an instructor. More specifically, a flight instructor like me.

"Which means there'll be no avoiding her," I said to myself, while her lithe figure grew smaller as she crossed the damaged shipyard. She deftly sidestepped scorched hulls and gaping holes in the ground, reminders of the Kronock attack and the fact that we were still in the process of repairing and rebuilding.

"Why would you want to avoid *her*?"

I twisted to see my colleague and friend Kann leaning against the ship's shiny, black hull and rubbing his silver Blades pendant between his fingers as he watched Ariana walk away. His dark hair was longer than mine, and he had a short beard, reminders that he'd only recently left our military's most elite battle division, Inferno Force, to teach at the academy.

I ignored his question and the flash of irritation that he was staring at the human who'd so unnerved me. "Did you know about this?"

"About what?" Kann had the ability to look completely unconcerned by anything, even though we were surrounded by rubble and were standing in the shadow of the damaged academy, its looming buildings scorched and riddled with the evidence of the enemy's unprovoked attack.

I bit back an exasperated sigh, reminding myself that I'd always admired Kann's ability to remain cool under pressure. It was what had made him such a skilled Inferno Force fighter, and now such a good battle instructor. It was also why he'd been my best friend when we'd been cadets at the academy ourselves. He'd taught me everything I knew about appearing cool under pressure, a talent I was still mastering. "About the humans coming to the academy."

He shrugged. "I might have heard something, but I assumed they meant male humans. If that's one of the new human cadets, I look forward to having her in class."

"She's not a cadet." Which meant she wouldn't be in Kann's class, a detail that made me happier than it should have. "She's a flight instructor."

Kann grinned at me. "Just like you."

I grunted but didn't answer as I pivoted and strode back inside the ship I'd been inspecting before I'd been distracted by Ariana.

To no surprise, Kann followed me in as I walked quickly to the cockpit. "Is she the only one?"

"Human instructor? Female?" It was my turn to twitch one shoulder. "I have no idea. I guess I've been too busy recovering from nearly being killed to have heard any rumors."

Kann grunted in response. He hadn't mentioned me getting shot during the alien attack, but that didn't mean he didn't care. As a former member of Inferno Force, he wasn't big on showing emotion. He was also a Blade, which meant he was a 'work it out on the sparring mat' kind of Drexian, and his version of making sure I was okay had been bringing me a bottle of Cressidian gin that we'd shared together. I preferred his way over my family's, which had been to ignore my brush with death and the fact that I might be the one to need help for a change.

I swallowed the disappointment that always filled me when I thought of my family and sank into the pilot's seat, quickly assessing that Ariana hadn't adjusted any of the controls. Kann flopped into the co-pilot's seat next to me and remained silent as I went through a mental checklist of the ship's functions, swiping my fingers across the sleek surface of the console and watching with satisfaction as lights flashed in response.

"I'm not shocked that Admiral Zoran would want to integrate the crew with humans, especially since he has a human mate."

I nodded, thinking briefly of Noora, the new Academy Master's wife. Despite enjoying a harmless flirtation with the woman, she'd never affected me the way Ariana had when she'd touched me. My heart raced as I thought of the short-haired female's hand pressed to my chest. Even through the fabric of my uniform, her touch and closeness had sent heat skittering through me and had made my palms sweat.

"He will be more openminded to change than Master Kerog." I rubbed my hands down the front of my dark pants, hoping that my friend didn't notice.

Kann choked back a guttural sound in his throat. "Considering Kerog's expulsion from the post and his suspicion of humans, I think it's safe to say that Zoran will have more of an eye toward the future."

"What do you think of the humans?" Unlike many of my Drexian brothers, I'd never traveled to the space stations where we were matched with human mates, and I'd never ventured to Earth. So far, the only humans I'd encountered were the admiral's new wife and now Ariana. I'd heard that the creatures from the blue planet were less delicate than they appeared, and Ariana's sharp wit and failure to back down when I'd challenged her had already proven that.

"If they all look like the flight instructor, then I fully support bringing them here."

I shot him a look. I knew why *I* did not have a human bride. I descended from a long line of grunts who'd never risen high in the Drexian ranks. Not only grunts, but grunts who were screw-ups and occasionally criminals, which meant I had little chance to elevate myself up the list for a tribute bride. Rumor had it that human women were now lining up for a Drexian warrior of their own, and the old lists based on clan rank were becoming obsolete. But until they were eliminated entirely, my family was the poisonous tree that continued to bear fruit.

Kann did not suffer the same fate or lineage, which meant he should have been high up a mate list somewhere. "Why do *you* not have a tribute bride of your own?"

"I am married to the academy," he said with mock severity, putting a fist over his heart.

There wasn't even the hint of truth in this since he'd only recently joined the academy staff. I glanced out the front glass of the ship, eyeing the wounded buildings and battered bridges connecting tall towers. "You need to find yourself a new mate."

He laughed at this. "Maybe I will. My only issue is having to settle on only one female."

My stomach did a flip as I thought about the way my battle instructor friend looked at Ariana, and a possessive growl tickled the back of my throat. "If you're lucky, the academy will soon be bursting with human females, and you can have your pick or choose an assortment."

I knew the four rules of the academy all too well. *Don't cross the Blades.* The Blades were experts in sparring and the use of the Drexian weapons. They were the ones who rushed into hand-to-hand combat, against even the most terrifying aliens. Only a fool would cross them, rule or not.

Even if I was a fool, I didn't want to fight my best friend over a female. Then why was I overcome with the urge to smash my fist into his face at the thought of him even looking at Ariana?

Kann reached over and patted my injured shoulder, causing me to wince. "Do not worry. I won't pursue your flight instructor."

I opened my mouth to say that she was not *my* flight instructor, but then I stopped myself. His fighting instincts were so tuned he'd sensed my hostility, which made shame prickle under my skin. I forced myself to laugh. "I suspect that Zoran will not want any of us openly pursuing our new female colleagues."

Kann groaned. "You're right. It would be so like Zoran to litter the academy with forbidden fruit now that he's got his delicious treat."

"Do not let the admiral hear you refer to his wife as a delicious treat."

Kann released an agonized breath. "I see many trips to the nearest alien outpost in our future."

"You can take the Drexian out of Inferno Force, but you can't take Inferno Force out of the Drexian." I sighed. "I hope these trips don't involve us running for our lives again."

My friend laughed and eyed the tattoos snaking around my biceps. "That only happened one time, and she didn't tell me she had a boyfriend who was a pirate."

I held up my fingers. "Twice. The second time it was a husband who was a smuggler."

Kann ran a hand down his dark scruff. "But you flew us out in record speed both times. I'm still surprised you were never Inferno Force. You know, it's not too late. I can put a good word in for you with my old commander."

I shook my head, even though at one time being in the elite fighting force of the Drexian military had been a goal. But the borderline lawlessness of Inferno Force danced too close to everything I despised about my family. I might enjoy the thrills of flying, but I also craved the order of the academy. Now that Ariana was going to be one of my colleagues, the academy was even more appealing.

"Leave the academy when you've just arrived?" I made a disapproving sound in the back of my throat. "Never. Besides, I can't abandon the academy when it needs me most," I said, which was partly true. "I want to help rebuild the school to its former glory so that generations of Drexian cadets can go on to be the best pilots in the galaxy."

"And the fact that you'll be working side by side with a beautiful female has nothing to do with it?"

"Nothing," I lied. It didn't matter how beautiful she was. A human female like Ariana was beyond the reach of the son of a grunt.

The roar of a landing ship made me jerk my head up and peer out the front of the vessel. "Is that another transport?"

"Looks like more arrivals." Kann rubbed his hands together. "Let's hope there's a female battle instructor for me."

I shook my head as I followed him from the cockpit, the thought of a female teaching Drexian battle so ridiculous I scoffed out loud. "How would humans be able to teach cadets how to fight with Drexian weapons?"

We stood in the opening of the ship and observed the arriving ship touch down on the hard ground. Kann nudged me in the ribs. "Maybe I would need to teach her first."

"Privately?"

My friend ran his fingers down his beard, his lips quirking. "Without question."

I watched the ship's hatch lower, and a group of humans emerged. The mix of males and females appeared unsure, their eyes widening when they saw the imposing academy. I sensed none of Ariana's confidence in these Earthlings. "I don't see a battle instructor for you."

"Maybe not, but I wouldn't mind flattening a few of them on the sparring mat." He jumped from the vessel and headed for the group. "Time to welcome our newest recruits."

I followed him off the ship, but not to the newly arrived humans. There was someone else I needed to see and some questions I needed answered.

THE WINGS

CHAPTER 4

ARIANA

I made a point not to look back as I walked away from the Drexian pilot who'd assumed I was a cadet. I did grin as I thought about the look on his face when I'd told him that not only was I *not* a cadet, but I was a new instructor at the academy. The cherry on top was his expression of total shock when I'd informed him that I was also a flight instructor.

It was almost worth the painfully long journey to the remote Drexian home world, although part of me was still adjusting to the idea of being light years from Earth. My posting had happened so quickly that I'd barely had time to dwell on the challenges involved in traveling halfway across the galaxy.

The part I really didn't want to focus on was what would happen if I failed. Failure meant everything I'd worked for would be gone. Failure meant I would return home in disgrace. Failure could not happen.

"You've had challenges before," I reminded myself, as I threaded my way across the shipyard and avoided the significant holes at my feet. Rising through the ranks on Earth as a woman hadn't been a cake walk, although at least on my own planet I understood the traditions and customs. From what I knew of the Drexian society, it was even more male-dominated. The few females they had didn't serve in the military. But breaking glass ceilings wasn't new territory for me, so there was no way I was going to let myself be intimidated by the alien academy, or its cocky staff. Shaking things up was my fucking specialty. I ran my short red fingernails through my hair. "Bring it on, Drexians."

I tipped my head back to take in the imposing buildings that made up the Drexian Academy and drew in a shaky breath for courage as I walked closer, my nose twitching at the sharp scent of smoke that still filled the air. None of the military schools on Earth were made of obsidian stone and had pointed towers like this one, whose peaks were dark against a granite sky. The holes and cracks in the buildings, courtesy of the Kronock attack, didn't do a thing to make the place look less like an evil wizard's lair.

"It's only a school," I said, as I entered through a high arched doorway with four emblems carved over the entry—a mask on top of a dagger, a pair of curved blades, a hammer, and wings—and my feet went from crunching over rubble to tapping on glossy stone.

Four emblems. Four schools. Four rules. This place had a thing for the number four.

Once inside, a pair of tall Drexians strode by me, their pace not faltering but their eyes roaming up and down me without hesitation. "Four schools filled with huge alien warriors who don't see a lot of women."

I squared my shoulders and defiantly gave them both a quick assessing look before flicking my gaze away. I knew I wasn't what the Drexians were used to seeing around the academy, but they'd better get used to the sight of human women quickly because I would not be the only one.

I wasn't sure precisely where I was going in the cavernous school—the spiraling staircases and bridges that connected buildings and towers made the place a maze, and the weapons hanging on the walls reminded me it was a training ground for war—but I didn't mind wandering the wide, stone corridors until I located another of the transplants from Earth, or a Drexian who looked friendly enough to be a guide. I fought the urge to wrap my arms around myself for heat since the interior of the school wasn't any warmer than it had been outside, and my uniform material wasn't thick.

"There you are!" A high, chirpy voice that couldn't belong to any of the Drexians echoed off the walls and made me spin on my heel.

The female hurrying toward me was not what I'd expected to see, but I instantly knew who she was, or at least *what* she was. She was tall and willowy with gray skin and a gravity-defying swish of blue hair that added several inches to her already impressive height. "You're a Vexling."

"Why, yes." The creature smoothed her spindly fingers down the front of a snug, pink dress that looked entirely out of place in a school where everyone wore dark uniforms with the academy insignia on the chest. "I'm Reina."

"My cousin told me all about you." I smiled at the alien, relief flooding through me that I'd found someone I knew, or at least someone I knew about. "Nina. She works on The Island."

The alien beamed at me, her enormous eyes holding mine. I'd heard all about the tribute bride liaison from my cousin, who was one of the holographic designers on the newest Drexian space station, also called The Island. I'd also heard that Reina had left the station when one of the tribute brides had been claimed by a Drexian admiral, the same admiral who now ran the school, and he'd taken her to the home world as his bride. Reina had insisted on accompanying her, which was how she'd ended up at the Drexian Academy.

Now, if Nina's report was correct, the Drexian admiral and the tribute bride were married.

"Then you're Ariana." Reina looped her slender arm through mine. "I was hoping to find you." Reina propelled me forward and past a hole in a wall. "It's been a bit of a mess since the invasion, as you can see. But Admiral Zoran is on top of everything so you shouldn't worry." She patted my hand that was linked through her arm. "He's the reason you're here. Well, one of them."

I knew that the new Academy Master was the one who'd pushed for an exchange of cadets and instructors, but I hadn't thought why until now. "Admiral Zoran? The one who has a human bride?"

"Noora?" Reina's face broke into a smile. "Oh, yes. Those two are quite happy, but it wasn't an easy road for any of us, let me tell you." The alien's cheeks mottled pink. "They've finally emerged from their quarters, so I'm sure you'll get to meet her soon. Between you and me, she was behind her husband's enthusiasm for bringing Earthlings to the academy."

I noticed more Drexians staring openly as we walked through the expansive corridors. "What do the rest of the Drexians think about humans at their school?"

Reina hesitated before answering. "I'm sure it will take some adjustment, just like it did when we brought humans to work on the space stations after the Reveal, but once the Drexians discover how smart and capable you are, they'll be as excited as I am."

I didn't think that was possible since the creature was practically vibrating as we walked.

Reina squeezed my hand. "You don't have a thing to worry about, hon. Nina told me how smart you are—top of your class on Earth."

I smiled at the mention of my cousin. "I wish I could have stopped off at The Island to see her before I came here, but the military doesn't like to delay."

"Nina is doing well, although I haven't seen her since I left. It's been a bit busy since the attack."

The attack. I'd been a part of it, but only from the air above as we'd beaten back the alien invaders. Seeing the effects on the ground made it even more personal. "I'm glad you weren't hurt."

Reina squeezed my arm. "Thanks, hon. It was scary, but I heard you were part of the reason the Kronock were defeated so swiftly."

"A small part. I was already training with the Drexian forces when they got the alert that an attack on their home world was imminent. I'm not going to say that I enjoyed all the jumps it took to arrive in time."

Reina nodded gravely as she led me to a staircase that went up. "Lucky for us the treachery and sabotage were discovered in time to send out calls for help." She lowered her voice to a conspiratorial whisper. "One thing you should know about this place is that things aren't always what they seem."

I cocked my head. "What do you mean?"

Reina let loose a nervous laugh, as we reached the top of the stairs and entered a wide entry hall that was swarming with broad-shouldered, dark-haired Drexians who were boarding transparent elevators that zoomed up the side of the building or were bounding up a sweeping set of stairs two at a time as their husky male voices filled the air. "This place was originally the largest defensive fortress on Drex. It kept out invading ground forces and protected them from vicious creatures that lived in the mountains and beyond. That's why it has dungeons and underground passageways and turrets for battle. A place like that would have to be filled with secrets, right?"

Before I could pin her down on exactly what secrets she meant—or what kinds of vicious creatures were roaming the alien planet—Reina waved a hand over her head. "I should probably give you the official tour, although there are parts of the academy even

I haven't seen." She leaned in conspiratorially. "And some I don't want to see."

She tugged me forward and out of the path of a determined group of cadets who looked at me like I was lunch as they stomped past. "This is the main hall, but it's more of a hub. It holds the library, the great hall where the welcome banquet will be held tonight, and Admiral Zoran's offices, but each of the schools has its own building of classrooms and offices, as well as its own tower." She pointed to staircases in the corners. "Then there are separate quarters for staff and cadets."

I tried to focus on all the information she was giving me, but my gaze snagged on a familiar Drexian as he moved through the crowd, his piercing, blue eyes locking on mine for a beat before he disappeared through a doorway. It was the cocky flight instructor I'd met earlier. The one I'd enjoyed shocking and was looking forward to continuing to surprise.

"I see you've met Volten."

I pulled my gaze back to Reina who was eying me with curiosity. "I was checking out the ships that hadn't been damaged, and I ran into him."

"He's quite the rising star at the Academy, and he was almost killed by the Drexian traitor before the attack. He's the reason Admiral Zoran was able to save Noora and the school."

I didn't bother hiding my surprise. "He didn't strike me as the hero type."

Reina tilted her head and quirked her bright pink lips to one side. "No? How did he strike you?"

Before I could tell her that she could wipe the smirk off her face because a cocky alien who assumed I was a cadet was the last kind of guy I'd like, hero or not, a voice behind us made me jump.

"Another human!"

THE ASSASSINS

CHAPTER 5

VOLTEN

K*EEP WALKING*, I TOLD MYSELF AS I PASSED ARIANA TALKING to the Vexling who'd come to the academy with Noora. *And don't look back.*

So far, I wasn't doing the best job of playing it cool. I'd never had trouble charming females before, but there was something about the human flight instructor that jangled my nerves and drained me of all my composure.

"Your composure is the last of your problems," I told myself harshly, as I wound my way through the damaged academy, noting the teams of Drexians working on the cracked walls and collapsed ceilings.

I coughed as I reached the door to the Academy Master's office, the dust from the rubble tickling my throat, even though it had been days since it had fallen. I raised my hand to rap on the door, when it slid open to reveal a Drexian leaving.

I backed up to avoid him. "Tivek."

I shouldn't have been surprised to see the Admiral's adjunct leaving his office. The Drexian had been Zoran's right hand for as long as I'd known the warriors. Rumor had it that the admiral had taken Tivek on as his assistant when he'd washed out of the academy, but I would have died before asking either of them to confirm that.

Loyal, intense, and brooding, Tivek had proved his allegiance to Zoran, but his suspicion of the rest of us was just as palpable. It probably had a lot to do with the sabotage and betrayal that Zoran had recently experienced, but Tivek seemed particularly wary of me. That might have had something to do with my friendly rapport with Zoran's wife, and his suspicion that I'd been pursuing her, which had been unfounded.

Zoran held no ill will, especially after he'd learned the truth. Tivek had been slower to warm to me. His pupils flared when he spotted me, and then they narrowed slightly.

"Lieutenant Volten." He inclined his head at me, the movement scant. "Do you have an appointment to see the Admiral, I mean, Academy Master?"

I was glad I wasn't the only one having a hard time with all the changes, but I wouldn't have dared smirk at his slip. "I don't, but—"

"The Master is occupied." He stepped forward, forcing me to step back. "Maybe I can address your concern."

"Let him in." Zoran's voice boomed from inside the room, and Tivek's lips pulled down at the corners as he stepped aside for me.

I returned the Drexian's nod of respect, aware that alienating him would be making it harder for me to gain audience with Zoran in the future. Some in the academy might view Tivek as someone to dismiss because he had no rank or status, but since I'd grown up around Drexians with no status and had none of my own, I knew all too well that they were often the most dangerous.

As I entered the room, it struck me that I'd spent almost no time in it before now. The previous Academy Master had been a strict adherent to protocol. There had been few reasons a new flight instructor would have been called into his office. I'd always been shocked that I'd landed the plum position at all. If anyone revered status and lauded the elite Drexian families more than Kerog had, I hadn't met them.

I flicked away old doubts about my position—Kerog was gone, and I was secure in my appointment—as the new Academy Master rose from behind a massive ebony desk to greet me. Unlike the odd, billowing robes his predecessor had worn that had made him look more like a sorcerer than an academic, Admiral Zoran preferred the dark Drexian uniform of the school. The only indication he was anyone of note was the fact that his academy insignia of two curved blades surrounding a flame was emblazoned on his chest in gold instead of the silver of instructors or the bronze of cadets.

"Fully recovered, I see." Zoran continued to walk around his enormous desk to greet me before I'd completely crossed the long room.

I thumped my right fist over my chest in salute, locking my eyes on his bright blue ones that weren't so different from my own. "As are you."

He returned my salute, which was highly unusual considering how starkly he outranked me. Then again, the Drexian had not been his usual gruff self since he'd taken his human mate. He studied my face for a beat, opening his mouth and then closing it again before he spun around and strode back toward his desk. "What can I do for you, Volten?"

I took a moment before answering. He'd been on the verge of saying something as he'd stared hard at me, then he'd reconsidered. Was he planning to tell me about the humans, but wanted me to ask first? I chalked up his hesitancy to the general uncertain feeling that pervaded the entire academy. We were all regaining our footing after such deep treachery.

"I met one of the new human instructors."

He reached the opposite side of his desk, pausing to look out the tall, narrow window. "The military strategist? Captain Douglas, I think? Earth names are so strange and difficult to remember."

I shook my head. "No, Admiral."

He turned and leaned his hands on the surface of the desk, his fingers splayed wide. "Not the new military strategy instructor? She did arrive earlier, but maybe more transports have come since then. I must admit I got caught up in the reports from the battle. Which of the new human instructors did you meet?"

How many human instructors were now at the Drexian military training school? "The female, sir."

Zoran straightened and folded his arms over his chest. "There is more than one female, but if it wasn't the strategy instructor then it must be the flight instructor." When I nodded, he continued, "She's supposed to be impressive, and she fought to defend the planet during the attack."

I didn't comment on Ariana's qualifications or her defense of my planet, though I valued both. I was stuck on the fact that such a dramatic change had been made at the storied school without mention to any of the staff. "When did you decide to allow females among our ranks?"

Zoran studied me, while I instantly regretted questioning his decision. "The academy has done things the same way for a long time, but considering recent events, it's high time to make some changes." His gaze dipped momentarily to my chest where I still wore the scar from my wound, even though it was not visible through my shirt. "Wouldn't you agree?"

I should agree. I, more than anyone, should welcome changes to the antiquated traditions that had ruled the school for so long. Even before I'd been a cadet myself, I'd known the rules like a mantra. Every Drexian boy did, even the ones like me who didn't come from elite military families or have a line of ancestors who'd been cocky Blades or proud Irons.

As much as I wished for change, I doubted that such deeply

ingrained rules and unwritten laws could be wiped away simply because humans would be joining us. And if the rules remained, so did the danger.

"I can tell you from personal experience that humans are more than they appear."

Of course, the admiral would say that. He was currently enjoying wedded bliss with his new human bride. But a human wife was not the same thing as a human fighter pilot. It took more than skill to be a Wing. Before I could remind the admiral of that, I questioned if I was being exactly the kind of Drexian I'd always despised.

I'd spent my life being on the outside of Drexian society because I did not come from a prominent house. I'd had to work twice as hard to get into the academy, twice as hard to excel against my privileged classmates, and twice as hard to graduate as a Wing. Now that I'd achieved some level of respect and status of my own making, was I truly going to advocate denying others based on their species and lack of status?

A gut check told me that I couldn't become what I'd always despised. "You are right, Master Zoran."

The admiral's blue eyes held mine. "It will not be so easy for them. The Drexian Academy is not like their military training on Earth. Even their toughest schools do not have the attrition we do. Or the trials."

My chest swelled at the reminder that not just any Drexian could make it through our military training. The rigor was what turned out the toughest warriors in the galaxy, the warriors who defended the rest of the planets from the Kronock, the warriors who'd been defending Earth for decades without their population's knowledge, the warriors who would continue to fight the enemy until their last breath.

"You believe the humans can keep up with their Drexian counterparts?"

Zoran rocked back on his heels. "We requested the best Earth had to offer, but we will see if they are as good as their superiors claim."

Part of me wished that the academy would return to its previous state—before the attack and before the arrival of the humans—but another part of me wanted Ariana to stay.

More than any of those things, I wanted to keep her from danger. But if she stayed, danger was part of the package. Danger had always been part of being at the academy.

Admiral Zoran opened his mouth as if to speak but hesitated and closed it again, much like he'd done earlier. Was there something else he wanted to tell me about the humans?

"Admiral?" I asked.

He gave a gruff shake of his head. "Nothing. You're dismissed, Lieutenant." He pivoted back toward the long, narrow window with the view of the craggy mountains in the distance. "Oh, and Volten, I'd like you to show your new colleague around the academy and make her feel welcome."

"Yes, Admiral." Welcome wasn't exactly what I wished to make Ariana feel, but that was the last thing Zoran—or anyone—could know.

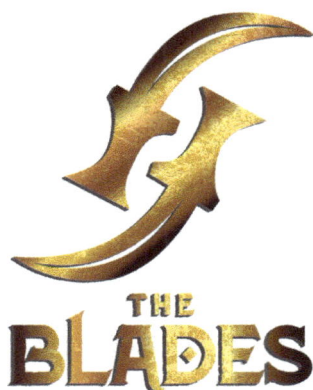

THE BLADES

CHAPTER 6

ARIANA

A TALL WOMAN STRODE TOWARD US, PARTING THE CROWD OF broad-shouldered Drexians in their cadet uniforms like they weren't there. Her long, blonde hair hung down her back and shoulders, but the soft waves didn't make her look any less tough and commanding.

The woman stopped and put her hands on her hips once she reached us. "I was starting to think I was the only female here." She swept her gaze across the brawny aliens. "Not that I'm complaining about the odds."

Even though she wore the same standard Drexian Academy uniform with the emblem of a flame and curved blades emblazoned on the chest, it was clear that she was used to being in a position of authority. Being smaller, or less of an obvious physical threat than the Drexians, didn't make her exude any less command, although I hesitated to salute her. Did I follow Earth military protocol, or should I adapt the Drexian custom of thumping one fist across my chest?

The woman ended my internal debate by extending a hand. "I'm Fiona. Captain Douglas if we're being formal."

"Ariana Bowman." I took her hand, admiring the firm handshake that wasn't bone-crushing. "Lieutenant."

"Since we're both instructors here and some of the only humans, let's go by first names."

I allowed myself to relax a bit. The woman might give off an air of confidence, but she wasn't the ballbuster I'd expected when I'd seen her approach. Then again, I had no balls to bust.

She took the Vexling's hand. "And you're Reina."

Reina's cheeks flushed a startling shade of pink. "You know me?"

"There will be less than a dozen females here." Fiona smiled at the willowy alien. "I figured we should all get to know each other."

"You mean stick together?" Reina's enormous eyes bulged even larger.

Fiona exchanged a grin with me. "Absolutely. I've never thought it was smart for women in the military to go it alone. We all benefit if we lift each other up instead of tearing each other down." She cut a glance to the aliens passing us. "Besides, we'll have enough challenges navigating this sausage fest."

Reina repeated the phrase 'sausage fest' quietly to herself as I sized up the blonde. She sounded sincere, and I would love having a woman ally—or a dozen.

"Were you heading to the female tower?" Fiona asked, as Reina continued to look puzzled by the idea of a celebration of sausage.

"We have our own tower?" I asked.

Reina's attention returned to us. "Oh, yes. It's the smallest one with only two floors of rooms, but it's females only. They thought it was best to keep the few women from Earth together—instructors and cadets—since the academy is mostly male."

Sausage fest, Fiona mouthed to me with a wicked smile.

I snorted a laugh—not my most feminine quality—but Fiona's grin only widened as she held up her hands. "I only speak the truth."

From what I'd seen so far—throngs of massive, dark-haired Drexians—she was right. We were the exceptions to the rule in a school where the only rules seemed to be unwritten.

"I can take her to the tower," Fiona said to Reina. "In case you need to meet more of the new cadets arriving from Earth."

Reina fluttered a hand to her cheek. "Could you? There's another transport arriving soon with human cadets, a few of them female."

"Don't worry," Fiona patted my shoulder. "I'll take it from here."

Reina gave me a finger wave as she backed away. "See you later, hon."

Once I could only see the top of Reina's blue, gravity-defying hair moving through the sea of Drexians, Fiona pointed to a high, arched opening. "This way."

She led me down a wide, spiraling staircase made of dark stone that had worn smooth in the center of the steps. Then we hooked a left and proceeded across a bridge that connected two buildings, the openings in the stone allowing me to see the ice-capped mountain range that ran behind the academy and how high up we were.

Fiona flapped a hand to her left. "The Restless Sea." Then she jerked her head toward the mountain range. "The Gilded Peaks."

I glanced at both the turbulent water that more than earned its name as it hurled white-capped waves at the cliffs and at the formidable peaks that bordered the back of the academy and appeared more frigid than gilded, then I averted my eyes. It made no sense for a pilot to be afraid of heights, but if I wasn't in a plane, I didn't like being in the air.

"I take it you've been at the academy for a while now?" I asked to distract myself from the dizzying drop.

Fiona shook her head. "Just got here." Before I could ask her how she knew where to go, she added. "I'm here to teach in the School of Strategy. Battle plans and maps are my jam. I memorized the layout of the academy before I arrived."

Smart, I thought, especially after seeing that the place was a labyrinth. "I'm here to teach in the School of Flight. I didn't even think of studying the layout of the buildings."

Fiona laughed. "I wouldn't expect a pilot to get excited by a complicated map. You'll learn your way by instinct."

"Pretty much. You know pilots."

Her husky laugh deepened. "Probably more than my fair share, but that's a story for another day."

Once we'd crossed the stone bridge, there were more holes in the obsidian walls being earnestly repaired by heavily muscled Drexians and a pervasive scent of char. This building had sustained more damage in the battle, or it hadn't been attended to as rapidly as the main building.

"It looks dodgy, but I've been assured that it's structurally sound," Fiona said as we passed some gaps in the walls with startling views to the rocky base below and even a glimpse of the stormy sea that bordered the school on the opposite side as the mountains.

For the hundredth time since I'd agreed to join the academy, tendrils of doubt wound their way through my brain. Before I could decide that I'd had enough odd encounters and huge aliens eyeing me, Fiona led us into an elevator compartment with clear doors that swished closed behind us.

"I thought the academy was unchanged for hundreds of years." It certainly looked like an ancient castle from outside, but the presence of the occasional elevator reminded me that the Drexians possessed more advanced technology than humans.

"From what I gather, they added inclinators when they added additional towers." Fiona turned to me as we zoomed up sideways and then twisted in another diagonal direction. "Maybe to cut down on the time it takes cadets to get to class?"

"Inclinators?" The word was vaguely familiar.

"I'll take that to mean you've never been to one of the tribute bride stations." Fiona said, as the compartment slowed, and the doors slid open. "They're in heavy use there."

"Nope. I managed to avoid them."

My new colleague laughed as we stepped out. "Smart woman. Computer powered alien matchmaking never appealed to me either, but I'm afraid we're in the minority."

She was right again. Since learning of the Drexians, Earth women had lost their damn minds for the aliens. Not that I entirely blamed them. The Drexians were hot enough to make any sensible woman swoon. But I guess I'd never been sensible.

We trudged our way up another staircase, this one tighter, until we emerged on a completely circular floor ringed with arched, inset doorways and an opening on the other side with more stairs leading up. Fiona spread her arms wide. "This is it."

If I'd been expecting something different than the uniformly black stone walls lit by flickering sconces of the rest of the academy, I would have been disappointed. The ceiling was high, but there were no windows to let in light, only the golden glow of the artificial and never-melting candles illuminating the curved walls of the tower.

Fiona approached a door and pressed her hand to a panel beside it until it slid open. "This is me."

I glanced inside the room without being too obvious, noting that the space was dominated by a tall, narrow window cut into the stone and an impressive view of the dark peaks in the distance. Despite having just stepped off a sideways moving elevator, the tower struck me as almost medieval in style.

"Each room is synced to handprints," Fiona explained with a wave at the closed doors surrounding us.

"This should be fun." I started making my way around the circle, testing the door next to Fiona's, and having no luck before crossing the hall and trying the door opposite hers. As soon as I pressed my palm fully to the panel, the door slid open.

"Easier than keys." Fiona lowered her voice once more. "Which is great because I always forget my keys."

A low chuckle made us both turn back to see a uniformed Drexian leaning against the wall near the other staircase with one leg bent and his foot flat against the stone. His brown hair was styled to look like it hadn't been, and he oozed arrogance.

"It does make it tougher to complete the academy's newest unofficial requirement though."

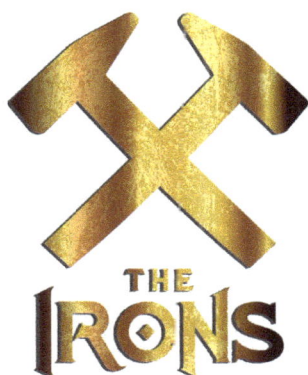

THE IRONS

CHAPTER 7

ARIANA

I exchanged a look with Fiona. Who was this Drexian douchebag, and what was he doing in our tower?

Fiona folded her arms over her chest and squared her shoulders, her easy smile vanishing, replaced by a hard-eyed glare. "Who are you, and what are you doing here? I know this isn't your floor."

He pushed off the wall and walked toward us, his arms loose by his side as he gave us both shameless once-overs. "Consider me your official Drexian welcome."

Fiona scowled. "Official?"

Her questioning didn't seem to faze him. He was either legit or possessed such copious amounts of self-confidence that even Fiona's aggressive stance couldn't dissuade him. I reminded myself that since Drexians were big, brawny, and tough, they could be afforded a decent amount of confidence.

I was less interested in watching the pissing contest play out than I was in what he'd said. "What about the academy's unofficial requirements?"

His mouth twitched at the corners. He knew he'd hooked me, but I couldn't help myself. As much information as I'd tried to find about the academy before I'd come, I hadn't heard of any unofficial requirements. There were plenty of official ones covering everything from dress code to curfew. So many that I'd been astounded that anyone graduated or survived, but unofficial ones?

"There have always been four unofficial requirements cadets need to accomplish before they can leave."

Four requirements. Four rules.

More fours.

Fiona hadn't relaxed her stance, and she didn't show any interest in what the Drexian was saying. "How does that apply to us?"

The Drexian allowed himself a wide smile as he opened his arms as if to encompass us. "You might not be Drexians, but you're still cadets, which means we all have to abide by the same graduation requirements."

Fiona let loose a low warning sound in the back of her throat, but I spoke up before she could school him on our ranks. "But these aren't official requirements, right?"

He shrugged as if he found little difference between the two. "Every cadet who's made it through has done them. It's a Drexian point of honor."

"Then lay them on us." I shot Fiona a meaningful look. "If this is what all the cadets do, then we should know them."

She caught my drift, and her scowl relaxed into a simple disapproving frown.

The Drexian cadet held up his fingers. "One, find the hidden underground passageways out of the academy which have been known to collapse in places. Two, slide down the long, spiral banister that runs through the center of the main building without falling to your death. Three, scale the forbidden tower. Again, without falling to a painful death. Four, spend a night in the dungeons, which are said to be haunted."

I'd heard of universities having unofficial rules, but most of them had centered around where you were supposed to have sex. These rules seemed a lot more dangerous and less fun.

"And the newest requirement?" I asked, as he walked closer to me, clearly deciding that I was the less hostile of the two of us and more susceptible to his charms.

"Now we have female cadets," he said, his smile spreading smoothly across his admittedly handsome face, "and a female tower?"

I waited for him to state what was obvious to him.

He arched one brow. "Spending the night in a human female cadet's room has to be the new requirement."

I didn't know how many human women were joining the alien academy, but if the size of the female tower was any indication, not enough for one per Drexian. This guy had high expectations of human women and our libidos or our tolerance for having Drexians loitering in our rooms overnight. We might like the alien warriors, but not *that* much.

"Thanks for giving us the heads up, Cadet." Fiona's voice was sharp. "Now I know to keep an eye out for any of you hanging around the cadets' rooms."

His confident grin faltered. "You aren't also cadets?"

I shook my head, enjoying watching the panic flicker across his face. "We're instructors."

He swung his head from me to Fiona and back again. "Both of you? You don't look like..."

"Both of us," Fiona said, smiling now that the Drexian was squirming.

"*Grek* me," he said under his breath.

"That sounds right." A deeper voice echoed from within the

stairwell and the lieutenant I'd met on the shipyard emerged from behind the cadet.

The cadet jerked to attention, the last remnants of his overflowing confidence seeping from him along with any traces of his cocky grin. "Lieutenant, I was—"

"You were leaving," Volten interrupted him, his expression fierce as he held the younger Drexian's gaze. "And do not ever let me catch you here again."

The cadet flinched but didn't respond, quickly retreating down the stairs and leaving the lieutenant standing ramrod stiff and seething. Then Volten's gaze went to me, the possessive heat of it stirring something within me, something I hadn't felt in a long time.

I ignored the fluttering of my pulse as I returned his stare. "We were handling that."

He grunted. "You are part of my school, and that makes you my responsibility."

The thought of being the tall, broad shouldered alien's responsibility made me both bristle and flush with unwanted pleasure. What was wrong with me? I shouldn't enjoy any part of this guy's protection. But when was the last time anyone had protected me?

Fiona swung her head back and forth between us without comment, folding her arms over her chest. Finally, her gaze rested on Volten. "Why are you here?"

His eyes didn't leave me, the black pupils expanding until they almost consumed the blue. "I'm here for Ariana."

THE WINGS

CHAPTER 8

VOLTEN

"THIS IS WHERE YOU'LL TEACH INTRODUCTION TO FLIGHT." I stood inside the doorway to a theatre-style classroom and waited for Ariana to peek inside.

She hadn't seemed particularly eager to join me for a tour, but I'd insisted. After all, Zoran had given me the task, and I did not want to let him down. Taking her around the academy was preferable to standing in the female tower and allowing my outsized rage at the cadet to smolder as the other human instructor had eyed us.

I was still startled by the fury I'd experienced when I'd come up the stairs and heard the cadet attempting to charm Ariana. The thought of him succeeding, the thought of him touching her, the thought of any male touching her had sent anger storming through me. It had been all I could do not to toss him down the stone steps.

I bit my bottom lip to keep from sighing audibly as she stepped closer to me to lean into the room, the faint flowery scent of her teasing my nose. I'd never experienced such a primal reaction to any female, and now I had the overpowering urge to draw my blade on every Drexian who so much as glanced at her. Why did Ariana have to be the one female I needed to work alongside, the one female I should not touch?

She gave the room a scant glance, like she'd done with almost every teaching space I'd shown her on our tour. "All first-year cadets take Introduction to Flight, even if they don't want to become pilots?"

"Every first-year takes basic courses in each of the schools during their first quarter." I stepped from the doorway. "Then they get placed into schools and focus their studies on that area. But every Drexian warrior must know the basics of flying, engineering, strategy, and battle before they can move into a specialty."

She ran her fingers through her hair, and the sideswept layers fell back across her forehead. "They only have a quarter to learn the basics?"

I forced myself to pull my gaze from her brown hair that had strands which looked like they'd been dipped in Garenthian spun sugar. "Drexians who enter the academy have already passed stringent testing and assessments. This is not a school for everyone."

Her posture stiffened as she walked beside me down the corridor and toward the main hall. "It's the same on Earth, you know. You have to work hard to get into one of our military schools, and most people don't make the cut."

"You went to one of Earth's military schools?" I was intrigued that such a pretty female would have desired to be a warrior. No Drexian female—of the few we had left—would consider joining the Drexian forces.

"The Naval Academy." When I didn't respond, she added. "It's highly selective."

I led the way through the smattering of cadets moving through the central hall and up the sweeping staircase. "The cadet dining hall is on the second floor."

"We eat with the cadets?"

I shook my head. "We have a staff dining room further up the stairs, but I thought you'd like to see where your students will be taking their meals."

I was hit with the aroma of yeasty bread and salty *padwump* as we approached the open archway leading inside the long dining room with a vaulted ceiling and tall windows on one side. Cadets were already filing in for the midday meal, which reminded me that I needed to speed up my tour so I could meet Kann for lunch in the staff dining room.

"Looks like the flight instructor's already nabbed himself one of the human cadets."

I bristled at the comment made by a Drexian as he strode by us and through the archway, giving Ariana a lascivious grin as he passed her.

Instinct told me to slam him against the wall and make him beg for her forgiveness, but I could not spend the entire term attacking anyone who spoke to her. Before I could think of a more measured response, Ariana had stepped forward and grabbed his sleeve.

She jerked him toward her with startling force. "What did you call me?"

The Drexian's arrogant smile slipped for a moment, but then he put his hand over hers and patted it. "Human cadet?"

She snatched her hand from under his as if it had been burned. "You're one for two, which I suspect is your usual track record, Cadet."

The Drexian's friends chuckled at the insult, but the cadet himself didn't look amused. "You're new here, so I'll forgive you for challenging a second year."

"This is not a—" I started to correct the cadet, but Ariana held up a hand to stop me.

"Not until this cadet apologizes for insulting an instructor."

"An instruct—?"

"Lieutenant Bowman is a flight instructor from Earth." I watched the cadet's face register confusion and then shock. Maybe this was better than dangling him over the stairwell.

"Humans are going to be teaching us? In Flight?" The disdain dripped from his voice, which made me almost groan out loud. This was not getting any better.

"If you don't like it, you can always change schools." Ariana spat out each word. "I don't want pilots who can't respect the chain of command."

The cadet held up his hands and backed away. "Sorry, Lieutenant."

The entire hall was silent as the cadets continued inside. We lingered in the archway, with Ariana glaring at the back of the retreating cadet. My own heart was racing, a mixture of desire to punish the cadet myself and the thrill of seeing Ariana put him in his place. Finally, she whirled around and stormed back into the hall.

I followed, exhaling with relief that she hadn't challenged the cadet to settle things on the sparring mat, which was how it might have ended if she'd been Drexian. I was lucky that *I* hadn't ended up dragging him to the sparring mat.

She stopped short and whirled on me. "Do *you* have an issue with humans teaching here?"

I was unprepared for her question, but at least I'd learned enough from the cadet's misstep to keep from admitting any doubts I might have about Earthlings and Drexians working side by side in a military setting.

She didn't let me speak before she'd jabbed a finger at my chest. "I have no issue proving that I deserve to be here, Lieutenant."

Her touch, even one finger poking the fabric of my shirt, did nothing to slow my racing heart. "Your issue isn't with me."

She cocked her head. "I'm starting to think my issue is with every Drexian who assumes I'm a cadet."

I knew that would come back to bite me. "I apologize for

being unaware of your posting, but you don't need to prove that you deserve it. Not to me."

"I think I do." Her chest was heaving as she locked eyes with me. "How do Drexians usually settle things?"

"On the sparring mat, but like I said, there's no need—"

She choked back a mirthless laugh. "I think there's every need. The last thing I need is a colleague who doesn't think I've earned my place." She started back down the stairs. "Let's go."

My pulse steadied. At least she wasn't going to make me grapple with her when I could barely breathe after a single touch. "You want me to finish the tour?"

"No," she snapped without a backward glance. "I want you to take me to the sparring mats."

THE ASSASSINS

CHAPTER 9

ARIANA

I DROPPED MY BOOTS OUTSIDE THE MAT, WONDERING EXACTLY how things had spiraled out of control so quickly.

Because you can never back down.

I scowled, sick of my inner voice always being right and always being righteous about it. The same traits that had helped me succeed in a male-dominated field could also get me in trouble, which they clearly had—again.

It's okay, I assured myself. I'd beaten opponents bigger than me before. I bounced from foot to foot to warm up, trying not to let my gaze linger on the huge alien on the other side of the mat, who wasn't nervously hopping from side to side. He wasn't moving at all, although he had shed his uniform shirt, which I would have said was playing dirty if I hadn't been the one to insist on fighting him despite his many protests.

My gaze snagged on the pendant hanging from a chain around his neck before he looped it over his head and dropped it on top of his shirt. The silver pendant was the same symbol that was chiseled into the stone arch above the entrance to the flight school. A pair of unfurled wings.

The Wings go as one.

I would have asked the guy what the rule of his school meant if I wasn't so focused on showing him that I deserved to be at the academy and could hold my own. If I wasn't also so preoccupied with the size of Volten and how staring at his bare chest made my mouth go bone dry.

Volten wasn't the first big guy I'd had to spar against, but he was by far the biggest, and none of my previous opponents had looked like they were chiseled from rock. My only consolation was the years of jujitsu I'd taken growing up that had inoculated me to wrestling guys. Still, no one competed in official jujitsu matches shirtless.

The Drexian stepped onto the mat. "I told you on the way here, this is not necessary."

Even if I wanted to back down, it was too late. I couldn't call off the match without appearing to be scared by his imposing physique, which a part of me was. It had been a while since I'd last grappled, although I assumed it wasn't a skill you'd forget, a lot like riding a bike.

"It's like riding something," I mumbled to myself, then promptly attempted to banish all thoughts of riding anything.

Volten twisted his torso, his back cracking loudly, and I got a glimpse of the raised bumps that ran along his spine. I'd heard of Drexian nodes, but I'd never imagined I'd see them up close and personal. I mean, I never imagined I'd see a half-naked Drexian either. That was tribute bride territory, and I had no plans to be anyone's bride.

Ignore and override, I reminded myself, as I focused on the match and not the alien warrior with hard bumps running down his back. "We fight until one of us holds a takedown for five seconds."

He bobbed one shoulder, as if this would be no problem, which fueled my determination to beat him. I rubbed my hands together and then raised one to pull on an imaginary bell. "Ding ding."

Confusion crossed his face, but when I started circling him, he got the idea. We'd begun.

If I'd expected the bulky guy to move like a linebacker, I'd have been wrong. Despite his size, Volten moved like a cat. A massive cat.

I took steps to the side as I watched the way he tracked me, my heart thumping loudly. He might not be an instructor in the Battle school, but the guy knew his way around a sparring mat. And he was patient, which wasn't something I was used to when facing off against bigger fighters.

After a few circles around the mat, I decided to lunge first. I went for his arm, but he deftly sidestepped me and spun away with a backward kick to my ass that was so unexpected it sent me to the floor. I rolled from his reach and leapt to my feet, cursing to myself.

This guy was fast, and he had skills.

Maybe more than you.

"Shut up," I told myself as I threw a decoy punch and then dropped down and swung my leg wide. My foot caught his, and he went down.

With a surge of satisfaction, I pounced on him and attempted to lock his arms to his side with my knees.

The Drexian grinned at me as I straddled him on the sparring mat. "If you wanted to be on top, you only had to ask."

"In your dreams, flyboy."

His eyes flashed heat as he expertly flipped me over until he was on top of me. "I've had worse dreams." He braced his hands on either side of my head and leaned down. "I think I prefer you under me. You're less dangerous this way."

"You're not the first person to think that." I jerked hard to one side and rolled him back underneath me. "And not the last to be wrong."

Before I could get him immobilized, he bucked me off and

sent me sprawling onto my back. I quickly rolled over and dodged his leg before it snagged mine, breathing hard when I jumped back to standing.

Volten didn't stand. Instead, he remained in a crouch with his head bowed. He must have hit the mat harder than I'd seen, which meant I had the advantage. I didn't hesitate to run at him, only realizing my mistake when he flicked his head up, grinned, and lunged for my waist.

Only when he was tackling me onto my back did I know he'd lured me into a trap. Son of a bitch. I flipped my legs up to hook around his shoulders and used the momentum of the fall to turn it around on him. I was on top for a second, straddling the huge alien's head as he grinned up at me.

"Why are you smiling?" My words were bursts between ragged breaths.

"You're better than I expected, especially for someone so much smaller." The bastard didn't seem to be breathing hard at all, which made me want to punch him in the face.

"Haven't you heard?" I grabbed for his wrists and held them to the mat. "Size doesn't matter, flyboy."

He flashed me another maddening grin before using his hips to power himself up and flip me onto my back. His hands rolled from my grasp, and he pinned my wrists over my head. "That's not what I've heard."

I huffed out a frustrated breath as I strained to hook my legs around his or jerk my arms from his grip, but the weight of his body kept me immobilized on the mat. As the seconds ticked by and I was unable to lift my shoulders from the mat, I groaned. "This means nothing."

"I never said it did. You are the one who insisted on sparring."

I hated that I'd lost. I hated that I felt powerless underneath him. I hated his charming smile. But most of all, I hated that I'd brought this onto myself.

"You don't understand," I rasped. "If a woman in the military backs down, she's done."

"I would never accuse you of backing down." He didn't release me, but he held my gaze. "But you don't have to fight me. We're in the same school. We're on the same side."

Some of the fight ebbed from me as I stopped straining against his hold. "The only way I know how to succeed is to be tougher than everyone else. If I don't succeed here, I lose everything. My rank, my career, my future." I drew in a shuddering breath. "What could be worse than that?"

"You don't know this place yet, but there are many worse things that can happen to you at the Drexian Academy." He kept my arms pinned down as he leaned close to my ear. "Let me keep you safe, Ariana."

His tone was so urgent, so desperate that I forgot how to breathe for a moment.

His warm breath and his hushed words sent heat pulsing through me, and I was suddenly acutely aware that there was a huge, hot, hard Drexian on top of me. Emphasis on hard.

It was impossible to ignore what was pressing into my hip and how impressively rigid it was. As much as my body was screaming for me to find out how much size actually mattered, there was no way I could let myself fall for Volten. I was at the academy to pave the way for other female officers. I was at the academy to succeed. I was not at the academy to screw an alien. I was not at the academy to stay safe or let a Drexian be my protector.

He gave a playful nip at my earlobe. "I'd hate to lose a colleague who's so much fun to fight." He laughed, and his warm breath tickled my neck and sent heat arrowing down my spine. "But if you wanted to get me on top of you, there were easier ways than challenging me to a sparring match."

I strained against his grip as he pinned me to the sparring mat, my own desire fueling my frustration. "I promise you, this is the last time you'll ever be on top of me."

He breathed in the scent of me before pulling back to meet my gaze, his blue eyes going molten. "I don't think that's true. Not if I have anything to say about it."

"Well, you don't," I whispered, my words a hush that lingered between us.

His gaze didn't move from mine, and for a moment I couldn't breathe. I might have been pinned beneath him, but I knew he wouldn't hurt me. My pilot's gut instinct told me that the only danger with Volten came from the fact that I didn't want him to get off me. I didn't want him to let me go. But I couldn't give in to what I wanted. Not when I had so much to prove.

I bucked against him again. "Get off me."

His gaze drifted to my lips for a moment before he inclined his head slightly. "Your wish is my command, Lieutenant."

When his grip on my wrists slackened, I wriggled from under him and got to my feet, steadying my breath as I walked away from him and didn't look back. That was the last time I was ever going to be pinned under a Drexian, I told myself, even as I fought the urge to steal a final glance at the warrior who was making me doubt my own resolve.

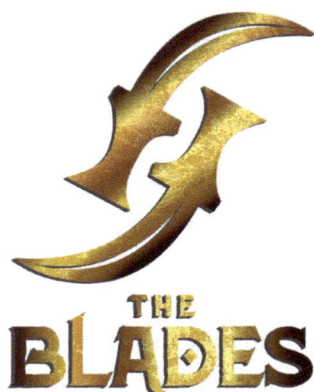

THE BLADES

CHAPTER 10

VOLTEN

I WAS LATE.

I hated being late.

Lateness reminded me of my father, who'd never been on time for anything if he'd bothered to show up at all. It reminded me of my brothers, who'd barely rolled into classes until they hadn't bothered anymore. It reminded me of my mother gnawing her bottom lip and trying to pretend it didn't matter that she was consistently made late by the worthless males in her life, constantly forgotten, always waiting.

And now I was late for the term's opening banquet.

"Just like them," I said darkly to myself, trying not to dwell on the disgrace of my clan, even though my face flamed at my own mental comparison.

My only comfort was the fact that it hadn't been derision or disdain that had prompted my lateness, but a malfunctioning console in one of the fighter jets. I'd lost track of time as I'd tried to determine the issue, and now I was hurrying down empty corridors, my footsteps echoing back to me and reminding me that I was the only Drexian not where I was supposed to be.

What I couldn't tell anyone was that I ended up in the ship-yard because I'd needed to cool down after sparring with Ariana, and nothing calmed me like sitting in a cockpit. Being in a ship was the only thing that could have distracted me from thoughts of her heaving chest and flared pupils as she'd been pinned beneath me. For a heartbeat, I'd considered kissing her, pressing my body to hers, provoking a moan from her curvy lips, but then I'd remembered who she was, and who I was, and why she was forbidden to me.

I walked faster as I remembered the unwanted desire to pos-sess her that had stormed through me, desire I needed to push aside before I reached the welcome banquet. I muttered a curse beneath my breath as I realized that there wasn't even one straggler loitering in the cavernous hall or rushing up the sweeping staircase with me.

So much for making a good first impression on the new humans joining the academy, although I'd already blown that with Ariana. Mistaking her for a cadet hadn't been a good start. Pinning her to the mat had not made up for it, but I suspected letting her win wouldn't have made her happy either.

I only hoped Zoran wouldn't regret giving me the commenda-tion and bump in rank he'd bestowed after I'd been injured in the attack. There was no doubt that he was aware of my clan's reputa-tion. Drexian clans were as much a part of us as our flesh, and my clan in particular, clung to me like a foul odor. I'd had to outperform everyone so they wouldn't have any chance to compare me to my forebears, and that included never being late.

Was the admiral being reminded of my lack of status even now as my seat sat empty? Were the other instructors from elite houses shaking their heads and thinking that I might not be so different from my disreputable clan after all?

The moment I stepped into the great hall for the welcoming

banquet, I was surrounded by the clatter of clanging platters, clinking glasses, and loud conversation that swelled all the way to the vaulted ceiling and almost drowned out the nervous chatter in my head. I entered from the back and made my way toward the staff table on the front dais, hoping the Academy Master wouldn't notice me slinking in after everyone else had started eating.

The long tables that ran the length of the room were packed with cadets jostling for more room as they prodded each other with sharp elbows and reached across bodies to refill their drinks from heavy pewter pitchers. It was too chaotic for one Drexian to be noticed slipping into his seat at the end of the table, too loud for my chair to be heard scraping across the stone floor, too packed with Drexians all in dark uniforms for me to draw attention, so I settled into my chair and drew in a breath of savory scents that hung heavy in the air.

"Volten."

I stiffened at the familiar deep voice from the center of the table.

"Apologies for my late arrival, Master Zoran." I chanced a glance down the length of the table, catching the curious eyes of other instructors and noting the presence of, not only Ariana, but also another human female at the staff table.

"Kann told us you were busy with one of your ships."

I stole a quick look at my friend seated beside me, but his gaze was not on me. Leave it to Kann to cover for me without question.

"I was." I straightened. "I wanted to ensure all our vessels were in flying shape before classes tomorrow."

The academy master inclined his head. "Admirable, but do not work so hard you forget to eat." He swiveled his head to the two new females at the table. "Lieutenant Volten, this is Captain Fiona Douglas and Lieutenant Ariana Bowman. I believe you're acquainted with the lieutenant."

Both women nodded at me, but Ariana's eyes narrowed in challenge. "We're acquainted."

I managed to smile at her, even though I was the only one at the table to know her veiled meaning. Then I returned my attention to the admiral. "I gave the lieutenant a tour of the academy as you requested."

Zoran glanced at the human. "As the two instructors assigned to our new cadets in Flight, I suspect you'll be working together closely."

"Lucky *grekking* bastard," Kann said, so only I could hear him. Since he was a battle instructor, the chances of a human female joining his school were remote. The humans might be clever and have decent flight skills, but it was hard to imagine one being able to excel against a much larger and stronger Drexian on the sparring mat.

"I look forward to it," I said, loud enough for Ariana to hear me at the other end of the table. If she wanted to pretend the sparring match never happened, I'd go along with her, but not without enjoying myself in the process. I would never let her know that being so close to her had unsettled me to the point of distraction.

Before I could say more, Zoran stood, and the din of the hall devolved to a hush. "Welcome to the start of a new term. We welcome our returning cadets." Cheers followed this. "And our new cadets." Whistles and hoots echoed off the high ceiling. "It is no secret that our academy has gone through turbulence and change, but this does not mean that it is weakened." Zoran's expression hardened. "We have never been stronger than we are now, and the changes we've made will make us an even greater training ground for the galaxy's finest warriors."

He paused for a moment as the cheering rose to a deafening roar and cadets pumped fists in the air. "There are some things that have not changed. There are still four schools that you will be divided into. After this first term, you will be either an Assassin, a Blade, an Iron, or a Wing. As always, it will be part effort, part talent, and part fate." He lifted his glass. "I wish you luck."

We all toasted, and the hall was once again filled with chatter.

I took a swig from my filled goblet, grateful as the drink slid down my throat to warm my belly. Then I leaned over to Kann. "Thanks for covering for me."

He flicked his dark hair off his forehead. "I know you. I know the only reason you'd be late was because you'd gotten caught up in work and forgot the time. You're a bit obsessive about those ships, you know."

"I am a flight instructor." And *those ships* had been my ticket away from home and to a life where I wasn't punished for my lineage, even if I did feel it hanging over me.

"A flight instructor who has a new colleague." Kann cut a look at the women who were in conversation with Zoran's wife, Noora, another human who'd relocated to the Drexian home world and academy. "Why do the flight and military strategy schools get all the fun?"

I let my gaze rest on the golden-haired woman next to Ariana. No one would deny that she was beautiful, but there was an intimidating air around her that made me want to keep a wide berth. "The captain is a strategist?"

Kann took a bite of his roasted *padwump*, the aroma of the meat wafting up from his plate. "Planning military attacks and wars is supposed to be her strength. She was part of the human contingent that worked with us to mobilize against the Kronock when they attacked Earth."

I eyed her again. She didn't look older than many cadets, but there was no denying she radiated command. While I was staring at her, she looked up and arched a brow at me. It wasn't curiosity. It wasn't an invitation. It was a challenge. I looked away.

Kann chuckled. "I'd keep my distance from her."

"I'm surprised to hear you say that." I studied my friend, who was as notorious with alien females as he was in the sparring ring.

"Why make life difficult for myself?" Kann swept his gaze

across the hall. "The new instructors aren't the only females at the academy now."

I followed his line of sight to the rows of cadets seated at the rectangular tables, my gaze instantly alighting on a group of humans near the front. There were several men, easily spotted because they didn't have shoulders as broad as their Drexian counterparts, and I counted six women. I'd been so focused on the fact that I'd be working with a human woman that I hadn't remembered that I'd also be teaching them.

"Female cadets," I said in a low voice.

Kann hummed beside me. "Aren't they enticing?"

I snapped my head to him. "And forbidden."

His eyes pressed together as he huffed out a breath. "Where's your sense of adventure?"

"I'm sure I'll get plenty of adventure this year." I cut my gaze to Zoran. "Do you think we'll still have the trials?"

"Why wouldn't we?"

I flicked a glance at the human cadets, but Kann shook his head, as if rejecting the idea of skipping the dangerous tradition that divided cadets into schools. "The maze has been a tradition since the start of the academy."

"A deadly tradition."

"I'm sure the humans know what they signed up for, Volt." He elbowed me. "But why are you worried? We've already survived the trials."

I swept my gaze across the raucous hall of cadets and lingered on the humans. *My* survival wasn't what concerned me.

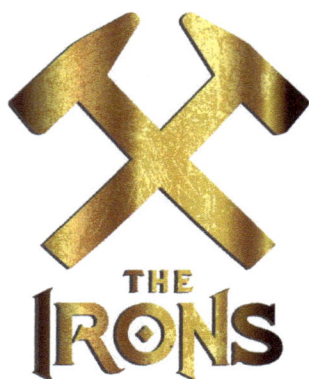

THE IRONS

CHAPTER 11

ARIANA

I SHOOK OUT MY HANDS AS I APPROACHED THE LECTURE HALL. The movement had always helped allay my nerves before, but no matter how hard I shook, my stomach was still a hard knot.

"Come on, Bowman. Get it together." I didn't have to worry that I'd be heard over the din of voices bouncing off the stone corridor. Every cadet was a foot taller than me, and so consumed with rushing to their own classes that they didn't even glance my way. Maybe the novelty of human women in their midst had already worn off, and I wouldn't feel the probing looks that had been almost palpable as I'd sat on the dais the night before.

I paused outside the massive doors leading to the room that would host Introduction to Flight. It was a basic class, and one I'd taught before as a teaching assistant when I was in school. This was nothing new. The only change was that I'd be looking at a sea of Drexian faces and not human ones.

"As if there's much difference," I reminded myself with a low laugh that sounded forced even to my own ears. Ancient strands of shared DNA meant that we had many of the same physical features, the main differences being size—they were bigger—and external arousal indicators—they had extra ones in the raised nodes that ran the length of their spines. It also meant that about half of the females on Earth were sexually compatible with Drexians, which was why the aliens had been procuring mates from Earth for decades. None of these facts that I quickly ran through my head meant that the cadets on this planet would go easy on me.

I rubbed my palms down the front of the dark fabric of my uniform pants then flicked them through my short hair, glad that at least that made me look more like my Drexian students. Finally, I threw back my shoulders, trying to channel Fiona's commanding stance and air of authority, and pushed open the door. I didn't wait until I'd reached the front of the theatre-style classroom to start talking, raising my voice to a bellow to be heard over the cadets talking and laughing.

"I am Lieutenant Bowman, your instructor for Introduction to Flight. Not all of you will be Wings, but every cadet must pass this class. If you are not supposed to be in this class at this time, now is the time to leave."

The volume plummeted as the Drexians took their seats, and I strode toward the lectern at the front. I noticed that no one left. I also noticed that the cocky cadet who'd appeared in the female tower and had assumed that Fiona and I were fellow cadets had taken a spot in the front row.

I had to give the guy credit for being either brave or stupid. Most would want to hide in the anonymity of the back row or bury themselves in the middle of the room surrounded by others, but he was front and center with a smile on his face. The smile was not comforting.

I took my place behind the clear lectern and used the controls inset in the top to dim the lights slightly and project a holographic image in the air to my side. I'd prepped my presentation the day before and even gone through it to ensure that the Drexian tech wouldn't throw me any surprises, but my fingers trembled as I pointed to the images of a Drexian fighter and a F-40 Lightning V from Earth. "Can anyone tell me about the differences between these two fighters?"

There were a few mumbles and then a voice called out. "One of them would blow the other to bits."

I stiffened at the clear implication that the Earth vessel was outmatched by the Drexian one, but I couldn't let anyone see my irritation. "Explain."

The voice didn't respond, so after a few beats, I asked again. "Does anyone want to defend the statement that one ship is more powerful than the other?"

More silence and a few low laughs. I took a breath and told myself that I could not let myself get rattled by my students—not on day one.

"Simple." The cocky Drexian in the front row stood and grasped his hands behind his back as he spoke. "The Drexian fighter is equipped with stealth shielding, which means that it can make itself undetectable to enemy ships. It also has a more powerful engine than any vessel created on Earth and better maneuverability. This particular fighter isn't outfitted with jump technology, but if it was, it could also leave any attack before primitive ships could follow."

Finally, a cadet who knew about ships.

Then, he added, "Basically, it looks better and performs better, like all things Drexian." He arched a brow at me, the suggestion impossible to miss.

Ugh. "Thank you, Cadet…"

He didn't drop my gaze and flashed a grin that bordered on a leer. "Torq of House Swoll. You can call me Torq."

A ripple of laughter passed through the room. Every cadet in my class knew what his suggestive tone meant. It wasn't the first time I'd been hit on by a student, but it had never happened during class or within the first five minutes.

I steadied my breath and forced myself not to react. "That will be all, Cadet."

"You sure?" He rocked back on his heels. "There's plenty more I'd be happy to teach you."

A few hoots followed this, and he shot a confident grin over his shoulder.

Okay, so this guy was clearly one of the alpha cadets. I could have already guessed that from his confidence when he'd sauntered into our tower, but now, I was sure. The other first-year Drexians looked up to this guy. If I let him get away with hitting on me in class, I'd never have their respect.

"Okay, Cadet Torq of House Swoll, I won't disagree with you that Drexian *ships* are better than human ones, but why don't you tell me why the Drexian fighters don't have jump capability?"

The guy opened his mouth, some of the glint fading from his eyes.

"Or you could explain Drexian jump technology to me, since I'm sure you know it much better than an Earthling would."

He clamped his mouth shut. Knowing the ins and outs of the technology that pulled Drexian ships across vast distances in space in the blink of an eye wasn't first-year-level material, but this cadet had broken the rules first. All was fair in love and war, or in this case, teaching war.

"Don't worry," I broke the silence. "I'm happy to help you out, Cadet. Take a seat with the rest of your first-year classmates."

He slowly sat, and there were no laughs or hoots that followed. Only hushed silence as I explained the technology behind the alien jump drives. I didn't add that it had taken me weeks to digest the physics of it or that it still amazed me. "So, Cadet, your people's ingenious technology cannot function in a ship as small as a fighter because of the space needed for the reaction that powers it."

I paused and the room remained silent. "I hope you're all taking notes. Unless I've been misinformed, Drexians do not, as a rule, possess eidetic memories."

A shuffling followed, along with the rapid tapping on devices.

I flipped to the next image, proceeding to show my class the cockpit of the fighters they would be training to fly and reviewing all the controls and displays. I was again grateful for the intense studying I'd done on the Drexian vessels, although my actual time in their cockpits wasn't significant.

"Once you've been thoroughly tested on the ship's controls, we'll get you in the simulators, but you'll be doing that with my colleague Lieutenant Volten." I clicked off the holographic display and raised the lights. "Tomorrow, there will be a test on what we went over today, so I suggest you study. Any questions?"

There were none, so I dismissed them, and allowed myself to finally exhale deeply as the sound of the cadets standing and moving toward the door masked my sigh. The last Drexians were filing out when I noticed Torq still sitting on the front row. He wasn't irritated that I'd shot him down in class, was he?

"Can I help you, Cadet?"

He stood and moved toward me, leaning one elbow on the lectern, and looming over me with an expression he must have thought was seductive. "When do we get time in a real cockpit?"

This guy was persistent and relentless. "Not until I'm sure you can handle it."

He winked at me. "Trust me, Lieutenant, I can handle anything you give me."

I opened my mouth to put him squarely in his place, but a booming voice from the doorway stopped me.

"Cadet! Can I have a word with you?" Volten stood at the top of the tiered theatre rows with his arms folded over his chest and his eyes flashing with fury.

Instead of showing concern, Torq gave a half shrug. "See you later, Lieutenant."

He made his way slowly up the steps to where Volten was waiting as I silently seethed. Who the hell did the Drexian think he was?

THE WINGS

CHAPTER 12

VOLTEN

I hadn't meant to observe the end of Ariana's first class, but since I didn't have one in the morning, it had been too tempting to sneak in the back when the lights were low. I'd been impressed with her knowledge of Drexian technology and vessels, and with her ability to shut down the cadet in the front row.

Once the lights were back on, and the students were streaming from the room, I stepped aside to let them pass. I also wanted the chance to speak to Ariana again and make a better impression than I had the day before.

Then my gaze snagged on the same cadet who'd challenged her earlier in the class. He hadn't left.

"Can I help you, Cadet?"

Ariana's voice was sharp and her facial expression wary as the Drexian ambled toward her. He propped one arm on the transparent lectern. I couldn't make out his question or her answer, but I heard his response.

"Trust me, Lieutenant, I can handle anything you give me."

His suggestive tone was unmistakable, and anger pulsed through me. Not only was I livid that one of our cadets was showing such disrespect to an instructor, but a possessive haze made me despise that he desired her. The thought of the handsome Drexian who exuded privilege and status laying a single finger on Ariana made my hands buzz with the urge to curl around his neck and squeeze. "Cadet! Can I have a word with you?"

Ariana's head jerked up, but the cadet didn't bother glancing at me as he twitched one shoulder in dismissal. Then he turned and made his way up the stairs with a cocky grin on his face.

I stepped from the room and let him follow, whirling around once we were outside the classroom doors. I was practically vibrating with rage, and I curled my hands into fists to keep myself from snapping. "Care to explain yourself, Cadet?"

He didn't look so confident now that he was facing me, and his gaze fell on the wing insignia on my uniform. "I was asking the instructor when we'd be flying real planes."

I allowed a growl to resonate in my throat. "I heard what you said to her. In case you hadn't noticed, Lieutenant Bowman is your superior officer and your instructor. You will show her the same respect you would show any Drexian instructor." I leaned forward. "Unless you do not wish to ever see the inside of a fighter."

He squared his shoulders as his gaze hardened. "Yes, Lieutenant."

I jerked my head to one side. "Dismissed."

He spun away, taking long strides away from me to where a group of other first-years waited for him. He mumbled darkly to them, and they all cast me brief glances before walking away.

"*Grekking* first-years." I raked a hand through my hair, my heart slowing and my temper waning. I'd expected that the new humans would have a bumpy start, but I hadn't imagined that cadets would be so bold as to make suggestive comments to an instructor. And

I really hadn't anticipated my own desire to pummel anyone who so much as glanced at my new colleague. Then again, none of my other colleagues looked like Ariana.

As if thinking of her summoned the woman, she pushed through the door, her eyes flaring and then narrowing when she spotted me.

"Don't worry," I said loud enough to be heard over the voices reverberating off stone as cadets flowed past us to their next classes. "He's gone. I talked to him."

Ariana swiveled her head to take in the busy corridor then grabbed me by the sleeve and tugged me with her. My steady heartbeat spiked. Where was she taking me? Some place quieter? Some place private? Maybe I hadn't made such a bad first impression after all.

She pulled me into a narrower corridor where few cadets were venturing and down far enough that the shadows from the dimmer light hid us. Maybe I'd made a spectacular first impression. Maybe she'd changed her mind after our sparring match. Maybe she did want me on top, after all.

Then she slammed me up against the wall and fisted her hands in the front of my uniform. My pulse quickened as I wondered if all humans were this assertive with their affection. I didn't think I'd made *this* good of an impression. Or was this because of what I'd done with the cadet?

"You don't need to thank me for what I did back there," I said quickly, before she could get the idea that I required some sort of payment for my actions. Not that I would object to her kissing me or pressing her body against me or—

"Thank you?" Her eyes flashed hot as she gripped my shirt more fiercely. "Why would I thank you?"

Clearly, I had seriously misjudged what was happening. Not that I had any clue why she appeared to be angry. "For handling that cadet for you?"

"Why did you think I needed anyone to handle him for me?"

"He shouldn't have spoken to you like he did," I stammered, finding myself firmly on the defensive and still not sure why. "He violated cadet code."

"No shit, Sherlock."

Sherlock? Had she already forgotten my name. "It's Volten."

She jammed her fists into my chest. "I know your name. I also know that the cadet was being a prick. You're not the only one with ears, flyboy."

"So why...?"

"Why don't I want you fighting my battles for me and making me look weak in front of my students? I thought I'd made that abundantly clear yesterday."

I opened my mouth to tell her she didn't look weak—especially now that she'd flattened me to the wall—but pinning her to the floor in the sparring mat probably hadn't helped.

"Tell me one thing, Volten," she continued, before I could respond. "Would you have jumped in if I was Drexian?"

A small breath left my chest as I realized that she was right. I wouldn't have said a word if Kann had a cadet talk back to him. I would assume he could handle it. But that was because he was Drexian and knew precisely how to deal with other Drexian males, especially overly confident ones. It was also because I wasn't consumed with a primal need to keep any other male away from Kann like I was with Ariana.

"No," I said, as she relaxed her grip on my uniform. "You're right. But I only stepped in because you're a member of my school and new to the academy. You don't know what Drexian cadets can be like—not yet."

She uncoiled her fingers and pressed her palms flat to my chest, bowing her head for a beat. "I appreciate the sentiment, but if I don't learn to deal with them on my own, and handle the pricks myself, they'll never respect me. This isn't the first place where I've had to prove myself because I'm not one of the guys. Believe me, I know how this plays out."

I stared at the top of her head, the short brown layers swept to one side and begging me to run my fingers through them. The ache in her voice made me desperate to pull her to me—and the warmth pulsing into my chest from her hands wasn't helping staunch the urge—but I also sensed that the last thing she wanted from me was an embrace. As it was, I was hesitant to move a muscle or even breathe too boldly. "I understand, Lieutenant. I apologize for undermining you. It wasn't my intention."

She let her palms linger on my chest for a moment longer before straightening and dropping her arms by her side. "Thank you. I promise you I can fight my own battles. I've been doing it for a long time." She looked up at me, locking her gaze with mine. "And don't think that pinning me once on the mat means you won."

Before she could turn from me, I grabbed her arm and spun her around so that she was flat to the wall, and I was blocking her in with my arms. "How many times do I need to pin you before you'll accept my help?"

She tipped her head back, her eyes darkening as she ran a hand up and through the short hair at the nape of my neck. "You really want to fight my battles for me, big guy?"

I shook my head as I'd momentarily lost the ability to speak. I might be bracing her with my body, but she was the one holding me prisoner with her eyes. Then, her grip on my hair tightened, sending a jolt of pain through me as she brought her knee up, halting it right before ramming it into my crotch.

"When I need someone to fight my battles for me, you'll be the first to know." She released my hair, dropped her knee, and ducked from under my arms. "And when I want a guy on top, flyboy, he knows it."

Then she spun on her heel and stomped back down the corridor, leaving me dragging in ragged breaths as I leaned my palms against the cool wall. I'd learned one thing for sure. I should never make Ariana angry again. I blew out a breath at the thought of her fury being directed at me and rubbed one hand on my shoulder where it had impacted the wall. I glanced down, grateful she hadn't kneed me. For a small female, she was remarkably strong.

She might be tougher than she looked, but she'd never been thrown into the Drexian Academy before. I knew all too well that in a place with so much unspoken, sometimes there was more danger in the battles being waged beneath the surface than the ones fought in the sky. And with so many cadets from so many clans battling it out, it would be easy to be taken down by their devious maneuverings.

I sighed as I brushed aside my own memories of being a cadet in the academy. I would not let *that* happen to Ariana. I would have to do a better job of protecting her without her knowing.

I shook my head, regretting my decision, but knowing I had no other choice.

THE ASSASSINS

CHAPTER 13

ARIANA

I LEANED MY HAND AGAINST THE PANEL TO THE SIDE OF MY DOOR, dropping my head below my slumped shoulders and not moving when the door slid open.

"That bad?"

I didn't need to turn to know that it was Fiona behind me. "Don't ask."

She laughed, the sound throaty and warm. "First days always suck. It doesn't matter which side of the classroom you're on."

I straightened and turned to see her leaning in the frame of her open door. After my first class and encounter with Volten, the day had improved—at least no other cadets had tried to hit on me, and no one had tried to be a white knight—but I was still regretting my overreaction to the lieutenant.

As irate as I'd been, I never should have dragged him down the corridor and slammed him against the wall. For a moment before I'd started yelling at him, I genuinely wasn't sure if I wanted to kiss him or kick him. There was something about the Drexian that made my heart lurch and my fingers tingle, something I needed to do a better job of ignoring.

"It will get better, right?" I asked, grabbing the back of my neck and attempting to squeeze out some of the tension.

Fiona tugged her own uniform shirt from her pants so that it hung loose. "Probably, but I know something guaranteed to make us feel better."

I hesitated. Usually promises of feeling better quickly led to regrets later.

She reached inside her room and produced a clear bottle filled with bright blue liquid. "I think both of us surviving the first day teaching cadets at the Drexian Academy deserves a drink."

My mouth watered even though my brain sent up warning flares. "I've never seen booze so brightly colored."

Fiona tilted the bottle and the contents swished from side to side. "It's Noovian something."

"Something drinkable?" I didn't want to end up in the infirmary after toasting with the alien equivalent of drain cleaner.

"Of course." Fiona waved me into her room. "I got it off one of the bartenders on the space station we stopped at before coming to the Drexian home world. But that Neebix is a story for another day."

That made me feel a bit better about it, although now I was wondering about the Neebix. I followed the captain into her quarters, letting the door slide closed behind me. Like my compact room, hers contained a bed, desk, and dresser, with bookshelves bolted into the walls.

Unlike me, Fiona had added her own decorative touches to the basic, black-and-gray decor of the space, with a lavender Angora throw across the foot of the bed, a hot-pink elephant figurine on the desk, and a row of bodice-ripper paperbacks filling one of the shelves. I wasn't sure which surprised me more, that the captain liked feminine colors or that she read romance novels.

She produced a pair of cups that looked unbreakable despite being clear and poured generous amounts of the blue liquid into them. She put the bottle on her desk and raised her glass. "Here's to the first two women to break into the ranks at the big, bad alien academy."

"And to making it out alive," I added before clinking her glass.

She laughed. "Maybe the Drexians will be the ones who feel lucky to survive *us*."

Maybe, I thought as I took a drink. Then I thought of the huge, muscled aliens and how firm Volten's chest had felt when my hands had been flattened against it. I was definitely the one who needed to keep my guard high.

The blue liquor looked like it should be used to scrub surfaces, but it tasted like candy. My lips puckered at the sour kick once the sweetness had faded.

Fiona eyed her glass before downing the rest in a single gulp. "I did not expect *that*."

I followed her lead, and then she refilled both of our glasses, pulled the chair from her desk, and waved for me to sit on the bed. I sank onto the bed, my tongue already feeling a bit numb, and held my glass with both hands. "You outrank me. Maybe you'll know."

"Know what?"

"The four rules of the academy. Any clue what they mean?"

She swirled the liquid in her glass before drinking. "Rules? You mean all those forms and releases we had to sign?"

I shook my head. "You know, the unofficial rules. Beware of the assassins. Don't cross the blades. Trust the irons. The wings go as one."

She held my gaze for a beat as if trying to determine if I was serious. "Never heard of them."

She clearly hadn't done a deep dive into the school lore like I had. She loved floorplans. I loved lore. "There isn't much information on this place, but that was one thing I found. I have no idea what it means though."

"Cryptic and a little ominous. Perfect for a school like this." Fiona ran a hand through her hair. "The Wings part must mean the fighter jets, right? Or the flight school?"

"That's what I guessed. Four schools. Four rules. One for each of the academy divisions."

She took a significant gulp. "Too bad that cocky Drexian cadet isn't hanging around anymore. I'll bet he knows."

I rolled my eyes. The drink might have been sweet, but that was obviously its trick. My skin buzzed from the effects, and my tongue had been robbed of all its restraint. "Speaking of that cocky cadet..."

"Don't tell me you saw him again?"

"In the front row of my first class."

Her lips curled into a gleeful grin. "I'll bet he was twitching."

"Not really. He hit on me."

Fiona's eyes bulged. "What? I hope you kicked him in the balls."

"I'm not sure if we're allowed to put a knee in the crotch for first offenses."

Fiona flapped a hand. "These are Drexians. They're notoriously tough."

That was true, but I didn't know if there was a male in the universe who was tough when it came to his balls if he were a species that possessed them.

"I didn't get the chance to do much of anything. Lieutenant Volten stepped in before I could."

"Volten, Volten." Fiona scrunched her lips to one side as she mulled over the name. "Which one is he?"

"Tall, dark hair, lots of muscles." I'd just described almost every Drexian.

She pursed her lips at my smart-ass reply. "Point taken."

"He's the one who was late to dinner last night."

Her eyes widened. "Him? Oh, he's cute. Too young for me, but hot."

"How can he be too young for you? We're probably the same age."

She met my eyes over the top of her glass after taking a sip. "I prefer my men a bit more seasoned. Personal preference, that's all."

"Well, it doesn't matter if he's hot. We're both instructors in the flight school. He's off limits."

"Really?" Fiona leaned forward. "Says who?"

I huffed out a breath. The last thing I needed was a devil on my shoulder telling me to give in to my urges. I'd only survived as long as I had and risen so high by controlling my feelings and being more focused, more disciplined, less distracted. And that meant no hot Drexians, especially not ones I had to work alongside. "Says me."

Fiona studied me for a moment. "I get it. Women in a man's world must be tougher and more disciplined, just to keep from falling behind."

I tossed back my drink and held it out for her to refill. "Something like that. Besides, Volten wants to be a savior, and I don't need saving."

"No, you don't." She filled her own glass again and tipped it to me. "I read your file."

I almost choked as I swallowed. "You what?"

"I had to know which other women were also being stationed with me. Captain's prerogative." She leaned back in the chair. "You were top of your class and ranked one of the best pilots in any of the branches."

"Like you said, work harder, be tougher."

Fiona inclined her head at me. "Not only that, but you also come from a long line of military heroes. This is in your blood."

Fear iced the warmth that had been bubbling inside me. Talk of my family never ended well for me. After my mother had died when we were young, my father had raised us like his own little soldiers, drilling discipline and toughness into us. The world saw a long heritage of military service while I felt nothing but shame where pride should have been.

My heart pounded as I held my breath, praying that she wouldn't mention the one military hero in my family I couldn't bear to think about and the reason I'd run from Earth and straight to the academy.

Fiona swung her gaze from me and to the bottle we were rapidly emptying. "Enough talk about family and hard work. Have you seen the new security chief for the academy?"

I blinked at her, my brain sluggishly absorbing such a brisk change of topic. "Security chief?"

"He arrived today. Total silver fox and one hundred percent my type." She released a tortured sigh. "Too bad he's a complete asshole and doesn't like humans. I've never had a guy be as dismissive to me as him, and that was even before I could be a superior bitch to him to deserve it."

I laughed out loud at this. At least Fiona had no problem owning her attitude.

She laughed along with me. "But that's okay. I guess neither of us need hot Drexians to make us feel complete, right?"

"Absolutely."

She pulled open the top desk drawer and her smile widened into something sly and dangerous. "Now, how are you at Drexian card games?"

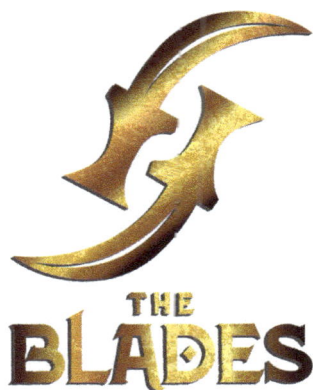

THE BLADES

CHAPTER 14

VOLTEN

T HUD THUD THUD.

I groaned in the darkness as I lay in my bed and tried to ignore the pounding on my door. What now? I'd retreated to my quarters after a long first day of classes and more green cadets than I would wish on my worst enemy. Actually, I might wish them on the Kronock. Maybe I should suggest that our new war strategy should be sending the first-years to infiltrate the enemy forces and destroy them from the inside.

Thud thud thud.

You're being too harsh, I told myself. You were just as green once.

But not as arrogant or entitled. Even now, my blood boiled as I thought about the cadet coming on to Ariana. Then I remembered the rush I'd felt when I'd chastened him. A dark part of me had savored the reverse of fortunes that a low-class Drexian like me could be putting an elite cadet in his place. Because that was what he was, a cadet from an elite Drexian family.

I didn't need to look him up to know. I didn't need to find his Drexian clan on the ancient scrolls. I didn't need to discover that his father was on the High Command or had been a general in the Drexian forces.

I knew the type. He exuded privilege, power, prestige. Drexians like him had made my time at the academy hell. I was a little surprised that there weren't more of them in the incoming cadet class, but even one was enough to make toxic memories force their way to the surface. *And now you wish to make his life hell to get a measure of retribution?*

Thud thud thud.

I sat up. "Maybe I do."

Throwing back the covers, I strode to the door and pressed the panel to allow it to open, growling when it was Kann looking much too eager and awake.

I turned on my heel and retreated within my quarters again. "I'm not interested."

"How do you know what I'm going to ask?" He followed me inside, laughing. "I haven't even told you."

"I know you, and I know when you're up to something. I also know that your plans usually land me in trouble."

"That was when we were cadets. I've matured since then."

I barked out a sharp laugh, some of my bitterness evaporating at the reminder that Kann had been my loyal friend since our academy days—and my frequent defender. "Have you?"

He ignored my question. "How much trouble can you get into if we're with the Academy Master?"

I craned my head to look at him, his face half illuminated from the light in the corridor. He didn't look like he was lying. "The Academy Master sent you to get me?"

"Invited is a better word." Kann grinned widely. "We've been asked to join the admiral in his private lounge."

"The admiral has a private lounge?" I'd never heard of the former academy master inviting instructors into any part of his private areas. Not that Kerog had been the type to allow anyone into his inner sanctum. He'd been as sly and unnerving as any Drexian I'd ever met, and there wasn't any part of me that missed the old master.

Kann opened his arms wide. "We won't know for sure by hiding out in your quarters."

I wanted to argue that I wasn't hiding out, I was resting, but the distinction would be lost on my friend who would always choose hanging out in a seedy bar or alien cantina over getting extra sleep. "Then let's go."

I slipped my feet back into my boots and followed Kann into the corridor lined with quarters for staff, including his own room, only three down from mine. The hallways were no longer bustling with activity since classes had ended and cadets were in the dining hall or skipping the meal to study.

I was grateful that academy staff and cadets didn't take all meals together—only the weekly all-academy dinners and special celebratory banquets—and that instructors had a small, informal dining space of our own. I was even more grateful that I was still friendly with the kitchen staff from my own cadet days and could sweet-talk them into letting me sneak bread fresh from their ovens.

Kann took a staircase two at a time, and I kept up with him, emerging onto the floor with the Academy Master's office. When we stopped at the large door, I put a hand on his arm. "This is his office."

Kann shook his head at me. "Have a little faith, Volt."

He rapped his knuckles on the door, and we waited until it slid open.

Tivek stood inside, his expression as stony and unreadable as ever. I wondered if the Drexian's permanent post was inside the door. "You came."

I couldn't tell from his tone if this was a good or bad thing, if he approved or didn't approve of our presence. The admiral's adjunct didn't say anything else as he pivoted and walked deeper into the long office which was empty.

"Are we the first?" I asked then immediately regretted my question. Of course, we were the first. There wasn't a soul in the room, not even the admiral.

Tivek didn't respond or turn as he walked to the side wall and pressed a finger into a groove in the stone. The previously seamless wall opened as a door slid aside to reveal an adjoining room.

I managed to keep my jaw from hitting the floor as Kann muttered "*grekking* hell" under his breath. We fell in step behind Tivek as he walked through the hidden doorway, and into a room that looked every bit like a hidden lair should.

A thick carpet covered the polished stone floor and a fire crackled in the hearth inset in the black wall opposite the entrance. Over the dancing blue flames of the fire hung a pair of Drexian battle blades crossed and curved to the ceiling, the light glinting off the polished steel. A pair of plush, smoke-gray couches were arranged facing each other on the rug with a low, clear table between them. Behind one couch was a wall of bookshelves filled with embossed leather volumes from floor to ceiling, and on the wall behind the other couch was a mirrored wall fronted with glass shelving that held bottles of more different types of liquor than I'd imagined existed.

"Welcome." Admiral Zoran stood near the fire with a silver-haired Drexian I'd never seen before. "I'm glad you could join us."

Tivek moved to the wall of bottles, plucking one down and pouring a measure of amber liquid into two glasses. When he handed one to each of us, I moved wordlessly toward the other Drexians, feeling like I'd fallen into a vortex to another dimension.

The older Drexian ran a hand down the short beard that was as silver as his hair as we approached, his gaze landing on me and not sliding away. He glanced back at Zoran, cocking his head and giving the master an inquisitive look.

"Lieutenant Volten and Lieutenant Kann, I'd like you to meet our new security chief, Commander Vyk."

New security chief? After my experience with the academy's former security chief, I stiffened at the reminder. I took a sip of my drink, welcoming the burn as the potent whiskey scorched my throat.

"Commander Vyk?" Kann thumped his fist across his chest before I could. "The Vyk from Inferno Force?"

The Drexian grunted. "That was a long time ago."

"Your battles are legendary, Commander."

I let the Drexian's name roll around in my brain. I knew I'd heard of him before. Had Kann talked about him to me? No, that wasn't it. Then where had I heard of this Inferno Force warrior before?

I took another sip, but before I could swallow, the memory slammed into me. I knew exactly where I'd heard the name. I knew exactly why the back of my neck prickled with unease. I knew exactly who he was.

The Inferno Force Commander was not as much legendary as he was notorious.

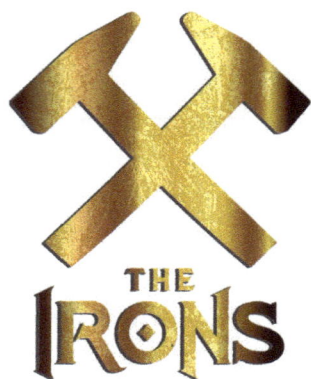

THE IRONS

CHAPTER 15

VOLTEN

The halls were silent when I finally extracted myself from Zoran's private lounge and office. Kann had been too busy discussing Inferno Force victories with the new security chief to do much more than glance at me when I'd slipped from the private room. Even though I'd managed to nurse the single whiskey, my head now swam, and my steps were heavy.

Deep-throated laughs from overhead made me tip my head back to peer up the opening in the wide, spiraling staircase. A cluster of shadowy cadets were straddling the banister at the top and urging each other to go. Wasn't it too soon for cadets to try to complete the unwritten graduation requirements?

"If you try to slide all the way down, I promise you won't reach the bottom," I called up, my stern tone silencing the laughter and urgent whispers.

I didn't glance up again to assure myself that they'd disbanded. I didn't care enough to trudge up to the top of the central staircase and ensure that no one was attempting to slide down the banister without slipping off and plunging to the atrium floor. My mind was too occupied.

I slid one hand along the cool stone of the banister as I made my way down, only stopping when I reached the final step and nearly ran into a figure significantly smaller than me.

"Ouch, watch where you're…" Ariana whirled on me and then her expression softened. "Oh, it's you."

I tried not to take offense at that, as I cut my gaze down the corridor that held classrooms. "What are you doing here so late?"

"In all the stairwells, in all the academies…" she murmured, before frowning at me. "Okay, fine, I'm lost. I was trying to find the kitchens because I forgot to eat dinner, and then I drank some Noovian liquor, and now I'm starving."

I stifled my impulse to laugh at her and her slightly slurred speech. "This definitely is not the level with the kitchens. It isn't even the right building."

She rolled her eyes. "Great. I should have studied the floorplans like Fiona instead of trying to learn all your goofy rules."

"My goofy rules?" *Grek*, she was cute when she wasn't trying to appear tough. Not that she wasn't gorgeous when she was furious, but I preferred the version of her that didn't glare daggers at me.

She waved a hand in the air. "Your academy's rules. You know, beware the assassins, double-cross the blades, trust in iron, the wings are number one."

Now a small laugh did slip from my lips as I took her by the elbow and started to guide her toward the kitchens. "Those aren't exactly the rules, but how did you hear about them?"

Her eyes widened, and she leaned closer even though the corridor we were moving through was deserted except for us. "Are they supposed to be secret?"

"Not secret, but they aren't something spoken about outside these walls."

"Nothing interesting about this place is. Not the rules, not the requirements."

"You've heard of the requirements, too?" Now I *was* surprised.

"From Torq. You know, that cadet you set straight." She held up two fingers on each hand and moved them up and down.

I mimicked her movement as we started down another set of stairs. "What is this?"

"Air quotes. Don't Drexians do air quotes?" When I shook my head, she sighed. "It means that I don't really think you set him straight."

Human customs were odd. "He told you the four unofficial graduation requirements?"

"Yes, but he said there was now a new one since there are females at the academy."

My spine went rigid. I could almost guess what the new requirement would be. "Torq does not speak for all Drexians at the academy."

She leaned into me as we reached a landing. "You wouldn't want to spend a night in a female's room?"

My pulse spiked as I inhaled the floral scent of her hair, and I bit back a groan. "Is that an invitation?"

She snorted and then slapped a hand over her mouth. "No." She gave me a harder glance as I led her across to another stairwell. "Not that you wouldn't probably be a lot of fun."

I tried not to focus on where the conversation was leading as I guided her down the dark and narrow stairs. "How much Noovian liquor did you have?"

She paused on a step and tipped her head back to lock her gaze with mine. "Are you suggesting that I'm too drunk to know what I'm saying?"

That was exactly what I was implying, but I wasn't going to admit it. Not with the way her eyes were narrowing.

She didn't wait for me to reply before she turned and resumed walking. "Maybe I should spend the night with you. Then I could sweet talk you into explaining the rules to me."

A jolt went through me as I contemplated what "sweet-talking" might entail, and I almost missed a step. Ariana really needed to stop talking like this, or I was going to end up rolling down a flight of stone stairs.

I drew in a breath and caught the scent of freshly baked bread. We were close. Once we reached the last step, I pulled her to the right down a dimly lit hallway as the savory scents grew more potent.

Ariana put a hand on her stomach. "I can smell food."

"They're already baking the bread for tomorrow." I spotted a shaft of light pouring from a wide opening in the corridor. I stopped her before we reached the doorway of the kitchens and flattened Ariana against the wall. "Wait here."

She seemed startled, but she didn't object as I left her so I could slink inside the warm, expansive kitchens and snatch a tray of rolls from one of the tall stacks of racks. I slipped out silently without being seen by the bakers who were intent on kneading dough at the long counters.

Ariana gaped at the golden-brown rolls, and at me, before snatching one and taking a big bite. Her eyes rolled into the back of her head as she chewed, and I followed her lead and bit into a yeasty, pillowy roll.

We ate in silence in the corridor, both finishing our bread at the same time.

Ariana took another and held it up. "This might be the best thing I've ever eaten." She smiled at me. "Thank you, Lieutenant."

"Volten." My whisper was hoarse. "You should call me Volten when we're alone."

One of her brows lifted. "Do you plan for us to be alone often, Volten?"

"No," I said so quickly that her lips quirked into a teasing smile. My mouth went dry as I let myself imagine what that would be like, but then I reminded myself that I was a Drexian officer, and we were both instructors at the Academy. And she's off limits, I reminded myself.

She twitched one shoulder and ran a finger down one side of my face. "Too bad." Then she took another roll and walked away from me, humming to herself.

The tray bobbled in my hands, and I almost dropped it before catching it and placing it carefully on the stone floor. I looked up in time to catch sight of her hips twisting as she turned toward the staircase, and I bit my bottom lip hard. *Grek* me.

THE WINGS

CHAPTER 16

ARIANA

THE WIND WHIPPED AT MY HAIR AS I LED MY FIRST-YEARS FROM the academy and across the shipyard. More of the rubble had been cleared, but that didn't mean the ground was even. There were still divots large enough to snap an ankle if you didn't watch your step.

The sky swirled gray overhead, but the Drexian home world seemed always on the verge of a storm that rarely came. It might smell like rain, but that didn't mean the drops would fall. Instead, the sky would greedily hold onto them until the clouds were so cruelly bloated, they were black.

The sky overhead matched my mood. Drinking so much Noovian booze hadn't been my best move, nor had been playing cards with Fiona. I really should have learned more about Drexian card games before I'd come like she had, although I'd never imagined that another human would be the one challenging me to play.

And then there'd been my trip to the kitchens with Volten. A part of me hoped that I'd dreamed it, and another part of me wished I hadn't walked away. An even bigger part of me wished I hadn't woken up with a wicked headache.

But I'd also woken up with a realization. I had to meet strength with strength. The Drexians didn't know anything about me, and they didn't hold Earth accomplishments in high regard. Not compared to Drexian ones because everyone knew that Drexians were bigger, stronger, tougher.

If I wanted to gain the respect of my cadets, I needed to show them that I was just as big of a badass in my own way. If I didn't, I might as well ask Volten to fight my battles for me. And that wasn't going to happen. The Drexian already thought he had some sort of responsibility toward me, and him finding me lost in the castle and taking me by the hand to get food probably hadn't helped my case.

I thought about my sister's letter. *Don't let them push you around and don't fuck up.* If all went according to my plan, none of the cadets would push me around ever again. If it didn't go according to plan, it would be a serious fuck-up. If it didn't go according to plan, I'd probably be dead.

I wondered what Sasha would say about that. Probably that I was being too stubborn again. As if she was any different. As if both of us weren't products of a father whose meager scraps of approval we'd always fought over.

"Well, you're not here, Sash, so you don't get a vote."

One of the female cadets hurried to catch up to me. "What was that?"

I shook my head and banished my sister and my father from my thoughts.

"What are we doing?" Torq was the only one bold enough to shout the question over the snapping wind as I reached a pair of long-nosed fighter jets with hulls as ebony as the academy itself.

"You asked when you would be flying, Cadet." I spun around to face my students. "The answer is now."

Even the cocky cadet who'd challenged me in my first class only stared at me. "We're flying in that?"

I shook my head. "*You're* flying in that."

His mouth gaped, as all his bravado leached from him. "A fighter?"

I gave him a clipped nod. "If you think you can beat my moves, that is."

Torq glanced around to the other cadets. They were all first-years. They were all inexperienced fighters, unless Volten had moved them into the simulators faster than I thought he would. And from the looks on their faces, they all thought I was crazy.

"I'm going to show you what one of these fighters can do. If you think you can do better, I challenge you to prove it." I jabbed a finger toward the turbulent sky. "Up there."

I hooked the toe of my boot into a virtually invisible notch behind the wing, hoisted myself up, clambered across the wing and dropped into the open cockpit. My heart was hammering, partly from the excitement from being in a plane again and partly because it was a plane I'd only ever flown once before.

"Like riding a bike," I said as I pulled down the cockpit glass, strapped myself in, and scanned the controls, "and all bikes are basically the same."

Despite the Drexians' technological advances that outstripped ours, and their space vessels that made ones on Earth look like toys, the controls weren't all that different. I reacquainted myself with the slight variations as I powered up the engines, welcoming the deep-throated hum that vibrated through me.

Glancing to one side, I noticed the first-year cadets backing away from the fighter, their faces slack-jawed as they watched me. Then I spotted Volten emerging from another ship, his hand above his eyes as he strained to see what was happening. I didn't wait for him to find out that I was making an unauthorized flight or that I'd challenged my own students to outfly me. I turned back, gunned it down the short runway, and blasted into the air.

THE ASSASSINS

CHAPTER 17

VOLTEN

TAPPED MY FOOT ON THE FLOOR OF THE TRANSPORT SHIP AS I inspected the controls. I'd set aside the morning to complete the check of all the ships in the shipyard, but my focus was not on the smooth console and flashing lights. It wasn't even on Ariana and her adorably drunk banter. If I thought about her, I'd be completely useless, so I'd banished my memories of creeping around the academy with her along with the flesh memory of her finger trailing down my cheek.

What I couldn't stop thinking about was the academy's new security chief. Despite Kann's enthusiasm for the Drexian, I was unsettled by the severity of the elder commander. He'd barely cracked a smile the entire time we'd been in Zoran's hidden lounge, but that hadn't been the most unsettling thing. It had been the way he looked at me, his blue eyes so probing I was sure he was on the verge of an interrogation.

Fitting, since interrogation had been what he'd been infamous for in Inferno Force. He'd been known to make enemies break when no one else could. I sincerely hoped he wasn't planning to use those skills at an academy filled with cadets.

No one else at the informal gathering had seemed to be bothered by Commander Vyk. Then again, he hadn't stared intently at anyone but me.

I shifted in the pilot's seat as a familiar unease suffused me like cold seeping into bones. Did he know my lineage? Was he aware of my family's lack of status? Or worse, did he know what my family was known for—deception, delinquency, disgrace?

If Admiral Zoran, the academy's new master, had no issue with my family, why should I care if the security chief did? I shouldn't, although being able to ignore suspicious scrutiny had never been something I'd fully mastered.

My device buzzed in my pocket, rousing me from my distraction, but I released a tortured sigh when I saw who was contacting me via a vid link. I considered ignoring it, but that had never gone well for me in the past.

I accepted the vid and forced myself to smile. "Mother."

The Drexian female's dark hair was pulled back from her face, making her wrinkles and pale thin lips more noticeable. She exhaled loudly as she said my name. "Volten. I hoped you'd answer."

I didn't respond, knowing that she would continue to talk without my prodding.

"Have you thought about what I asked?"

Now I released a breath, although the weight on my chest remained. "I have no influence here. I cannot get my father a job at the academy. Not with his record. You know that."

"Have you even tried?" Her voice was low, which meant that my father was close enough that she feared being overheard.

There was no point in trying. The Drexian Academy would never accept a Drexian with so many criminal infractions. I knew this. She knew this. Anyone who knew anything about the elite military training school knew this.

She pressed her lips together into a hard line. "So, you rise up the ladder and don't reach a hand back for your family?"

It was a bold thing to say, considering I'd risen the ranks in spite of their infamy and disrepute. I'd received nothing but mockery and derision for wanting to attend the academy, nothing but scorn when I'd graduated with commendations. A graduation only my mother had attended. "He wouldn't take it if I did."

She didn't respond to this because she knew it was true. My father would no sooner accept help from his oldest son—and the only one who hadn't followed his path—than he would light his own hair on fire.

Her shoulders sagged as if the only thing keeping her upright had been invisible strings that I'd snapped. "He's going to end up in a labor camp."

"Would that be so bad for you?" It was no secret that he did not make life easy or pleasant for her, and for the millionth time in my life, I wondered why she stayed.

She straightened as if electricity had been shot through her veins. "He's the only one who hasn't left me."

Because you're the only one who'll put up with him, I thought, but didn't say aloud. I could feel the conversation unraveling as it always did. "I didn't leave you. I went to the academy and to work."

"I heard the new head of that place is Admiral Zoran."

The sudden change in conversation caught me off guard. "You know the new Academy Master?"

She shook her head as her gaze shifted down. "No." She looked up again. "What do you think of him?"

"He's good. Better than the last one." Why were we suddenly talking about my boss? "I should go. I have a class soon."

"Always working." A hint of a smile that wasn't so haunted

twitched the corners of her mouth. "Some things never change." Then her image was gone.

I sank back in the pilot's seat and allowed myself to breathe normally. Why did every conversation with my mother have to devolve into my being blamed for my own success and my father's and brothers' failures? Why did I always feel like I'd failed my mother by rising above the muck? Before I could fully dissect the conversation, I glimpsed movement outside the front of the vessel.

What was Ariana doing with her class, and why was she climbing into a fighter? Dread tingled my skin as I watched her drop into the cockpit and pull the dome closed. Was she demonstrating how to get into the ship? She couldn't be taking an unauthorized flight in front of her class, could she?

I raced from my vessel in time to watch her kick the engine into gear, tear down the runway, and blast into the sky. What the *grek*?

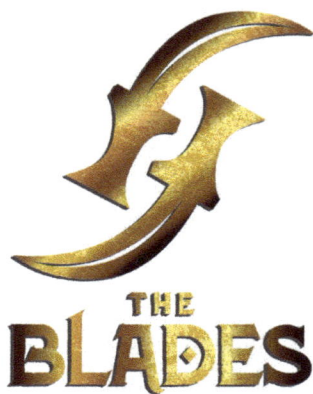

THE BLADES

CHAPTER 18

ARIANA

MY HEART POUNDED AS I STOOD UNDER THE STREAMING water, steam billowing around me. The academy might look like a castle that shouldn't even have indoor plumbing, but my private shower boasted great water pressure.

I pressed my hands against the slick stone wall as hot water cascaded over me and my mind raced. My plan had been to take a cold shower to bring me down from the high of the flight, but I hadn't worked up the courage to switch the knob from hot to cold. Besides, was it so bad that I was still jacked up from showing my students what I could do?

After taking off and hurtling through the hazy atmosphere, I'd taken a breath to get my bearings and feel the ship. After all the uncertainty of my first few days on the alien world, being in the cockpit had made me feel like myself again.

I'd banked hard to one side, dipping below the cloud cover so the cadets on the ground could see me execute a hard stop, flip the fighter onto its nose, hover completely vertically for a beat and then spin around and fly in the other direction. It had all come so naturally that my breathing had synced with my moves, as if I was one with the vessel.

It was only when I'd landed the ship back in front of the academy that my nerves jangled. I hadn't officially gotten permission to take out a fighter, and I was almost sure that using one to show up my first-years wouldn't have been deemed a legitimate reason. Still, seeing the looks of admiration and respect on their faces when I'd slid down the side of the hull and landed on my feet had been worth it.

Torq hadn't suggested trying to best me, and to save him the embarrassment, I didn't press the matter. He now saw that I knew my shit, and I hoped I wouldn't have to deal with him second-guessing me as an instructor again.

It wasn't Torq I was worried about anymore. He hadn't been the one staring at me as I'd led my students back inside. He hadn't been the one to fold his arms with a look of fury on his face. He hadn't looked like he was a second away from ratting me out.

Would Volten do it? Would he turn me in? He'd looked furious enough as he'd watched me from the opening of a transport, but was that what Drexians did? Did the instructors turn on each other? We were in the same school, so I had to believe that he wouldn't want to make Flight look bad.

A little voice in the back of my head reminded me that he wasn't the one who'd most likely broken half a dozen rules. But weren't Drexians known for pushing boundaries and being unorthodox? It wasn't like the aliens had a reputation for being clean-cut and straight-laced. Far from it. But would a brand-new female instructor from Earth be allowed to push the limits?

You sure you didn't do it to get his attention?

That voice wasn't mine, and I hated that it had followed me all the way to the Drexian home world and into the shower. Sasha always accused me of needing attention, mostly our father's and taking risks to get it. She wasn't always wrong—although in this case she was—but I hated when she called me out.

There was no way I'd shown off in the fighter jet to get anyone's attention but my students'. If Volten had seen and been impressed by my pilot chops, that wasn't a bad thing, was it? Maybe now he'd think twice before coming to my rescue.

I shook my head, sending droplets of water flying. The last thing I wanted to think about was Volten, or my father, who could never be impressed. And I didn't want to think about my older sister, either. Neither of them could help me now. Not that I would have asked. The only thing I craved more than attention was the knowledge that I could do anything on my own.

"Including fucking up so badly they toss your sorry ass to the curb," I said to myself, the words getting drowned out in the deluge of the shower.

I finally flipped off the water and stood in the quiet. My heart had steadied itself, and I'd almost convinced myself that I wouldn't be kicked out of the school for something that was typical, brash Drexian behavior by the time I heard rapping on my door.

Shit. Had Fiona heard what I'd done? I scoffed at my own hesitation to answer the door. There was no way she'd have a problem with it. I got the sense that she broke lots of rules.

I wrapped a gray towel around me and padded from the bathroom and across the floor, leaving soggy footprints in my wake. I opened the door, fully expecting to see the blonde in the hallway, but it wasn't her.

Volten strode into my room without asking to be invited, without even glancing at me, without saying a word until he reached the window and spun around. "Did I really see that?"

I tried to regain control of the situation, even though I was only wearing a towel, and my hair was dripping water onto the stone floor. "Did you see me display flying techniques to my class?"

"Is that what you're calling it?" His voice vibrated with barely suppressed anger as he focused on me, his pupils flaring as he seemed to notice my attire.

I was on thin ground, claiming it was a simple flying demonstration when I'd clearly been showing off, so I decided to take a different approach. "Okay, maybe I was showing them that I have skills, something I wouldn't have felt compelled to do if you hadn't undermined me to that cocky-as-shit cadet. I promise you, if I hadn't challenged him to do better and shut him up, I never would have gained his respect. And pricks like him are the kind who always sway opinions."

Volten closed the distance between us, his eyes flashing. "Are you saying that I'm the reason you took an unauthorized flight and executed dangerous maneuvers in front of a bunch of impressionable first-years?"

I had to tip my head back to hold his gaze as my heart resumed its uneven patter. When he put it like that, it didn't sound great. "They weren't that dangerous. I know how to fly."

"Clearly, but that's not the point."

"What is the point?" Now I was starting to get as mad as he was. How dare he barge into my room and try to act like my superior officer. Clearly, our little night adventure to the kitchens had made him think I needed his guidance.

He scraped a hand roughly through his hair. "You don't know what this place is like. You don't know what can happen…"

"So, this is all about protecting me?" I jutted out one hip. "I thought I was clear that I don't need or want a protector."

He barked out a laugh that was more of a growl. "You should."

Maybe he was right, but I would never admit it. "What I really *don't* need is a guy telling me what I should want, especially not you."

He visibly stiffened. "Especially not me? You'd prefer one of the high-born Drexians to advise you?"

What was he talking about? "I couldn't care less who's high-born or not. I don't even know what that is."

His scowl didn't soften, but he strode so close to me I had to back up until my ass hit the wall. I held out one palm in an attempt to put distance between us as I struggled to keep my towel from slipping. "What the hell?"

His breathing was ragged, and he closed his eyes for a beat, finally opening them and locking his blue gaze on me as he towered over me. "If you don't learn the dangers of Drexians and our academy, you might not survive it." His gaze drifted to my lips, and he drew in his own breath sharply. "Despite how much you fight me, I won't let you get hurt. Not on my watch."

I was given no opportunity to snap back that I didn't need anyone to watch over me before he stormed from my room as quickly as he'd rushed in. I followed him to the door, waited for it to slide closed, and slammed my palm against the surface, flinching from the sharp sting. Why did so many of my encounters with Volten leave me torn between wanting to throw him against the wall and throw him out a window?

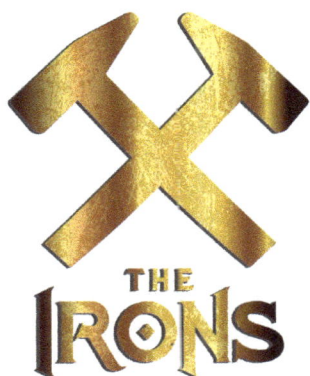

THE IRONS

CHAPTER 19

VOLTEN

Stumbled from her room, grateful that the dimly flickering light from the wall sconces hid my tenuous grasp on control. I'd been so close to her and so close to touching her. All I'd had to do was brush a hand over her damp shoulder or lean in until my chin had touched down on her wet hair. Even now, the flowery scent of her lingered in the air around me—or maybe it was my imagination.

"Or maybe I'm going mad."

I cast a look back at her door, battling within myself whether I should go back and apologize. But for what? I hadn't touched her, despite every cell in my body aching for contact. I'd fought each dark demon lurking in the recesses of my brain as I'd kept myself from crushing my lips to hers, if only to stop her from challenging everything I said. Things meant to help her.

Despite her assertion that her flight hadn't been a big deal, I knew that I hadn't been the only one to see her, and I knew someone would have to come up with a legitimate reason she shouldn't be punished for it.

"Which will be me." I walked jerkily to the stairwell and took the spiraling steps quickly, my feet moving by rote memory as I thought of how I could defend her actions. When I reached the bottom, I almost bumped into a figure leaning against the carved stone banister.

"You're not a female."

I put distance between us, before recognizing the cadet I'd pulled aside after Ariana's class on the first day. What was he doing at the bottom of the stairs leading up the female tower?

I didn't respond to his statement, although I tried to hide my shock that he would be so bold as to say it. This first-year didn't seem to care that I was an instructor or that I was one of *his* instructors. "Shouldn't you be in class, cadet?"

He also chose not to answer my question, instead straightening and giving me a thorough once over. "You were with the tribute who teaches flight, weren't you?"

"She's not a tribute."

"Sorry." He wasn't sorry. "I'm used to calling human females tributes. That's what they've always been to us before."

I might still be adjusting to having human women as colleagues, but I instantly took offense at the way this Drexian belittled Ariana. It was a casual disdain I knew all too well. I'd been on the receiving end of cruel, callous comments like his all my life. "The ones at the academy aren't tributes. I suggest you catch up, first-year."

His top lip curled at this, and his gaze narrowed. I also knew that look. If he hadn't been a cadet, I would have braced myself for an attack. But even a cocky Drexian like this one wasn't foolish enough to challenge an instructor.

He angled his head at me like a predator sizing up his prey. "She sent you away?"

I opened my mouth before remembering that I owed this cadet no answers. "What is your name, Drexian?"

His shoulders popped back as if the mere thought of his name made him proud. "Torq of House Swoll."

House Swoll. One of the oldest and finest clans in Drexian history. His family tree was littered with High Commanders and Admirals. I knew all this because his elder brother had ensured that I did when he ground my face into the dirt with his boot our first year at the academy. He'd also made sure that I knew how little I was worth in comparison. None of that had helped him when he'd been unable to bully his way through a required engineering course and had left the academy.

But I didn't indicate to Torq that his clan meant anything to me. "You also don't look like a female, Torq of House Swoll."

"Afraid that if I present myself at her door, she won't turn me away?"

My spine stiffened, rage pulsing through me at the prospect of him going near Ariana. Then I decided there was a greater chance that she would do serious damage to the cadet than let him through her door. "I would be more afraid that lurking in the female tower might make your stay at the academy of an even shorter duration than your brother's."

His eyes flickered shock and then confusion before the mask of arrogance slipped snugly back on. "I'm not my brother."

"I hope not."

He might be cocky, but his smug expression had faltered since I now knew more about him than he did about me. Not that the imbalance would last. High-born Drexians were never in the disadvantage for long in a school where tradition and legend ruled.

Before I could leave him and proceed to the staff quarters, he leaned closer. "There's no point, you know."

"In you lingering at the bottom of the stairs hoping to lure a female? I agree with you."

A muscle ticked in his tight jaw. "There's no point in you trying for a human female, even if they aren't tributes. Only worthy Drexians can take brides, and I don't need to know anything more about you to know that you're common born." He sniffed the air. "You reek of it."

I considered planting a fist on his perfectly square jaw but decided that the explanations to Zoran weren't worth it. This green Drexian cadet wasn't worth it. "You seem to know as little about Earthlings as you do about flying. Their societies are not based around clan names. None of the females who've notched enough achievements to land here would care about your elite status."

He backed away from me. "You tell yourself that, but you're the one whose ignorance is showing. Our pretty new flight instructor isn't the first of her name to fly with Drexians. Her clan is legendary."

When I stared at him trying to figure out if he was telling the truth and how he knew this, he added. "Haven't you heard of her sister, the battle hero? The one who died in the Kronock attack on Earth."

I was unable to speak. Ariana spoke of her sister as if she was still alive. Had she been lying all this time or was she delusional? My face flushed with heat as I realized that the arrogant cadet was right. I knew nothing of the female who occupied my thoughts and made me crazy.

I managed to focus on the smirking cadet again. "You should concentrate more on your classes and less on scrounging information on the humans, especially if you plan to make it through your first term." I swept my gaze around the bottom of the tower. "Don't let me find you loitering in the female tower again, Torq of House Swoll."

Torq spared me a withering, superior look before he left me standing at the base of the stairs, wondering what else I didn't know about Ariana.

THE WINGS

CHAPTER 20

ARIANA

PAUSED IN THE DOORWAY, WONDERING FOR A MOMENT IF I WAS in the right place for the instructor meeting. Instead of being held in one of the classrooms or even the Academy Master's office, I'd been directed to a room at the top of a tower. A room that held nothing but a single, oblong table that stretched from one end of the long room to another. But it wasn't the massive, black table that drew my full attention, it was the wall of glass behind it, with the view to the Gilded Peaks on one side, their jagged tips reaching for the roiling clouds, and the Restless Sea to the other, frothy waves pounding the cliffs.

"Are we early or in the wrong place?" Fiona whispered as she stood beside me.

"If you're not early, you're late." I parroted my father's words without thinking.

Fiona laughed. "Spoken like a true military brat."

"You are in the right place."

We both jumped at the deep voice behind us, turning as the Academy Master walked past us and into the room. His dark uniform was pristine even if his hair fell long over the collar. I'd come to learn that the Drexian military did not require its warriors to be clean cut or clean shaven as the scruff on the admiral's cheeks proved.

He strode to the end of the table nearest the window with his assistant, who did appear more like military officers on Earth—short hair, no stubble—walking alongside him. "Take a seat anywhere."

Fiona and I exchanged a glance before entering the room, our shoes tapping on the stone floor as we took seats in the middle of the table. Before we could pull out the clear, high-backed chairs, more Drexians entered the room and started to take seats around us. Unlike us, they were not whispering and didn't seem awed by the stark room or imposing view.

I sat and put my hands on the table with my fingers interlaced, hoping that the stance made me appear relaxed and attentive. When the chair beside me scraped out, I glanced up to see Volten dropping into it.

I hadn't seen him since he'd made a scene in my room a couple of days earlier, but I also hadn't been called to task for my unauthorized flight, so either he'd decided not to tell anyone else, or he'd managed to smooth things over for me. Either way, I should say something, even if it pained me.

"Thanks," I said, as more chairs scraped against the hard floor and instructors filled the table.

He tilted his head to me without pivoting his body. "For what?"

I couldn't help letting out an impatient breath. "For keeping my secret."

"Which one?" His face was inscrutable, but his question was barbed.

Was this his idea of teasing? "The flight." I lowered my voice even though the chatter around me meant that no one was listening to me. "Thanks for not ratting me out."

He held my gaze for a moment longer than was comfortable, and I shifted in my chair before he nodded. "I have no desire to lose a member of my school so soon in the term."

Not what I was expecting to hear, but at least I knew that he'd decided not to disclose what I'd done. I thought about bringing up the fact that he'd barged into my quarters, but a sharp rap from the front of the room drew my attention.

Admiral Zoran stood in front of his chair, with his assistant slightly behind him. He took a moment as the talking ceased, and he swept his gaze across the Drexians and humans seated around the table. "Welcome to another term at the Drexian Academy, and welcome to our new instructors, especially the ones who come from Earth."

All eyes swiveled to me and Fiona. Fiona's spine straightened, but I fought the urge to drop my eyes under the alien scrutiny.

Do not look down. Do not show weakness.

"Despite the recent challenges and internal changes, the academy is resilient and with your hard work, will emerge stronger." Zoran continued. "Now, more than ever, we must hold tight to our traditions and standards. We must ensure that our cadets are tough and prepared for the battles they will face. We must continue the legacy of the Drexian empire."

Fists pounded on the table as the males rumbled their agreement, and I snuck a glance at Fiona, who displayed no surprise as she thumped her own fist on the hard surface.

"Accordingly, this term will proceed exactly as all others, including the upcoming trials to divide the first-years into schools."

Trials? I remembered reading something vague about testing used to separate the cadets into the four schools. After their brief introductory period at the academy, during which cadets took introductory classes in all areas, they would be assessed and placed into the various schools according to their abilities. But I didn't remember the word trials, although it was fair to say that I'd found scant details about the inner workings of the school. Secrecy seemed to be as big a part of their traditions as anything.

Volten cleared his throat loud enough that the Master swung his gaze to him. The Drexian next to me stood, his chair dragging loudly across the stone as he pushed it back and pounded his fist across his chest in salute. "What about the humans?"

I bristled, thinking he meant me and Fiona.

"Earth has sent us their best." Zoran didn't so much as glance at me or Fiona as he answered. "If they wish to graduate as Drexian cadets, they must pass the same tests as their Drexian counterparts."

Volten pressed his lips together but sat without another word.

Zoran turned to the side and inclined his head to his assistant, who pressed a device. A holographic image appeared to the side of Zoran and took up a sizable portion of the empty space between him and the wall.

I narrowed my eyes as I studied the unusual, illuminated map that was augmented with curious moving elements. It was some kind of game board or grid.

"We were fortunate that the maze was not damaged in the Kronock attack, although the power surges that resulted from it did require reconfiguring of some of the technical challenges."

Maze? The cadets were divided into schools by way of a maze?

I could tell from the way the others at the table looked at the hologram that this was news to only me. I noticed Fiona's mouth open as she stared at the image. Okay, it was also news to her.

Another chair scraped across the floor as the Drexian seated to the admiral's right stood and strode to the hologram. His hair and short beard were silver, although he looked as buff as every other warrior at the table. This must be the new security chief that Fiona had mentioned, the one who'd been dismissive to her. Before he opened his mouth, I disliked him.

"Each maze is unique." His voice boomed as he stood facing us with his arms clasped behind his back. "All of you experienced different challenges which tested your abilities in strategy, battle, engineering, and flight." His sharp gaze lingered on me and Fiona, and his gaze hardened. "Almost all of you."

My face blazed with heat at his obvious meaning and undisguised slight. Fiona and I had not gone through the Drexian Academy tests and trials, which meant we were not worthy of being one of them. My hands curled together in front of me, my knuckles going white as the other Drexians followed the security chief's lead and stared at us.

"Commander Vyk has devised this year's maze," Zoran said, breaking the brittle silence. "It will not be easy, but at the end, you will know that the cadets who emerge and are placed in your schools are of the highest caliber."

The security chief rocked back on his heels and gave the room a smile that was more chilling than his scowl. "You have the rest of the quarter to prepare your first-years. I suggest you use every moment of it."

I tried to focus on the details of the maze as Vyk continued to outline the different challenges, but I couldn't shake the sick feeling that the Drexian security chief was using these trials to rid the academy and himself of the human cadets.

Not on my watch.

THE ASSASSINS

CHAPTER 21

VOLTEN

I wished I didn't know Commander Vyk's reputation. I wished I hadn't heard of his brutal interrogations. I wished I wasn't certain of his goal for the trials.

Once he'd finished explaining how cadets would need to use strategic reasoning to make it through the complex maze, how they would have to employ their engineering and technical skills to get past barriers, and how they would be met with creatures to battle—all to emerge in the center where an array of ships awaited them to be successfully piloted away, the holographic image vanished, and Zoran dismissed the meeting.

I sat digesting the information until a heavy hand clapped my shoulder. "You plan to stay here all day?"

I peered at Kann, giving myself a mental shake as I realized that everyone else had gone, including Ariana and Fiona. I cursed at myself for my distraction. I'd wanted to talk to Ariana and tell her that I didn't agree with Vyk or his cruel tactics.

Standing, I cut a glance at the front of the room, which was now empty. There was no admiral, no Vyk, and no floating image of the maze.

I grabbed Kann's arm before he could walk toward the door. "Do you agree with this?"

"With what?"

I eyed him. Had he not seen what I had, heard what I had, sensed what I had? "Why is Vyk making this term's maze tougher than ever? Do you think it's a coincidence that it's the first time we've had human cadets?"

Kann frowned. "Commander Vyk is tough, but he's fair."

I scoffed at this. "He clearly despises humans."

Kann shifted from one foot to the other. "He's from the older generation. Not all of them support the idea of Drexians co-mingling with humans."

"They'd rather our species die out, comforted by the knowledge we remained pure bloods until the end?"

"You know *I* don't believe this. I'm all for tribute brides, especially since our species was dying out before them." He grinned. "Not to mention, the human females are quite appealing."

"And what about working with them and serving with them?" I snapped. "Are you for that?"

"If they meet the same standards as their Drexian counterparts, then I'm all for them."

Kann didn't see that the odds were already in favor of the Drexians. He didn't see what I did. The humans were already at a disadvantage by the mere fact that they didn't come from Drexian families with a long history of academy graduates. I knew because I'd once been them.

I'd been an outsider like the human cadets. When I'd come for military training, I'd had no knowledge of the school's rules or traditions that were passed down in secrecy. Unlike other cadets, with a long line of graduates in their family, I'd never heard of the maze trials. I had no clue that we could wash out if we didn't make it through. I'd been unaware of the dangers I'd have to survive before I could even be placed in one of the four schools. I'd been just like the humans were now.

"You don't think Vyk is trying to eliminate the human cadets from the academy because he thinks they don't belong here?"

Kann hesitated, which was all the answer I needed.

"There's nothing you can do, Volt. Not without getting yourself kicked out."

I held my arms wide. "What do you think I'm going to do? Sabotage the maze? Rig it so that the humans can win?"

He opened his mouth and closed it again. "No, but only because you're a pilot and not an engineer."

I shot him a look as I released his arm and we headed for the door. "I'll try not to be offended by that. You know we both made it through the maze our first year."

Kann grinned at the memory. "Because we worked together. I fought off a Verellen gerendella while you worked on rewiring that power relay."

"We were both lucky that it was exactly like the power relays in fighters."

"There's a reason you were chosen for Flight, and I was chosen for Battle." Kann paused at the door. "The trials work, Volt. They've been working for generations. They're still the best way to see what the cadets can do under pressure, which is what they'll be under when they're in the middle of a battle against the Kronock. It's better to eliminate the weak before they can put a Drexian crew in danger."

I sighed. I understood his point. Life as a Drexian warrior was anything but easy, and if cadets couldn't make it through the maze, they probably couldn't hack it on a military mission or in a battle. That didn't mean I agreed with Vyk's tactics, or the theory behind them.

There were skilled and talented humans in our ranks now, and it should be our job to make them ready to fight alongside Drexians. As our two species worked together more and more as allies, it was a necessity.

Kann pressed his hand to the side panel, and the door swished open. All the other instructors had quickly dispersed, but there was one who lingered outside.

My friend's eyebrow quirked when he spotted Ariana, but I gave him a hard pat on the back. "I forgot that I agreed to meet with my fellow flight instructor after the meeting to go over our upcoming curriculum. "All lies. "I'll see you in the staff dining room later."

Since Kann knew me as well as he did, I had no doubt he saw through my lies, but he merely gave me a crooked grin and walked away, which told me that I'd have some serious explaining to do later.

When the corridor was empty, Ariana approached me. "Thanks for the cover story."

I folded my arms across my chest. "I seem to be doing a lot of that for you lately."

She ran a hand through her short hair and the long layers sweeping across her forehead fell back into place. "I guess I deserved that."

"What can I do for you, Lieutenant?" I didn't trust myself to be anything less than formal with her.

"You can tell me what the hell that was all about and why that old prick has it out for humans."

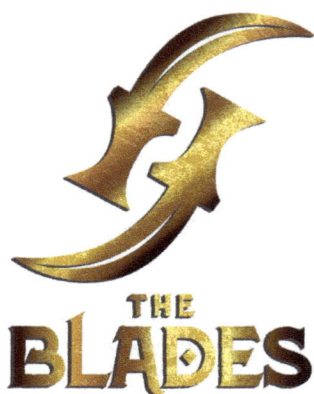

THE BLADES

CHAPTER 22

ARIANA

I PUSHED MY WAY THROUGH THE THRONGS OF CADETS ON THEIR way to classes, trying to remember which corridor to take. If I'd thought that talking to the one Drexian I hoped would have my six might make me feel better about the upcoming trials and my belief that the head of academy security despised me, I was wrong.

I cursed as I stood at the top of a staircase. Why hadn't I taken Fiona's advice and memorized the layout of the school? Going off hazy memories was not a sure way to find the kitchens, and after missing breakfast, I was dying for some Drexian bread.

Who was I kidding? I also wanted to soothe myself and my growing anxiety by shoving as much warm bread into my mouth as possible. There was nothing like carbs to make you feel better, or at least make you feel like taking a nap.

I decided to chance the staircase, even though the stone steps looked like every other set of stairs in the labyrinth academy. Volten had class soon, but I wasn't teaching until the afternoon, which meant I had time to get lost hunting for the kitchens and untangle everything he'd told me and everything he hadn't.

As I wound my way down the steps worn smooth from so many boots over so many centuries, the stream of cadets dissipated until I was walking alone when I reached the bottom. My footstep echoed when I stepped into the dim corridor, and I sucked in a greedy breath, hoping to pick up the yeasty scent of bread. There was none.

Odd. When Volten had brought me down to the kitchens I'd been able to smell the heady scents from the bottom of the stairs. Maybe that had been because they'd been busy baking the next morning's bread and now we were between meals.

I turned to the right like I remembered Volten doing and walked further down the hall. Why did the Drexian flight instructor have to be so maddening? One moment he was helping me sneak bread from the cooks, and another he was bitching me out for trying to prove myself to my first-years.

When I'd asked him about the maze after waiting for him outside the instructor meeting room, he'd only told me marginally more than the asshole who'd outlined the trials. All I knew now was that the maze was different every time, so no Drexian had an advantage by learning how to navigate it from a previous term. But he did admit that Drexians with predecessors who'd been through the academy would have heard about it.

"Not all Drexians have that advantage though." His voice had been a hush even though we'd been alone. "I didn't, and I made it through. There are few elite Drexians in this first-year class, so it might not be as one-sided as usual."

That wasn't much comfort. Volten might not have known about the maze but that didn't mean he still wasn't a Drexian who was bigger and brawnier than any of the human cadets, especially the females.

When I'd said this, he'd emitted a low rumble in his chest. "If you want to help the female cadets, tell them that the best thing they can do is to work together. The maze isn't a time to go it alone.

Nothing in the academy is about personal glory, no matter what it might look like on the surface. They won't succeed," he'd corrected himself, "they won't survive if they don't work together."

That had sent a chill through me, but then he'd mumbled something about saying too much and having to go to class, and he'd left me standing in the hall with my mouth open and my stomach growling.

What Volten had told me had only made me more convinced that I couldn't let the women at the academy be forced out by trials designed to be tougher and less forgiving to humans without the size and background of the Drexians. "If they want to stack the deck against the women, then it's up to me to even out the score."

As I said the words, I knew exactly what I had to do. I had to personally prepare the human cadets for the maze, and I had to do it without the Drexians—especially the security chief—knowing. Earth's top cadets were not going to be purged from the academy—not if I had anything to say about it.

I'd picked up my pace as I'd become more and more certain what I had to do, but my long strides hadn't brought me to the kitchens. They'd taken me down a sloping corridor that had gotten darker and colder. I inhaled the pervasive scent of moisture that wasn't even a close second to the delicious, yeasty aroma of baked bread that had made my mouth water.

"This is definitely not the kitchens."

I rubbed my hands over my arms as I stopped and peered down the dark hallway, the flickering sconces fading from view. An odd clanging noise made me jump, but it was the tormented moan that made cold fingers of terror curl around my heart. A tortured moan that wasn't human or Drexian.

My chest lurched as I stumbled backward, wishing I hadn't tried to find the kitchens or wander the bowels of the academy without knowing where I was going. Just as I righted myself and was preparing to run, one hand gripped my arm from behind and another closed over my mouth.

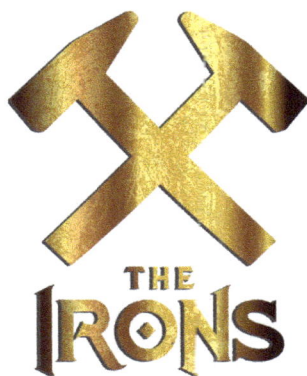

CHAPTER 23

VOLTEN

"**D**ON'T SCREAM," I WHISPERED AS I STEADIED ARIANA, MY FIRM grasp on her keeping her from falling backward. I removed my hand from her mouth one finger at a time, in case she decided to shriek, and I needed to silence her.

Her eyes were wide when she twisted her head around, and her body sagged. "It's you. What the hell are you doing sneaking up on me like that?"

I released her so she could turn fully, and I marveled at how quickly she went from terrified to outraged. But she was not as out-raged as I was. "What the *grek* are you doing, going to the dungeons?"

I inhaled the all too familiar smells of soil and water, and I knew without venturing further that the corridor's ceiling would descend before revealing a rusted gate leading to slick stairs that spiraled to the depths of the castle.

She opened her mouth to snap back, and then cut a look over her shoulder. "The dungeons? That's not a myth or something to scare cadets? I hoped that unwritten graduation requirement was a joke."

I shook my head as her anger morphed into confusion. "I assure you the dungeons are real, and are not some place I'd suggest you visit, especially not alone." I remembered that it was Torq who'd told her about the unwritten requirements. My pulse spiked at the thought of the cocky cadet. "You didn't agree to meet anyone here, did you?"

She gave me a side-eye glance. "You think I'd agree to meet someone in the dungeons?"

I forced myself to swallow the possessive growl tickling the back of my throat. "So, you wandered down here alone?"

Ariana shuddered and crossed her arms in front of herself. "I was trying to find the kitchens. I missed breakfast. When we have morning staff meetings on Earth, there are usually pastries or bagels or coffee."

"Drexians don't drink coffee."

"I know, and it's one of the great failings of your society."

I grinned at this. She'd almost wandered into the dungeons, and she was still managing to complain. "Come on. I'll show you the way to the kitchens."

She walked briskly as we left the sloping corridor that led to the dungeons, humming nervously until we'd reached the stairs that led back up. She stopped before stepping onto the bottom stair. "Wait a second. Why are you down here? Is there anything in this corridor aside from the dungeons—which are a super creepy thing to keep in a school, by the way? I don't even want to know what you're keeping down there or what made that sound."

"*I'm* not keeping anything down there." I had my suspicions who was and why, but I didn't want to tell Ariana and scare her even more. "I'm down here because I spotted you heading down the staircase. I thought either you were lost, or you were on a mission to find the dungeons, neither of which would end well. So, I followed you."

"What about your class?"

"They'll survive me being a bit late. I can't say the same thing about you if I hadn't stopped you."

Ariana emitted an indignant huff. "If you must know, I was about to leave when you grabbed me."

I smiled and waved for her to go first up the stairs. "I'm glad to hear it."

"I thought we'd established that you're not my protector." Her voice echoed off the stone as we wound our way up the stairs, but it sounded more weary than hostile.

"I'd stop protecting you if you'd stop…"

"Doing stupid shit that might get me killed?" She pivoted when she reached the top step so that our faces were at the same level. "You're not the first person to say that."

I held my breath as I stared into her eyes, and my pulse quickened. Again, I was so close to her I only had to tip forward for our lips to brush. I fought the urge to look at her soft lips, losing the battle and letting my gaze drift to her pursed mouth. Then I tore my gaze away and focused on her eyes. "The Drexian Academy is not like your schools on Earth, and there is a lot that you don't know about it."

"Like the fact that you have to survive a crazy maze in order to even make it to one of the schools?"

I held her gaze, allowing myself to enjoy the heat in her eyes, and imagining that it was for me and not from her irritation at the school. Then, I sidled past, so that I was standing on the landing with her. "Like that."

She shook her head slowly. "None of this was in the briefing I got before I came here, although I'm guessing the humans who gave the briefing didn't know about any of this."

"Like I have told you, there is much about the academy that is not common knowledge outside its walls."

She grumbled something about how that went for inside the

walls too. "The location of the kitchens isn't one of those secrets, is it?"

"Only if you keep forgetting the way." I resumed walking, listening for the rapid patter of her feet behind me and grinning to myself when she mumbled something about me being a typical, cocky Drexian.

"You're almost as infuriating as my sister," she grumbled, as she caught up to me.

"Your sister?" According to the mouthy cadet and the war records, her sister had died defending Earth, but she spoke of her as if she were still alive.

"Sasha would agree with everything you've said about me being stubborn and taking dumb risks." She flicked a sideways look at me. "You two would get along great."

I didn't reply, not sure what to say to someone who was delusional.

THE WINGS

CHAPTER 24

ARIANA

"I don't know what this stuff is, but it's delicious." Fiona held up a crispy strip of meat that looked remarkably like bacon as she sat across a table from me.

I'd selected the corner of the staff dining room so we wouldn't be overheard, although with the cacophony of voices bouncing off the beamed ceiling, that wouldn't be an issue.

"*Padwump*," I told her as I took a sip of tart alien wine. The Drexian meat did taste a lot like bacon—smelled as salty and savory too—but it wasn't as fatty. I knew this because fried *padwump* had been one of the things Volten had helped me sneak from the kitchens earlier in the day.

I wouldn't admit that to Fiona. I didn't want her to think there was anything between me and the Drexian but a working relationship. I knew what she'd suspect if she was aware of the number of encounters where one of us had pinned the other to the wall or mat.

"*Padwump*," Fiona repeated. "I like it. It almost makes up for Drexians not having coffee. Almost."

I swept my gaze across the room again, making sure I didn't see the security chief or the head of the academy at the wooden tables that looked worn and nicked from centuries of use. I doubted either of them frequented the staff dining room, but this was one conversation I didn't want them to hear. If I was being honest, it was a conversation that probably should have waited until I could get Fiona alone, but I was too impatient for that. Besides, if my plan was going to work, there was little time to waste.

Leaning over the table, I dropped my voice. "I've been thinking about the meeting this morning."

Fiona swallowed the last bit of *padwump* and wiped her lips with a napkin. "I haven't. I didn't want to walk around all day plotting the security chief's untimely death in my head."

"I thought he was your type."

"Looks-wise, yes." She wrinkled her nose. "But his asshole levels are too high, even for a girl who likes the occasional alpha hole."

"Alpha hole?"

She grinned at me. "You clearly don't read enough romance novels."

"I guess not." I was still grappling with the fact that the badass captain loved romance novels.

"You're missing out." She took a swig from her glass. "But that's not what you want to talk about, is it?"

I shook my head. "I've been thinking about the maze trials. Obsessing about them, actually."

Her grin morphed quickly into a scowl. "If you're asking if I knew about them—"

"I'm not," I interrupted. "I saw your face when the admiral put up that holographic map. You were as shocked as me."

"I shouldn't have been." She put her elbows on the table and fanned them to the side as she leaned closer to me. "As an instructor in the School of Strategy, I should have been told about a test like this. I should have been a part of developing it."

"I don't think Vyk wants humans involved in any part of the testing process because I'm pretty sure he intends to use this to force out all the human cadets."

Fiona opened her mouth as if to provide a counterpoint, but then sighed. "I hate to admit it, but I don't disagree with you. That prick clearly wants us all gone."

I cast my gaze around us to ensure no one was listening. "Why bring us here if they're only going to make it impossible for anyone from Earth to succeed?"

"Vyk didn't bring us here."

"Reina said that the Academy Master probably had a lot to do with humans integrating into the school."

"Then why isn't he stopping his security chief?"

"The maze isn't new. It is how they divide cadets into the four schools, and they've been doing it this way forever. The only problem is that most of the Drexians have heard about the maze from fathers or brothers who've come before them. It might not be common knowledge outside the academy, but those who made it through have passed on their experiences, which means that most of the Drexians have been preparing for this trial. None of the cadets from Earth have any clue what's coming."

Fiona ran a hand roughly through her hair. "Even if it's somewhat different every term, the basic skills to succeed don't change. Growing up hearing about how your brothers or father got through the maze is an advantage, even if the Drexians wouldn't want to admit it. It's an institutional bias."

"Exactly." I waited until a pair of Drexians who were obviously instructors in the Battle school—males so muscular their arms couldn't hang straight at their sides, with curved blades at their waists—passed us. "Which is why I propose that we even the playing field."

Fiona's eyes flared. "Are you suggesting we rig the maze?"

I recoiled slightly. "Cheat? Never." I leaned in and lowered my voice again. "I don't think the cadets from Earth need to cheat to make it through. I think they need to know what's coming and how to handle it."

"The cadets have been told that they'll be going through trials to be divided into schools at the end of the quarter."

"But they haven't been told that the trial is a crazy maze filled with obstacles they need to fight or configure their way through." I thought of the holographic map. "They're probably expecting assessments like we have on Earth."

Fiona nibbled the corner of her bottom lip. "So, we tell them about the maze."

"Not only that. I suggest that we coach them after hours." I waited for Fiona's response, watched for alarm to register on her face, braced myself for her to tell me why my idea was going to get us both kicked out.

"Hell, yeah." The grin returned to her face. "Count me in."

"Really?" My voice rose a few octaves, drawing the attention of the Drexians a couple of tables over who had the intense, studious look of engineers. When they returned to their own conversation, I steadied my racing heart by taking a sip of wine. "You're sure you don't mind breaking the rules?"

"For one, I'm not aware of any rule prohibiting instructors from helping cadets after hours. I think it's only fair to give our cadets from Earth the same knowledge that their Drexian counterparts have, and for another, I would love nothing more than to see the look on Vyk's face when all the humans make it through his maze and get placed into schools."

"Maybe then he'd have to admit that humans are as valuable as Drexians." Somehow, I didn't think the silver fox Drexian would ever do that, but it was nice to imagine.

Fiona leaned back in her chair and folded her arms over her

chest. "I'll tell you one thing. They were wrong about their weird rules. They say to beware of the Assassins, which is the School of Strategy. But I think you've proven that the Wings are just as dangerous."

I liked thinking that I was dangerous, even though that terrifying sound in the dungeons told me that I was far from the greatest danger in the academy.

THE ASSASSINS

CHAPTER 25

VOLTEN

THE DOORS OF THE HOLOCHAMBER SWEPT OPEN, AND I WAS hit with a blast of hot air. I shifted the Drexian battle blade in my hand, my finger buzzing as my heart pounded. I wished that it was anticipation of the simulation I'd programmed, but the agitation was more than the knowledge that I'd soon be fighting off jungle beasts from the planet Ancarra.

Ariana was the one who was consuming my thoughts and making my pulse spike. I couldn't focus on teaching without thinking of her standing at the lectern. I couldn't operate a flight simulator without remembering her blasting off in a fighter. I couldn't even talk to Kann about sparring without remembering the feel of her body underneath mine on the mat.

Then I remembered her talking to me about her sister as if the woman was still alive, and all the good feelings withered in my chest and died. Should I tell the admiral that my colleague was delusional, or was this some weird human ritual of pretending the dead were still alive? If it was a human custom, I hadn't heard of it. Between thoughts of Ariana making my heart race and conflicting worries that she might be mentally unstable, I'd been unable to focus on anything but her.

So, I'd decided to take drastic measures. I couldn't be distracted by the beautiful human if I was busy trying to stay alive in the holochamber. The creatures might be holographic simulations, but they looked and felt real. They had to be, since the holochambers were used by the School of Battle to train cadets on real-life combat situations. The bruises and pain would be real, even if my opponents would not be allowed to draw blood or strike death blows.

I strode into the jungle, the humid air already sending trickles of sweat down my bare chest as the doors closed behind me. Birds cawed and insects chirped, a welcome change from the constant sound of boots thumping on stone and cadet chatter echoing down the corridors. I was glad for the break from so many Drexians constantly surrounding me and even the break from the cool, dry air of the academy.

I stepped gingerly, the holographic undergrowth crackling softly beneath my boots as I listened for anomalies in the environment. I'd never been to the actual planet of Ancarra, but it was my preferred holo-program, and it felt as real to me as the Drexian home world.

Crickle crunch crick.

With each step, I moved deeper into the jungle. Tall, spindly trees were draped with purple vines that curled toward the ground and swayed in the warm breeze. I breathed in the loamy scent, inhaling deeply so I could forget the wet, rancid smell of the dungeons.

Dungeons. My mind was instantly back with Ariana, and my chest hitched as I thought of standing on the stairs with her, my face so close to hers I could feel her breath on my cheek. I'd ached to touch her skin, to feel her softness, to taste her—

Ooof! I barely had time to register the blur of movement to

my right before I was knocked off my feet. I hit the ground on my back, the air rushing from my lungs as pain shot through me. A green-scaled Villaraith stood on top of me, his front legs pressed to my shoulders as his long snout opened to reveal hundreds of sharp teeth in jagged rows.

Grek. I'd let myself become distracted again. With a grunt, I used my legs to power myself up and toss the creature to the ground. I leapt to my feet and spun around to be ready for another attack, slashing my blade as the four-legged creature lumbered toward me. Without the element of surprise, the monster wasn't as deadly, and I quickly dispatched it with a slice across its throat.

I had little time to catch my breath as a snapping sound behind me made me whirl, and a screeching tree ape hurtled through the air toward me, baring his massive fangs. I thrust my blade into its chest and tossed it aside moments before another came at me, emitting a horrifying scream.

It seemed like an entire tribe of the alien beasts was attacking me, and I could think of nothing but fending off the ferocious creatures as they flew at me one after another. My training in the sparring ring against Kann came back to me, and I was grateful that my friend had ensured I was well-versed in hand-to-hand combat, even if I had more than a few scars from him to prove it.

Once the final ape was dead on the jungle floor, I sucked in lungfuls of air and swiped a hand across my sweaty forehead. There was nothing like fighting for your life to keep your mind occupied. The holographic systems safety protocols might have been on, but the battle had felt as real as any I'd experienced, and I put a hand to the ache in my side from slashing so hard and fast.

My fingers slipped on my slick skin as I scanned the jungle for danger, and when I pulled them back, my breath caught in my throat. My hand was covered in blood. My blood. From a gash in my side that should have been impossible.

THE BLADES

CHAPTER 26

ARIANA

"Is this everyone?" I asked Fiona as we stood in the room with the flight simulators.

"All the women."

We'd decided to start our after-hours coaching with the women since we were all in the same tower, and it was easier to gather them. I'd decided we should start our training in the flight simulator room, because I knew it would be empty, the repairs to the walls had been completed, and it was in the corridor of the School of Flight that was farthest away from the central hall.

A woman with long, dark hair huddled with a taller woman with dark skin and hair cropped close to her head. "Should we be here after hours?"

I recognized the long-haired woman from my introduction to flight class and also because she had the room next to mine. "You're Jessica, right?"

"Jess," she corrected with a slight twang, and I suspected she was from somewhere in the American South.

"Well, Jess, there's no rule against getting extra tutoring after class."

She looked stricken. "I need extra tutoring?" Then she glanced at the women gathered. "We all do?"

"It's not that you need extra help because of your classes." Fiona jumped in as the women started to exchange panicked looks. "You need extra help because of the upcoming trials."

A woman with silvery hair that spilled down her back shoved up the sleeves of her T-shirt. "The tests that will place us into the different schools?"

Fiona leaned against one of the shiny flight simulators. "They aren't exactly tests."

More confused expressions.

A blonde tugged her high ponytail tighter. "Then what are they?"

"To get into one of the schools, you have to get through a maze," I said talking quickly before anyone could pepper me with the questions I knew would come. "But it's not like any maze you've ever seen. To get through it you'll have to figure out technical puzzles, fight off opponents that could be pretty dangerous, and figure out the one correct path through. Then once you're out, you'll need to pilot a ship away from the maze."

The woman with short black hair crossed her arms and eyed me with suspicion. "You're kidding, right?"

Fiona shook her head. "We're not kidding. We just learned about this, but it's always been the way the academy sorts its cadets."

"Is there anything about this place that isn't dangerous?" Jess asked.

After stumbling onto the dungeons earlier, I wasn't sure if there was. "The important thing is that we now know about the maze, and we're going to help you prepare for it."

"You know what's going to be in the maze?" The blonde narrowed her eyes at us. "Isn't that cheating?"

"This isn't cheating," Fiona answered sharply. "We don't know what will be inside the maze. No one does aside from the sadistic, human-hating fuck who's designing it."

I cleared my throat and took over. "What she means is that we don't know the specifics of the maze challenges, but we do know they represent each of the schools. So, you'll be challenged in engineering, battle, strategy, and flight."

"Aren't our intro classes giving us an overview of all those things?"

I nodded to the silver-haired woman who was younger than me despite her iridescent locks. "They are, but one quarter's worth of classes isn't the same thing as what the Drexian cadets have, which is a lifetime of hearing about the mazes their family members defeated."

"I've already heard enough about all these Drexian cadets' legacies to last me a lifetime," the blonde muttered.

"Morgan isn't a fan of Drexian bragging," Jess said with a laugh.

"Is anyone?" Fiona rolled her eyes. "If you want a chance to put these cocky assholes in their place and show them that we're every bit as good as they are, then let's get to work."

"Either that or get ready to pack your bags," I added when I saw that not everyone was convinced.

"Pack our bags?" Morgan put her hands on her hips. "I thought the tests were to assign every cadet to a school within the academy."

"They use the trials to weed out cadets. If you don't make it through the maze, not only do you not get placed into a school, but you also wash out."

A ripple of dark murmuring passed through the group as they digested this information.

Jess's frown deepened. "They'd bring us all the way here only to send us home?"

"Not every Drexian is happy we're here," Fiona said.

I remembered the way Commander Vyk had looked at me and Fiona. That was an understatement.

"Then I guess there's only one thing to do." Morgan interlaced her fingers and extended her arms so that her knuckles cracked. "Every single one of us has to kick some serious ass in this maze."

Jess gave her fellow cadets a single nod before turning to face us. "Agreed."

All the women exchanged glances and bobbed their heads their agreement.

Fiona smiled at me. "Then Ariana and I would like to welcome you to the first official unofficial session of after-hours maze boot camp."

I rubbed my hands together and motioned to the simulators. "Let's do this."

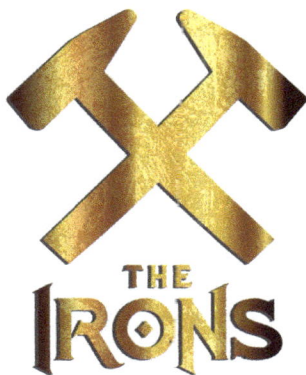

THE IRONS

CHAPTER 27

VOLTEN

I HELD MY HAND TO MY SIDE AS I EXITED THE HOLOCHAMBER with blood dripping through my fingers. The cut wasn't deep, but it was bleeding a lot.

It was a cut that never should have happened, I thought as I cast a final look at the dense jungle behind me and let the metal door slide shut. I tapped my finger on the panel by the door, ending the program, and powering down the chamber.

"I should report the malfunction before someone gets killed," I said to myself as I made my way down the corridor flinching as my steps sent pain through my body. At the least, I needed to tell Kann before he used that particular chamber for a battle simulation and lost a few cadets to lethal holograms.

One good thing about getting slashed by a holographic ape was that I was no longer obsessing over Ariana. The pain in my side was making it impossible to think about much else.

The halls were deserted as I walked from the School of Battle and crossed toward Flight, my gaze flicking to the stylized wings carved into the stone arch leading to classrooms and offices. Like the darkened halls of Battle, the corridors in Flight were dim. But unlike the ones I'd left, the School of Flight wasn't silent.

I paused and strained to hear, sure that I was imagining voices echoing to me from deep within the corridors. It was well after instruction hours. No one should be in any of the schools. No one should be out of their rooms. I ignored the hypocrisy that I was not in my quarters as I held my breath and listened.

No, those were definitely voices, and not only one or two. There was a group somewhere within the halls of the flight school.

"*Grekking* hell." I should have ignored the voices and proceeded to the academy surgeon, but I couldn't walk away especially if a bunch of cadets were causing trouble.

It wasn't unusual for cadets to sneak out after hours, especially if they were trying to knock out the unofficial graduation requirements that Drexian cadets seemed compelled to complete, even though the tasks were both foolish and dangerous. I'd already saved Ariana from the dungeons. I did not want to top off my already unpleasant evening by catching cadets in their search for the tunnels that ran beneath the school and had multiple hidden entrances, one of which was in the School of Flight.

I gritted my teeth and pressed my hand hard against my side as I made my way toward the voices. Now that I wasn't in a steamy jungle, the cold air of the academy chilled my skin and made me shiver. I didn't miss being attacked by vicious apes, but I did miss the warmth.

"When I find these cadets," I muttered as my teeth started to chatter, "I'm going to throw them in the dungeons myself."

I turned down a hallway and the voices grew louder. Ahead, light crept from beneath a door. My chest constricted when I saw which door.

The flight simulators. *My* flight simulators.

How could cadets get into the room? It was coded so that only instructors had access, precisely to prevent cadets from taking virtual joy rides after hours.

I moved slowly to the door, more from the pain that was now making it challenging to walk than from an abundance of caution. When I reached the door, I hesitated, putting my ear close to make out the conversation. Unfortunately, the steel door was too thick for words to reach me, only garbled sounds.

I drew myself up to my full height, realizing only when I was about to press my hand to the side panel that I wore no shirt. I pushed aside any hesitation. It didn't matter what I was wearing or that I was both sweaty and bloody—and shivering so hard my teeth were rattling. I was still an instructor, and they were cadets.

I assumed my sternest expression as I pressed the panel for the door to slide open and stepped inside, preparing to launch into a tirade. But I stopped in my tracks when I saw that it wasn't only a bunch of cadets. It was all the female cadets. All the human female cadets and the two female instructors.

Ariana stood next to one of the flight simulators coaching the blonde who sat inside it on her landing. When she spotted me, her eyes went wide.

"Volten! It's not what you th—" Her gaze dropped to my bare chest and my bloody hand. "Are you bleeding?"

Everyone's eyes were huge as they turned to me. I tried to compute what I was seeing as the room started to spin, and my knees wobbled.

Ariana rushed forward and slipped her arm around my waist. "What happened to you?"

I cocked my head at her as she steered me from the room. "You tell me yours, and I'll tell you mine."

She sighed. "Fine, but first, you need to tell me how to get to your quarters."

Even as my head swam, I knew that a female would be noticed on the Drexian staff corridor. "What if someone sees you going into my room?"

"I think we've already established I don't mind breaking the rules, flyboy." She tightened her grip on my waist. "Now, before you bleed out on me, where to?"

THE WINGS

CHAPTER 28

ARIANA

THIS IS SUCH A BAD IDEA.

I readjusted my grip on Volten, trying not to press my hand to so much of his bare flesh. Bare flesh that was slick with sweat and pulled over rock-hard muscle.

Concentrate, Lieutenant, I told myself sternly as we made our way through the academy corridors, the air whistling through cracks in the stone and the lights flickering from high perches in the wall sconces. At night, the dark, damaged buildings felt ominous, while during the day they were too jammed with rowdy cadets to seem anything but crowded.

At least the creepy vibe of the academy at night was distracting me from the large, half-naked Drexian pressed to my side. I was slowly recovering from the sight of Volten walking into our after-hours training session, but I had no doubt that the women I'd left behind were still talking about the shirtless, sweaty, bloody male who'd burst into the room.

My first reaction when I'd seen Volten should have been shock that he'd discovered our illicit training so quickly, but that hadn't been what had gone through my brain at all. I hadn't been able to focus on anything but how good he looked without his uniform, how his corded stomach glistened with sweat, how his muscular chest looked like it was chiseled from stone—warm, bronze stone. That had even been before my gaze had drifted lower.

I bit back a groan and focused on guiding him down the corridor, chiding myself for getting distracted again. I should be worried about what he'd seen and what he might do about it. I should not be thinking about that vee of muscle that started below his ridged stomach and disappeared beneath his waistband.

It's his fault for being topless and wearing the Drexian version of gray sweatpants.

I fought the urge to glance at the snug, stretchy, slate-gray pants that he clearly wore during workouts, although I didn't know what kind of workout resulted in bloody gashes.

"You still haven't told me why you're bleeding," I said, as we started up a staircase.

"Holochamber accident," he gritted out flinching with each step.

"Holochamber?" I knew that the Drexians possessed holographic technology that was far superior to ours—their holograms were not only projected light but could take solid form—but I hadn't seen evidence of it at the academy. "I thought you guys only used your holograms on the fancy tribute bride space stations."

"The stations are where we use the technology the most, but it's too useful a tool not to access for teaching."

I'd heard tales of the wild environments that the Drexian tech created on the space stations used for matching Drexians and humans—my cousin worked on that tech on one of the advanced stations—but no one had mentioned holographic technology being used in classrooms here. Then again, there was a lot that hadn't been explained to me. "How am I only hearing about this now?"

Volten paused when we reached the top of the stairs and looked at me. "The holochambers are in the School of Battle so the cadets can train on realistic war simulations. I would have shown them to you on our tour if you hadn't been so determined to get me on the sparring mat."

I started to snap back before realizing that, despite the guy being injured, he was teasing me. Instead, I shot him a look. "You want to go again, flyboy?"

He managed a weak laugh. "In my current state, you would certainly end up on top. Not that I'm complaining."

If he hadn't been bleeding from his side, I would have elbowed him in the ribs. "You're lucky I'm excessively loyal to my work colleagues. Otherwise, I might not let all your stuff slide."

"My stuff?" His words spluttered then he coughed and hissed in a pained breath. "What about everything you've done?"

My face warmed at the reminder of what he'd stumbled upon and that he'd covered for me when I'd taken an unauthorized flight in front of my class.

"I would not have ended up on top of you if you hadn't insisted on sparring," he said.

"If you say, 'not that I'm complaining,' I will leave you here."

His laugh was a low rumble that reverberated through me as I held him upright. "Can we call a truce? At least until we're not in the middle of a corridor at night?"

"Agreed."

We started moving forward again, this time down a corridor with arched doors evenly spaced on both sides. Volten led me to one and pressed his hand to the side panel, glancing around the empty hall before the door glided open.

I helped him into his room, noticing that the layout and furnishings were almost identical to my own, but he had even fewer personal effects than I did. There were no photos, no well-worn books, no mementos on his spartan desk. Even I had an old, framed picture of me and my sister on my nightstand along with a digital reader, but Volten had nothing on his nightstand but a small token with the Wings emblem embossed on it.

He sank onto the foot of the bed, his jaw tight as blood seeped through his fingers.

"Holochambers can do this, and cadets are allowed to train in them?" I shook my head. "Drexians have more of a death wish than I thought."

He lifted his fingers gingerly and peeked under them. "The holochambers should not do this. They're equipped with safety protocols that are supposed to prevent the attacks from killing you."

"Looks like the safety isn't on," I said under my breath as I eyed his wound.

He looked up at me and a muscle ticked in his jaw. "Thank you for helping me to my quarters."

Was he dismissing me? I took in the blood now smeared across most of his abdomen and his pale face. "If you think I'm leaving you so you can pass out and bleed to death, you don't know me." I headed to the attached bathroom, snatched a towel from the rack, and ran warm water over it. "We need to wrap that cut."

"I should have gone to the surgeon," he said, once I emerged with the damp cloth.

"The surgeon? You mean, there's a medical bay here?" I huffed out a breath. "One more thing I didn't know about this place." I knelt in front of him as I shook my head. "You know, it wouldn't kill you guys to have a map or something."

"The academy has always operated on a policy of survival of the fittest and the fastest learners."

"How many don't survive?" I asked then shook my head. "Don't answer that. I don't like to know how high the odds are stacked against me."

I wiped the cloth gently over his uninjured skin, then moved his hand and pressed the fabric over the wound.

Volten let out a tight breath at the pressure before inclining his head toward his desk. "There is tape in the top drawer."

He closed his hand over mine, and I met his gaze for a second, my mouth going dry before I slipped my hand free. I stood and cleared my throat, wiping my damp hands on the front of my pants and then pulling open the drawer. I was glad to see that, even though Volten kept no personal items, he did have a roll of bandages and medical tape.

I grabbed both and turned back to him. "I'm not even going to ask why you have these."

He managed a weak grin. "The sparring rings don't have safety protocols."

I rolled my eyes. Not a surprise from the testosterone-fueled aliens. "Is anything at this place not about killing or being killed?"

"It *is* a military academy that trains us for war."

I squatted in front of him again, unrolled the bandages, and proceeded to wrap them around his torso. He moved his hand enough for me to cover his gash, and I could feel his gaze on me as I leaned close to pass the roll of bandages behind his back.

"Did you train as a medic as well as a pilot?"

I didn't glance up as I worked on bandaging his wound. "I have a friend on Earth who's one. She improved my technique, but I've bandaged lots of cuts. My sister and I played rough as kids, and we patched each other up so we wouldn't have to tell our parents we'd gotten injured again."

"Is violent play common with females on your planet?"

I laughed. "Probably not, but Sasha and I have always been different from other girls. My dad wanted boys he could train to be soldiers like him, and he got girls. After my mom died, he trained us to be soldiers anyway."

"Your sister is—?"

I cut him off before he could finish his question and make me talk about Sasha. "She's probably jealous that she doesn't get to be the one at this crazy school. Sasha would be all over the spooky, dangerous stuff."

He didn't respond as I finished the initial patch over his gash, and I breathed easier, my stomach unclenching.

"You can trust me, Lieutenant."

I glanced at him briefly. "I know."

He huffed out a breath. "You don't have to worry about me."

"I'm not worried." I taped over the bandages so they would stay in place, glad that my medic friend had practiced her skills on me. "Not now that I have you wrapped up."

"I don't mean about my cut."

More than a cut, I thought, catching sight of the blood that had dripped onto his pants and trying not to let my gaze dwell on what was creating a noticeable lump in his pants.

"Ariana."

His solemn tone got my attention, and I met his gaze. It was then I realized that I was kneeling between his knees so close to him that my breath was probably tickling his stomach. I jerked back and almost flipped onto my back.

He caught me by the arm, wincing from the sudden movement, but releasing his grip when I popped to my feet.

He stood as well, keeping one hand on his newly taped side as he tilted his head at me. "I meant that you don't have to worry about me telling anyone what you're doing after hours."

I considered doubling down and denying everything, but the look in his eyes told me that he knew. Something else in his gaze told me I could trust him. My shoulders sagged with defeat and relief. "Really? You aren't mad?"

"Does this have anything to do with the maze trials?"

I considered lying but decided against it. "Yes."

"Then I'm not mad. The human cadets are at a disadvantage.

They haven't grown up hearing about the maze from their family members, and the tricks or strategies they used to beat it."

"That's what I said to Fiona."

"I know what that's like." He winced again, but this time I didn't think it had anything to do with his injury. "I will not tell anyone, but I do want something from you in return."

My pulse fluttered as I realized that I was willing to give him more than I wanted to admit.

THE ASSASSINS

CHAPTER 29

ARIANA

I paused outside the doors to Volten's room, my heart still hammering so hard I was surprised the sound wasn't echoing off the walls. He hadn't wanted what I'd thought he would, and I was trying to wrap my head around what he'd requested.

Why would a Drexian—especially an instructor who'd graduated from the academy and been through the maze trials—ask to be part of coaching human cadets in secret? It didn't make sense to me, but I also wasn't going to question it too hard. If he agreed to keep our secret, and also wanted to help, who was I to say no?

As if you would have said no to anything he'd wanted.

I frowned at this, annoyed at the snarky bitch in my head who knew me too well. It had been a long time since I'd been as attracted to anyone as I was to the Drexian flight instructor. But we were colleagues, a fact that clearly meant more to him than it did to me since he'd sent me away to sleep by himself. Not that I would have jumped on him when he was injured.

Liar.

I huffed out a breath and attempted to banish the devil on my shoulder who seemed to be running the show in my brain.

"Ariana?"

I spun around and let out a tiny yelp at the Vexling who'd appeared behind me. If her body-hugging, acid green jumpsuit with flared legs was what she slept in, it was the most unusual pajamas I'd ever seen. "Reina, what are you doing here, I mean, what are you doing in the staff quarters, I mean, is your room on this corridor?"

She blinked her large eyes rapidly as she joined me. "My room isn't here, but it's not far. What are you doing here?"

I tried to shift my mind into gear. If I told her that I'd helped Volten to his room because he was injured, I'd have to tell her why I was wandering around at night and why he was. I didn't know if his injury was my story to tell, or if Volten wanted anyone to know he'd been hurt in the holochamber. Were Drexians as unwilling to admit weakness as human males? Chances were high.

"I was heading to the kitchens," I finally said, the words bursting from me.

Reina nodded, her bright-blue, gravity-defying swish of hair quivering. "I've been known to sneak extra nibbles for myself and Noora." She looked at my empty hands. "You haven't found your way there yet?"

I looked down as if startled that I wasn't carrying a loaf or two of bread. "I already ate everything."

Reina cocked her head at me. "You did? What a curious way to return to the women's tower."

I decided to be truthful, at least about one thing. "To be honest, this place is a labyrinth. I can make it from my quarters to Flight and the staff dining room, but anything else means a lot of wandering."

Her gray skin mottled as she pressed a bony hand to her chest. "This is all my fault. I never finished giving you a tour on your first day."

"No worries. You have a lot to do…" My words drifted off since I didn't know what Reina did at the academy.

"Helping Noora in her new role as the Academy Master's wife."

"That must be interesting," I said as diplomatically as I could. "I don't get the feeling that human input is welcome around here."

Reina looped her arm through mine and started moving me forward. "Noora had a background in Earth politics before coming here, so she's quite skilled at—how does she put it—finessing others to get what she wants. It's how she got human instructors and cadets to be admitted to the academy."

I faltered at the top of the stairs leading down. "She's the reason I'm here?"

Reina glanced behind her although the corridor remained empty. "Zoran had to approve it, but she's the one who convinced him to suggest the integration of the academy."

"I'll bet that didn't make Commander Vyk happy," I muttered more to myself than to her.

Reina's expression darkened. "It happened before he came, but I can tell you that the new security chief doesn't approve."

"Tell me something I don't know."

"Hmm." Reina tapped her chin, obviously taking my words seriously. "Did you know that Vyk is tight with the Drexian High Command?"

"I barely understand the Drexian High Command."

We started down the stairs. "It's the ruling body of the Drexian empire made up of high-born Drexians. Admiral Zoran may be the Academy Master, but only at their direction."

The more I learned about the alien society, the more the antiquated traditions seemed to conflict with their advanced science and technology. "So, Zoran needs to keep Vyk happy?"

Reina bobbed her head and leaned closer to me even though there was no one else on the winding staircase but us. "That's why he's been given free rein to design the maze so that it's the most challenging one to date."

I clenched my jaw as Reina started narrating her tour of the academy. Commander Vyk was why I was going to train the human cadets so hard that every single one of them would beat his twisted maze.

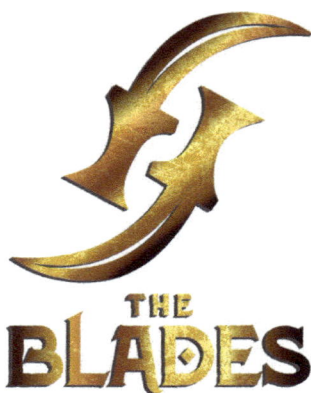

THE BLADES

CHAPTER 30

VOLTEN

I spotted Kann in the packed main hall the next morning, cadets pushing by him as he stood against the wall with one leg bent and his foot flush to the stone. How did he always manage to look calm in the sea of chaos that was the morning rush to class?

I made my way to him, taking care not to twist my side and open my wound. "What are you doing?"

"Waiting for you." He flicked his gaze down at me. "Why are you walking like that?"

I sighed. Leave it to the infuriatingly astute Drexian to notice me favoring my side. That was the problem with being best friends with an expert in battle. He was always sizing me up and assessing my worthiness as an opponent. "Injury last night in the holochamber."

His brows peaked. "You got injured? How? Did you fall on something?"

I glared at him. "Have you ever known me to fall on something during a battle?"

"No," he admitted. "You have a pilot's reflexes. What happened?"

I didn't bother to lower my voice since the din around us was so loud. "I was using the Ancarra simulation."

"The jungle?" His expression brightened. "That's a good one."

"You know the apes?"

"Nasty things. Viciously sharp fangs."

"Well, those fangs sliced open my side."

Kann's gaze dropped to my waist, even though I was fully dressed in my academy uniform, then lifted to meet my gaze. "That's impossible. The safety protocols prevent actual injuries."

I started to tug my shirt loose. "I'm happy to show you the gash."

He waved me off. "I believe you." He dragged a hand through his hair and a loose strand flopped back over his forehead. "Did you get checked out by the surgeon?"

I paused, considering how much I should tell my friend. Not everything, but I didn't want to lie. "No. Lieutenant Bowman assisted me in wrapping the gash."

Now Kann straightened, a grin curling his lips. "You mean the pretty human flight instructor? *That* lieutenant?"

I gave him a shove. "Yes, that lieutenant. She did nothing but wrap my wound, I promise you."

"Well, that's disappointing."

"Even though we agreed the humans are off limits?"

He stroked a hand down his short beard. "If you were up for relaxing the rules—"

"I'm not," I said quickly, watching his eager expression fade. "I do think you should have the holochambers checked out before you send cadets in there for training. I had enough experience not to suffer a serious injury, but an untrained cadet might not be so lucky."

Kann crossed his arms over his chest. "There must be a malfunction in that specific chamber. It's rare, but possible."

I hoped he was right, and the malfunction was limited to one chamber. "Let me know when they're cleared for use. There are some apes I need to pay back."

He laughed and slapped me on the shoulder. "Will do. Now how exactly did the female lieutenant happen to be near the holochamber?" His eyes popped wide. "Don't tell me she was in there with you?"

"No, she wasn't." Now how was I supposed to explain running into Ariana without betraying the secret I'd promised to keep? "I ran into her on my way back to my quarters."

"The female was wandering the corridors after hours alone?" His eyebrows were so high I feared they might vanish beneath his errant locks of hair.

"I showed her how to get to the kitchens," I admitted, trying to stay as close to the truth as possible.

Kann smiled. "So, you're revealing all the best parts of our cadet years to your new colleague? Will I be seeing the two of you in the old sparring rings, too?"

I forced myself to think of anything but the time I'd already pinned her to the mat. Kann might be my best friend, but he didn't need to know everything. "I doubt she's as obsessed with sparring as you."

He tipped his head to one side. "True." Then he drummed his fingers on his chin. "Speaking of the old sparring rings, I guess I'll have to put them to use to prepare my cadets for the trials if I can't use the holochambers until they get checked out."

"There's nothing wrong with using the old methods."

"Says the Drexian who still has full use of his flight simulators," Kann grumbled as he eyed the thinning crowd.

"Which I should get to before my cadets decide to teach themselves."

My friend took a few steps toward the arch leading to the School of Battle, the pair of curved swords carved into the stone overhead. "I'm sure your new colleague would be willing to help."

I ignored the wicked grin he gave me before walking under the arch and into his school. Guilt stabbed my gut as I turned toward Flight. I hadn't lied outright to my friend, but I still felt a pang of regret that I hadn't told Kann the entire truth. Of all the secrets swirling around me at the academy, I knew that this one was going to be the one that gnawed at me.

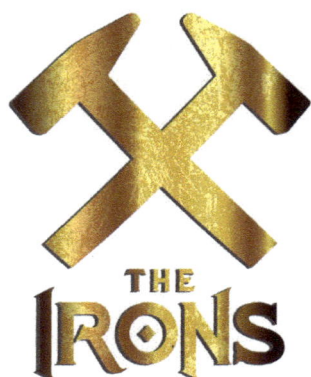

THE IRONS

CHAPTER 31

ARIANA

I PAUSED OUTSIDE THE OPEN DOOR OF THE OFFICE, HOPING THAT I'd found the correct one in the Strategy school. I poked my head inside, exhaling when I spotted Fiona standing behind a desk covered with papers and uneven stacks of books.

As if sensing me, she looked up and beamed. "You found it." She beckoned me with one arm. "Come in."

I held up the scrap of paper that I'd found wedged under the door to my room. "Your note was cryptic. I'm shocked I figured it out."

When I reached the desk, she snatched the paper from my hand. "You were supposed to destroy that."

"Is that why you didn't send me an electronic message?"

She nodded. "No paper trails." She tore the note into tiny pieces. "Literally."

Either she had something significant to tell me, or she'd gotten considerably more paranoid since I'd last seen her. "What's going on? Did something happen after I left?"

"You mean after you left with that hottie pilot who looked like he'd been in a cage match with a panther?"

"I didn't leave with him; I helped him back to his quarters."

Her grin broadened. "I take it you did what you had to do to make sure he wouldn't talk?"

I narrowed my eyes at her. "I didn't have to. He promised he wouldn't tell anyone what he saw."

Now she frowned. "Can we trust him?"

I thought about the expression on his face when he'd said he understood being at a disadvantage. "I trust him, and he wants to help us train the cadets."

"He does?"

"I think he gets that this is an unfair test for humans who have no clue about the academy traditions, including the trials to place them into schools."

"Okay." She didn't sound fully convinced. "I guess him helping is one way to ensure he doesn't talk. He'd be burning himself." She considered this for a beat. "How did he end up so bloodied anyway? The rest of the women were convinced there was some kind of monster on the loose in the academy."

I laughed at this, although after the sound I'd heard near the dungeons, I couldn't entirely discard the possibility. "He injured himself in a holochamber."

"I thought those things were supposed to be safe."

"You knew they had them here?" Then I shook my head. "Forget I said that. Of course, you knew. You memorized the layout of the academy."

"Schematics come in handy." She tapped a finger on the papers unrolled on her desk. "Especially ones of past mazes."

I drew in a sharp breath when I realized what she'd said. "How did you find these?"

"I'm a military strategist. I know how to find things, especially ones that are hidden in the bowels of the stacks."

I'd never even been in the stacks, what the Drexians called the academy's library—the night before Reina had only waved her long fingers at the imposing double doors on the level below the main hall—so it hadn't occurred to me what might be buried in there that could help us in training our cadets. "Do they know you have these?"

She gave me a look that told me that was a foolish question as she spread the pages wide with both hands. "None of these are recent. I assume the recent ones were only stored digitally and hunting for those will leave a footprint, which I don't want to do."

I peered at the elaborate, faded drawing on the top yellowed paper. It was undoubtedly a rectangular maze with smaller drawings within the path and notes scrawled in the margins. "Are those animals?"

"Some of them." Fiona pointed to a drawing of something with multiple legs. "I'm hoping that these are coded in some way or representative. Otherwise, this maze appears to be filled with bizarre but deadly creatures."

I leaned closer. She was right. Almost all the sketches were of creatures with six legs or enormous fangs or long talons. "You said these were old, right? Maybe the mazes in the past were different than the more modern ones now."

Then I remembered what Reina had said about Vyk wanting to make the maze the most challenging it had ever been. I lifted the top scroll, glancing at the one underneath then at the one under that. All of them contained drawings of creatures I'd never seen before lurking in the labyrinth meant to test the cadets. I swallowed hard as cold dread settled over me.

Now I knew why they called them the trials and why not everyone made it through.

THE WINGS

CHAPTER 32

VOLTEN

"THIS HAD BETTER BE WORTH MISSING DINNER FOR," I TOLD Kann as I approached him outside the holochambers. The corridor was deserted—no shock since classes were done for the day—aside from my friend and an instructor I remembered from the staff meeting.

"Like you won't sneak down to the kitchens anyway. The cooks still spoil you."

He knew me too well, but that didn't mean my stomach wasn't rumbling from a long day of classes and no breaks.

"You know Drux from Engineering, don't you?" Kann motioned to the Drexian who was intently studying the open control panel outside one of the holochambers.

Drux lifted a hand to me without taking his attention from the exposed wiring and blinking motherboard. "Kann told me you're the one who discovered that the safety protocols are malfunctioning."

I instinctively touched a hand to my bandaged side, which no longer throbbed like it had earlier in the day. "The hard way."

He grunted, still not taking his gaze from the internal components of the holo-technology that powered the chambers.

"Drux is the best at holo-technology." Kann gave the Drexian an appreciative nod. "He's the reason our simulations are so realistic."

That explained how a Blade knew so much about an Iron, especially since this particular engineering instructor hadn't been with us when we'd attended the academy. If anything, the clean-shaven Drexian with wavy, brown hair appeared to be younger than us. Even though the Blade and the Iron instructors seemed like an odd pairing—one all about muscle and the other all about brains—the engineers were the ones who kept the holochambers updated with new battle simulations.

I thought about the flash of the apes' fangs and the sting as they broke flesh. "A little too real."

"Your injury had nothing to do with my program," Drux said before straightening and finally glancing at me. "And the system isn't malfunctioning."

I crossed my arms over my chest. "If the program is working according to its design and there isn't a malfunction, how do I have a bloody gash?"

"I didn't say that the program was working according to its design."

I suppressed an exasperated sigh. Leave it to an Iron to be clever with his words. "Then what do you mean?"

Drux matched my stance with his arms folded over his chest. "The program has been altered from its original design, my original design."

"Altered?" Kann strode to the open control panel inset in the black stone as if he could see the changed program. "You mean someone sabotaged the holo-simulations?"

Drux tilted his head back and forth. "It isn't as crude as sabotage.

There is no damage to the program itself, but the safety protocols have been disabled and the difficulty levels have been raised."

Kann spun back to us. "The safety protocols of the system have been disabled?"

"Not the system," the engineer corrected. "The alterations are within the program. That way it's not as easy to detect. The safety protocols would appear to be active at first glance."

"*Grekking* hell," I whispered as the gravity of what he'd said sank in.

Kann shook his head, as if willing this to be untrue. "So, someone who knew about holo-technology altered the programs so that anyone using it could get injured?"

"Or killed," Drux added as he bobbed his head up and down.

Suddenly, my bloody gash didn't seem so serious.

"How many of the simulations have been altered?" I asked, my voice cracking.

"I haven't gone through all of them." Drux glanced back at the control panel, "but it seems like most of the battle simulations have been changed to make them more deadly."

"So, all the ones I usually use to train cadets?" Kann blew out a breath before tilting his head to the ceiling.

I shared my friend's frustration. It was our job to protect our cadets to the best of our ability especially the first-years. They would face enough challenges as they moved through the academy. Despite what someone else clearly believed, they didn't need to risk death in training, and we should not be risking cadets who might become valuable warriors.

"Is there any way to know who did this?" I asked while Kann was still muttering curses under his breath and vowing revenge.

"It's true that engineers have individual styles when it comes to designing, but the architect of these changes did not design enough to leave any distinguishing marks." He sighed. "It could be anyone with a decent understanding of holo-technology."

"Which eliminates you and me," I told Kann.

"Why would we sabotage the holochambers?" Kann waved a hand wildly at me. "Why would you go into a simulation if you knew it could kill you?"

At least my injury and our general lack of engineering prowess eliminated us from suspicion, but that left a large pool of potential saboteurs.

"Any of the Irons could have done this," I said which gained me a scowl from Drux, "but we shouldn't bother with who *could* have done this. We need to be focused on who would *want* to do this."

"What Drexian would want to put cadets at risk?" Kann asked.

I waited a beat to see if he would come to it on his own, but I finally released a breath. "There are Drexians here who have no problem putting cadets at risk. One in particular is hoping to rid the academy of its newest cadets by making the maze for the trials more difficult than it's ever been."

My friend shook his head. "Commander Vyk would never sabotage the holo-simulations. He's the head of security, which means he's the one who should be preventing things like this."

I wasn't convinced by this argument. "He's Inferno Force, and you know better than I do that Inferno Force plays by its own rules."

Kann flinched at this. He'd fought as an Inferno Force warrior, which meant that he'd seen firsthand the way the elite fighting force pushed the limits. "Inferno Force never turned on our own."

I swept my gaze down the empty corridor. I didn't want to be overheard darkening the good name of the academy's security chief especially by the Drexian himself. "You know Vyk doesn't consider all the cadets worthy of being here. Why wouldn't he take matters into his own hands and try to cull the field before the trials?"

Kann was silent as he considered this, his dark eyebrows pressing together and sending deep furrows across his brow.

"If it isn't Vyk," I asked my friend, "who else has the stomach to kill cadets?"

"Admiral Zoran would never," Kann said in a hush, "not after taking a human as a bride."

Drux closed the control panel. "The academy has been purged of the traitors who despised the intermingling of Drexians and humans. There are some cadets who have been slow to accept that they are competing with humans, especially human females, but none would have the skill to do this. And only a foolish or overly confident cadet would risk his own life by removing the safety protocols from a simulation he would use."

The Iron made a good point. Even the cockiest Drexian cadets wouldn't be brazen enough to alter a program they would use for training, even if they did have the technical skills to pull it off.

Kann drew himself up to his full height and pivoted to Drux. "Can you fix the programs so they're safe again?"

"Already did, and I added a feature that will shut down the program if the safety is disabled again."

Kann thumped the Iron on his arm. "Thanks. I owe you one."

When my friend started to stride off, I jogged a few steps to catch up. "We aren't going to report this to the Academy Master?"

"Who would he ask to investigate the issue?"

My stomach dropped. Vyk, his head of security. "So, we keep this between us?"

"The danger is eliminated. We have no proof who did it. If we want to know who was behind it, we stay quiet and watch."

I was used to my friend's policy of striking first and asking questions later, so I gawked at him. "Odd advice from a Blade."

He cut his gaze to me. "What can I say? You've been a horrible influence."

THE ASSASSINS

CHAPTER 33

ARIANA

"I THINK I MIGHT BE GOING BLIND." I RUBBED AN EYE WITH ONE hand as I gingerly turned a page in an enormous book with sheets so papery thin I could see my fingers on the other side. Light seeped down from wrought iron chandeliers suspended from thick chains, leaving most of the high ceiling draped in shadow.

Fiona laughed low as she sat across from me, her messy, blonde bun peeking from behind a towering stack of books. "We haven't been here that long."

I scanned the cavernous space that was divided by towering shelves that created lots of narrow passageways. Passageways that were made even tighter by the placement of rolling ladders so you could reach the top shelves. I'd only made a few trips up the ladders before getting serious vertigo. "I think time might pass slower in the Stacks."

Another chuckle from Fiona echoed off the stone ceilings that loomed over us and a shiver went through me. The fact that the academy's library was called the Stacks only added to the overall sensation that the tomes on the dusty shelves hadn't been touched for decades. Since the alien species had adapted sophisticated technology into so much of their society, I doubted the young cadets had much reason to visit the rows of ancient books that had been inked onto parchment and vellum long before they were born.

I moved my translator screen over another passage in a Drexian book on zoology, watching as the alien language morphed into English. "Are we sure they will even have records of the creatures we saw on those maze schematics?"

"I don't know, but it can't hurt to try." Fiona closed a book and a puff of dust swirled into the air. "I, for one, would feel better if I knew what kinds of creatures the Drexians plan to have waiting for cadets in the trials."

My eyes stung as I scanned the page of tiny writing. "Those maps were so old, we can't even be sure they still include live creatures in the maze. I'm sure technology has changed the way they do the trials."

Fiona released an audible sigh. "Even if they're holographic creatures now, they're probably based on something real, right?"

I shrugged, not sure if this was a safe assumption. The Drexians did not do things the way we did on Earth. They didn't test cadets the same way. They didn't enforce rules the same way, and they certainly didn't divide students into specialties in the same way. I smiled as I contemplated the public outcry if the military academies on Earth started weeding out candidates by using a giant maze stocked with lions, vipers, and bears.

I closed my book and pulled another from the pile. "What happens if we do find what kinds of creatures they used to use in the maze? How will that help the women cadets?"

"Knowledge is power." Fiona said this with complete assurance, and I was reminded why she was a captain and why even Drexian cadets moved out of her way when she strode through the academy.

"The more we know about the challenges that might appear, the better we can train our cadets."

Fiona and I had already started referring to the women at the academy as "our cadets." It seemed fitting, since we were spending almost every evening with them and getting to know them better than we did any of the Drexians. If I ever experienced a twinge of guilt that I was treating the women differently I just had to think of the silver-haired Drexian security chief and his disdain for humans, especially female humans.

The odds were against anyone at the academy who wasn't Drexian. Anything Fiona and I did was only an attempt to even the score. An attempt I wasn't sure would be successful.

I rubbed the back of my neck as I wondered if we were wasting our time. Was any of this going to make a difference when the cadets were thrown into an unfamiliar maze full of obstacles they didn't know? Would there even be beasts, or was that a relic of the old mazes? Would the cadets be fighting off actual creatures or holographic ones? Or would the more modern trials be based on advanced technology, in which case, all our research in the stodgy books would be pointless?

"I can hear that, you know."

I jerked up, my gaze meeting Fiona's over the books. Had I been talking out loud?

She grinned and shook her head. "You're worrying so loud that I can practically hear the gears grinding from my side of the table."

"I'm not worrying," I lied. "Okay, maybe I'm a bit concerned that we're shooting into the dark with a lot of this."

"Not all of it. Our cadets have gotten much better in the flight simulators."

This was true. I was confident that every one of them could now pilot a fighter without crashing or stalling. "But that will only come into play once they've made it through the maze."

"Which is why your Drexian pilot is such an asset. He's been through the maze before."

I didn't even bother to correct Fiona and remind her that Volten wasn't *my* Drexian because I knew she was teasing me on purpose. I also knew that I wouldn't mind him being my Drexian, if we didn't have to work together. But we did, so he wasn't.

Volten had already been instrumental in working with our cadets on the flight simulators, and he'd promised to start drilling them on sparring once his gash had healed. He hadn't told me much about his own experience going through the trials when he was a cadet, but that was probably because we hadn't talked much since I'd helped him back to his quarters. We'd either been passing in the corridors between classes or busy with cadets after hours.

I opened the next book, flipping through the pages that were warped with age until an image made me stop. I peered down at the sketch of a creature that looked remarkably like one of the drawings in an old maze. I hovered my translator screen over the text below it. "Why would the Drexians use a one-eyed Parnithian Vantha in the maze?"

Fiona stood up so fast her chair flipped to the floor, but she ignored it and hurried around to my side of the table. "*Grek* me! You found one of the creatures from the old maze maps."

I grinned at her use of the Drexian curse, but my smile faded when I returned my gaze to the book. "This means that the Drexians were bringing creatures from other worlds to the academy to test their cadets."

"You don't think they're still doing that?" Fiona's gaze was riveted to the sketch of the terrifying creature with a snakelike neck, four legs, and a spiked tail.

"I can answer that."

We both swiveled our heads at the soft, female voice as the Academy Master's wife emerged from one of the rows of shelves with Reina behind her. I put a hand to my racing heart.

"Sorry to startle you, hon." Reina gave me an apologetic smile. "Noora and I thought we could help."

"Help?" Fiona positioned herself in front of the open book.

Noora smiled warmly and didn't seem offended that Fiona was trying to hide what we were doing. "With you coaching the human cadets, of course."

Reina bounced up and down on her toes, the iridescent fabric of her turquoise column dress shimmering in the ambient light. "We want to be part of the team."

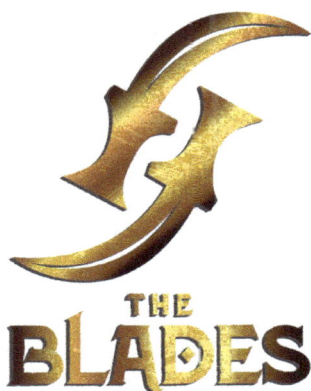

THE BLADES

CHAPTER 34

ARIANA

I EYED THE DARK-HAIRED WOMAN AS THE HEM OF HER FLOWING, gossamer gown fluttered in the drafty stacks. I knew little about her, except that she had been a tribute bride who'd been claimed by the admiral against her will and then brought to the academy. Somehow, she'd fallen for the Drexian, although even I had to admit that the alien was unmistakably handsome and did have a distinguished air about him.

But the fact that she'd volunteered to be a bride for one of the warriors was a sticking point for me. As a woman who'd fought bitterly for my achievements, I couldn't wrap my mind around the idea of prioritizing a guy. Much less, one I'd never met. The tribute brides could marry the Drexians. I wanted to fight with them.

"I understand if you don't trust me." Noora smiled. "I get that I'm technically sleeping with the enemy."

"I never said the Admiral is our enemy." I didn't want it to get back to the head of the military school—my commanding officer—that I considered him a foe.

"Of course, you didn't, hon." Reina giggled, and the high-pitched sound echoed around us.

"I might be the Academy Master's wife, but that doesn't mean I'm not still human." Noora pulled out a chair and sat, motioning for us to do the same. "When I was on Earth, I worked as a political advisor for a U.S. Senator. I understand political machinations, and I can tell you that there is plenty going on here beneath the surface."

Fiona and I both sat and exchanged a look before moving the tall stacks of books aside so we could see Noora across the table. Did we trust this woman? She was literally in bed with the head of the academy, and we were secretly coaching cadets and hunting for information about the upcoming trials. But she was one of us—a female from Earth—and if rumors were true, the impetus behind humans coming to the academy in the first place. If there was any-one who should want us—and the human cadets—to succeed, it would be her.

I gave Fiona a nod I hoped would be imperceptible.

"You said you want to be part of the team coaching human cadets." Fiona chose her words carefully. "What makes you think that's what we're doing?"

"How do you think you've been able to work every night in the classrooms without detection?" Reina asked.

I looked at Fiona again. We'd tried to keep the noise down, and we'd been careful about sneaking the cadets through the academy after hours. At least, I thought we had.

"I saw you processing through the main hall one night, and I fol-lowed you." Reina beamed at us. "From a distance, of course. Once I realized what you were doing, I made sure to keep watch and shoo away any cadets who happened to be out of their quarters at night."

"You did?" I guess I should have been suspicious that no one had happened upon us the entire week we'd been sneaking around, but how had we not noticed an alien with blue hair who favored wearing neon and bright patterns?

Reina bobbed her head and her tower of hair followed suit.

Fiona cleared her throat "Thanks for that."

"Don't mention it, hon. It's the least I could do." She put her spindly fingers on her chest and leaned forward. "Noora and I know what it's like to be outsiders here. The Drexians are not used to females at their academy, no matter what they might say about wanting to integrate. We have to stick together."

"Reina is right." Noora stood again and started to pace a small circle in front of us. "I might have been able to encourage the placement of humans and especially women at the academy, but I'm aware that things are in no way equal. I've tried to explain it to Zoran, but there's only so much tradition he can change without the Drexian High Command objecting."

"Are we talking about the trials now?" Fiona also stood.

Noora's expression darkened. "I'm learning a lot of the school's secrets along with you, but Zoran had never mentioned the trials—or that they consist of a maze filled with obstacles. So much of Drexian military culture has been kept hidden over the generations so that they could maintain their strategic advantage over their enemy."

"We're supposed to be allies," I reminded her.

Noora sighed. "Drexian culture is slow to adapt despite its technological advancement."

"I don't mean to be rude," Fiona braced her hands on her hips, "but how can you help us prepare the human cadets for the maze? Political experience won't be much help against technical challenges."

Noora laughed as if Fiona hadn't just told her that she was useless to us. "You're right. I'm not offering to help coach the cadets. Aside from not being able to teach them applicable skills, I doubt my absence every night would be so easy to hide."

I eyed her flowing, ivory dress. As one of two females in the academy who didn't wear a uniform, she didn't blend.

Reina made a face. "I'm not a magician, and I don't want to make excuses to your husband."

"What I can do is provide you with some clues as to what might be in the maze." Noora turned to Reina who handed her an electronic device. "Zoran isn't the one designing the maze. The new security chief is doing that." She wrinkled her nose, making it clear that she was as much a fan of the Drexian as we were. "But Zoran does have to approve all of Vyk's acquisitions, and most of those have to do with what he's hiding in the maze."

She tapped the device's screen and then held it out. "The information won't tell you how to beat the maze, but at least you'll have a general idea of the type of challenges the cadets will face, which is something most Drexians already know courtesy of their family members."

Fiona took the device, and I jumped up to peer at it with her. This would be helpful.

I glanced at Noora. "Will you get in trouble for sharing this with us?"

She winked at me. "No one knows I'm here. No one has any idea that I'm watching and hearing everything that my husband is doing."

"No one would guess that someone so pretty could be so cunning," Reina whispered.

Noora put a hand on the Vexling's arm. "You flatter me."

I couldn't help smiling at the two women, and it was hard to suppress the optimism that was bubbling inside me at this new information. Until Fiona spoke.

"Why did the academy order so many tranquilizer guns?" Her voice sent a chill down my spine. "And enough sedatives to knock out ten bull elephants for a week?"

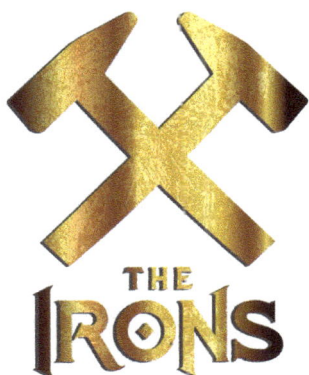

THE IRONS

CHAPTER 35

VOLTEN

I SLID MY GAZE ACROSS THE GROUP OF HUMANS ASSEMBLED IN the rarely used sparring ring. Steel fencing encircled us, rising high and then curving to create a dome overhead. There was no escape except through the single iron mesh door that was currently bolted shut from the outside. There was no hiding from the sound echoing off the rigid surfaces. There was no avoiding the scent of sweat and blood that stained the floor and permeated the warm air. It was the ideal setting to teach the cadets what it would be like to be trapped in the maze.

At my suggestion, Fiona and Ariana had widened their after-hours sessions to include the human males, although the men looked equally nervous to be in the training area that had been all but abandoned after the introduction of holochambers. They also appeared less sure they should be there at all as if attending extra coaching was admitting to weakness they didn't possess. As a Drexian, I understood them more than I wished to admit.

Part of me was glad I'd agreed to help Ariana train the humans, but another part of me was certain I was signing my own termination papers. I'd never done anything as reckless before, but I'd also never had as good a reason to break the rules, if we were breaking rules. There was nothing in any regulations that prevented giving cadets extra help, although I doubted that the academy's new security chief would agree with that assessment.

Not that I cared what Vyk thought, especially since he was the one who was making it harder for all cadets to survive. Helping the humans train for the trials was only evening the playing field, something that was never done for me when I was thrown into the academy. I didn't view my actions as breaking the rules as much as making them fair for everyone.

"Lieutenant?"

I snapped my head to Ariana as she stood to one side with an expectant look on her face. I cleared my throat and held up a sparring blade. "The Drexian blade is something that you will be allowed in the maze. It is also the weapon that every Drexian cadet will have been practicing with since they were children."

I ran my hand across the dulled edge of the practice version of the curved blade that every Drexian carried. I hadn't come from a military family, but even I'd possessed a small, curved blade as a boy. Fighting with it was something the humans would need to learn if they were going to make it through the trials to enter one of the schools.

"Are these the weapons we'll be using during the trials?"

I sought out the female cadet who'd asked the question—a blonde with her long hair pulled up high. "These blades will not cut you. The blades you will have for the trials will be real and will slice you to pieces."

Eyes widened and mouths gaped, but I ignored their shock. I was getting the sense that testing at human schools did not involve the possibility of death.

"Who will they be fighting with these blades?" Ariana asked.

I thought back to my own experience in the trials, and my fingers tightened around the hilt of the weapon. "I cannot say for sure, since each maze is unique, but you should not be startled to find yourself facing off against third-year cadets."

Groans rippled through the group. "Third-year cadets who would rather not share their school with humans."

I couldn't tell who had said that, but they were right. Few of the oldest cadets were eager to share their academy with Earthlings, and I suspected they would not go easy on the humans. But I couldn't let them think that the older cadets were their only concern. "You will also be sharing the maze with your fellow Drexian first-years, who will be armed."

"Are you saying that other contestants in the trials might attack us?" The shocked voice was deep and male.

"There are few rules inside the maze, and some cadets believe that eliminating the competition improves their chances." I pinned the group with a hard gaze. "To survive, you must do the opposite."

"Which is…?" A dark-skinned female returned my intense gaze.

I shifted the blade from one hand to the other, barely feeling a twinge in my injured side. "You will have better odds if you work together. There are no quotas on the number of cadets that can be chosen for each school, so eliminating your fellow first-years does not boost your chances. There will be Drexians who wish to be chosen for Blades, and they will wish to show off their sparring skills by besting you. Do not engage."

"Are you telling us to run?" One of the tallest males scowled at me.

"I'm telling you to be smart and remember that your goal is to make it through the maze. To do that, you will most likely have to fight off challengers, and to prevail, you will need to work as teammates."

The females exchanged subtle but determined glances. I had a feeling they had already established an alliance and were better suited at putting aside their egos. Maybe I'd been mistaken when I'd suggested involving the men in the coaching sessions. Maybe Ariana and Fiona understood something that I didn't.

I shook off this thought, reminding myself that every cadet deserved a fair chance. "I'm here to teach you Drexian sparring techniques, and most importantly, how to counter them."

"Aren't you in Flight?" The tall man's scowl had faded, but his arms remained crossed over his chest.

"He made it through the trials, which is what matters right now," Ariana said before I could answer. "Lieutenant Volten is the only one here who knows what it's like inside the maze, so I suggest you listen and learn."

Ariana's pointed words had the intended effect, and even the most suspicious cadets relaxed their stances. She took the opportunity to pass out sparring blades while Fiona put the group in pairs.

"I know you've all had basic battle training, so I'm going to show you the kind of moves you'll need in the maze." I scanned the group for a possible sparring partner then pivoted to Ariana. "Lieutenant Bowman is going to help me demonstrate."

What was it about her that drew me back again and again? I knew that beating her would only enrage her, but I couldn't resist the chance to touch her. Even if I drew her ire, I would be inducing an intoxicating argument. If I couldn't possess her, at least I could provoke her.

She tilted her head at me before grabbing one of the sparring blades and granting me a challenging grin.

As I stepped closer to her, she dropped her voice. "You sure, flyboy?"

"More than sure," I said matching her low tone. "Come at me."

Her pupils flared a beat before she lunged forward and slashed her blade through the air. I deftly stepped to the side and used the momentum of her thrust to push her to the ground. She almost dropped her weapon, but keeping her grip on it meant that she was slower to rise. I was able to come up swiftly behind her, coil a hand around her waist, and yank her flush to me while pinning her blade hand to her side and positioning my own blade at her throat.

"A Drexian blade can slow you down if you're not used to fighting with it." I held Ariana to me as I spoke. "Even the fiercest of fighters can be bested if they aren't used to blade battles."

Ariana's chest was rising and falling, and I could feel her seething beneath my unrelenting grasp, although she refused to struggle and reveal her frustration. My own breath caught in my throat as heat pulsed restlessly through me, the nodes running down my spine prickling as they hardened. If I was being honest, there was more than one reason why I hadn't released her yet.

"Now, I will show you how to fight as if the blade is an extension of your own arm." I loosened my grip and reluctantly let Ariana slip from my arms, ignoring the daggers she was shooting me from her gaze as I plucked a cadet from the group for the next part of the demonstration.

THE WINGS

CHAPTER 36

ARIANA

"GOOD WORK, JESS." I PATTED THE BRUNETTE ON THE ARM AS she turned in her sparring blade, wincing as she walked.

She rubbed the back of her leg, which had taken a few hard hits during the training session. "I never imagined I'd need to use hand-to-hand combat so much, since I'm not trying to become a Blade."

I inhaled the steamy air, made even hotter from all the heavy breathing and sparring that had taken place in the enclosed room, and blew out a breath. There was a lot I'd never expected when I'd agreed to come to the academy, but I didn't want to admit the extent to which I'd been clueless. "Once you get chosen for a school, your need for grappling should drop considerably."

At least, I hoped it would. To be honest, I knew little about what came after term one, and the moving of cadets into separate schools. Something to add to my growing list of things to research, after uncovering exactly what was being brought into the academy for the maze trials.

The cadets drifted from the open sparring cage, the steel stairs rattling as they descended from the elevated and illuminated enclosure and into the shadows, leaving the area in pairs or alone so as not to draw attention as they crept through the academy after hours and returned to their quarters.

When it was only Fiona, Volten, and me, the blonde captain eyed the pile of sparring blades. "Where do we stash these?"

"I can handle it." Volten dragged a hand through his hair and let it scrape across the scruff on his cheeks.

Fiona shot me a grin before spinning on her heel and heading for the door. "Thanks, Volt."

I suppressed a flash of annoyance that she'd left me, but it did give me the chance to tell Volten exactly what I thought of his earlier demonstration with me, something I suspected that Fiona knew I'd want to do. She'd noticed my irritation when he'd released me and we'd started sparring in pairs, but she'd told me to save it until we were done. Well, we were officially done.

"What was that all about?"

Volten had crouched low to arrange the pile of practice blades, and he tipped his head back to meet my gaze. "What was what all about?"

I braced my hands on my hips. "At the start, when you used me as an example."

Volten stood, unfolding his body until he was looking down at me. "You're still upset that I beat you—again?"

Irritation pulsed hot through me. Just when I thought the Drexian wasn't like all the rest of the cocky aliens, he said something arrogant, something annoying. "You don't fight fair."

His dark brows peaked. "You think I've cheated when we've sparred?"

I didn't exactly mean to accuse him of cheating, but he knew that he had an advantage when it came to fighting with Drexian blades. "I think you've used an unfair advantage. You grew up fighting with these blades."

His pupils darkened as we stood alone in the battle ring, the faint jingle of the cage and our voices echoing back to us. "I did grow up with these blades, but that might be the only advantage I have ever had over another."

I wasn't sure what that meant, but I didn't have the chance to argue back before he was holding his empty hand up as if in surrender.

"You wish to challenge me again, this time without blades?"

I had a stitch in my side from sparring with the cadets, but since I'd been the one to start this, I couldn't exactly back down. My gaze dipped to his injured side, which was covered by his shirt. "You are sure you should be fighting before you're healed?"

"Drexians heal quickly. Besides, it wasn't a deep cut, and it's been long enough that I can survive some sparring."

I thought back to the sight of his hard muscles and the blood trickling down them, and my fingers tingled with the fresh memory of pressing my hands to his bare skin. I gave my head a slight shake to knock those images and sensations from my mind, before I frowned at the implication that fighting me wouldn't be strenuous enough to reopen his wound. Then I reminded myself that reinjuring him shouldn't be my goal. It was only the two of us in the bowels of the battle school, and I didn't relish the idea of dragging him back to his quarters from here.

You're being stubborn, Ariana. You don't need to prove yourself to him.

I brushed aside the warning voice in the back of my head. That wasn't true. I did have to prove myself to him and to everyone. If I wanted them to respect me, I had to show them I was more than I appeared.

Volten took several steps backward until he stood in the center of the ring where the lighting from above was the brightest.

"We're doing this?" How had my desire to call him on showing me up in the sparring mat turned into me ending up on the sparring mat again?

He held out his arms with his palms up. "No blades. No cheating." Then he dropped his hands to his knees and assumed a battle stance. "Isn't this what you wanted?"

I bit my bottom lip. As much as I seemed to pick fights with this particular Drexian, sparring was not my favorite pastime. Why hadn't I suggested we compete with the flight simulators?

"Because you're a headstrong idiot," I mumbled to myself as I walked toward him in the ring. I should be thanking the Drexian for agreeing to help us coach the human cadets, but instead, I was challenging him to hand-to-hand combat. Again.

I was moments away from admitting that this was a bad idea, and we should head back to our quarters, when Volten grinned at me. "I'll even let you attack first."

I closed my eyes for a beat. Why had he said that? When I opened my eyes, I returned his smile. "You're going to regret this, flyboy."

Then I lunged for him.

THE ASSASSINS

CHAPTER 37

VOLTEN

HER EYES FLARED THE MOMENT BEFORE SHE DOVE FOR ME, AND all thoughts of letting her hit me fled my brain. My body pivoted instinctively to avoid her attack, all the years of sparring with Kann kicking in and overriding my intentions.

She was quick, something I'd noticed the first time we'd sparred. Her smaller size made it easy for her to change direction swiftly, which she did as soon as I'd spun around her. She made another fast run for me, almost catching my leg with a sweep of her own.

I dodged her, the gust of air from her slashing leg reminding me that she wasn't as delicate as she looked. "Where did you learn to fight? The Earth academy?"

She feathered a hand through her bangs to push them off her forehead as she shook her head. "My sister."

I was used to fighting with my brothers, but it continued to surprise me that females on Earth would do the same. But what startled me more was her constant mention of her sister without acknowledgment that the woman was no longer alive. "Your sister?"

She faced off against me, her lips curling into a grin. "I told you our father encouraged us to settle our differences by sparring."

"You didn't tell me who would win."

"Sasha has always been a cheat." Her grin faded. "Now, are we going to fight or exchange family stories?"

In her fierce expression, I recognized the same need to be enough that I'd been chasing my entire life. Her hunger to prove herself was both palpable and familiar, and it slammed into me as if it was my own.

She dove for me again, and I forced myself not to sidestep her attack. Instead, I allowed her to take me down to the mat and straddle me, pinning my arms to my side with her legs.

Her eyes shone with triumph as she sat on my chest, but her exhilaration was short lived as she braced her hands on either side of my head. "Did you take a fall?"

"You pinned me."

She narrowed her gaze. "Last time, you flipped me off like I weighed nothing."

"Last time, my side wasn't bandaged." This wasn't the whole truth. I could have flipped her off me.

She sat back and her grip on my arms with her thighs loosened. "I didn't ask you to let me win."

"But you want to win." I held her gaze with mine. "You need to win, don't you?"

She flinched at this. "I was trained for war. Winning is the point."

I used my hips to power up and flip her over and onto her back. When she was pinned beneath me, I leaned down so that her heaving chest almost brushed mine with each breath. "But we're on the same side. Beating your allies is not the point of war."

She strained against me. "If we're on the same side, why am I trapped beneath you?"

Blood pounded in my ears as her movements awakened something primal within me. "You're dangerous."

"Me?" Her laugh was light and musical. "Don't tell me you're threatened by a human female half your size."

Despite her teasing tone, I knew that she was a deadly threat. A threat to my control. A threat to my position. A threat to everything I'd overcome.

"You could undo everything."

The laughter left her eyes as she peered at me. "You're wrong about me. I'm not the dangerous one."

I shook my head. She had no idea how deadly she was to me. No one had ever threatened my grip on control like she had. No one had made me break the rules. No one had made me forget everything I'd thought mattered.

"Before you arrived, I was a respectable flight instructor."

Her breath hitched in her chest. "And now?"

I pulled her hands over her head and trapped her wrists beneath one of my hands. "Now I'm sneaking around the school in the middle of the night and helping train human cadets to survive the maze trials."

Her breath was thready as she peered at me, her dark eyes flashing. "There's no rule against that."

I huffed out a rough laugh as I lowered my head to the side of her neck, breathing in the scent of her skin. "There aren't any rules when it comes to humans at the Drexian Academy, but I doubt our superiors would approve of what I'm doing right now or of what I want to do."

She drew in a shaky breath, the pulse in her neck throbbing. "What do you want to do?"

I brushed my lips so softly beneath her ear that she whimpered. "You don't know?"

Her body went rigid beneath me as if every molecule was at war with her desire. "I know that what *I* want is wrong."

My nerves jolted at her words and the torment barely contained beneath the surface. "And what do you want?"

She turned her head to catch my earlobe in her mouth, nipping the tender flesh before pulling away and letting her hungry words send heat skittering down my spine. "I want you to fuck me, Volten."

My body imploded, all resistance melting as I was consumed with a carnal fire that tore through me without remorse. My mouth devoured her neck as I kissed my way across her jaw until I'd reached her lips, parting them and letting my tongue tangle wildly with hers.

When I ripped my mouth away, I released my grip on her hands. "You don't know what you're saying."

She raked her hands through my hair, yanking my head back so that she could meet my gaze. "I know exactly what I'm saying, and I know exactly what I want. I'm already risking everything to help the human cadets survive. Why shouldn't I risk even more for something I want, something I need, something we both need?"

I didn't want to fight with her anymore. I didn't want to argue with her. I couldn't. I moaned as I let Ariana roll on top of me, and I realized that I'd never been any match for the woman.

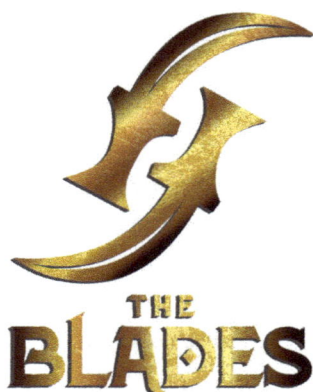

THE BLADES

CHAPTER 38

ARIANA

Now that I was on top of him, I pressed my hands to his chest, enjoying the shift in power, even though I felt like things were quickly spinning out of my control.

Volten sat up, curling his arms around my back, and holding me to him as his gaze burned into me. "Did you change your mind?"

I curled my fingers around the fabric of his shirt and tugged him closer, rising to the challenge in his eyes. My heart hammered as I wrapped my legs around his waist, needing to feel more of him. "Not even close, flyboy."

"Good. Let's see if you can handle my cock as well as you can handle a fighter jet." He threaded one hand through the back of my hair, fisting it and tilting it back so he could nip along the length of my throat. A moan escaped from my lips as his hot breath scorched my skin and made my core clench.

He shouldn't have felt so good. Nothing should have felt as good as Volten's mouth did on me, but I could barely think of all the reasons why I shouldn't want him, shouldn't be doing this, shouldn't need his touch. My thoughts were a useless muddle as I tore at his shirt, tugged clumsily at it, and freed it from his pants.

He released his grasp on my hair so I could pull his shirt over his head, hissing out a breath when I tossed it aside and scraped my fingernails down the tight muscles of his chest. I touched the silver Wings pendant dangling between his pec muscles, the metal cool compared to the heat of his naked flesh, but I hesitated at the small bandage on his side, letting my fingertips brush over it. "I don't want to hurt you."

Volten's jaw was tight as he cocked his head at me. "Don't you?"

I thought back to my valiant efforts to strike a blow against the Drexian as I allowed my fingers to trail down to the ridge of hard stomach muscles. I bit my bottom lip as I traced the ridges that led down beneath the waistband of his pants, dipping my fingers under the fabric. "Not anymore."

All the stress of the assignment, the threat of failure, and the pressure to save the human cadets from death bubbled up in me, desperate for release. I didn't care that Volten was my colleague. I didn't care that he had the power to enrage me. I didn't care what our superiors here, or on Earth, would think. All I cared about was slaking the hunger that barreled through me like a rampaging fire.

"The sight of you on top of me is making my cock ache to fill you." Volten growled as he pulled my shirt up and over my head in a single movement, his gaze taking in the black lace bra underneath. "Hurt me all you want."

I snatched his attention by claiming his mouth with mine, sinking into the kiss, and letting myself descend into a reality where there were only his lips moving with mine and our moans melding together. The lingering scent of sweat vanished, the steamy air was no longer oppressive, and I couldn't even feel the hard sparring mat beneath us.

I gripped his shoulders as he shifted and stood without breaking the kiss or dropping me. I tightened my legs around his waist as he walked me to the side of the steel cage and pressed my back to the interlocked chains. The rattling of the metal snapped me from my pleasure haze, and I snatched my lips from his, gasping for breath.

"So beautiful." He held my gaze for a beat before he dipped his head and kissed the hollow of my throat. "So tough, but so beautiful."

I reached overhead and coiled my fingers through the wire cage to take some of the weight off him. He flicked his gaze up, his comprehension instant as he took the opportunity to slide my pants over my hips and slip them all the way down my legs. When they puddled on the floor and I wore only the thinnest snippet of black lace panties, he released a shuddering sigh.

"You're so perfect. Now I know why my people have lost their minds for human females."

I detected hesitation in his voice, and I put my hands on his shoulders again, digging my nails into his flesh. "Don't stop now, flyboy."

He cupped my chin in one hand and dragged his thumb across my lower lip. "You are sure? You could have anyone, any Drexian—"

"I don't want any Drexian. You're the only Drexian I've ever wanted and ever will want. And I'm sure if you don't fuck me right now, I'm going to kick your ass for real."

With a guttural sound, he crushed his mouth to mine as one hand slid down to grab my ass and the other clasped one of my breasts, his finger caressing the hard nipple through the lace. I crossed my ankles around his waist and rocked into him, sucking in a breath when the hand on my ass slipped down so that his finger darted beneath the fabric of my panties.

I angled my hips, needing him inside me, needing to take him, even if it was only his finger. But, instead, he dragged his finger through my slickness until he found my clit. The heat that had been pooling in my core was now burning me alive as I moved desperately with his quick strokes.

Breaking our kiss, he dropped down and slid his finger from me. He palmed my ass, holding me up while he opened my legs so he could bury his face between them.

I gasped as he nudged my panties aside and parted me with his tongue, and I tightened my grip on the metal cage when he found my clit and began to swirl the tip of his tongue over it.

"How are you so good at this?" I managed to ask between desperate breaths. I didn't think he'd left Drex or visited one of the space stations filled with human women.

He lifted his head for the briefest moment. "Drexian's talk. I've been eager to taste one of these magical human pleasure buttons for myself."

Magical human pleasure button. I liked the sound of that. I liked it even more when he resumed sucking it, and I loved the sounds he made as he devoured me—growly and deep-throated—as if he was enjoying the most delicious treat he'd ever tasted.

I let my legs curl around his shoulders as pleasure built within my core, hot and restless. I threw back my head as my body trembled, detonating in a torrent of trembling and moaning, until I was barely holding onto the metal rungs over my head.

Volten emitted a satisfied growl, and the sound buzzed the tender skin of my thighs and sent euphoric aftershocks through me.

Fresh waves of desire pounded through me as my pussy clenched in anticipation. "Please, Volten. I need you inside me." When he feathered his lips across my sensitive clit, I shook my head. "I want you to fuck me. Now."

I unwound my legs from his shoulders and slid down his body until I looped them around his waist and braced my feet on his ass. I reached for the top of his pants, hunting for the buttons or zipper or whatever it was that was keeping him from me. Volten closed his hand over mine, but instead of pushing it away, he helped me tug down the fabric and release his cock.

When it sprang up, long and thick, with veins curling around

181

the rigid flesh, I bit back a groan. "If you ask me if I'm sure again, you'll regret it. But I do have a birth control implant, and I'm clean."

He met my gaze, the blue of his eyes almost devoured by the molten black of his pupils. "I also have an implant and am clean."

I nodded, glad to get that out of the way, but how did I not know that Drexian males had birth control implants? It might be the first thing that wasn't completely male dominated about their society, not that I wanted to dwell on that now.

I didn't wait for Volten. I was too needy, too desperate. I used my feet braced above his ass to lift myself so I could notch the crown of his cock at my entrance. Before I could have any kind of doubts about his size versus mine, I sank down on him. Gritting my teeth as I took the first few inches of him, I let his girth stretch me slowly until I sank fully onto him with a cry of pleasure.

Volten's jaw was clenched as he held my gaze, his eyelids flickering. "Are you okay?"

I managed to take a breath and move my head up and down. "Are you?"

"I am much better than okay," Volten gritted out. "I did not think you would take me so well."

I flushed at this, absurdly proud that I had taken all of him. I'd never been with a guy so big, and I loved how completely he filled me.

"Everything about you is perfect, Ariana," he whispered as I adjusted to having him so deep inside me that I wasn't sure where he ended, and I began.

The steel cage rattled behind me as I leaned back and grasped it overhead again. Volten took hold of my hips and started moving me up and down the length of him, slowly at first, but then faster. The clanging of metal became a metallic cacophony, and for the first time, I wondered if anyone would hear us even though we were in the depths of the battle school.

As if thinking the same thing, Volten stepped back so that I had to release the cage, spun me around, and lowered me onto the sparring mat. Having him on top of me was even better than riding him, and I looped my legs around him again.

"What if someone walks in on us?" Even as I said this, the possibility made my pulse spike. I was a pilot who loved risk. The idea of being caught was like gasoline to a flame.

"Then they'll see me claiming you as mine." He thrust inside me, holding his cock deep as he held my gaze. "They'll know that no one can touch you, no one can fill you, no one can make you moan but me."

My eyes rolled back in my head. I should rebel at his possessive words, his primitive need to mark me as his, his primal desire to claim me. But his desire sent a thrill through me. I wanted his hunger for me alone, I needed his dominance, I craved being his and only his.

Volten pressed his forehead to mine as he drove into me so deep and so hard that stars danced in front of my eyes, his frenzied movements slowing enough that he slid his cock out and over my clit after each thrust inside me. I almost wished that someone would stumble into the sparring area and watch him fuck me. Instead of needing him to be a secret, a part of me wanted everyone to know that I was his.

My hands slipped on his slick back as I wrapped my arms around him, my fingers brushing over the hard, hot bumps that ran the length of his spine.

Volten growled. "If I'd known stretching you with my cock is what it took to tame you, I would have fucked you the first day you walked onto my ship."

"Who says I'm tamed?" I stroked his nodes harder, matching his movements and savoring his quickened breath, until we were both panting. "And who says I would have let you?"

"Tell me you would have stopped me," he said between thrusts and hitched breaths. "Tell me to stop now."

I closed my eyes and let myself imagine him pinning me to the wall of the ship like he was pinning me to the floor now. I scraped my fingers along his back. "Don't you dare stop."

He arched his back, inhaling sharply as I scratched him. Then he looked down and grinned. "That's my girl."

My body imploded again, and I clutched Volten's back, rasping my nails across his nodes. At that, his control shattered, and he threw back his head and roared. Waves of pleasure were sending tremors through me when he exploded inside me, and I held on as he shuddered and finally sagged to the floor beside me.

"You win," he managed to say, through ragged breaths.

I swiveled my head to him, flush with pleasure at the thought of being his girl. "I'm pretty sure we both won that round, flyboy."

THE IRONS

CHAPTER 39

ARIANA

"Do you want some?" Fiona held out a ladle filled with *chidi* berries, which we'd both discovered were one of the few sweet foods enjoyed by Drexians.

I held out my plate, which so far held a few rounds of bread and nothing else. "Do you have to ask?"

"How do the Drexians survive without dessert or coffee?" Fiona spooned the blue berries onto my plate and shook her head as we proceeded through the two-sided display of breakfast foods in the staff dining room.

"They don't seem to be suffering much." I watched a pair of instructors from Battle enter the high-ceiling room crossed with dark beams. "They have *chidi* berry tea."

My friend gave them a quick once-over, her gaze lingering for a moment on the uniforms stretched tight over their broad shoulders. "Are you suggesting that their fruity tea compares to a shot of espresso, or that a lack of sugar and caffeine might be good for you?"

I choked back a laugh at her horrified expression and led us through the heavy wooden tables to one in the corner. Once we were seated, I allowed myself a breath of relief. At least Volten wasn't in the dining room this morning, which meant that I didn't have to pretend not to remember every delicious moment we'd shared in the sparring ring.

At least Fiona had no clue what had happened after she'd left. She hadn't even mentioned it.

"You and that hot pilot weren't stuck putting up sparring blades for too long last night, were you?"

So much for that. I tried to look as casual as possible, shaking my head thoughtfully. "Not really."

"I didn't hear you come back to our tower." She flicked her gaze to me. "Then again, I was pretty wrecked after all that fighting and practically fell asleep in the shower."

I glanced around us, grateful that none of the other staff were sitting close enough to overhear. "You didn't run into anyone on your walk back through the castle?"

She shook her head as she speared several berries onto the tines of her fork. "Only Reina, but she'd positioned herself outside the entrance to Battle, in case anyone wandered by and needed to be steered in another direction."

Crap. I hadn't remembered that Reina was acting as lookout. There wasn't any chance that she'd overheard us, was there? My stomach did an uncomfortable somersault that had nothing to do with the muddle of savory scents that filled the air.

"What about you?"

I stared at Fiona, forgetting what she was asking me as my brain swirled with memories of making plenty of noise with Volten.

She laughed. "Did you bump into anyone when you left the sparring ring?"

I exhaled a bit too loudly. "Nope. The place was deserted." That much was true. By the time Volten and I had remembered how to breathe normally and forced ourselves to get up and retrieve our clothes, all the human cadets were tucked away in their quarters, and even Reina had been nowhere in sight.

I thought back to those blissful moments when we'd been lying side by side, before reality had started to creep back in and hints of regret had teased the corners of my brain. I didn't regret what had happened between us. Not really. But I was afraid he did. The Drexian was the kind of guy who played by the rules, until I'd showed him how much fun it was to break them.

"Do tell."

I jerked my head up to see Fiona eyeing me with blatant curiosity. "Tell you what?"

"Why you're grinning like the cat who caught the canary."

Had I been smiling? Shit. This was why I never won against her at cards. Although, to be fair, I'd never played Drexian card games until Fiona had introduced me to them, so she had even more of an advantage. Regardless, I was garbage at hiding my feelings or apparently not smiling like an idiot when I thought about Volten.

"Nothing. I was thinking about how much progress the cadets are making."

Fiona's brows arched, but then she reached for her goblet and took a long gulp. "You were right about bringing on Volten. Having a Drexian who's been through the trials is a game changer."

"His tips on blade work were good," I admitted.

"Now if we could figure out what the cadets will be fighting against, aside from the third years." Fiona dropped her voice even lower. "Do you think Noora has made any progress on figuring out what all the tranquilizers are for?"

I didn't want to mention the dungeons, or the sounds I'd heard in case Fiona thought exploring them was a great idea. I might take risks in the cockpit, but dark, subterranean lairs were not my thing.

I lifted my shoulders absently as my gaze snagged on Volten and Kann walking into the dining room. Even thinking about Volten hadn't inoculated me from the jolt of desire seeing him gave me. I shoved a bite of bread into my mouth to distract myself with the chewing, but my cheeks burned with unwanted heat.

Fiona followed my gaze, even though I tried to glance away before she noticed my reaction. Her pink lips curved into a smile, and she leaned back in her chair. "It looks like the canary walked in."

I tried to swallow, but choked on the mouthful, coughing loudly enough that Volten couldn't help but notice me. He paused in the doorway, his gaze locking on me with an intensity that did nothing to help me swallow.

Fiona shoved my goblet in my hand, and I managed to take a drink of the *chidi* tea.

So much for playing it cool.

"You want to tell me what actually went on last night?" Fiona asked in a whisper.

"We're colleagues," I insisted, even though I was unable to stop myself from stealing a glance at Volten as he crossed the room.

Fiona patted my arm. "You're a shit liar, babe, but don't worry." She mimed zipping her lips closed. "I'm an excellent secret keeper."

I could feel Volten's gaze on me, but I managed not to look at him again. If we were going to be regular fuck buddies, we needed to get better at hiding it.

THE WINGS

CHAPTER 40

VOLTEN

I T WAS IMPOSSIBLE FOR ME TO BE IN THE SAME ROOM AS ARIANA and not look at her. Everything about the woman begged me to touch her. I could imagine my fingers tangling in her short, brown hair. I could imagine my mouth capturing her curved pink lips. I could imagine my—

"Volt!"

I jerked my attention back to Kann, and the long table of food spread out in front of us. Cadets might have simpler fare, but the staff dining room always served dishes worthy of a feast. I stood on the side of table that afforded me an unobstructed view of Ariana's table in the corner while Kann stood across from me serving himself.

"You think you have enough?" Kann waved a spoon at my plate.

I followed his spoon to the obscene pile of fried *padwump* on my plate. *Grek.* So much for serving myself while thinking about all the things I wanted to do to Ariana.

"Sorry." I used the metal tongs to offload some of the strips of salty, savory meat back onto the serving dish, while Kann reached across and snatched a piece from my plate.

"What's got you so distracted?" He glanced over his shoulder. "Is it still the sabotage of the holochamber?"

I was so relieved that he hadn't noticed where I'd been staring that I nodded. "I've almost healed, but that doesn't mean the danger is gone. Without knowing for sure who altered the program, we can't prevent it from happening again."

Kann's jaw tensed, and a muscle quivered on one side. "It won't happen in the holochambers again. I have Drux checking them daily."

We moved down the table, and I added a round of bread to my plate, now that I'd made room for food other than fried *padwump*. "If someone wishes to put the human cadets at risk, they won't let that stop them."

Kann grunted, as we finished taking food, and moved to the end two chairs at a long table already half filled with Iron instructors eagerly discussing a new weapon augmentation. We tipped our heads at them, but their return acknowledgments were brief before they went back to their bent-heads discussion.

"I know we're supposed to trust the Irons, but I'm glad the rule isn't that we have to socialize with them," Kann muttered so only I could hear him.

I cut my gaze to the intense Drexians, fighting the urge to peer past them to Ariana. "They aren't bad. They just like their tech."

"And thinking about tech and talking about tech." Kann rolled his eyes, telling me exactly what a Battle instructor thought about such a boring fixation.

When we sat, I angled myself so Ariana wasn't in my line of sight, although her presence in the room made it impossible for me to breathe normally. "What about Drux? He's an Iron, and he's the reason you could use the holochambers again."

Kann moved his head back and forth as if admitting that I was right. "Drux is one of the good ones." He picked up a long strip of *padwump* and pointed it at me. "He could have ended up in Battle. Apparently, both schools wanted him, but the Irons got lucky."

"Isn't that rare?" I hadn't heard of a cadet being fought over by two schools as disparate as the Blades and the Irons. I'd also never heard of a cadet knowing the inner workings of how he was chosen. My memory of going through the trials was mostly shrouded in the fear I'd had of being taken out by a fellow cadet, or not being clever enough to make it past the strategic puzzles that opened passageways and shortened the maze. I'd been so grateful to have made it into Flight that I never cared about the details.

"Who knows? They don't talk about the selection process, do they?" He paused with another slice of *padwump* halfway to his mouth. "But I guess this term we'll have some insight into it, won't we?"

It hadn't occurred to me that we would be part of the process of deciding which cadets would be part of our schools, and I was suddenly filled with questions. I tore off a bite of bread, savoring the warmth on my fingers before I popped it in my mouth.

Kann leaned over the table and one of his longer locks of dark hair fell onto his forehead. "Since we're talking about Drux, I should tell you that he hasn't been able to find any sort of digital footprint for the sabotage."

I swallowed the yeasty bread and reached for more. "Nothing?"

A sharp shake of his head. "Anyone can access those panels, but it does take skill to disable the safety protocols without setting off alerts. He thought if he examined it more closely, he'd be able to find a trace, but he's found nothing."

"Do you think that means it was an Iron?" The thought of one of the engineers tampering with the holo-technology made a chill snake down my spine.

Kann stole a glance down the table before frowning. "I don't know of any Irons who are against the human cadets. If the cadets can keep up, they don't care if they're Drexian or not. At least, that's what Drux says."

It made sense. Of any of the schools, the Irons were the least concerned with politics or status. They were all about intellectual ability. You couldn't use status or influence to get into the Irons.

"So, it's someone who knows the holo-technology enough to tamper with it but isn't good enough to be an Iron."

My mind whirred as I tried to think of anyone who would fit that description. As much as I wanted to pin the treachery on Vyk, did he know anything about rewiring a holochamber?

Kann stood, and his chair scraped the stone floor as he pushed it back. "You figure it out while I get us both some *chidi* tea."

I'd barely convinced myself that Vyk remained a possibility when I sensed someone standing next to me. I tipped my head back, but Ariana was already leaning down and holding out a device as if she needed to show me something important on the screen.

"You're going to have to stop looking at me like that when we're in public."

There was no point in me asking what she meant, since I'd been gawking at her earlier. I opened my mouth, but no sound came out. Having her so close had short-circuited my ability to speak.

"Don't look at me. Look at the device." She leaned closer, her attention fully on the device but her voice a seductive hush. "If you don't play it cool, everyone's going to know our secret."

How had this female—this human female—rendered me a mute fool who could barely remember to breathe? I couldn't breathe because I knew what she was going to tell me. I knew the words were on her lips. I knew she would say that we could never let what happened between us happen again. That it had been a mistake. That we needed to pretend it had never happened.

She clicked the side of the device, and it went blank. "I'll see you in Flight, and in your quarters later, flyboy."

It took me a few moments to compute her whispered words. "My quarters?"

"I'd prefer something softer than the sparring ring next time." She gave me a quick wink, straightened, and walked away without giving me a single backward glance.

"Is the lieutenant giving you headaches again?" Kann returned to the table with two goblets and handed me one.

I took it and hid my smile behind the rim, as it sunk in that Ariana hadn't come over to tell me what had happened between us could never happen again. She wanted a next time. Tonight. In my quarters. My heart tripped as I tried to pretend like I wasn't elated. "Something like that."

CHAPTER 41

ARIANA

I couldn't help bouncing as I entered the top of the classroom, which was already swarming with chatter from the packed seats. We were three quarters of the way through the first quarter and the intro-to-flight class that was meant to give cadets enough information to make it through the trials. I scanned the tops of the heads—most of them Drexian—and it hit me that my next class would be considerably smaller, since only a fraction of the cadets would be slotted into a space in the School of Flight.

My gaze lingered on the humans grouped at the front of the steeply sloped classroom. There were a few among them who would make good pilots. Then I swallowed hard as I remembered the key part of the whole selection process I was forgetting. *If* they survived the trials.

There was no guarantee that anyone in my class would make it into Flight, and if the tales I'd heard were true, there were some who would not survive the selection process, period. My bubbly mood evaporated as I stood at the top of the stairs leading down to my lectern and observed the cadets laughing and talking. Which of them would not make it out of the maze?

A sick feeling churned in my gut. If we were on Earth, I would have something to say about the way the academy chose cadets for their specialties. But we weren't on Earth, and I had no power here.

I was an anomaly among the big, alien warriors. I was their guest. But if I were being honest with myself, I was an experiment. The future of females at the Drexian Academy hinged on how well I performed, Fiona performed, the women cadets performed. There was no room for me to tell the academy leadership what I thought of their brutish methods, even if they had cared for the opinions of a female from Earth.

I squared my shoulders. "That's fine. If we can't change the system, we work around it."

I didn't need to make a scene at the academy to disrupt the way they did things, and I had never minded being subversive. All the best pilots had a rebellious streak in them, even Volten, who liked to think he followed the rules.

Thinking of Volten returned a grin to my face and made me bound down the steps with renewed enthusiasm for my class. If there was one thing I enjoyed more than Volten's outrage when I pushed boundaries, it was watching him lose control. Breaking the rules with him was the most fun I'd had in years, and like an adrenaline junkie who'd just been reminded of the sweet succulence of danger, I couldn't wait to sneak into Volten's quarters later.

Until then, I was going to do my damnedest to prepare my cadets for the trials, even the ones I wasn't coaching in the dead of night.

"Let's talk about combat takeoffs and landings," I said as I reached the transparent lectern and spun to face the class. "These will be crucial during a battle, and they might be crucial during the trials."

The cadets shifted in their seats, sitting up straighter at the mention of the upcoming trials. The Drexians would not have been surprised by my mention of what they might need during the assessment, and thanks to our illicit coaching, neither would the humans.

I still didn't know what types of ships—or how many—would be waiting for the cadets who made it through the maze, but I'd been assured by Volten that the cadets would have to fly themselves safely away to be considered successful.

A hand went into the air, and I fought the urge to release a tortured sigh when I saw that it was Torq and that he wore his usual cocky smile.

"Is this related to combat takeoffs or landings?" I asked, hoping my sharp tone would tell him that I wasn't in the mood for his alpha bullshit.

"It's related to the trials." He stood and clasped his hands behind his back as he tilted to partially face the rows of cadets behind him.

I couldn't shut him down if he had a legitimate question about the trials. "Go on."

"How can you instruct us on the trials, if you've never made it through them? You've never even seen one of our mazes, have you?"

I stiffened. His questions were barbed and meant to make me look weak in front of the class, but he had a point. It was something that had been gnawing at me since I learned of the trials.

"My flight knowledge is pertinent to the trials, whether I've been through this particular test or not."

He choked back a laugh that dripped with derision. "The trials are more than a test. How many tests on your planet can end in death?"

"If you believe that serving in Earth's military is free from danger, you haven't seen the vast graveyards of fallen soldiers." My voice caught in my throat as I thought about the one soldier who wasn't buried beneath a white cross, the one whose body had never been found, the one who's ship had exploded, leaving us with nothing to bury and no way to properly say goodbye. "Now do you have a question that might help your fellow cadets?"

"No." He pivoted so he fully faced me. "But if you ever need someone to tell you about the trials, I'm happy to help *you*."

I ignored his sultry smile. Not this shit again. "I would never take time away from all your preparations for the maze."

"It would be my pleasure *if* you have any free time after classes."

His emphasis on the word *if* made the back of my neck prickle with unease. Did this arrogant Drexian cadet know about how I was actually spending my time after classes? Did he know about the covert training sessions? The roiling sensation in my gut returned. Did he know about Volten?

I bit back the urge to put him firmly in his place. "I'll take that under advisement, Cadet. Now, we'll start with combat takeoffs, which are harder to pull off than the landings, but less painful."

Touching the lectern, I swiveled to the holographic image of a Drexian fighter that flashed into the air and hovered beside me. If the Drexian knew either of my secrets, what was I going to do to keep him quiet?

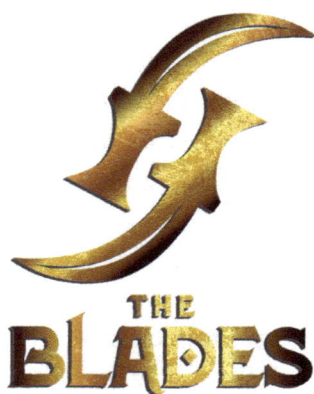

THE BLADES

CHAPTER 42

VOLTEN

I STOOD IN THE MIDDLE OF MY QUARTERS AS I TRIED TO ASSESS the overall sex appeal of my room. Drexian Academy quarters were not known for creature comforts, although my room as an instructor was light years ahead of the shared room I'd occupied as a cadet. At least shared showers and a snoring roommate were a thing of the past.

That didn't make the gray blanket covering my bed and the bare window overlooking the stormy sea any more appealing for a romantic rendezvous. If I was giving myself a small break, I didn't think that even Kann, who considered himself to be constantly on the brink of a sexual conquest, had his quarters outfitted for an encounter with a female. Until recently, there had been zero chance of a female entering my room.

I tugged at the foot of the blanket again, but it couldn't get any smoother. I'd thought of asking Kann for anything he might have that would appeal to a female, but that would be all but admitting what was going on. My friend might not have the razor-sharp intellect of an Iron or the strategic brain of an Assassin, but he was no simpleton.

"She won't care," I told myself. "After the sparring ring, this is luxurious."

My heart rate spiked at the mere thought of taking her in the sparring ring. Maybe I should suggest we meet there? Then I shook my head so hard my ears rang. Wasn't it enough I was fucking another instructor in my school? Risking getting caught was not something I wanted to do again. Or did I?

I scraped a hand violently through my hair. How had I gone from a disciplined, honorable Drexian, to one who was worried about how to best seduce a colleague?

A shrill bleep forced me to abandon my self-torture to pull out my device. *Grekking* hell. Why was my mother pinging me again? I rarely heard from her anymore, especially since I'd taken my post at the academy and earned my father's disgust, but this was the second time she'd reached out since the start of the new term. There was little doubt in my mind why she was calling, why she ever called.

"Volten." Her strained face sagged with relief when I answered her vid call. "I hoped you'd pick up."

"What do you need?"

I hadn't meant to be so direct, but I was weary of pretending with her. There was only one thing she cared about, had ever cared about.

She reared back as if I'd reached through the screen and across the vast surface of Drex to slap her face. "I wouldn't have to call if you'd helped your father the first time."

I wondered if she'd had too much deep-outpost alien gin, or if she really didn't recall what I'd told her the last time she'd begged for my father. "I can't help him, even if he would accept help from me."

"You have to try." Her voice quavered, and she darted a nervous glance behind her. "Things are bad. Worse than they've ever been."

My stomach tightened. As tired as I was of my mother's unwavering support of my father to the detriment of everything else—including me, including my brothers—I wasn't heartless. "What has he done?"

She shook her head quickly—too quickly. "Nothing, but you know how he gets. Since the new regulations after the attack, he can't do much."

You mean, since the Drexian security forces are cracking down on criminal activity? I pressed my lips together to keep from saying that out loud.

"He would not work at the academy," I told her. "Even if he didn't have a record."

She opened her mouth, but I continued talking. "He would hate the rules. He would hate the cadets. He would hate being reminded that he didn't get accepted."

"He should have." My mother's tone was crisp as she reopened an old grudge she'd nursed right alongside my father. "If he had a decent house, he would have."

I didn't bother to remind her that I didn't possess a decent house—made even worse with my father's aversion to the law—yet I'd been accepted into the academy. That would only stir up past resentments that I'd chosen to attend an academy that had dared to reject my father.

"You have to ask your new Academy Master." My mother changed tone and tactics. "You said Zoran was better than the last one."

"He's less concerned with rank, but that doesn't mean—"

"Promise me you'll try." My mother was almost begging now. "Zoran will do it. I know he will. Does he know who you are?"

"He knows me." Although him knowing who I was and the fact that I came from nothing wasn't what I'd consider an asset. "But I'm one of the newer instructors. I don't have any leverage."

"You don't need leverage to ask. Promise you'll ask."

I paused, not wanting to lie to her but knowing that I couldn't dare ask Admiral Zoran for a job for my dishonorable father. Even reminding him of my questionable lineage made my face blaze with shame.

"You owe him, Volten." She didn't wait for me to object to this laughable statement. "You owe me."

Since childhood, my mother had told me how I owed her and how much she'd sacrificed for me. If that meant that becoming pregnant with me had tied her to my father, I had long since paid for that sin. As the oldest, I'd always been treated more harshly, held to higher standards, been expected to step in each time my father fell through.

"I do not owe you this, mother."

Before she could launch into a fresh assault, I disconnected. I wasn't sure if I despised her more at that moment or myself.

The rapping on the door put an end to my internal war, but I could only stare at it. My mother had not convinced me to talk to Zoran, but she had reminded me where I came from and how unworthy I was of someone like Ariana.

Letting the human into my quarters, my life, my mess would be a mistake I couldn't undo.

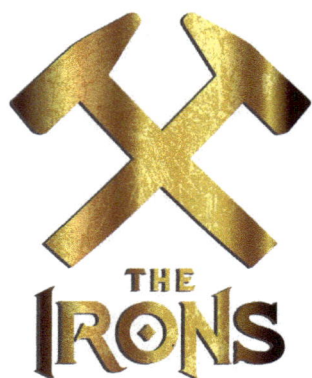

THE IRONS

CHAPTER 43

ARIANA

'D WAITED UNTIL EVERY CADET HAD DRIFTED UP THE STAIRS and out the top door before I flipped off the holographic image of a perfect combat landing that was playing on loop. I'd been able to resume my class and focus on the lesson, but now that I'd powered through, the paranoia crept back into my brain.

What did Torq mean when he'd pointedly asked about my free time? Had he somehow uncovered the clandestine training sessions, or had he stumbled onto me with Volten in the sparring ring the night before? I wasn't sure which I thought would be worse. Neither was good.

"If he knows anything," I told myself. One comment didn't mean that he knew. It was, well, one comment. But if he did know something…

I groaned as I trudged up the steps. I needed to talk to someone. I thought of Fiona, but to explain my concern and uncertainty I'd have to tell her about Volten. She might have suspicions, but she didn't know anything for sure, and she did not know that he'd had me pressed up against the metal cage half naked after she'd left.

My cheeks warmed at the memory, but I brushed it away and pushed through the doors to the outside hallway. No, I wasn't ready to confess all to Fiona, even though she was my closest friend at the academy. Whatever had happened with Volten was so new that I didn't even know if it was a thing worth mentioning. If we were one and done, then I definitely didn't want to tell anyone. It would only make things awkward, and the last thing I wanted was for there to be a weird vibe between my fellow flight instructor and my best friend at the school.

For a flicker of a second, I thought about Sasha. Who was I kidding? Even if she'd been around, we'd never had the kind of relationship where we shared our deep feelings and dark desires. We'd been too competitive for that, something I now regretted. What I wouldn't have given for a sister I could confide in, trust with my secrets, share my fears. But Sasha and I had never been that for each other, and all the regret in the universe couldn't change the past.

That left Volten. He was the only one who knew everything, the only one who would be able to tell me if I was being paranoid. He was the only one who had as much to lose as I did.

I picked up my pace as I maneuvered through the flow of cadets and headed for the tower that housed the staff quarters. I hadn't spotted Torq, which was a good sign. The cadet hadn't been waiting for me outside the classroom doors or in the high-ceilinged corridor that led to it. He wasn't loitering in the main hall that filtered students up the wide, curling staircase or into inclinator cars that whizzed up the interior of the towering, stone building. He didn't grab me as I skirted the four arched entrances to the schools, each with their emblems carved into the black stone overhead and slipped up a side staircase.

Maybe I was being overly anxious about what he'd said. It had only been a single ambiguous comment. Then I recalled how he'd cocked his eyebrow and given me a knowing look.

I broke into a jog as my feet tapped the steps that had been worn smooth, echoing my brisk pace back to me as I coiled up the twisting stairs. When I emerged on one of the floors that contained the Drexian staff quarters, I paused and released a breath as I scanned the arched doors inset in the polished, ebony stone. The only light in the dim corridor came from the sconces on the walls and danced in long, contorted shadows on the ceiling even though it was daytime.

"Why do all the doors look the same?" I cursed under my breath. "Why do all the halls look the same?"

Drexian culture—at least Drexian Academy culture—wasn't big on diversity. They valued uniformity and consistency and discipline. Not all that different from Earth military, if I was being honest. And now that most of the holes in the academy walls had been repaired, I couldn't even use those as landmarks.

I pawed through my memories of helping Volten to his room as I walked slowly down the door-lined hall, finally pivoting to a door that I was reasonably sure was his. I hovered in front of it, my fist hesitating before pounding on the surface. What was my story if it wasn't Volten who answered? How did I explain my presence in the staff quarters that were so far from my own tower?

Voices, garbled behind the door I was somewhat sure was Volten's, gave me more pause before I knocked. I leaned closer, almost pressing my ear to the door. Was that Volten's voice? If so, who was he talking to? Did he talk to himself, which would be curious but not concerning? I'd been known to talk to myself more than a few times. But what if he wasn't talking to himself? If it was his friend Kann, I did not want to knock on the door.

My back went rigid when I heard one of the voices again. *That* was not Volten. That voice was female.

A wave of indignant anger washed over me. Was he seeing

another woman? My raised fist tightened into a fierce ball. Who else could he be seeing? I knew all the females at the academy, and not one of them had any reason to be in the flight instructor's quarters. I barely had a reason, and I'd screwed him.

This is why you don't sleep with people at work.

I growled at the annoying voice in my head. I hated that that bitch was always right. "Insufferable know-it-all."

My ear was still flattened to the door when I heard the feminine voice again, this time sharper. "You owe him, Volten. You owe me."

I pulled back, instinctively recoiling from the rebuke that felt so personal that I flinched. This was no lover.

"I do not owe you this, mother."

Silence followed Volten's statement, and I held my own breath as I backed away from the door. I was on the verge of leaving, but then the sound of footsteps in the stairwell reached me. Someone was coming. I glanced to the far end of the corridor. I wouldn't make it to the other staircase in time.

I tapped my knuckles on Volten's door as I kept my gaze locked on the top of the stairs. "Come on, open up."

The door didn't budge. What was taking him so long? I knocked harder as the footfall grew louder until I was pounding my fist against the unyielding door.

CHAPTER 44

VOLTEN

"Took you long enough!" Ariana rushed inside and ducked out of sight.

I stood in the open door, baffled by her rush, and how flustered she was, until two Iron instructors walked by on the way to their rooms. I nodded to them and shut my door, but they were too engrossed in their conversation to wonder why I was standing with my door open.

"What are you doing here?" My question was more direct than I'd meant it to be. I tried again. "I mean, I thought you were coming here later."

She rubbed her palms down the front of her uniform pants. "I am. I was." She sank onto the foot of my bed without even commenting on how neatly it was made. "I had to talk to you."

Talk? I'd completely misinterpreted what she'd meant in the staff dining room. Human females were even harder to understand than Drexians, and I didn't consider myself an expert on them either. "You wish to talk?"

She peered at me. "I need your opinion on something. You're the only one I can ask."

I stood in front of her as she jiggled one leg up and down. After my mother's vid call, talking was the last thing I wanted to do, but I waited for Ariana to continue.

"It's Torq."

My mind tripped over the Drexian name. "The cadet I pulled aside?"

She frowned. "I don't think you pulling him aside did much. He said something to me today in class."

Heat prickled the back of my neck. "Again?"

"This time it was specific. He questioned my ability to prepare them for the maze if I've never gone through it myself."

"He did what?" A Drexian cadet should never question an instructor, human or not. Not only that, but I'd also seen the way Torq looked at Ariana—the hungry, predatory gaze—and the memory sent anger pulsing through me.

She waved a hand in the air. "That's not the part that bothered me. He said he'd be willing to tell me about the maze *if* I had any free time after classes."

I waited for her to say more, but she only looked at me intently. "And that bothered you?"

She jutted out her chin. "Doesn't that sound like he knows something? Like he's suggesting I don't have any time after classes because I'm already busy with..." She flapped her hand again.

"You believe he knows about the after-hours coaching sessions?"

She lifted one shoulder. "Or he knows about..." She moved one finger back and forth between us.

"You think he knows that you seduced me in the sparring ring?"

Her mouth fell open, and a strangled sound emerged. "*I seduced you?*"

I couldn't keep the serious expression on my face, and Ariana caught the quirk of my lips.

She exhaled loudly. "Ha ha ha. You shouldn't be joking about this, you know. Torq could blow up both of our lives."

"The cadet is cunning. If he knew something, he would have already tried to use it against me or you in a more direct manner. Drexians do not dabble in subtlety."

Her shoulders sagged. "So, you don't think he knows anything?"

"I don't. I think he was trying to undermine you again, but I do not believe he knows about the extra training for the humans or about what you did to me in the ring last night."

A grin pulled at the corner of her mouth. "I should kick your ass for that."

I was glad that she was no longer vibrating with worry. Her empty threats were much better than the fear that had trembled her voice. "You can try."

She swept her gaze around my compact room. "In here?"

"You said you preferred some place more comfortable than the sparring ring." I stepped closer to her, and she had to lean back to maintain eye contact.

"I did say that." She hesitated. "But we can wait if you're not… in the mood."

Why was the previously bold, almost-always reckless female suddenly so hesitant? "I promise that Torq has no idea about us."

"It's not that." She glanced at the door. "Before I knocked on the door, I heard you."

It took me a moment to realize what she meant. She'd overheard me talking to my mother. "How much did you hear?"

She shook her head and the side swept layers of her hair fell into her face. "Only the end. I wasn't trying to listen in, but I thought you had company." Faint patches of pink appeared on her cheeks. "I didn't want to disturb you." She took a breath. "I know what it's like to have a demanding parent, if you want to talk about it."

The last thing I wished was to discuss my family with Ariana. Not if she did not trust me enough to admit that her sister was dead. The last thing I wanted was for her to know that I didn't deserve a female with her status. I moved my head back and forth. "I do not need to talk about it." Then I thought about what she'd said, everything she'd said. "You thought I had a female in my quarters?"

"I heard a female voice. I didn't know what to think."

I reached for her hands and pulled her to standing. "You are the only female who will ever be in my room."

She twisted her lips to one side. "You can't know that."

"You have seen the number of females at the academy. I *can* say that." I turned her small hands over in mine. "I also know that you are the only female I desire."

"Oh." Her pursed lips curved into a smile. "Then I'm sorry I suspected you of being a player."

"Player?" The word did not make sense to me. I did not play any sports.

"It means someone who dates lots of people at the same time."

Human language had so many words that did not mean what they should mean. "I am not a player. Why would I be with anyone else when I only want you?"

Ariana pressed a hand to my chest. "It's hard for me to resist you when you say things like that, flyboy."

I curled a hand around her waist and backed her up until her legs bumped the edge of my bed. "Then don't."

THE ASSASSINS

CHAPTER 45

ARIANA

I pressed a hand to his chest. All the doubt that had flooded me when I'd heard him talking with a woman was gone, especially after I'd figure out that it was his mother. As he gazed into my eyes with his striking blue ones, it seemed impossible that I'd ever doubted him. "It's hard for me to resist you when you say things like that, flyboy."

He curled an arm around my waist and backed me up until my legs bumped the edge of his bed. "Then don't."

I fisted my hands into his shirt and fell backward onto the bed, bringing him with me. Volten grinned as he braced his arms to keep from crushing me, his biceps bulging as he then slowly lowered himself to kiss me.

I wasn't any kind of muscle worshiper, and I'd never chased gym rats, but I couldn't resist releasing his shirt and running my hands over his flexed arms. Every bit of him was so big and hard, which made it even more shocking how soft his lips were as they moved expertly against mine.

I forgot all about his soft lips when he lowered his torso, and I could feel the part of him that wasn't even remotely soft. Memories of his long, thick cock made my pulse jackknife and my hands drop to the waist of his pants and fumble.

Volten broke our kiss and coiled up and out of my reach. "Not so fast, flygirl."

I laughed and made a swipe for him. "Flygirl? I don't think that's a thing."

"It should be." He deftly unfastened my uniform pants and yanked them, along with my panties, over my hips and down my legs in a single, swift movement.

I gave a small gasp of surprise but managed to agree with him. "It definitely should be."

He shed his own pants and shirt just as briskly, and I tugged my uniform shirt over my head fast enough to enjoy the sight of him standing with his huge cock protruding from his body. My pussy clenched in anticipation, and I stretched my arms toward him.

"Last time was fast," he said as he lay down on the bed next to me and then pulled me across him so that I was straddling his chest. He scooted my bare ass higher, until I was bracing my knees on both sides of his head and lowering myself onto his face. "This time will not be."

There was no way I was arguing with that or with the amazing things his tongue was doing. "How did you get so good at this so fast?" This I glanced down at his occupied mouth. "Don't bother answering that."

I tilted my hips forward, shamelessly opening my legs wider for him as he grabbed my ass cheeks and squeezed. Arching my back, I ran my hands through my hair and down my neck, pausing to caress my own breasts.

Volten's eyes went wide as he watched me, but his pace didn't falter as he sucked my clit and then flicked his tongue quickly over it. I brushed my own fingers across my taut nipples, squeezing them as I rocked my hips back and forth to meet Volten's urgent tongue.

The sight of him between my legs made it impossible for me to fight the wave of pleasure that barreled through me, and my body detonated as I quivered and moaned and finally dropped one arm behind me as I bowed my back and let my head fall between my shoulder blades. "Fuck me."

Volten sat up with his hands still clasping my ass cheeks and lowered me all the way onto my back, as I let the last tremors of my release reverberate through me. "That was my plan."

He pulled me down farther on the bed so that my head wasn't dangling off and then spread my legs on either side of him. He was on his knees with his cock jutting from his body and he dragged the broad crown through my slickness. "This time I want to watch you while you take me."

I bit my lower lip as he guided my hips up and notched his cock at my entrance, his gaze never leaving my eyes. As he pushed inside, I rolled my head back.

He stopped suddenly. "Eyes on me, Ariana."

My instinct was to challenge him, to challenge any order, but I wanted his cock inside me, I needed it, so I obeyed him. I locked my eyes on his as he slowly pushed in and my body stretched to take him. My eyelids fluttered, and I released a moan of pleasure but I didn't look away.

When he bottomed out, I closed my eyes to savor the sensation of being filled so completely. When I opened them, Volten was staring at the place our bodies met.

"You stretch so perfectly around my cock."

I flushed with pleasure then flushed even more because I couldn't believe how much I craved his praise. What had happened to me? I was helpless when it came to Volten, especially when it came to his cock. I twitched my hips. "Are you going to fuck me?"

His eyes glinted as he stared hungrily at me. "Tell me how you want me to fuck you."

I reached for his hands. "Hard."

He released my ass and tipped his body forward so that he was on top of me and my legs were coiled around his waist. He gathered my hands in one of his and pinned them over my head. "Last time was about me fucking you hard. This time is about me going slow."

I strained against his hands and made an impatient sound.

"You can fight all you want, but you won't escape. Not until I've made you come on my cock at least two more times, Lieutenant."

I stopped wriggling as he started to move in and out deliciously slowly, hitting all the right spots and provoking more desperate sounds from me. Maybe submitting to Volten wasn't so bad.

"Yes, sir," I whispered before he crushed his mouth to mine.

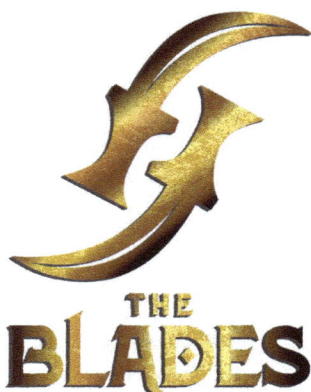

THE BLADES

CHAPTER 46

ARIANA

"THERE HAS TO BE A BETTER MEETING PLACE THAN THIS." I stepped closer to Fiona and away from a bucket filled with rubble.

"Not if we don't want anyone to hear us." Reina's head was bent low so her vertical swish of hair wouldn't brush the low ceiling.

The maintenance closet in a back corridor was one of the few spaces in the school that didn't have a high or vaulted ceiling. It was also a pretty sure bet for places where we couldn't be overheard.

"Even the Stacks aren't safe." Noora gave Reina a brief glance. "Too many spots for hiding and snooping."

Reina giggled then put a hand over her mouth to stifle the echo. "I know because I've overheard plenty in there."

I breathed in the scent of dust and oil soap as I shuffled my boots on the gritty floor. "What was so important we had to meet in here?"

Fiona lowered her voice even though it was only the four of

us standing in a tight circle with our shoulders touching. "Did you discover anything new?"

Noora produced a device from somewhere within her gown, and I wondered how many hidden pockets were in such a gossamer dress. "I've had to be careful about what I research."

"She doesn't want her hunky husband to know she's sneaking onto his accounts," Reina added with a giggle.

"I'm guessing you can't simply ask your hubby?"

She flicked her gaze to me. "I don't think anyone has ever called Zoran my hubby before." She grinned. "He would hate it." Then her smile dimmed. "I can't ask him without him asking me a million questions. He has no idea that I know anything about the trials or what it might mean for the human cadets."

"But you're the reason he supported incorporating humans into the academy, aren't you?" Fiona asked.

"I am but trust me when I tell you that I finessed that."

"Finesse is when you don't run into a situation with guns blazing," Fiona said to me with a gentle nudge to my ribs.

I shot her a sideways look. "Sounds like a waste of time."

"I don't like going behind Zoran's back, but I don't have time to finesse this," Noora said. "I know he isn't involved with anything treacherous here, but I also know that some decisions aren't within his control."

"The Drexian High Command again?" Fiona gave the woman a sympathetic look.

Noora made a noise in the back of her throat that I took to mean yes and swiped the screen of her device. "Since we know that the academy has procured an unusually large amount of animal sedative, I could work from there." A selection of sketches of animals, much like the ones Fiona and I had seen on the old maze maps, appeared on her screen. "I used the documents pertaining to past trials to determine which types of creatures had been included in the mazes."

I leaned closer as I spotted beasts with wings and long snouts, creatures with snake-like necks and equally long tails, and animals with fangs that had spikes covering their backs. "But these must be mythological, right? They aren't actual, living creatures, are they?"

"They aren't any animal found on Earth or Drex," Noora said without looking at us.

"But they can be found on other planets." Reina tapped a skinny finger on one of the scary beasts on the screen. "The *ridanthian* is rare, but it still roams on Parnisia 3."

"That's a real animal?" I shuddered at the image of a furry beast with wide wings and a tail like a platypus.

"Real and deadly." Reina's usually chirpy voice was subdued. She slid her fingertip across to a squat creature with horns in front and back. "And the *zigtroll* is prevalent on Harellen, although they're hard to catch."

I shivered and rubbed my hands briskly up and down my arms. Fiona wrapped an arm around my shoulder and squeezed. "Better to know than be surprised, right?"

I wasn't sure if I was happier that I knew that the horrifying alien creatures existed or if I'd preferred my blissful ignorance.

Noora swiped her finger, the images disappeared, and a grid took its place. "I did a deep dive into each of the creatures that still exist."

Fiona nodded her approval. "You made a chart for comparison."

"I needed to know their size and their general biology if I wanted to figure out how much sedative it would take to knock them out."

I ran my gaze down the chart, which appeared to be arranged in order of the creatures' size by weight. "From this chart, you can tell which creatures the Drexians might be planning to put in the maze?"

"Only in the most general sense." Noora released a sigh that betrayed frustration. "There are too many variables for me to know anything for sure."

"We don't know if the sedative is for one creature or more than one," Reina said. "Or if it's intended for one dose, or more than one per animal."

My nerves jangled as I stared at the long list of creatures and the numbers associated with each. The thought of having to encounter any of them made my pulse spike, and I hated that the cadets were being thrown to the wolves. Or, in this case, the *ridanthians* and *zig-trolls.* "So, what *can* it tell us?"

Noora wasn't bothered by my pointed question. She swiped to another screen. "It tells us that these creatures are not a match. Despite the number of sedatives that the academy has procured, it wouldn't be enough for these guys."

I released a breath that the largest beasts from the original collection were eliminated. "That's a good thing, right?"

Reina and Noora exchanged a look—a look that did not calm my worries.

"The largest creatures aren't necessarily the most dangerous. They can be slower and less agile in a maze." Noora straightened and looked at us. "In fact, some of the smaller creatures are significantly more deadly and more difficult to outrun."

She swept her finger to the left and a final image of the remaining creatures appeared, each one of them a combination of talons and claws and spiked tails. Each one making me regret that I'd ever agreed to come to the Drexian Academy.

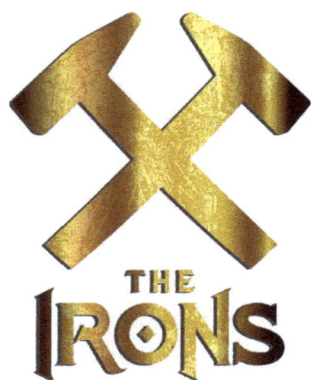

THE IRONS

CHAPTER 47

VOLTEN

I slipped into my chair, glad to see that I wasn't the last member of the staff to join the weekly all-academy dinner. My gaze went to Ariana's chair, but it was empty as was the other female instructor's seat.

"Looks like you aren't the late one this time." Kann leaned over and gave me a maddening grin. How did he always seem to know what I was thinking?

"This time it's a female thing," he added, glancing at the empty chair by Zoran. "Maybe they had a meeting."

He laughed, but a part of me wondered if there was some kind of gathering of the women. A glance to the long cadet tables told me that it wasn't. The female cadets were all in place and already laughing and talking to the other humans around them.

"Something happened," Kann said as he handed me my filled wine goblet.

"What?" My mind was still on the missing females, and my breath hitched in my chest. "Something happened to the women?"

Kann laughed and scraped a hand down his dark scruff. "No, with the holochambers."

"Oh." I took a drink to calm my racing heart and reminded myself that I needed to play it cooler with Kann. Then I remembered that we'd been waiting for someone to attempt to sabotage the safety controls of the holochambers again. "Someone tampered with the systems again?"

Kann held up a finger. "They attempted to tamper with it, but they must have noticed the additions that Drux made and realized that they'd been discovered. The only way we know someone accessed the systems at all was because Drux set up a trigger."

I took a larger gulp, hoping the Drexian wine would dull the anger that was swelling within me. "So, the saboteur realized that cadets weren't getting injured, and went in to remedy the situation."

Kann pressed his brows together until they were a solid line. "Looks like it. I guess they don't want to wait for the trials to take out the new recruits."

I snuck a glance at Zoran, who had Commander Vyk seated on his other side. "We still can't tell our superiors."

"Zoran is loyal," Kann said, his statement brooking no argument. He eyed Vyk, then tore his gaze away. "I cannot imagine a member of Inferno Force being a traitor."

"Maybe he doesn't see ridding the academy of weak cadets as being a traitor." I'd heard too many Drexians spout off against humans and the intermingling of our species to believe that a Drexian like Vyk couldn't harbor such opinions.

"Then we have to be vigilant." Kann's jaw was set as he inclined his head to the human cadets. "They won't die on my watch or in my school."

Kann was as loyal a Drexian as I'd ever known, and he'd stood by me when no one at the academy had, when I was a nobody, when it would have been the easy thing to join the Drexians who tormented me. But he never had. He'd never taken the easy path.

It was on the tip of my tongue to tell him another way he could help protect the humans. I desperately wanted to tell him about the after-hours coaching and invite him to join the cause. There would be no one better to train the cadets in battle than Kann and no one who would fight harder for them to succeed.

If I told him, I would no longer be keeping a secret from my closest friend. The subterfuge weighed heavy on me as I sat next to Kann. I was sure that he'd never kept something important from me, although one of the best things about Kann was that he was an open book. He wasn't like an Assassin who relished in subterfuge. He was a Blade—bold, brave, straightforward.

But it wasn't my secret to reveal.

As I thought about Ariana, she and Fiona walked onto the dais and took their seats. I must have missed Zoran's wife arriving because when I looked, she was seated beside him. I returned my gaze to Ariana, hungry for her eyes to meet mine. When they did, and she gave me the slightest of smiles, my chest constricted with the most intoxicating blend of pleasure and torment.

Being so close to her was both euphoria and torture. I longed to touch her again, but instead I drained my wine and forced myself to look away, over the heads of the cadets and across the great hall.

Then I saw the figure standing at the back of the long room, and I almost lost my grip on my goblet. Her hair was pulled back tight, making her cheeks look sunken. Her gaze darted like a cornered animal looking for escape until it landed on me. The threat in her eyes sent fear arrowing through me.

What was my mother doing at the academy?

THE WINGS

CHAPTER 48

ARIANA

I wasn't a fan of the weekly all-academy dinners, preferring to grab my meals in the staff dining room, or sneak snacks from the kitchen. But once a week, at the end of the last day of classes before the single day off—Drexians didn't have such a thing as a two-day weekend—the great hall was filled from end to end with raucous cadets eager to stuff their faces with food that was a step up from their usual fare in the cadet dining room.

The din of conversation had signaled that we were getting closer to the hall even before the savory aroma of the food reminded me that I hadn't eaten since the morning. I glanced at Fiona walking briskly beside me. "We aren't too late."

"You think we gave Noora and Reina enough time to slip inside?"

I paused outside the open doors of the long hall with vaulted ceilings that amplified the sound of laughter and chatter so much so that I could feel the hum of it through my feet. "I don't think anyone will notice them going in late, or us, and they'd never suspect we were together."

Fiona brushed remnants of dust from her uniform. "Or huddled in a maintenance closet."

I took a second to glance at my uniform and make sure it didn't look like I'd been practically standing in a bucket of rubble. "Let's do this."

We walked purposefully into the back of the room and cut sharply to the right, proceeding up the far side and skirting the wall until we could walk onto the dais and slide into our seats. No one at the staff table seemed to notice our arrival except Volten. I felt his gaze on me before I met his eyes, smiling at him unconsciously, my mouth betraying my desire to play it cool.

His gaze was hot, and my breath stuttered in my chest before he looked away, and I reached for my wine, grateful for the tangy beverage to distract me. My pulse fluttered, my heart constricted, my cheeks warmed. Why did this Drexian make me feel like a horny teenager instead of an accomplished pilot and officer?

If this was going to be a thing, if I was going to be unable to resist him, if he was going to have the power to make my insides turn molten, then I was going to have to learn to hide my feelings better. I looked anywhere but at Volten as I settled myself at the table—Noora sharing a smile with her husband, the security chief scowling at the room, one of the female cadets in the front of the hall clinking her goblet with another cadet.

I concentrated on sipping my wine, grateful that distracting myself by observing the rest of the crowd was working. It was working so well I almost missed Volten jerk to his feet. I almost missed him leaping from the dais. I almost missed him making a beeline for a Drexian female walking toward the front between two tables.

When I realized what was going on, I looked to his friend Kann to see if I should be concerned. Kann's mouth was open, as if he'd been struck in the chest and all the air had left his body. Not good.

I glanced back to the female that Volten was quickly near-ing. Like almost all Drexians, she had dark hair. But unlike the male Drexians, she wasn't huge and muscular. This female almost appeared shrunken, with shoulders that sagged in on themselves, and skin that was stretched tight over sharp cheekbones. It was clear that she'd once been beautiful, striking even, but that her beauty had been drained from her.

I suspected the fury in her eyes had something to do with that. I'd never known anyone who sheltered such seething anger who could also hold onto beauty. Rage devoured everything in its path, and as I watched her stride toward Volten, a pang of fear went through me that her vitriol would devour him as well.

"Who is that?"

Fiona's words broke my focus and made me realize that I wasn't the only one paying attention to the unfolding scene. The buzz of chatter had faded, and everyone on the dais watched the female advance on us. Cadets were turned around to track her as she stalked between the tables, and they murmured questions to each other and shook their heads. She was no one they knew. She was no one anyone knew.

Except for Volten.

Like an animal sensing an impending storm, my body vibrated with the need to stop whatever was about to happen. I could feel Volten's pain as if it was my own, and I wanted to run at the female and take her down. I didn't know why she was there or what she was planning to do, but I wanted to stop her, silence her, shut her down.

"Ariana?"

I cut my gaze to Fiona only to discover that I'd risen halfway, my palms planted on the table as if I was preparing to bolt. I scanned the dais to see all eyes on Volten marching across the room. All eyes, but Kann's. His were on me.

I could see in an instant that he knew. I'd given myself away.

Before I could think of any reason to explain my agitation on behalf of Volten, a voice pierced the undercurrent of whispers.

"You won't help your own father, so I'm here to talk to Admiral Zoran myself."

The female's voice was shrill and insistent, each word stabbing the air like a well-honed blade. Her face had contorted into a mask of spite that made her look monstrous as she sidestepped Volten's attempts to quiet her.

His usually square shoulders had contracted, and his own head was bowed low as he tried to talk to her in low tones I couldn't hear. As soon as she'd spoken, I'd recognized the voice from the one I'd heard berating him on the vid call in his room. Volten's mother had come to the academy to demand something from the Academy Master that Volten wouldn't do for her.

Blood rushed hot in my ears as I flashed back to my own father's scalding lectures, his stern expression as he told Sasha and me that we needed to be tougher; his stony, unforgiving face when we'd fallen short. I knew what it was like to have family who only demanded and never praised. I knew the blistering humiliation that was being heaped onto Volten like sizzling coals.

Admiral Zoran stood, and a hush washed over the room. Even Volten pivoted to him, his face twisted in pain and embarrassment that I wished I could take away.

The female pushed past Volten, her menacing gaze locked on the Academy Master. "You are Zoran of House Vorran?"

"I am." His voice was a menacing rumble that would have made anyone else hesitate.

"If my son won't help me, won't help his family," she drew herself up and thrust out her chest, "then maybe his brother from the illustrious House Vorran will."

THE ASSASSINS

CHAPTER 49

VOLTEN

THE GREAT HALL WENT QUIET AS IF ALL SOUND HAD BEEN sucked from the room and secreted away. No one coughed. No one shifted in their seat. No one breathed.

My mother's words—her accusation—was a bomb that had first frozen everything around it before it exploded. I looked from my mother with her hands in angry fists by her sides and her tightly clenched jaw, daring anyone to challenge her. My gaze touched on Ariana for a moment, but the agony in her eyes—the pain for me—was too much to bear. It finally landed on Zoran as he stood unmoving in the center of the staff table.

His fingers were spread wide and braced on the table as his eyes slid from my mother to me. Then he closed them for a beat before giving an almost imperceptible nod and opening them. "Lieutenant Volten is descended from House Vorran. I do not deny that he is my half-brother."

The bomb that had sucked away all sound and motion

exploded. My mother let out a bark of triumphant laughter as if even she couldn't believe that Zoran had admitted it. Gasps rippled through the room like a hungry flame, and then the sound of disbelief and shock consumed everything, consumed me.

I staggered back as my mother turned from Zoran to me. Her victorious smile slipped when she saw me gaping at her.

"You lied." My words were hoarse, and I doubted she could hear them over the swell of scandal swirling around us. But she knew what I'd said.

"I did it to protect you, Volten." Her own voice had softened to the pleading tone I knew so well as she tried to reach me with her arms outstretched. "Everything I did was to protect you."

Bile rose in the back of my throat, the bitter bite of it threatening to make me double over. I pressed my lips together to staunch not only the bile, but also the cruel words I wished to unleash on her.

I kept my hands at my side as she tried to take them. "Does my father know?" I choked back a guttural laugh as the truth slammed into me. "I guess he isn't my father after all, is he?"

Her eyes lowered. "He doesn't know. He couldn't. He wouldn't have taken me if he'd known I was carrying another Drexian's baby."

I shook my head. I didn't want to know the details. I didn't want to know about how she'd tricked the man I'd grown up thinking was my father. I didn't want to think about who my real father was, even if he was in House Vorran.

"You've lied to me for my entire life." I didn't care that cadets were staring at us and could hear every word. "You made me think I was someone I wasn't."

Her mouth set in a stubborn line. "You are the same Drexian you've always been."

"I never fit in. I never understood why I wasn't more like my father or my brothers. I never knew why my father disliked me."

"He doesn't dislike you. He couldn't. He doesn't know."

I scoffed at this. The Drexian might be a criminal, but he wasn't a fool. On some level he knew, he'd always known, and he'd held it against me and probably against my mother. So many scenes from my childhood replayed in my head, suddenly making sense through this new lens.

I stepped back, lengthening the distance between me and my mother. In an instant, she'd become a stranger to me. She might still be my mother, but all the lies that had held me to her and had tethered me to my cruel father and useless brothers were snapped like the thinnest threads.

Pivoting from her, I looked to Zoran. He hadn't moved, even though his wife was now standing and talking into his ear. I pushed past my mother and strode toward the dais, leaping onto it and planting my hands opposite his. "Have you always known?"

"No." His blue eyes held mine, and I was struck by how familiar they were. We had the same eyes. How had I missed that? Who hadn't missed that?

My gaze flicked behind Zoran to his adjunct Tivek, who did not look surprised or shocked. I sucked in a breath as I registered another gut punch. Of course, Tivek had known. Was that why he'd been awkward around me?

"I was not told until recently," Zoran's expression was dark, "and it was only as a threat that it was revealed at all."

"A threat?" My head swam. How would I be a threat?

"My father—our father—always used our status and inheritance as power over his children. Our older brother, who now leads our clan, is the same. He only mentioned your existence when he wanted to threaten my right to lead our house." He shook his head. "It was not the threat he thought it was. I do not care about leading our house."

Our father. *Our* brother. *Our* house.

My mind couldn't compute what he was saying.

"Why didn't you tell me?" My voice cracked, and I was aware of the entire staff table watching us.

"I didn't want to ruin your life." He inclined his head to one side as if to indicate the chaos that had erupted because of the revelation. "If your mother had not told you, or the rest of your family, I did not believe I had the right to upend a family."

Even though my body was trembling with confusion and anger, Zoran's reasons made sense. He must have been equally as shocked when he found out, although he'd had the advantage of being able to process his surprise in private. My entire past, my family, my clan had unraveled in front of the entire academy.

"I can't," I managed to say as a scream of frustration and humiliation welled in my chest. "I have to..." I staggered off the dais, my vision blurry as I passed Kann and slipped out a side door.

As soon as I'd walked a few steps from the hall, the cacophony dissipated and I could hear again, but the only sounds were the th-thump, th-thump, th-thump of my heart and the slapping of my boots on the stone floor. The cool air cocooned me, and I sucked it in greedily, glad to be away from the stifling warmth of the hall filled with bodies. Bodies that now knew truths about me that never should have been unearthed.

I pressed a palm against the wall, the chill of the stone dampening the fire simmering beneath my skin. The one thing that had defined most of my life—my lack of status, my lack of a notable clan—had been a lie. My struggle to get into the academy had been pointless. The bullying I'd suffered because I had no clan to speak of had been needless. I'd endured hardship in service to a secret, a lie, a cowardly betrayal that was not of my making.

My father was not my father. My mother was a liar. My clan was not mine. I was not the Drexian I'd thought I was.

When a hand touched my arm, I jerked away, recoiling at the

assumption that my mother had followed me. But it wasn't her. It was Ariana.

Relief flooded my body, but shame and humiliation followed briskly on its heels. What female wanted to align themselves with such scandal and disrepute? I despised myself for allowing her to share in my shame even by standing near me now.

"You shouldn't be here." I hated the hard edge of my voice, but I couldn't help it.

"I wanted to see if you're okay." Then she shook her head. "Of course, you're not okay. What happened in there was awful. I'm so sorry, Volt. What can I do to help?"

I shook her off and shook my head. What could anyone do? "You can't do anything."

She stepped closer and tipped her head up to meet my gaze. "You can talk to me, Volten. You can trust me."

Inexplicable anger at her surged within me, desperate for release. "Can I, or have you been lying to me, too?"

She jerked back. "What? When have I lied to you?"

I'd known my mother all my life, yet I hadn't seen her lies. How many other webs of pretty lies were being spun around me? What did I know about Ariana aside from the fact that she stoked my most primal desires and clouded my judgment? What did I know that she hadn't told me? What did I know to be fact aside from the truth of her sister's death that she ignored?

I stared at her, seeing only another female who hid the truth. "How can I trust you if you don't trust me?"

Her brow wrinkled. "I do trust you."

"But not enough to tell me about your sister? I know what happened to her."

"What?" She reared back, her pupils flaring. "You know about Sasha?"

How could she be so startled when her sister's death was

public record? How could she have thought I wouldn't find out? "Everyone seems to know your sister is dead but you."

As soon as the words left my lips and her face crumpled, I hated myself for lashing out at her. Witnessing her shrink from me as if I'd struck her was another body blow, but one I deserved. "Ariana, I'm—"

She shook her head so hard her hair flopped over her eyes before spinning on her heel and running away from me.

Grek grek grek. Now I'd truly lost everything.

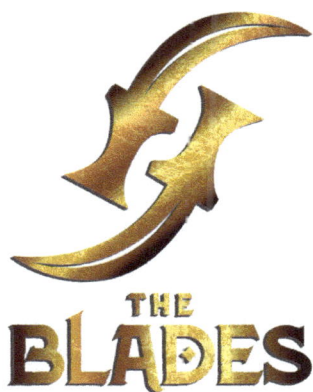

THE BLADES

CHAPTER 50

ARIANA

"**Y**OU NEED TO STOP LOOKING FOR HIM."

I swung my gaze back to the blonde across the table from me as she took a sip of *chidi* berry juice. "I'm not looking for—"

"Don't try to pretend with me." Fiona held up a hand as she cut off my lame protest. "I saw the way you reacted when shit went down with his mother. I know you two are involved. I teach Strategy, remember? I notice details. Not that you did a great job of hiding it."

I cut my gaze left and right, hoping no one heard her. Luckily, the staff dining room had thinned out with only a handful of Irons at a far table, distinctive for their intense conversation. If they'd been arm wrestling, I would have known they were Blades. If they'd been surveying the room with analytical calculation, they would have been Assassins. Flight I would have known by the strut in their walk. It hadn't taken long, but I'd gotten adept at recognizing members of the schools at a glance.

"We're not involved," I said confidently. At least that was the truth. Whatever had been between me and Volten had ended when he'd pushed me away outside the great hall. Even thinking of his face when he accused me of not being honest, and he'd told me he knew about my sister made my stomach clench and my appetite for breakfast vanish.

I didn't want to think about whether he was right or not. Just because we'd screwed a couple of times did not mean I owed him the contents of my soul.

Which is exactly why you'll always be alone, the small voice in the back of my brain teased. *You never open up to anyone or let them get close.*

I almost groaned aloud. The last thing I needed was to be reminded why I'd never had a relationship that lasted more than a few weeks—by my own bitchy inner voice.

"Okay," Fiona conceded. "You might not be involved now, but it's clear you care about the guy. You did go after him when he left the great hall. Have you heard if he's okay?"

I shook my head. I hadn't heard anything since I'd run from him, although I did know he hadn't missed his classes. The cadets were still being drilled on the flight simulators even if I steered clear of that area of Flight.

Avoiding him was cowardly especially after what had happened. But if I searched out Volten I'd have to tell him why I hadn't told him about Sasha, and I wasn't even sure if I fully understood that. What did it say about me that I couldn't accept my sister's death? What kind of badass pilot couldn't admit that another pilot had been killed in battle?

It was easier to pretend to myself that Sasha was alive some-where, that she was being the thorn in my side she'd always been, that she was the older sister blazing the way so I could follow and attempt to beat her. If I didn't lie to myself, I'd have to admit that one of the only remaining constants in my life was gone and that the person I'd always chased would never be caught. It was impossible to compete with a ghost.

I picked at the cold strip of *padwump* on my plate. Volten had said that everyone knew my sister was dead but me. It wasn't like her death in combat had been off the record, but somehow it was strange to think of others knowing. And if I could convince myself that no one knew, then I could trick myself into thinking it wasn't true.

Ignore and override. It was how I'd survived my rigid childhood. It was how I'd made it through flight training. It was how I'd dealt with losing fellow pilots. It was how I'd been able to keep breathing after I'd lost Sasha. So why wasn't it working now?

Why wasn't I able to ignore my feelings for Volten and override my protective instinct to forget about him, forget about how he'd made me feel, forget that it was the first time I'd felt something for someone else in a painfully long time?

I looked up and pinned Fiona with a hard gaze. "You know about my sister, don't you?"

Her eyes widened. "That was unexpected." She studied me for a beat. "I do. I told you I researched all the other humans who'd be coming here."

I exhaled, shifting into the strange sensation of talking about Sasha. "Do you think it's unusual that I don't mention her?"

Fiona considered this for a moment. "There isn't one specific way to grieve. If you aren't ready to talk about her, then you aren't ready."

"Volten said that I act like I don't know she's gone."

She moved her head back and forth as if bobbling between two thoughts. "You're protecting yourself."

I braced my elbows on the table and scored my hands through my hair. "I'm a fighter pilot trained to kill and be killed. I shouldn't have to pretend someone is still alive to keep myself from feeling pain. I shouldn't have to read the one note from her over and over so it feels like she's still with me."

"Why not? Because you're a Wing you think you aren't allowed weaknesses?"

I dropped my voice and was glad our usual corner spot wasn't near any other occupied tables. "I'm pretty sure weakness is something the Drexian Academy despises. Why else would they put their cadets through tests that might kill them?"

"If it makes you feel better, I doubt any Drexians think you not talking about your sister is a sign of weakness. They probably see it as a sign that you're cold and heartless and unaffected by death."

"That makes me feel tons better," I grumbled.

Fiona winked at me. "What are friends for?"

It hit me that this was the first time I'd talked about Sasha's death out loud, and that Fiona *was* a friend. There hadn't been much room in my rise to the top of my classes and my steady advancement in rank for friendships. I'd been too busy striving to be the best, but now I'd found some true friends, at the Drexian academy of all places. I'd only had to cross the galaxy for them.

The back of my eyes prickled, and I blinked rapidly, looking away and clearing my throat as Kann approached us.

He took the chair next to Fiona and across from me without asking. "Lieutenant." He tipped his head at me then looked at Fiona. "Captain."

"Kann." Fiona twisted to fully face him. "I'm not sure if we've had a conversation before."

He put a hand to his chest. "My loss."

I couldn't stop myself from asking about his friend. "How is Volten?"

His charming smile faltered. "He'll be fine."

That wasn't comforting, but before I could ask him to elaborate, the Blade instructor leaned closer. "He's the reason I'm here, but before you get angry at him, you should know that he only told me because he believes in what you're doing."

Fiona glanced at me, her expression guarded.

"Volten can't help you with your project anymore. Not right now, at least."

I stared at him, unwilling to say anything before I knew exactly what the Drexian meant.

"Project?" Fiona's voice was impressively curious yet revealed nothing. How did the woman do it?

Kann swept his gaze across the almost empty dining room. "The one that takes place after hours."

"He's quitting on us?" I couldn't keep the hurt from my voice or the feeling that this was my fault. If I hadn't run off, he wouldn't be quitting. It was me he wanted to avoid, not the cadets who needed training.

"Not quite." Kann grinned brightly. "I'm taking his place. Since I'm a Blade, I'm the best one to teach the human cadets how to defend themselves in the maze."

Fiona and I looked at each other, unsure of what to say and if we could trust this Drexian we barely knew.

"Volten said to tell you that he trusts me with his life and that I would never betray him or you." He put his hand to his chest. "That's true. You might not know much about the Blades, but not only are we brave, we're loyal. To the death."

"Let's hope it doesn't come to that," Fiona said.

Kann leaned back in the chair, shifting his attention from me to Fiona. "At the Drexian Academy, death is always a possibility," he blew out a breath, "especially when it comes to the maze."

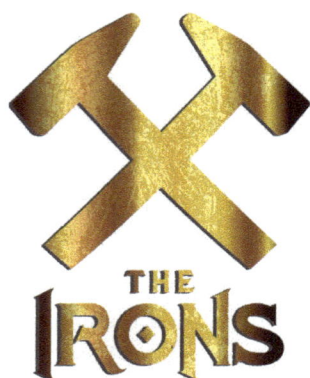

THE IRONS

CHAPTER 51

VOLTEN

T HIS TIME I DIDN'T HESITATE WHEN I WAS ON THE THRESHOLD of the Academy Master's door. I knocked loudly, the sound louder and more insistent than I'd intended.

Why should I be careful or worry about what impression I might make? I was no longer coming to see my superior as a lowly instructor. Zoran was part of my clan. He was family. He was my brother.

Half brother, I reminded myself, the distinction crucial to me, and I was sure, to the admiral. I still couldn't bring myself to think of *our* father and *our* family. Zoran's father was not my father. House Vorran was not my house. Not really. Not yet.

I might have spent most of my childhood longing for a different father and a house that wasn't tainted by scandal and shame, but I'd never imagined that it could be real. I'd never once thought that my entire life was built on a lie, that my existence was mired in betrayal, that I hadn't felt a connection to my father because there was no connection. Not by blood, at least. And in the Drexian empire, blood and clan were everything.

The door swung open, and Tivek stood on the other side. He inclined his head formally to me as if he hadn't been the one to summon me to an audience with the Academy Master.

Since my mother's disruptive appearance at the academy dinner, Zoran's adjunct had looked at me differently. He no longer eyed me with suspicion, and I wondered if he'd suspected me of knowing my connection to the Drexian he served. Had he thought that I'd been secretly trading on my connection? I almost laughed out loud at this. If he'd doubted me, I felt sure my violent reaction to the revelation by my mother had convinced him that I'd been in the dark.

But he hadn't been in the dark. I scowled at the Drexian. Zoran's assistant had known my own bloodline before I did, and like everyone complicit in the lies, he'd kept quiet.

"The admiral is ready for you."

I grunted and strode past Tivek, uninterested in playing nice or continuing to play games that involved my life. When I reached the wide desk, I thumped a fist across my chest, even though Zoran stood facing the tall narrow window instead of me. "You asked to see me?"

The admiral turned slowly, the silver at his temples glinting in the fading daylight that reflected off the sea. "I thought we should talk."

I pressed my lips together so hard that it hurt. Talking was the last thing I wanted to do. Talking was the reason I'd been humiliated and exposed in front of the entire academy. Talking wouldn't undo any of the betrayal that had been heaped upon me like smoldering cinders.

I grasped my hands behind me and stared over his head. "So, talk."

There was a sharp intake of breath behind me, but I didn't care what Tivek thought about my disrespect. Zoran had known I was his brother and had said nothing. Tivek had known and had kept the secret. They could both *grek* themselves.

The admiral held up a hand as if to forestall his adjunct's protests or maybe his rebuke of my rudeness. "You are still upset."

"I discovered that my entire past was a lie. Nothing about myself—my father, my family, my clan—is what I thought it was. I am not who I thought I was. Do you fault me for being upset?"

Zoran sighed and shook his head. "You should not have found out the way you did."

I snapped my gaze to him. "Maybe I shouldn't have found out at all? Did you ever intend to tell me, or was it better for you that I remained ignorant?"

"The admiral wanted to tell you a hundred times—" Tivek's rushed words burst from behind me before Zoran interrupted him.

"You do not need to defend me, although I am grateful for your loyalty." Zoran inclined his head slightly. "Maybe I should speak to Volten alone."

I pivoted to watch Tivek's expression shift from outraged to stunned, but he accepted his superior's wishes, walked to the door, and slipped outside.

"My apologies. Tivek is so loyal he is often blind to my flaws."

"He knew." I wasn't asking; I was telling. If we were talking, if I was going to be forced to talk, I wanted to know the entire truth. "About me. About my connection to you."

"He did, but only after I did, and only because I was wrestling with the question of when to tell you and how."

"Tivek didn't believe I was ignorant of our connection." Once again, it wasn't a question.

Zoran tilted his head at me in silent acknowledgment. "It's his nature to be suspicious especially after the betrayals that nearly took down the academy, but I knew just as surely that you didn't."

"You said you haven't known for long?"

His face darkened, and he swung back to look out the window.

"I'm sorry to say that our father was not ignorant of your existence. Knowing the Drexian, I suspect he always knew." Bitterness dripped from his voice as he spoke of the Drexian who'd sired both of us, but whom I'd never met. "He made it his business to know everything that concerned him and everything that could possibly concern him."

"Your father...our father is no longer living?"

Zoran gave a curt shake of his head without facing me. "Our older brother is the head of the house now, and he is much like our father. Just as cruel, just as manipulative. He is the one who told me of your existence as a threat."

"Why would I be a threat?" My head ached from all the new information about my family, the family I'd never known was mine. "I was never acknowledged, and I am younger than you."

Zoran glanced at me over his shoulder. "None of that matters if my brother decides to choose you to succeed him as leader of the clan."

The admiral wasn't making sense. I couldn't be named the head of a clan I barely knew. House Vorran was as unfamiliar to me as any of the prestigious clans I'd grown up hearing about. I knew the name. I knew it was more revered than my clan. I knew Drexians who belonged to it were more important than me and would have an easier life because of it. "Why would he do that?"

"To punish me." Zoran whirled around and walked around the desk until he stood in front of me. "I defied him. I allowed his son to make a love match instead of the one he arranged. Then I took the bride he'd selected for his son as my own."

"Your brother would do this because you took Noora as your mate?" Maybe I didn't want to be a part of a notable clan. They sounded as crazy as my sordid one.

"He would, but that doesn't matter to me. Noora is more important to me than being the head of our clan, so my brother's threat is powerless," Zoran smiled at me, "which enrages him."

I wasn't sure if I was supposed to return his smile. The conversation had taken a bizarre turn and had reminded me why I had avoided my own family for so long.

"His threat backfired. He believed that I would want to hide you and your connection to our clan to keep my place in the family secure. He made the mistake of thinking I was like him, desperate for power. He was wrong. I welcome a new brother to our clan especially one as honorable and loyal as you. My only hesitation was when and how to tell you."

"Two problems now eliminated."

He moved his head up and down slowly. "If I had any idea your mother would do what she did, I would have told you myself. I thought I had time to figure out the best way to disrupt your life."

I released a breath, some of the anger draining with it. "I doubt there was a good way."

"I have ensured that your mother will not return to the academy and that her needs will be met." He held up a hand before I could warn him from pouring money into a well that could never be filled. "I have arranged for your father and brothers to be given jobs that will take them far from home for long periods of time. I have also arranged for it to be impossible for them to lose them."

A familiar prickle of shame crept up my neck. "You didn't have to—"

"I did." He clamped a heavy hand on my shoulder. "We are family, and after everything, it was the least I could do."

I thought of all the years of torment I endured because of my lack of clan. I thought of how I'd had to work harder for every scrap of respect. I thought of every Drexian who believed me to be beneath him simply because of my clan. And all the time, I'd been a member of one of the most illustrious and powerful clans that existed.

But would I have risen as high, strived as hard, or learned to rely on myself if I'd known? Would I be the Drexian I'd become if I'd had an easier path? My shoulders sagged as the rage that had been simmering beneath the surface drained from me, and I was struck with the realization that I regretted nothing of my past. It had brought me to where I was now, and there was a lot to like about my life. It was a life I'd made, not one that had been forged for me.

"You do not owe me a debt because of our father's actions, although I am grateful for what you have done. But if you are honoring requests, I would like to know more about House Vorran."

Zoran gave me the first broad smile I'd ever seen from him. "I'll tell you the stories, but hearing about our forefathers might make you regret your lineage."

After spending my life questioning who I was and where I came from, I doubted that. Knowing the truth was better than a mountain of regrets.

Zoran took a seat and waved for me to sit across from him. "Did you know that our ancestors inhabited this academy when it was merely a fortress built to keep out Drexian marauders from across the sea?"

"Those marauders were probably from my clan," I said with a shake of my head. "My old clan."

Zoran barked out a belly laugh, the sound so spontaneous that it made me laugh. How was it possible that this Drexian already felt like more of a brother to me than the ones I'd been raised alongside?

CHAPTER 52

ARIANA

"**W**HAT DID I SAY ABOUT LOOKING FOR HIM?"

I wrenched my gaze away from the doors and whipped toward Fiona. "I wasn't." A big lie. "I thought I heard something." Not as much of a lie. "You know I've been jumpy since that cadet said something about what I did after hours." One hundred percent true.

"That cocky little shit was just being his usual charming self." Fiona tightened her ponytail and jerked her head behind her at the human cadets spread around the room. "There's no way he knows what we're doing. Not with Reina acting as lookout."

I remembered that the Vexling had appointed herself official corridor monitor, and she'd so far been extremely effective at steering wandering cadets and even instructors away from wherever we were training. She was convincing as a lost female needing assistance finding her quarters, and more than one Drexian had found themselves going in the opposite direction of their intended destination.

Tonight, we were in one of the classrooms in the School of Strategy going over maze techniques. With all the fretting over alien creatures, grappling and blade techniques, and teaching cadets how to get fighter jets off the ground fast, we'd all but neglected one of the key elements of the trials. It was a maze.

If you couldn't find your way through the labyrinth, it didn't matter how good you were at combat or flying. If you couldn't use logic to avoid dead ends, your engineering skills would be pointless. If you couldn't keep from retracing your steps or wandering aimlessly, the deadly creatures had more chances to attack.

Fiona beckoned for me to follow her to where the cadets were gathered around the old parchments of past mazes. She was right. There was no point in worrying about Torq with Reina guarding us. Besides, if the cadet truly knew something, he would have gone to Zoran about it or Vyk.

I shivered at that thought. Despite Fiona insisting that the silver fox security chief was not a sociopath determined to kill all the humans at the academy, I wasn't convinced. Where she saw sexy and gruff, I saw cold and calculating. But for an Assassin, calculating and cunning wasn't a bad thing. And Vyk had been in the School of Strategy when he'd been a cadet.

"You can see from the documents that the mazes are all square." Fiona strode ahead as she raised her voice to be heard by the cadets. "So, we're not dealing with a seven-circuit labyrinth. From the maps, it looks like there are sliding panels, which indicates that it's a dynamic maze."

One of the women looked from where she'd been poring over the unrolled parchments. "Does that mean it could be different for each one of us?"

"That's exactly what it means."

We all pivoted to the deep voice, and my heartbeat quickened. Then my pulse slowed again when Kann entered the room.

"They wouldn't call them the trials if they weren't challenging," he continued, flicking a grin to me and Fiona. "Sorry I'm late."

Fiona brushed off his apology. "So, the challenges are different for each cadet who enters the maze?"

"In a way." He took long strides to the front of the room, but he didn't go to the old maps. "When you come to a barrier that can be opened by solving a puzzle or repairing a bit of tech, it will reset for the next cadet who encounters it, but with a different puzzle."

A male cadet rocked back on the heels of his boots. "So, we can't watch someone else and follow their lead?"

"You can, but not always, but you can usually go through challenges two or three at a time. Most of the time." Kann swept his gaze across the cadets as they watched him with rapt attention. "The maze does reward teamwork."

"How does it reward teamwork if you can't get through all the challenges in groups?" I thought the cadet with long, dark hair asked a good question.

"Do you know the fable of the *kerrenwolf*, the feasting bird, and the bag of grain?"

We all stared at Kann in confusion. Then Fiona barked out a laugh.

"You mean the fox, chicken, and bag of grain?"

Kann wrinkled his nose. "Is a fox like a *kerrenwolf* and a chicken like a feasting bird?"

"Sounds like it." Fiona tapped one finger on her chin. "You're saying that it matters what order cadets choose to get their group through the challenges."

"Obviously." Kann smiled brightly as if what he was telling us wasn't confusing everyone even more. "Even the strongest and smartest cadet cannot make it through the trials alone, and only a foolish one would try. Aside from skills to make you deadly warriors, the academy is teaching you that you must work together to be victorious. No single Drexian wins a war. No one ship can bring down an enemy fleet." He cut a glance at me. "The Wings are not the only ones who should remember to work together as one."

The Wings go as one.

I felt like a bit of a dolt that only after Kann spelled it out did I understand the meaning of the Flight school rule. Of course, a squadron of fighters had to work as a single unit in the air, flanking each other and providing cover. We drilled formations for a reason.

It seemed that the lessons I'd learned in the air also transferred to survival at the academy, although we'd already stumbled upon that ourselves. We were working together to ensure that the human cadets had a fair shot at survival, and they'd been practicing skills as a team so they could make it through the maze.

"If you've looked at those ancient maps for long enough, are you ready to see the maze?"

Eyes widened at Kann's question, and when he turned and walked from the room, Fiona and I exchanged bewildered glances. The cadets did the same. Did he mean the actual maze? I knew it was somewhere near the academy grounds, but I'd also understood that it was shrouded in secrecy until the day of the trails.

The Drexian popped his head back into the room, a dark strand of hair falling over his forehead. "Do you want to see the maze, or am I going on this excursion by myself?"

THE ASSASSINS

CHAPTER 53

VOLTEN

THIS WAS A MISTAKE.

I stamped my feet on the frozen ground and huffed out a breath, the puff from my mouth visible in the frigid night air before it cooled and slunk away. Why had I agreed to this?

"You've gone from an exemplary Drexian instructor to a rule-breaking reprobate." I crossed my arms over my chest for warmth and wished that the Drexian uniforms were thicker.

At least I didn't need to worry about the rules as obsessively as I had for my entire life. I'd been terrified that if I stepped one toe out of line that I'd lose all the ground I'd gained, knowing there was no rank or powerful family to help me.

But that was no longer true. I wasn't the cadet with no clan worth mentioning. I wasn't the warrior hoping that my record was enough to secure me a post. I wasn't the only instructor at the academy with no notable family.

My skin prickled uneasily, like it had since I'd learned my true identity, as if it no longer belonged to my body. I might now be a part of a prestigious clan, but that didn't mean I felt different. I was still the same Drexian who'd struggled and been mocked. I was still the same Drexian who had been nothing to so many. It was impossible to shrug off the burdens of the past and accept that everything had changed even if Zoran was welcoming and eager to share clan stories.

At least some things hadn't changed. Kann treated me no differently than he always had, and his steadiness had been my anchor as I'd tried to right my world.

That was why I found myself standing in the cold in the dead of night. Kann continued to possess the talent to talk me into making foolish decisions, but I could only grin about it now. At least he would never change, and his infuriating and intractable nature was more important to me now than it had ever been.

A low whistle roused me, and I squinted through the darkness. Like he'd promised, Kann rounded an outcropping of bushes with the cadets in tow.

Only the faintest glow of moonlight sifted through the thick clouds, but I could make out the two female instructors right behind Kann. My chest constricted at the sight of Ariana, and as much as my gaze begged to roam the familiar contours of her face and body, I forced myself to look away.

"All clear?" Kann asked as he approached.

We were far enough from the academy that it took some effort to get there and the flat plain that housed the maze held few hiding spots. The bridge that crossed a deep gulch separating the maze from the academy had even fewer. "As long as Drux disabled the sensors like he promised, we don't have company and shouldn't expect any."

Kann gave a single, certain nod. "He did. He's the one who created the sensors. He knows how to make it seem like this place is as deserted as a pleasure house on prayer day."

I rolled my eyes at my friend. As if a prayer day had ever stopped him.

"This is it?" Fiona stepped forward, and her gaze locked on the towering black stone walls looming behind me. "The maze is the same stone as the school?"

Kann tipped his head back as he admired the imposing structure with smooth walls that gleamed in the dim light. "It was all mined from the Black Mountains in the East."

"These aren't the Black Mountains?" The cadet's voice wasn't more than a whisper, but it carried in the hush of the night.

I glanced at the ridge that cocooned the academy on one side. "These are the Gilded Peaks." I pointed to the icy tips that glinted. "The Black Mountains are not topped with ice."

"And they're so dark they suck away all light and warmth," Kann added, repeating something we'd both heard about the mysterious and dangerous ridges that had claimed many lives during the mining of the stone to build the ancient school and testing ground.

"That's not ominous at all," Ariana muttered without glancing at me. Her gaze was also tethered to the high walls of the maze that seemed to simultaneously warn anyone from approaching and dare them to enter.

Nervous murmurs passed through the cadets. Not surprising, considering that Kann had led them out of the academy through one of the defunct underground passageways and across uneven terrain to reach the maze that sat on the opposite bank of the deep gulch. They shifted their feet and rubbed their arms and were probably rethinking all their life choices.

"How does a stone maze change each term?" Fiona walked forward and placed a palm on the black rock. "How can something this solid be a dynamic maze?"

"The exterior is stone." Kann joined her, thumping his palm next to hers on the unyielding wall. "The interior is not. Some of it will look like stone, but that's the holographic technology."

Fiona shook her head. "Drexian tech is pretty badass."

"You're talking about a maze that could kill people," Ariana said. She hadn't stepped closer to the walls even though the cadets had started to drift over.

I took advantage of everyone's preoccupation with the massive maze wall to move closer to Ariana.

She didn't pull her gaze from the dark wall as she spoke. "I'm surprised you're here. I thought you'd abandoned us."

Her words were like sharp, well-targeted daggers. "I didn't abandon you. I sent Kann. He's better at teaching battle techniques anyway."

She made a sound in her throat that I couldn't read. "You've been avoiding me."

"I've been avoiding everyone."

She finally swiveled to face me. "I'm not everyone."

Even through the darkness, her gaze bored into me, hot and accusatory, before she snatched it away and faced the maze again. "Or maybe I am." I opened my mouth to tell her that she wasn't like everybody, but she continued speaking without taking more than a quick breath. "I think you were right about us."

What had I said about us?

"We don't really know each other, and we clearly don't trust each other. As fun as it was, we should just be colleagues. Anything else is too messy. Not to mention the potential fallout. I know you don't want that. Not after you've already broken so many rules."

My throat closed on the words clawing their way up my throat, denying my desperate attempt to tell her that I did trust her, that I'd spoken out of anger, and that she'd been more than a bit of fun for me. I wanted to tell her that I didn't care about breaking rules, not anymore, not if it meant I could be with her again. But I couldn't speak. The words were lodged in my throat as I opened and closed my mouth. I couldn't explain that I didn't care about the mess or the fallout, because her hard, determined words had rendered me mute.

As I impotently watched the cadets run their hands along the exterior while Kann expounded on the merits of the dark stone that was harder than any other rock on the planet, I remained stiff and speechless, broken from the torturous silence only when the Vexling rushed up to us flapping her bony hand and fighting for breath.

"Reina?" Ariana spun and grabbed the alien's flailing hands. "Why are you here?"

"Had to tell you…" Reina gasped between words as if she'd run the entire way, which I was starting to think she had. "The monsters for the maze…"

"The alien creature they got for the cadets to fight," Ariana prodded. "Do you know which one it is?"

Reina shook her head. "Not one creature."

Fiona had abandoned the maze wall and stood beside Ariana as Reina's wide eyes pinged back and forth between the women. "What do you mean?"

"They didn't get one monster," Reina dropped her voice and stole a look over her shoulder. "They have four, and they're bringing them to the maze now."

THE BLADES

CHAPTER 54

ARIANA

REINA'S WORDS HAD AN ELECTRIFYING EFFECT ON EVERYONE. Kann and Volten instantly rushed past her toward the path leading to the academy, and the cadets huddled around us, voices low and tension bristling the air.

Volten returned first. "Reina's right. Four cages are being brought from the dungeons and across the bridge."

Reina emitted a high squeak as if shocked and horrified by what she'd told us moments earlier.

"We can't be here when they arrive." Fiona swung her head around, and her ponytail flew in a wide arc. "There must be another way back to the academy."

Volten jerked his head at the maze. "The other side."

"We have to go through it?" The cadet's voice trembled.

"Only around it." Volten started walking to the corner of the maze, and I followed so the cadets would fall in step behind me.

When we reached the side, my breath hitched in my chest.

There was a path that ran between the maze and the gulch, but it was narrow, and the drop was perilous. "You never mentioned that the maze is clinging to a cliff."

Volten glanced back at me without breaking stride. "The maze wasn't always abutting the gulch, but time has claimed some of the surrounding land."

I bit back the urge to tell him that it looked like the gulch was what had claimed the land, but the more we talked about it and the more I thought about it, the less I'd be able to follow him.

Volten didn't slow his pace as he stepped onto the path that was little more than a body's width wide. I sucked in a breath when he didn't even turn and edge along with his back pressed to the maze wall, which was what I desperately wanted to do.

You can do this. You're a fricking pilot.

My irrational fear of heights was probably all tied up with my jumble of control issues, but I wasn't about to untangle them now.

I paused before I took a step, my pulse jackknifing and making it impossible for me to hear anything but the thundering of blood in my ears. I didn't know if the cadets were behind me. I didn't know if the caged beasts were getting closer. I didn't know if Kann and Fiona were coming. All I knew was that I was putting one foot in front of the other and trying not to look beyond my feet at the sheer drop below.

Step. Breathe. Step. Breathe. Step. Shit!

A clump of ground gave way under my foot, and I pitched forward, my knee almost slamming down before two hands grabbed me. I looked up and Volten's face was so close to mine I could see the black flecks within his blue eyes.

"Thanks," I managed to whisper.

He moved his head down brusquely, sliding his hands down from my shoulders and taking hold of one hand before he started moving forward again. The firm grip of his large hand around mine gave me something solid to focus on instead of the insane galloping of my heart, the petrified jangle of my pulse, and the screaming voice in my head telling me that I was going to die.

I pushed aside all the internal noise and only allowed myself to notice the strength of Volten's grip, the surprising softness of his skin, and the warmth of his hand even in the freezing air. Following his steps and allowing myself to think of nothing but how good his hand felt cocooning mine, we made it to the far end of the maze and stepped onto a flat space that stretched toward another path leading toward the academy.

Once we were no longer in danger, I allowed myself a deep exhale and Volten dropped my hand. I instantly missed the warmth of him and how safe and protected I'd felt, but he was already walking briskly toward the second path.

I looked behind me as the cadets walked off the ledge one by one, a few of them with linked hands and a couple sliding with their back along the wall. Fiona and Kann were the last off, and Kann ran the final few steps.

"Come on." He hurried us all forward. "We need to be out of sight once those cages and whoever is escorting them rounds the rocks."

I found myself separated from Volten and next to Fiona as we threaded our way down a path toward the mountains and between squat trees. She gave me a sideways glance and a crooked smile that told me that she loved the thrill of this.

Fucking Assassin.

Give me the roar of an engine and the weightlessness of flight any day over death-defying escapes in the dark. The back path was longer than the one we'd used to arrive at the maze, but soon we were ducking through a creaking iron gate.

"Where are we?" I whispered, casting a look at the dark mountains rising above us.

"The back passageway goes under the tributary," Kann said, waving us forward.

Under? I drew in a breath as I soldiered forward, wishing with every ounce of my being that I was high above the planet in a cockpit. Darkness consumed us as we entered the underground passageway that led underneath the stream and into the academy, and my nostrils twitched from the dank scent of standing water.

The passageways were almost as cold as the air outside, but it was the damp that made me shudder. The damp and the pitch blackness. And the memory of how cold I'd been to Volten.

I hadn't meant to put it all on him. It wasn't only his outburst that had made me rethink what we'd been doing. As much as I cared about the Drexian, he'd reminded me that getting close meant getting hurt. I hadn't been able to cope with losing the one person I'd cared about before Volten. I didn't know if I could survive losing another, but I would lose him since I had no plans to stay. My assignment was to pave the way for other women to succeed at the academy, then return to Earth with a promotion and command of my own aerial fleet.

None of that had changed, even if Volten did give me butterflies or make me feel safer than I had in years. I still had no intention of being anyone's tribute bride or even a Drexian girlfriend. I was a pilot sent on a mission. A mission I would complete.

We trudged in a silent line through the tunnel, our boots splashing in puddles as we proceeded along the pitch-dark path. Then we were emerging into a dim corridor beneath the school, our feet squishing on the dry stone. Once we were standing in a group, and Fiona and I had completed a quick head count to ensure we hadn't lost any cadets, I allowed myself to exhale normally.

"Well done, Cadets." Kann thumped a few backs. "It might have been unplanned, but that was good practice for the maze."

Volten had walked to the far end of the corridor and poked his head up a stairwell. "We should disperse in small groups to draw less attention."

"Straight to quarters everyone," Fiona ordered. "See you at the trials."

I'd almost forgotten that the trials were the next day, and my heart constricted as I watched the cadets leave in pairs and trios.

"You're with me." Fiona looped her arm through mine after the cadets were gone and then turned to Kann. "If you were twice as old, I'd give you a proper thank you, but thanks for everything."

We left him with his mouth dangling and me shaking my head. "You're horrible."

Fiona gave me a wicked grin. "I'm honest. He's hot, but he's too young for me." We ascended the stairs, and she slowed her pace. "Speaking of hot Drexians…"

I followed her gaze to where Volten was lingering across the main hall that was now free of rushing cadets and whizzing inclinators.

Fiona unhooked her arm from mine and sidled away. "Later."

I wanted to grab her and keep her with me, but I didn't want to tackle her, so I shot her retreating back a dirty look and waited as Volten approached. My heart shifted into overdrive as he closed the distance between us until his body almost brushed mine.

"About that mess." His husky voice was like velvet as it slid over me, making my knees wobble and my resolve crack.

"What about it?" My question was so high and breathy it sounded like it had come from a stranger.

"Yes, what about it?"

I went rigid at the sound of Vyk's voice and the menacing slap of his boots as he emerged from the shadows and closed in on us.

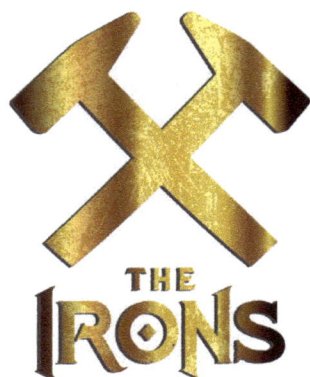

THE IRONS

CHAPTER 55

VOLTEN

INSTEAD OF LIFTING MY HANDS TO CARESS ARIANA'S FACE, I curled them into fists by my side as the security chief advanced on us, and I stepped away from the human. The fizzy feeling in my chest, the excitement that buzzed my skin before I touched her, the tripping pulse that made my heart tighten, all evaporated and drifted away with one of the cold drafts that crept through the gaps in the stone walls. How long had he been lurking in the shadows? How much had he seen and heard?

"Two instructors out after hours," Vyk said, his voice like gravel being dragged over rock. "Two *flight* instructors. Don't tell me this is a late-night staff meeting."

Ariana opened her mouth to answer, but I beat her to it, afraid her response would be something sharp and challenging. The last thing I wanted was for the security chief to have a reason to scrutinize Ariana. I knew his reputation in Inferno Force. I knew of his interrogations. I knew I could not let him get his hands on Ariana.

"I asked the lieutenant to meet me," I said loudly as I stepped forward.

Vyk narrowed his eyes at me, and he dragged a hand down the silvered scruff on his cheeks. "Why?"

"It is my duty as a Drexian to keep my colleagues in line," I gave the security chief a knowing look, "especially humans who do not understand our customs and standards."

I didn't need to look behind me to see Arian bristle with outrage. I could feel it, but I hoped she wouldn't contradict me and ruin my strategy.

"You brought her here to reprimand her?"

I wasn't sure if Vyk was impressed or incredulous, but I gave him a conspiratorial grin. "It was nothing a verbal correction couldn't handle, but it wouldn't be appropriate for me to go to the female tower."

The Drexian crossed his arms over his chest, and I noticed that he wasn't wearing his academy uniform shirt and instead had a tight, black top with the orange flames of the Inferno Force emblem emblazoned over his heart. "Are you done? Tonight is not the night to be loitering in the corridors." He flicked a gaze at Ariana. "Tomorrow is a big day."

"We were both about to return to our quarters, Commander." I pivoted to Ariana so that Vyk couldn't see my face. "I hope you will carefully consider what I said, Lieutenant."

She must have caught the play-along-for-both-our-sakes look in my eyes because she managed to give me a strained smile. "Absolutely, sir."

I jerked my head to one side, indicating that she should leave. "Dismissed. I will see you on the maze field tomorrow."

I held my breath that Vyk might countermand my order or even point out that I was the same rank as Ariana and should not be giving her orders, but he didn't comment as Ariana threw back her shoulders and strode off toward the female tower.

I was both flooded with relief and regret—relief that Ariana escaped further scrutiny from the former Inferno Force commander, and regret that I'd lost my chance to talk to her. After I'd held her hand along the narrow path around the maze, I'd hoped that she might be more willing to talk to me and rethink her decision to go back to being only colleagues. But now that I'd dismissed her in front of our superior officer, I had a feeling I would owe her an even bigger apology.

At least, Vyk didn't seem to know where we'd been, or why we were out after hours. That was the crucial thing. I could only imagine what the commander would say about a group of Drexian and female instructors conspiring to covertly coach human cadets. Even my newfound clan wouldn't save me from that wrath.

"I should also return to my—"

"Why don't you accompany me to my office, first?" Vyk said, the demand disguised as an invitation cutting off my words.

"Your office?' Maybe I'd been hasty in assuming he didn't know the truth of where we'd been. A weight pressed on my chest, and I fought for a regular breath. I caught a final glimpse of Ariana before she disappeared around a corner, her gaze hesitant. I looked away sharply and hoped she would get the message that she should go.

"I have a matter to discuss with you." He turned and motioned with his head for me to follow.

Since I had no other choice, I fell in step with him, our boots hitting the floor in time with each other and echoing off the stone as we trudged up the central winding staircase in the main building, until we'd reached the floor that held the offices of the academy leadership.

I cast a brief, longing look at Zoran's door, knowing that he was probably long asleep in his own suite with his bride. At the end of the hallway, Vyk pressed his hand to the wall, and the heavy door slid open.

Instead of a long room with light that came in through a tall window like Zoran's, the security chief's domain was dark and lit by a flickering holographic fire inset in the stone wall at the far end. The side walls were hung with a collection of Drexian weapons— blades with ornamented hilts and the daggers with etched symbols on the sharp steel. It was truly the office of a warrior, and a chill iced my skin as I followed him deeper inside.

"Whiskey?" He opened a drawer in his dark wood desk and held up a bottle. "It's Noovian."

I'd never been a connoisseur of any type of liquor, so I nodded mutely, wondering what exactly was happening. I got the impression I wasn't there to be reprimanded, and if this was an interrogation, the Drexian's techniques had changed.

Vyk pulled two glasses from a shelf behind his desk and put them on the pristine surface of the desk before he poured generous amounts of the whiskey into them and handed me one. "I need your help, Lieutenant."

I took the glass, but it almost slipped from my hand at his statement. Why would the Drexian who'd barely acknowledged me before now desire my help? Was this part of some ploy to extract information? I eyed my glass. Was he drugging me? Then my heart lurched. Was he poisoning me?

Vyk let loose a rumbling laugh and took a significant gulp of his own whiskey. "The whiskey is untainted. Poison is one technique I never mastered."

How reassuring, I thought, but I took a small sip. "Why do you need my help?"

"The trials this term are unique. For the first time, we have humans taking part."

Humans you'd like to eliminate, I thought, but didn't say.

"There are several members of the Drexian High Command coming for the trials." He started to pace a small circle in front of his fire. "They are mostly old-guard members from notable clans."

I wanted to ask if there were any other types of Drexians on the

High Command, but instead I took another sip of my drink. Better to be drugged than talk back to the security chief. "Do any of them have family members taking part in the trials?"

Vyk stopped pacing and pivoted to face me, his face oddly illuminated in the dancing artificial flames. "None. Not this term." He took a breath before continuing. "The High Commanders do not want the humans to succeed. I need you to help me ensure that they do."

I choked on a mouthful of whiskey, the alien booze burning my throat as I coughed. I must have misunderstood the Drexian. He was the one who despised humans. He was the one designing the maze to be as hard as it had ever been. He didn't want them to succeed. "You need what?"

A slight smile twitched the edges of his mouth. "I was put here to restore the academy to its previous rigor and to ensure that another attack like the one that damaged our school could never occur. The High Commanders who chose me did so because they know I am tough and believe in the old Drexian traditions of honor and hard work. They forgot where I came from."

I managed to stop coughing as I eyed the security chief. I knew that he'd been Inferno Force, and I knew he had a reputation for being tough, but I knew little else.

Vyk lifted his nearly empty glass in my direction. "I'm like you. I came from a clan that had no status and no influence. I had to battle my way from nothing to get into the academy, make it through, and get into Inferno Force."

I couldn't keep my jaw from dropping. The security chief of the Drexian Academy came from nothing?

"I know what it's like to be counted out," he continued. "I know what it's like to be you, and to be one of the human cadets. I may not be convinced that the humans have what it takes to be Drexian warriors, but I've come to believe that they should have the same chance to prove themselves as every other cadet."

I gave my head a shake, not convinced by what I was hearing. "But you've made the maze tougher than ever. You've brought in more deadly alien creatures than have ever been in a single maze before." I decided to take a chance and make an accusation I couldn't prove. "You sabotaged the holochambers."

His jaw tightened and his expression was fierce in the shadows of the fire. "I hoped that if enough cadets got injured, the humans would be recalled to Earth. I wanted Zoran to think the academy was unsafe for our allies."

"That's twisted logic." And I didn't know if I believed him, but at least I now knew it had been him. A part of me wanted to punch the Drexian in the gut as repayment for my gashed side. "How did you manage to alter the program? That doesn't seem like something a Blade would know how to do."

He eyed me over his glass. "Who said I was a Blade?"

That silenced me. I'd assumed he'd been a Blade since so many Inferno Force warriors were Blades.

"I was an Iron." His fingers tightened around his glass. "A proud Iron who enhanced many Inferno Force ships before becoming known for my less technical talents."

An interesting way to phrase enhanced torture, but I let him speak.

"I did not instigate the procurement of the creatures, but I also could not stop them. Neither could Zoran. We both serve at the bidding of the High Commanders. But even as the High Command instructed me to make the maze the most challenging it's ever been, the challenges remain fair." He downed the rest of his drink in a single, violent motion and turned to face me, most of his face in shadow. "Until now. Until the High Commanders decreed that upper class Drexian cadets could not enter the maze to battle the first-years. Until they made me suspect that there is a reason they don't want cadets from elite houses in the trials."

The Noovian whiskey turned rancid in my stomach. "You think--?"

Vyk wouldn't meet my gaze. "I believe the maze I've created to test cadets will not be survivable by the humans. I fear there has been sabotage beyond my control, but I do not know what it is. That's why I need you to help me make sure the human cadets survive." He poured himself another slug of whiskey and swirled the liquid in his glass. "In case the High Commanders decide I'm a loose end that needs to be eliminated."

THE WINGS

CHAPTER 56

ARIANA

I RUSHED THROUGH THE ACADEMY, DETERMINED TO GET AS far from the security chief as possible. I'd deal with Volten and his ridiculous claims later.

Volten.

I'd been so sure when I'd told him that we should remain colleagues only. I was certain it was the right decision, the smart move, the shrewdest thing for a woman desperate to keep her position at the academy and return to Earth a success and not a cautionary tale. Then he'd grabbed my hand when I'd slipped and held it until I was safe, and all my tightly held beliefs had fallen away like a sheer scrap of fabric that I'd thought was armor.

Volten had kept me from falling and protected me from Vyk, taking the heat from the Drexian who was clearly looking for an infraction to punish. I thought about Volten being ordered to accompany the security chief to his office. That couldn't be good.

I'd almost gone back for him. I'd almost abandoned my own

escape to return and confess that we hadn't been in the corridor so I could be reprimanded—Volten would get an earful about that gem later—but then I'd thought about everyone else I'd be risking. I couldn't let Volten's noble sacrifice be for nothing even if it pained me to see him take the brunt of getting caught.

My stomach was in knots as I thought about Volten. Then those knots unwound themselves and transformed into butterflies as my mind lingered on the warmth of his hand and how solid he'd felt, how solid I'd felt holding onto him. Was I being an idiot to cast aside someone who made me feel solid and safe and secure?

Who was I kidding? It wasn't the safe feeling that made my stomach do loops. Memories of being pressed up against the sparring ring and flattened to the mat sent heat arrowing through me. Was I an idiot to give up great sex?

I crossed the bridge to the women's tower, grateful that I was almost back to my quarters. Between the late-night coaching session, the journey through the old passageways to the maze, the perilous expedition back into the academy before we were caught outside, and the encounter with Vyk, I was ready for a hot shower and bed.

"You know you want to tell me."

The voice was low and silky, and it did not belong to any resident of the tower—or any female. I stiffened as I moved toward the base of the staircase. Why was a Drexian in our tower, and who was he trying to charm?

I almost groaned when I recognized the Drexian cadet with his arms braced against the wall on either side of a woman with long, chestnut-brown hair, pinning her in and keeping her from escaping. "Torq, why are you harassing my cadet?"

He spun around at the sound of my voice, his expression rapidly morphing from startled to suave. "Another human wandering around the academy the night before the trials."

My heart stuttered, but I gave him a smile I hoped was as

smooth as his. "I hope you haven't been loitering in our tower harassing women." I stepped closer and gave him a quick once-over. "What are you doing here?"

He straightened, cutting a glance at the woman I remembered was called Jess as she slipped up the first few steps of the winding staircase. "Wasn't that my question?"

"Aren't I the instructor? Don't I ask the questions and you provide the answers?" I cocked my head at him. "Or have you forgotten how this works, Cadet?"

"I was merely helping Jess back to her tower."

I stifled a bark of laughter. I knew enough about Jess to know that she was smart and quick, a studious type who was probably angling to be in the school of Engineering or Strategy. The suggestion that she wouldn't know her way back to her own tower was comical.

I flitted my gaze to Jess, giving a subtle jerk of my head to tell her to go upstairs. Then I swiveled my attention back to Torq. "Were you following her? You know on Earth when a male follows a female around, we call it stalking."

"She wishes I was stalking her."

I folded my arms over my chest. I was liking this guy less and less. "Doubtful."

He changed tactics, his taciturn expression gliding into one that made my hair stand on end. "I heard that Volten cast you aside."

My body went rigid. He'd heard what? Before I could snap back that Volten hadn't cast me aside, I'd decided to end things, I caught myself. The cadet was fishing for information. Maybe he'd heard a rumble, a rumor, but there was no way he knew about what had happened between me and Volten. No one did.

I didn't have a chance to deny the rumor before he'd leaned closer. "I would never do something as dumb as that. The Drexian clearly doesn't know how to handle a female with spirit. Now, I—"

"You should not finish that sentence," I interrupted, knowing that if he said what I thought he was going to say, I'd have an impossible time keeping myself from decking him. "Do I need to remind you again who is the cadet and who is the instructor?"

His smug smile didn't droop, and he lifted a blasé shoulder, as if I was the one making the error in judgment. I'd often longed for the confidence of Earth men, but the cockiness of Drexian males was next level. What I wouldn't give for an ounce of their self-assuredness that danced dangerously close to breathtaking arrogance on many occasions.

"What you should remember is that I could be an asset to you." He touched my arm. "My clan has power and pull. With my influence, you could become more than an instructor."

I snatched my arm away. "I like being an instructor, and I don't need anyone to pull strings for me."

"Some free advice, Lieutenant?" Torq stepped past me, brushing against me as he did. "If you want to survive on Drex and at the Drexian Academy, you need to learn to play the game. And with Drexians, the game always has to do with power and status. Volten didn't play the game because he couldn't—until now." He turned when he reached the archway leading from the tower. "I wonder if that's why he dropped you. Now that he has a clan with influence, he doesn't need you anymore?"

I bit the inside of my mouth to keep from snapping back at him, the metallic taste of blood reminding me that he was spouting nonsense. If there was one thing Volten didn't do it was play games. At least, that's what I'd thought. I'd barely spoken to him since he'd learned of his true lineage. Maybe his priorities had changed, and maybe I wasn't one of them. Then I thought of him waiting for me in the hall and the husk of his voice as he'd said something about a mess. No, Volten was nothing like this Drexian who was clearly used to manipulating and charming his way through life.

I ignored everything he'd said, smiling instead. "Shouldn't you be getting some rest before the trials tomorrow?"

"Don't you worry about me in the trials. I'm a legacy." He winked at me. "Which means I'll be seeing much more of you after I'm inducted as a Wing."

I watched him walk away, rage churning within me. "Over. My. Dead. Body."

THE ASSASSINS

CHAPTER 57

VOLTEN

HEARD THE MAZE BEFORE I SAW IT. HEARD THE EXCITED SCUTTLE of voices, the drone of announcements, the ebb and flow of nervous laughter. But I heard my own hammering heart over all of it.

What was I doing? How did Vyk expect me to protect the human cadets? I'd already done what I could by helping coach them, although he didn't know that. Despite his revelations the night before, I hadn't revealed anything of the cadet training.

I stomped from the academy to the maze, using the well-worn outdoor path and bridge, instead of the one we'd taken the night before. I didn't want to think of everything that had happened then. I didn't want to dwell on the warmth I'd felt when I'd held Ariana's hand or the rush of hope I'd experienced the moment before Vyk had appeared.

Everything that had happened after that had brought me to my current impossible situation. If I believed Vyk, which I had to admit that I did, then he wanted to ensure the survival of the human cadets. If he was lying, then he was leading me into an expertly laid trap, in which I might be ending my own career almost as soon as it had started.

Either way, I had to make sure the cadets lived. The problem was, I didn't know how. Not without jumping into the maze with them. I didn't know the challenges any more than the cadets did, and Vyk hadn't given me any tips to help. He'd told me that the challenges were tough and there were more alien creatures than usual—a fact I'd already known—but he hadn't been able to tell me how he thought the maze might be sabotaged. He claimed he didn't know and that it was what he'd surmised from the actions and orders of the High Commanders, but could I believe him?

My gut clenched as I thought about how I was flying blind, and I was grateful that I hadn't been able to eat anything. The scent of sizzling *padwump* had turned my stomach and sent me straight from the staff dining hall. Not only had I not been able to eat, but I'd also barely slept. "Some help I'll be."

I was running on pure nerves and fear, which seemed to match the atmosphere as I neared the maze. The air was charged as if currents were whizzing through it. Even the usual blanket of gray overhead had parted, and slats of light beamed down as if the energy of the day had blasted holes in the clouds.

I gazed up longingly, wishing I was flying instead of being stuck on the ground, waiting for first-years to go through the maze and be chosen by the four schools—or not make it through and be sent home. Then I reminded myself that Drexian warriors were the toughest in the galaxy and defended alien worlds from invasion, so we had to take only the best into our forces, which was why Vyk's request had startled me.

Of anyone, I thought the security chief was one to hold tight to the Drexian belief that only the best deserved to serve in the Drexian military. I agreed that the human cadets deserved a chance to prove themselves, but it did no one any favors if I allowed an unqualified cadet to succeed. Unless the dangers in this term's maze were truly beyond what was survivable. Unless the maze was sabotaged to make it impossible for the humans to complete as Vyk believed.

I shook my head as a horrible thought teased the back of my brain. Would the Drexians who despised integrating humans into the academy be willing to risk an entire first-year class to ensure that no humans made it to the second year? Would they ruin any chance of humans sending more cadets by making the trials a bloodbath?

I shook my head, telling myself that this wasn't possible. Even the most intensely separatist Drexian wouldn't send an entire class of cadets to slaughter, would they?

Then I remembered Vyk saying that none of the High Commanders coming to watch the trials had family members taking part in them. None. *Not this term.*

His words echoed in my mind as I thought back to Kann noting that the class was light on elites and then him noting that the upperclass cadets would not be entering the maze to battle the first-years like they usually did. Bile churned in my core as I turned the possibility over and over in my head, willing it to be impossible, willing it to be a lie, willing it to be anything but the most logical explanation I'd discovered so far.

I stumbled on a rough patch of ground and caught myself on a boulder, slapping my hand hard against it and peering up to see the top of the black maze around the cluster of rocks. My mouth went dry, and my heart raced as the truth slammed into me as hard and dark as the maze stone itself.

This term's trials were going to be a bloodbath. A bloodbath to rid the academy of the human cadets.

And I was supposed to save them.

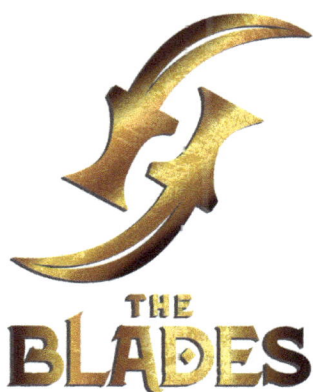

THE BLADES

CHAPTER 58

ARIANA

I RUBBED MY ARMS, MORE FROM NERVOUSNESS THAN COLD. EVEN though there was a breeze, the air at the maze wasn't much cooler than the drafty corridors of the academy.

As much as the fortress-turned-military-school had seemed foreign when I'd arrived, I missed the dark walls and echoing passageways as I stood in the shadow of the maze. The ebony structure looked no less ominous than it had the night before, and there was something perverse about the contrast between the excited chatter of the cadets, and the challenges that awaited them.

Reina hadn't been able to tell us any more about the creatures that were placed inside the maze but knowing there were four made a sick feeling roil my stomach. I knew I was on an alien world, and that the Drexians had been fighting fierce aliens for longer than I'd known they existed, but did they really need to put their cadets through this? Was it necessary to risk their lives and even lose cadets, all to place them into their specialties?

I cast a disapproving glance at the Drexian dignitaries who stood to one side on a small dais. Unlike the instructors and cadets and even the school leaders, the High Commanders wore robes that flapped around their legs as if they were waving to beckon attention. They might have been tall and broad-shouldered like every Drexian I'd seen, but their faces were heavily lined, their hair tipped with gray or white, and they wore hardened expressions. I guessed powerful assholes looked the same everywhere.

"Did you get a load of the cake eaters?" Fiona sidled up to me, talking from the side of her mouth. Her blonde hair was pulled up into a high bun, making her cheekbones look sharp and her demeanor scream 'boss ass bitch.'

"Is that the whole High Command or whatever they call themselves?"

She shook her head without glancing at the Drexians huddled together as we all awaited the start of the trials. "Only the ones who are overseeing the rebuilding of the academy. Apparently, there's a committee, although I don't think the Drexians call them committees."

Why was I not surprised there was a committee? If there was a hell, it would have committees.

"Do you think our cadets are ready?" That was the question that had been haunting me all through the night when I couldn't sleep. I hadn't given much more thought to Torq after I'd stomped upstairs to my quarters. After all, I was used to blowhards. Earth was full of guys who loved to hear themselves talk, and the military had more than its fair share.

Torq was nothing I hadn't encountered before, and even if he had suspicions, last night had told me that he didn't know anything for sure. He didn't know about the after-hours coaching, and he didn't know details about what had happened between me and Volten. The Drexian had been fishing, and he'd come up empty. His cockiness was annoying as was his belief that he'd be in my school, but I had a feeling he wouldn't be so arrogant after the maze.

Fiona nodded, her bun remaining immobile. "They're as ready as they can be."

"You didn't hear anything else about the creatures released into the maze either?"

She swung her head to take in the flat land at the entrance to the maze. "Reina told us everything she knew, and I'm guessing Noora couldn't sneak away from her husband once all the dignitaries arrived."

I let my gaze linger on Noora and Zoran as they stood slightly away from the High Commanders. Her pale green, flowing dress danced around her ankles as she kept her gaze fixed to the looming maze walls and a smile locked onto her face. She'd done all she could without getting caught, and we'd prepared the cadets as well as possible.

"They do this every term," Fiona reminded me. "First-years have gone through the maze to be chosen for a school since the academy was established. It will be fine."

I wasn't sure if fine was the word I'd have chosen, but at least it would soon be over. I spotted Volten on the other side of the dais, and my pulse spiked. I hadn't seen him since I'd left him with Vyk. What had Vyk wanted with him? Had he been punished for both of us?

Fiona nudged me in the ribs. "Go."

"What?"

She huffed out an impatient breath. "You're staring a hole into the guy. Go talk to him."

So much for me being casual about looking at Volten. I shot her a look. "Are you sure you aren't a witch?"

She gave me a wicked smile. "All the best women are witches."

I laughed at this, some of the tension releasing from my chest as I left her and walked toward Volten. He hadn't seen me yet, and

I wondered why he looked so jittery and why his gaze was darting around like an animal about to be pounced on by a predator. Had something bad gone down with Vyk?

I didn't see the security chief, but he must be around somewhere. He'd been instrumental in creating the maze, so he wouldn't miss the running of it, would he?

I slipped behind the dais so I wouldn't cross in front of the important Drexians, which meant I had to sidestep my way behind them and skirt the edge of a copse of scraggly bushes. As I passed behind them, I caught snatches of their conversation.

"You aren't having regrets, are you?"

"About restoring glory to the academy? Not for a moment."

"But you regret the sacrifice?"

Sacrifice? I paused when I was directly behind them, realizing that they were facing forward and had no clue I was within earshot. I held my breath as I stood still, my legs refusing to move.

"I regret that it has come to this." A throat was gruffly cleared. "Humans never should have been allowed at the academy."

Wait, what? Chills went through me, but I forced myself to remain motionless.

"Not everyone agrees with us. There will be an outcry."

"Which will result in Earth refusing to send its people to our dangerous military school. They will not risk losing all their cadets again."

My spine went rigid. These arrogant asshats assumed that all the human cadets were going to die? I bit my lip to keep from telling them that they were about to be proven wrong.

"True, but the cost will be high for Drexians as well."

"We have never lost an entire first-year class before," one of the white-haired Drexians growled.

"We can't be sure they'll all die."

"Even if a few make it through the challenges and past all the monsters loose in the maze, the escape ships will not take them to safety. The thrusters have been externally disconnected. I saw to it personally."

My knees wobbled. The entire thing was a trap, and the final deadly jaws of the trap were ships? My ships?

"There will be questions."

"And Zoran can answer them," another said with a malevolent chuckle.

"It will be good to get someone into the position of master who is more malleable. It's a shame we'll have to get rid of Vyk. He would have been ideal."

"In the end, he could not do what was required. It is a shame and a waste of a good Inferno Force commander."

"As long as the new Master has less fondness for humans than the current one, I will be happy." Their heads went to Noora, which gave me the chance to start moving again, even though my steps were jerky, and my breath had become stuck in my throat. The pounding of drums masked any sound I made stumbling away and finally gasping for air.

I cleared the dais, sucking in breath and rubbing my arms as if cleansing myself from the poisonous words I still couldn't believe I'd heard.

The trials were rigged. The human cadets had no chance of survival, and neither did the Drexians. Somehow the High Commanders had made it so that every cadet would perish, and that the tragedy would convince Earth not to send any more cadets. And if all the cadets perished, I would most certainly be summoned home in disgrace for letting the cadets from Earth die on my watch.

I picked up my pace, looking desperately for Volten. He would know what to do.

But he was nowhere in sight.

Then a voice blared above the insistent drumbeat. "Cadets, prepare to enter the maze."

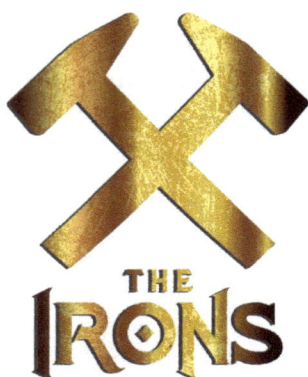

THE IRONS

CHAPTER 59

VOLTEN

I couldn't look at the High Commanders standing together like a flock of Verridian vultures, rubbing their veiny hands together and hungrily waiting for the carnage. The carnage that would be of their making.

I couldn't look at the nervous cadets as they gathered near the maze entrance, unaware that they wouldn't be running into a test to determine their school for the rest of their time at the academy. They would be running to their deaths.

And I couldn't look at Ariana, knowing that she had worked so hard to train the humans so they would have a fair shot at making it through the maze. Not when I knew it was all a lie.

I searched the maze grounds for Vyk. He'd sent me away the night before with a head filled with questions and little else. I knew that the monsters had been roaming the confines of the maze and guards had patrolled the exterior, which meant it had been impossible for me to do anything about the maze itself, even if I had a clue where to start.

Did he want me to warn the cadets not to enter? But wouldn't that be suspicious and result in them all being dismissed, if any of them even listened to me? Dismissed was better than dead, I reminded myself. Even if I could convince the humans that the maze had been rigged, the Drexians would never refuse to enter. It would be a stubborn point of pride. And who would believe that Drexian leadership at the highest levels would sabotage the trials and kill every cadet? Even I didn't believe it. Didn't want to believe it, was more accurate.

The only answer was Zoran. I allowed my gaze to rest on the Academy Master. He had to be why Vyk had taken me into his confidence. Maybe he thought that as his brother, I would have more influence. Maybe he thought that Zoran wouldn't believe such a tale from the Drexian who'd been installed by the High Command. Maybe Vyk couldn't bring himself to stop a plan he'd had a part in implementing or maybe he knew if he stopped it, he'd face harsh censure.

I thought back to what he'd told me of his own past. The Commander had no high-ranking family to save him from the fallout. The elite High Commanders would undoubtedly emerge unscathed, but Vyk would take the blame. That was probably why they'd picked him for the job in the first place. And that was why he'd picked me to tell. He knew that I would understand.

I swept my gaze around me, taking in the bridge leading over the gulch, the dark spires of the academy, and the ominous peaks of the mountains. Vyk should have been there, but he wasn't. I'd thought his fears of being eliminated as a loose end had been paranoid, but now I wasn't so sure. Dread engulfed me as I considered where the security chief might be and what might have been done to keep him from talking.

The pounding of heavy drumbeats told me that I didn't have

much time. I strode toward Zoran, even as the cadets surged forward toward the maze entrance. I was swarmed by a crush of bodies as they eagerly moved forward, clueless about what awaited them.

If I could delay the start of the trials, I thought, at least that would buy me time to prove the sabotage.

"Cadets, prepare to enter the maze."

The booming voice sent ice sliding down my spine. I pushed roughly through the cadets, desperate to reach the academy master before—

"Let the trials begin."

Grek. Grek. Grek. I barely cleared the cluster of cadets as they raced forward. I wanted to grab at least a few by the arms and tell them to wait, to stop, to turn around and run. But I couldn't. I had no proof, and there was no sign of Vyk.

I had a sinking feeling that either he'd left so he wouldn't have to witness the horror he'd set into motion, or he was sitting back and waiting for me to take the rope he'd given me and hang myself. Or he'd tried to put a stop to the madness and been silenced. No matter the reason, I'd officially run out of time and options.

I strode to Zoran, grabbing his arm tightly. "These trials must be stopped."

He looked at me as if I was insane. "What do you mean? They just started."

"All the cadets are going to die."

Noora leaned in, her brow furrowed. "The four monsters?"

Zoran's head pinged to her. "How do you—"

"More than the monsters," I said, uninterested in the admiral's discovery that his wife knew more than he'd thought. "The High Commanders don't intend for the cadets to survive. None of the cadets."

Zoran shook his head. "The cadets can battle the monsters. There have always been beasts released into the mazes. Not always four but—"

"It's more than that." I hesitated. This was where I ran into problems with my story. "I don't know exactly what, but the maze is intended to kill them all."

Zoran eyed me, his own blue eyes narrowing. "How do you know this and why can't you tell me how?"

"Vyk was put here by High Command to ensure that the humans fail so that this integration experiment will fail. But they can't kill only humans without causing an uproar and a breakdown of the treaty with Earth and the tribute bride program." I took a breath. "I think they're going to kill them all."

"Where is Vyk? He should be here." Zoran pivoted to scan the emptied field then cut his gaze to the imposing black stone structure. "All the cadets are inside."

Reina rushed up in a dress such a bright shade of yellow I almost flinched. "Ariana!"

I glanced around but didn't see the lieutenant. Was the Vexling suffering from delusions?

"What about her?" Noora's voice was patient but insistent.

Reina flapped long fingers toward the maze. "Ariana ran inside."

I swung myself to the entrance of the maze as my body went cold. Why would Ariana go into the maze? It made no sense. "Into the maze?"

Reina nodded, wringing her hands in front of her.

"You're sure it was her?"

Reina's enormous eyes were filled with dread, which told me she was sure.

I pivoted to the admiral. "We have to stop this."

Zoran cut a malevolent gaze to the High Commanders behind him. "There's no way to stop it now that the cadets are inside. The challenges are all automated from within the structure."

I couldn't let Ariana die. I'd always known that I would break any rule for her, break anyone who dared touch her, and break the

Drexian Empire to save her. In that moment, I knew that I would break myself into a thousand pieces for her.

As soon as that realization hit me, as soon as I knew that I loved her and couldn't survive without her, a calm settled over me. There was only one thing to do.

"I'm going in." I didn't glance back at my brother as I ran toward the maze.

THE WINGS

CHAPTER 60

ARIANA

MY HEART THUNDERED IN TIME TO THE DRUMS, THE SOUND reverberating through my body and making my hands tremble. The cadets were going to enter the maze, but they didn't stand a chance especially since the ones who survived the roaming alien beasts wouldn't be able to fly away once they reached the center of the maze. All my lessons on vertical combat takeoffs would be pointless since the thrusters were externally disabled.

But not removed.

That thought made my breath hitch and a calm settle over me. If they weren't removed, then I could get to the ships and enable the thrusters. I was the only one who knew they wouldn't work but also knew how to fix them.

If there was one thing I was grateful to my father for, it was instilling the importance of knowing how your ships worked and how to fix them. I didn't claim to be an expert at flight mechanics, but I knew the basics. I knew how to enable the thrusters on Drexian ships. Which meant, I knew how to save the cadets.

"Let the trials begin."

The second announcement made me jerk forward and follow the flow of cadets toward the opening of the maze. My presence in the group drew a few curious looks, but the Drexians around me were more concerned with getting inside the maze and proving their ferocity and skills than in questioning why an instructor was tagging along.

I was at the back of the crowd and was the last to step through the opening in the polished black stone. The instant I was inside, the sound of the drums faded as I was cocooned within the obsidian walls.

At once, I was presented with a choice—go straight or turn to the left. I cast my mind back to the maps of past mazes, trying to remember the general layout, even though I understood the maze was dynamic. The interior walls could shift or even disappear as a result of solving a successful challenge, which meant the path was different each time. This meant that what had worked for past mazes might not work this time. Still, I wished I'd paid more attention to the layout.

"You didn't think you'd enter the maze yourself," I whispered as I chose to go left.

I tipped my head back to note that the walls were high and smooth, spaced far apart, and had no gaps for footholds. There was no climbing the walls or walking up them using the other side as a brace. Even if I could get up the walls, there was a ceiling that I assumed covered everything but the open courtyard in the center.

A thud behind me made me jump, but it also told me that the maze entrance had closed, locking the cadets—and me—inside and preventing anyone from trying to escape the way they'd entered. A shiver skated down my back, and I swallowed hard. No going back now.

I continued around three turns until I was heading in the same direction as when I'd entered the maze. I might not be great at memorizing maps and floorplans, but I had a spot-on sense of direction.

After walking straight and then taking a slight bend to the right, I almost bumped into someone.

"What are you doing here?" Jess had her brown hair tied up in a ponytail as she stood in front of a wall with her head craned to look at me.

"I need to get to the center of the maze."

"That's kind of the point of the trials, Lieutenant."

We both spun toward the male voice who'd rounded the corner, and I let out a string of curses in my head. Of all the Drexians in all the mazes.

Torq lifted an eyebrow at me. I'd been on the verge of telling Jess why I was in the maze, but I hesitated now that the Drexian was there. He would never believe me. Then I realized I didn't care if he believed me or not.

"The ships in the center of the maze—the ones you need if you're going to escape from this maze and the multiple alien monsters they released into it—have been sabotaged. I'm trying to get there to fix them."

Torq's slightly amused expression remained on his face. "Who would sabotage them?"

"The High Commanders who want the human cadets to die so that the Drexian Academy will go back to the way it was. The same ones who don't care if they take out Drexian cadets at the same time." Now I lifted a brow. "Have you ever wondered why there are so few elite Drexians among the first-years?"

His face fell, and he suddenly looked more like a boy than a big, alien warrior. "You aren't lying."

It had been a statement, not a question, but I still answered it. "Why else would I be here, risking my life?"

His usual arrogant smirk vanished, and he jerked a thumb behind him. "That way is a dead end. Looks like this is, too."

"Not exactly." Jess turned back to the wall. "Don't you see the panel in the stone?"

I hadn't, since she'd been blocking it with her body, but when she leaned away, I noticed the sheen of metal covered with unusual shapes and a dial like you'd find on a safe. "It's a combination lock?"

Jess nodded. "I assume if we crack the code, the wall opens for us."

"Or we could try another way," Torq said moments before a terrified shriek pierced the air from somewhere else in the maze.

A cadet had found one of the alien beasts or been found by them. Jess and Torq must have thought the same thing because they both moved closer to the wall.

I blinked at the symbols. "Is that Kronock?"

"We have to know the language of the enemy," Torq said, squinting at the panel. "But I've never been great at it."

"The first line says left two." Jess said, spinning the knob two clicks without glancing at either of us. "I pick up languages easily, and Kronock is an interesting one."

I was overcome with gratitude that I'd stumbled into Jess, but it was a brutal reminder that I'd been reckless to run into the maze by myself. I might be an instructor, but I wasn't a Drexian, and I'd never had to complete the maze myself. I hadn't even done all the cramming that the cadets had done, which meant that I might be the least prepared one in the maze, despite my rank.

"The next one says five to the…" Torq hesitated for a beat, "right. Five to the right."

Jess immediately spun the knob five clicks in the opposite direction, which made me think she'd already figured that one out in her head. Another sound from behind us—this one an inhuman growl—made my chest seize.

"And six to the left." Jess turned the knob six clicks the other way almost without pause.

I held my breath, hearing heavy breathing advancing on us, but nothing happened. Jess's shoulders drooped, then the knob popped flush into the panel, and the entire wall slid aside.

We all rushed through the wall, turning to see a purple creature with three heads and a snake-like tail turn the corner behind us. Torq drew his blade, but the wall with the puzzle slid back again, blocking the monster from reaching us.

"What was that?" Jess's voice wavered as she stared at the sliding wall that had saved us.

"Something that will probably look for another way to find us." Torq kept his weapon raised, and walked backward, watching our six, as we moved toward another fork in the maze.

I hated to admit that I was glad the Drexian was there. His Kronock translation skills weren't the fastest, but I had no doubt that he was better with a Drexian blade.

There was another choice to make, and Jess took us to the left and down a short passage, which then veered left again. Torq brought up the rear with his blade at the ready, only pausing when a deep roar of pain tore through the air.

I tried not to think of the male who'd emitted that sound or what was happening in other parts of the maze. If I did, I might not be able to keep putting one foot in front of the other.

"That was a battle cry," Torq said, even though he didn't sound confident. "A Drexian cadet must have encountered another beast."

I thought he was right about half of that statement. More screams and shrieks emanated from all directions, which prompted Jess to walk faster. I stayed close at her heels, allowing myself a full breath as we made another turn and started down a long, empty corridor.

If my mental calculations were correct, we were at least halfway through one side of the maze and walking in the same direction that we'd entered. We'd encountered one strategic challenge and one alien creature. So far, so good.

Then Jess stopped short, inhaling sharply. The alien beast that lumbered around the corner at the far end of the straightaway only had one head, but its jaw was elongated, and its body was covered in barbs, including one viciously sharp one on its slashing tail.

Jess drew her blade to match Torq's battle stance, and I put a hand to my waist before remembering that I wasn't armed.

Just *grekking* great.

THE ASSASSINS

CHAPTER 61

VOLTEN

WHAT HAD HAPPENED TO MY USUAL ADHERENCE TO RULES? What had happened to my desire to avoid trouble? What had happened to my devotion to the Drexian chain of command? Ariana had happened.

Before I'd met the Earth pilot, I'd been content to serve at the academy. I'd been proud of how I'd worked my way to a position of honor. I'd been happy to help produce well-trained warriors to serve the Drexian empire.

Then I'd met a human who'd shaken my beliefs in the Drexian ways, shown me the cracks in the academy, and provoked me to defy my own desires in pursuit of what was right. If it wasn't for her, I wouldn't be racing toward danger. But I experienced no pangs of regret that I was risking my life for hers, only fear that I wouldn't find her in time.

Many times, I'd wanted to kill anyone who dared touch her

or look at her. Now I knew without a doubt that I would be killed to save her.

My feet ate up the hard ground and kicked dust behind me as I barreled toward the black structure. I was vaguely aware of shouts behind me and the drums beating their steady *thum-thum-thum,* but my focus was on the entrance of the maze, the place where she'd disappeared, the mouth of the deadly trap.

A panel between the tall walls of the entrance started to slide when I was a few strides away, and my chest constricted. The maze was sealing so the cadets couldn't run out the way they'd entered. It was going to shut me out.

I dove forward, leaping through the shrinking opening and doing a somersault to cushion my landing. The panel thudded behind me, sealing me in and sealing my fate.

I stood and brushed off my pants. It was done. I'd made my decision, and now there was no changing my mind, no turning back. Not that I had the smallest urge to be anywhere but inside the maze searching for Ariana.

The urgent beating of the drums had gone, along with the voices of the spectators. Inside the sealed maze, it was quiet. Too quiet. I'd seen all the first-year cadets rush into the massive structure, but as I stood inside with my choice to go forward or turn to the left, I heard no quick footsteps, no deep Drexian voices, no ominous sounds of alien creatures prowling the labyrinth.

It took only a heartbeat to decide to go straight, my strides long as I drew my blade from my waist, glad that at least I'd armed myself. The walls led me to the right and then I went straight—right into a dead end.

Grek. The maze had changed since I'd gone through it my first term. I knew that the interior changed for each class, but it would have been nice if my experience had given me an advantage. A shriek from somewhere deeper in the maze made my spine go rigid.

I turned and ran back the way I came. The noise hadn't been

from Ariana—I knew her sounds well enough to know that her cries were huskier—but the path I'd chosen wasn't getting me closer to her. I returned to the newly sealed entrance and took off in the other direction, curving to the right and then left and then left again.

Did I hear voices ahead? My pulse tripped in the hopes that Ariana wasn't far, and I raced around another turn and then another until I was thoroughly turned around and facing another dead end. Frustration seethed through me, and I slashed my curved blade through the air as I spun around and retraced my steps. Where had I gone wrong and taken a turn that had led me away from the voices?

I was mentally unwinding my path when I rounded a bend and almost bumped into the long, swishing tail of an alien creature with purple skin. Three heads whipped around to pin me with six eyes, all black and narrowed as it opened its three mouths to reveal rows of razor-sharp teeth. In all my simulations in the holochamber, I'd never gone up against a beast like the one that was advancing on me.

I might not be a Blade, but that didn't mean my best friend hadn't drilled me in battle techniques. All Kann's training flashed through my mind as I sized up my opponent. It had me on sheer size. It had me on number of heads and teeth. It had me when it came to length and power of a tail.

It did not have me on speed or agility, though, and its arms were negligible. The beast would have to get me with one of its jaws or swipe at me with its tail, but the pathway wasn't wide enough for it to do both. I decided that I'd rather take on a single tail than all the teeth.

I ducked under the creature's lunging heads, jumping over the tail and slashing at it as I landed. The beast shrieked, but it couldn't turn fast enough. Now its tail was injured and unable to swipe at me with force, so I took my momentary advantage to leap onto its back.

Three heads swiveled and snapped at me, but I was already too close to them for the mouths to crane back far enough to capture me. One of the sharp teeth ripped my pants and gashed my leg, but

I ignored the pain. I squeezed my legs tight to hold on as the animal thrashed around and tried to dislodge me, and I stabbed my blade into the thick, reptilian skin to pull myself closer to the top of the spine where the heads converged.

Pain shot through me as another knife-like tooth punctured my calf, but I was already plunging my blade into the creature. It reared up, releasing a horrific screech before collapsing to the ground, its trio of heads rolling to their sides and the glittery eyes going wide and glassy.

Sliding down from the beast's back, I landed and cringed from the pain. I didn't have time to dwell on my injuries or revel in defeating one of the alien monsters, so I continued through the maze, straining to hear any voices over the sound of my heavy breathing.

I reached a wall with a steel panel inset in it, grateful for the chance to stop and catch my breath as I deciphered the Kronock code and twirled the combination lock to open the panel. The Kronock symbols were one of those things I'd never forgotten from my time at the academy, even though a shiver went through me every time I had to read the language of our enemy.

The wall slid open, and I walked through it, now on high alert and my blade, slick with green alien blood, extended. A pained roar came from the other side of the maze, a stark reminder that the cadets were spread throughout the large labyrinth of passageways, and so were more alien monsters. Then why hadn't I come across any cadets yet?

Just as I was wondering if the first-years were getting sucked into a vortex, I went around a corner and spotted the last one I'd hoped to see. Torq faced me in a battle stance with his blade drawn, but my gaze was drawn to what was behind him—two females, one of them Ariana—and in front of them, a hulking beast covered in barbs.

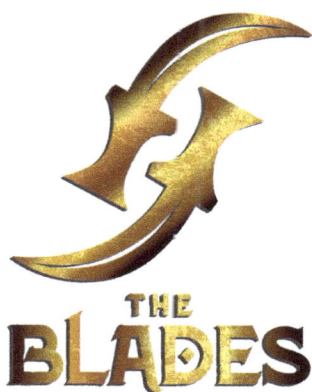

THE BLADES

CHAPTER 62

ARIANA

BACKED UP AS JESS EXTENDED HER BLADE, MY FINGERS ITCHING to hold something as the spiked beast slowly moved toward us. It wasn't fast, but its heavy paws or hooves or whatever they were rumbled the ground with each step, which did not help my already erratic heartbeat.

"What the *grek*?"

I chanced to look away from the monster and at Torq, who was staring behind us. "The problem is up here, buddy."

Then I glimpsed a figure moving toward us. Not an alien beast. A Drexian. But not a cadet. My chest squeezed as the Drexian got closer. "Volten?"

His uniform was torn and dirty, and sweat smeared his face along with…was that blood? Before I could ask what he was doing in the maze and if he was okay, he reached us and locked eyes with Torq. "Ready?"

The cadet readjusted his grip on his blade, his trembling grip shaking the weapon. "Ready."

Volten pushed me and Jess aside as he and Torq stepped between us and the monster. Instinct made me open my mouth to protest being pushed out of the way, but Jess grabbed my arm as if she sensed what I was about to do.

"How about we let them be the first line of defense against this thing?"

I clamped my mouth shut. The woman was right. The Drexians were bigger than us, and they had the advantage of both being armed. If they failed to kill him, then I'd have my chance to face off against an alien monster with a spiked tail—and I'd get to do it without a weapon.

Still, I hated being a spectator, especially when it came to watching Volten go up against a creature that was ten times his size. My heart hammered as he and Torq moved to flank the creature, and I tugged Jess back a few steps with me.

The creature snapped at them, and both Drexians dodged. It slashed its tail around and in front, but they jumped back and missed the swinging spike. Then Volten jerked his head to one side, and Torq made a quick dash to follow. The beast swung his elongated snout to follow him, and Volten used that moment to race around the back of the creature. While Torq dodged the snappy jaws, Volten used the spikes on the animal's back as steps, leaping from barb to barb until he was behind the head.

As if it had just realized what was happening, the creature threw back his head, but not before Volten thrust his blade deep into the back of the skull. The force of the beast rearing back sent Volten flying from his back, and he hit one of the walls of the maze and slid to the ground.

I slapped a hand over my mouth to keep from screaming as the alien creature thudded to the ground and Volten remained a motionless heap at the base of the maze wall. Torq was the first to react, leaping over the dead animal and reaching Volten. He gave the Drexian a shake, and Volten groaned.

Jess clutched my arm, and we both released loud breaths of relief. He was alive. The beast was dead, and we were all still alive.

I hurried over to Volten, the relief that he'd survived quickly turning to confusion and then irritation. I knelt as he propped himself up on his elbows. "What are you doing here? Are you following me?"

"Yes, I'm following you," he snapped with an impressive amount of vigor considering how hard he'd hit the wall. "You ran into a sabotaged maze where every cadet is supposed to die, and you didn't have a clue how to survive."

"I'm sorry." I held up my hands. "No clue? I've made it this far, haven't I?" I flapped a hand at his ripped uniform and blood-smeared face. "I look better than you do."

His pupils widened. "I look like this because I just saved you from being eaten."

Okay, he had a point there.

He motioned to one side with his head. "I also killed another beast before it could find you."

I blew out a breath. "It's not like I had a choice. I had to come in here." I paused. "How do you know that the maze has been sabotaged?"

He narrowed his gaze slightly. "How do you know?"

"I overhead the High Commanders talking about sacrificing the entire class of first-years so the academy can go back to being human-free."

Torq stood and released a low litany of Drexian curses.

Volten's jaw tightened. "So, the worst-case scenario is true."

"You mean that your old leaders are bloodthirsty assholes? Yep, it's true. It's also true that even if any cadets make it through this deadly maze, the ships in the center have disabled thrusters so they won't be able to take off. That's why I came into the maze. That's why I'm trying to get to the middle."

Volten held my gaze for a beat before he pushed himself to standing. "Then we'd better keep moving." He thumped his fist across his chest at Torq. "Good work, Cadet."

Torq squared his shoulders and a genuine smile that wasn't smug or edged with cockiness lit up his face. He returned the salute. "Thank you, Lieutenant."

Volten glanced behind the Drexian. "Would you mind...?"

Torq pivoted to follow Volten's gaze then ran to the dead creature and yanked Volten's blade from its head. He wiped it on his own pants before handing it back to Volten, who grinned as he took it. "Thank you, again."

Jess was already at the far end of the corridor, waving for us to follow. "I think I see another challenge."

Volten fell in step behind Torq, and we followed Jess, but his gait was uneven as we walked side by side.

"Are you limping?"

"The other beast had three heads and ten times the sharp teeth. I couldn't avoid all of them."

"Purple guy with a long tail?"

He tipped his head forward, grimacing with each step.

I shook my head and slipped a hand around his waist, taking as much of his weight off his injured leg as I could. "You don't have to be stubborn all the time, you know."

He draped one arm over my shoulders as he leaned on me. "Are you giving me advice on taking help?"

I didn't look up at him. "Fine. Maybe we both could be less stubborn."

He snorted out a laugh. "Maybe."

I pressed my lips together to keep my own laugh from erupting. We might be stuck in a deadly maze, but my happiness at seeing

Volten again and my relief that he was alive were making it hard for me to feel anything but grateful.

We hobbled along in silence behind Torq until we'd caught up to Jess, who was standing at a dead-end and studying an open panel on the wall. We'd encountered a challenge that had seemed to fit the School of Strategy, we'd used skills worthy of the School of Battle to defeat a monster, and the middle of the maze held planes that would test cadets' piloting skills. Chances were good we'd discovered our first test from the School of Engineering.

Jess glanced back at us, her ponytail flying as she swiftly returned her gaze to the mess of exposed wires. "I'm no expert in this stuff, but I think we need to reconnect the wires."

"Reconnect them to do what?" Torq asked, showing that he really wasn't an expert.

"I don't exactly know, but—"

Pounding footsteps made us all whirl around while Torq and Volten reached for their blades. Then we all exhaled when two female cadets rounded the wall.

The blonde scanned our group, her eyes flaring when they landed on me and Volten. "Are we glad to see you!"

The cadet with long, silvery hair glanced behind her. "And thanks for killing the monsters back there."

Before she could turn back around, a panel slid closed behind them and enclosed us all with the wiring panel. Then there was a hiss at our feet, and gas started to swirl around our boots.

"Now we know why we have to reconnect the wiring," Jess said as she put a hand over her mouth. "And we know we need to do it before the gas knocks us out."

The bitter odor started to burn the inside of my nose, and I pulled my shirt up to cover it.

Or kills us, I thought.

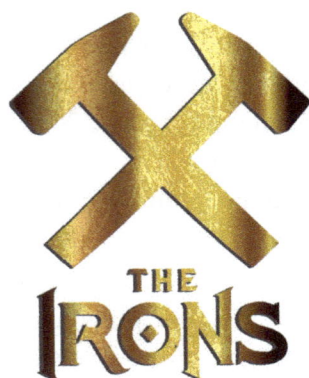

THE IRONS

CHAPTER 63

VOLTEN

HELD MY BREATH, BUT EVEN THAT COULDN'T STOP THE WHITE gas from creeping into my nose and burning my throat. Was I really going to be poisoned after surviving attacks by two vicious monsters?

Ariana coughed next to me, and I pulled her into my chest, hoping to block the gas from overpowering her. Not that I would be much good if I collapsed, but I couldn't focus on that. I tipped my head back and took a sip of air that wasn't yet tainted.

The woman with silvery hair pushed past me, blinking rapidly from the irritating gas. "I can do this. It's a basic loop-in system. If I reconnect the blue ones, then it should shut off the venting."

"I don't remember going over this in our coaching sessions," the blonde said through the crook of her elbow that she held over her mouth and nose.

My head started to ache, and Ariana's weight against me became heavier. Torq leaned against one of the walls, and I saw him grab Jess under the armpit before she sank to the ground.

"Got it!" The cadet slapped her hand against the wall beside the wiring panel, then kept it there as she leaned forward and pressed her forehead to the black stone.

"Nice going, Britta," Ariana managed to say in a weak voice.

As my vision blurred, the wall slid open and fresh air poured in. The woman who'd figured out the challenge—her name was Brittanis, I reminded myself—fell forward and crawled from the space while the rest of us stumbled out around her.

Jess straightened as Torq released her, and she hoisted Britta to her feet. We all sucked in greedy breaths as we fled the quickly dissipating gas.

"Thanks, Jess." Britta put her hands on her knees and shook her head as if to cast off the remnants of toxic gas.

Torq took a few long strides down the empty corridor. "We should keep moving. We can't be far from the center now."

Unless we were going the wrong way or in circles, I thought. Between the throbbing wounds in my legs, the ache in my back from being thrown to the wall, and the fire in my lungs, I was starting to wonder if we would make it, or if the High Commanders would get their way.

Ariana straightened and coiled her arm around my middle again. "You good?"

I nodded, hoping that she couldn't sense my worry or my doubt. We continued in a loose group, turning to the right and then again to the left.

At the next corner, Torq stopped and stared. Jess joined him and bent over again, dragging in a breath as her dark ponytail flopped forward.

I was already preparing myself to face another alien beast as Ariana and I picked up our pace to join them at the next challenge.

When I got a good look at the corridor with climbing holds

covering the walls and a floor that looked like molten lava, part of me wished it was another monster.

Then I peered beyond the terrifying floor. There was a half wall blocking my complete view, but I could see the tip of a ship's wing. The way out was within our grasp. If we could all make it across the last, deadly gauntlet.

"Screw this!" Ariana shook her head roughly. "No one said the maze might have a lava floor."

Torq squatted near the edge of the bubbling red substance and took a deep breath. "I think it's from underneath the black mountains."

I'd heard that there was a molten core beneath the treacherous peaks, the very place they'd mined the stone used to build the academy millennia ago. Bringing it here to be a part of the maze that would restore the military school to its ancient traditions—traditions forged hundreds of years ago—was almost poetic. It was also twisted.

Fantasies of dropping the High Commanders in the bubbling, red pool cavorted through my mind as I eyed the holds that stretched across the walls on both sides. "We have to climb to the other side."

Ariana looked up at me. "Can you make it across?"

It wasn't a matter of if I could. I had no choice. Besides, a climbing wall was something I'd mastered long ago. "Of course, I can. I'm Drexian."

She rolled her eyes. "As long as you don't die, I can put up with your cockiness for a little while longer."

"Um, guys," Morgan frowned as she studied the walls. "The holds move."

"What?" Jess squinted at the gray holds on the black walls.

They were like the holds on the towering climbing wall in the School of Battle, except for one detail. Like the blonde cadet had said, they moved. As I watched, a V-shaped hold swiveled from pointing up to pointing down and went from being a decent hold to being impossible to grip.

I was going to have serious words with whoever designed this challenge, assuming I survived.

"We have to move fast, that's all." Torq slapped his hands together. "No stopping. Don't overthink it. Go as fast as you can."

Jess shook her head. "That does not seem like the best strategy for dealing with a lava floor."

"It is if you can't trust the holds." He took a breath and reached for a hold.

Morgan surged forward and grabbed his arm. "Wait. Give me a few seconds, and I can figure out the pattern."

"She's right." A satisfied smile twitched Jess's lips. "There is a pattern. The moving holds aren't moving randomly." She glanced at the blonde. "Morgan and I can stay back and tell you when to move and which hold to grab."

"Are you sure?" Ariana asked.

Both women gave us determined nods. "We've got this."

Ariana clearly didn't like the situation, but she sighed and turned to the rest of the cadets. "Keep your hips close to the wall and your arms long. That will keep your arms from tiring and help you not fall."

"I can go first," Torq offered.

Again, the cadet surprised me with his willingness to rise above his cocky persona. If the women were wrong with any of their predictions, he could easily end up falling to his death.

He paused before he reached for the first hold and looked at the women. "Just so you know, they were wrong about humans and about human females. I'd go into battle with any of you, any day." Then he pivoted to the closest wall and stepped onto the nearest foot hold. "Climbing."

I wasn't sure who 'they' meant, but I suspected a high-born like Torq had heard plenty about Drexian superiority and human inferiority from his family. I hoped the cadet would live long enough to learn about more ways he'd been wrong, and a part of me wished I'd get the chance to know the less aggravating version of him.

"Grab the round hold above your head." Jess's gaze was riveted to Torq. "Now move your foot to the next low hold."

"Move your hand to the hold below the round one!" Morgan yelled, and Torq grabbed the next hold before the one he'd been holding twisted.

I could barely breathe as I watched the Drexian make his way across the wall and the holds spun. At one point, his foot slipped on a rotating hold, but he was able to hold himself up with his arms, his boots dangling over the scorching red lava. When he reached the opposite side, we all cheered, and I allowed myself a quick breath before Britta started across.

The woman moved surprisingly quickly, following the other women's direction, and jumping to the ground on the other side in half the time it had taken Torq. Ariana didn't hesitate as she left my side and stepped to the wall.

"See you on the other side."

I could only move my head up and down mutely as she made her way across the holds, swinging her arms loosely as if she'd been climbing trick walls her entire life. Her feet danced above the bubbling, fiery floor like it wouldn't burn the skin off her bones if she made a wrong step. When she reached safety, I choked back the emotion that had welled in my chest.

"Your turn, flyboy," she called.

I pivoted to the two women, but they waved me forward. "Like the boss said, you're up."

My leg screamed as I stretched it to balance on a hold, but I fought through the pain. I was almost to the middle of the maze. We'd almost made it.

I grabbed the holds I'd seen everyone else grab, moving my hands quickly to avoid the now predictable turns and following the instructions as they were called out behind me. I grasped a shelf hold, letting my body hang from my fingers for a beat, but instead of hearing the female cadets call out the command for my next move from behind, I only heard a shriek.

Spinning my head back, I spotted the enormous, furry monster that was advancing on them with blood dripping from its mouth. Then the hold that was keeping me upright rotated and sent my legs flying.

THE WINGS

CHAPTER 64

ARIANA

I RUBBED MY HANDS AND SNUCK A GLANCE OVER MY SHOULDER at the open courtyard behind me. We were so close. Half of our group was already over the molten pool, with only Volten and the two women calling out the route left to cross.

I didn't know where things stood with Volten. He had run into the maze after me, and saved me from a being eaten alive, but considering this was the Drexian Academy, I didn't know if that meant anything had changed in our status. Sure, I'd put my arm around him to help him walk, and he'd cocooned my face with his chest when the gas had started to overwhelm us, but that was more about helping fellow warriors, wasn't it?

He flinched as he extended his leg to start climbing across the wall, and it took all my resolve to watch him as he grabbed the hand holds. Watching others cross the deadly course was worse than doing it yourself, even though I was relieved that I would never have to experience the sensation of heat sizzling up my legs as I dangled inches above boiling lava.

Volten moved loosely, his arms long and his legs stretched wide for balance, and it was impossible not to admire the body on the guy. Despite being undeniably big and stacked with hard muscle, his movements were graceful. Even through his shirt, his core muscles rippled with each turn and pivot.

He reached for the next hold, but a scream made him jerk his head behind him. Morgan and Jess were edging closer to the lava pit, as a creature with matted fur ambled toward them on all fours, leaving a trail of blood dripping from his mouth.

I didn't want to think about whose blood it might be, or about the fact that the two cadets had nowhere to run. The beast was too wide for them to get around, and Volten had barely started crossing the wall.

Then Volten's feet flailed in the air as he lunged for new hand holds just before the ones he'd been clutching spun upside down.

A scream was stuck in my throat, but I was too petrified to make a sound as I watched Volten lurch his way toward me without the aid of Morgan and Jess warning him which holds would move. Both female cadets were now on the wall, sidestepping their way toward Volten and away from the alien beast, who'd begun to move faster now that his prey was escaping.

"Go, go, go!" Jess screamed as she brought up the rear of the group and flattened herself to the wall as the furry creature swiped a sharply taloned paw at her.

Volten grunted with exertion as he moved faster, and the blood from his exposed leg wound ran down his torn pants. He paused for a breath to wipe one palm on his shirt, and I realized that the blood and sweat were making his hands slip.

I slapped a hand over my mouth to stifle my scream as he continued his fast but unsteady progress. His legs shook and his fingers trembled as he reached for a hold that twisted before he could grab it.

"Above you," I called out, my voice hoarse.

Behind Volten, the alien creature was roaring in frustration as it tried to slash at Jess, who was now beyond its reach. It paced in front of the red bubbling pool, lowering its head to sniff at the surface and then snorting in impotent rage. Finally, it locked its gaze on its escaping prey, backed up a few paces, and made a desperate, running lunge for the wall.

My heart seized as the monster's outstretched arms and impossibly long claws tore through the air, barely missing Jess. It hit the wall, scrambled at the holds, and then fell into the lava. I instinctively turned my head away as it let out a gruesome scream. When I allowed myself to look again, it was floundering and sending heavy drops of red through the air. The cries of agony made the hairs on the back of my neck prickle. Even though I had no love for the vicious creature, I couldn't help feeling sympathy for its horrific end.

I ran to the edge as Volten approached, reached for his arm, and pulled him off the wall. He staggered into me while I helped him rip off his shirt that sizzled with flecks of lava burning through the fabric toward his skin. The beast was still emitting horrifying sounds as it was consumed by the fiery pit, sounds that would be the stuff of my nightmares for years to come.

Torq and Britta helped the last two cadets as they reached the end of the wall, but instead of Morgan and Jess ripping off their lava-flecked uniforms, Torq took off his shirt, wrapped his hand in it, and brushed off the small, fiery clumps. Then we stood together, breathing heavily, the two Drexians shirtless, and two of the cadets wearing uniforms with holes burned into them.

I tried not to gawk at the ripped Drexians. I'd already seen Volten without a shirt before, but seeing the muscular cadet and the hard, flushed nodes running down both of their spines was unnerving. And why did I like the look of grime and blood smeared over the sweaty muscles rippling across Volten's chest and back so much?

"No offense." Jess glanced around the group. "But I don't know if being in the Drexian Academy is worth all this."

Morgan brushed a strand of pale hair off her sweaty forehead. "Even SEALS don't have to play a real-life version of The Floor is Lava."

"But we made it." I swiveled toward the center of the maze, my euphoria tangled in the sharp bite of adrenaline that was making my hands shake.

Volten and I walked around the wall so that we could finally see the ships that would take us from the maze, but as soon as we stepped into the open courtyard, I stopped breathing.

"These aren't..." My voice cracked and then died on my lips.

"What the ever-loving hell?" Britta whispered behind me as the rest of our group rounded the wall.

I fought for breath that wouldn't come, as I realized that the ships in the center of the maze, the ships that were intended to be an escape for those who made it, were not Drexian fighters. The hulls were not the glossy black of the Drexian vessels, and they weren't sleek and aerodynamic. The ships waiting for us were muddy-gray and covered in metal that looked like scales.

They were the same ones that had filled the sky over Earth during the attack. They were the same ones that I'd fought against when they'd attacked the Drexian home world and the academy. They were the same ones that had shot my sister's ship from the sky.

The ships were Kronock.

THE ASSASSINS

CHAPTER 65

VOLTEN

D READ SETTLED OVER ME, AS I SAW THE MAZE'S FINAL DIRTY trick. Instead of racing victorious to the fighters the cadets had been training on, we'd been met with enemy ships. Flying Kronock vessels was not a first-year skill or something that any of the cadets would be able to do.

But I would.

I steeled myself as I took a step toward the gray ships hunched on the ground, then I stopped. Ariana hadn't moved since we'd entered the courtyard. She stood rooted to the spot, her eyes wide and her breaths quick and shallow.

"I think she's having a panic attack." Jess touched her arm, but Ariana's gaze was locked on the ships.

I stood in front of her, blocking her view of the enemy vessels. "Ariana." She didn't meet my gaze, her own eyes wide and unfocused, so I raised my voice and hardened my tone. "Lieutenant Bowman."

She snapped her gaze to me, refocusing with a wrinkled brow, as if she'd only now remembered where she was and who was with her. "These aren't ships I can fix."

I grabbed the sides of her shoulders. "Ships are ships. The Kronock ships might be brutal in design, but they aren't so different. And I think you've forgotten something."

She blinked rapidly. "What?"

"The Wings go as one. We will do this, and everything else, together."

"Together." Her shoulders relaxed beneath my hands as she repeated the word. Then, a roar from somewhere else in the maze made us both stiffen. The final monster in the maze was still out there. A series of screams told me that there were still other cadets alive as well.

I released her and turned to the cadets. "Our group only needs one ship to get out of here, but we need to fix the rest."

Morgan finished my thought for me. "We don't know how many other cadets are still out there, and who will make it to the middle."

"From what Ari—the lieutenant—overheard, the ships' thrusters have been externally disabled." I started walking toward the closest enemy ship, suppressing the urge to shudder. "I'll show you how to re-enable them, and then we'll split into pairs to fix the rest of the ships."

Ariana stayed close to me as we went to the rear of the ship, and I flipped open a panel. Luckily, learning about Kronock ships was something I'd mastered in my final year at the academy, although it wasn't something I'd used since then. If pilots did their jobs well, there would never be a case where we needed to hijack a Kronock ship.

It took me a moment, staring at the tangle of wires and circuitry, for me to locate a dangling cable. "Take this and reattach it here." I reconnected the cable, hoping that my memory was correct.

"That looks nothing like the thruster cable on Drexian ships," Ariana muttered.

"Got it." Torq gave me a sharp dip of his head and turned to Jess. "You're with me."

She gave a curt nod, tightened her brown ponytail, and the pair ran off to the next ship. Morgan and Britta didn't even need to announce that they were pairing up, leaving side-by-side and picking the ship farthest away.

"Thanks," Ariana said, when we were alone.

I snapped the outer panel closed. "For showing you how to reattach the thruster?"

She shook her head as she met my gaze. "For keeping me from losing my shit and embarrassing myself in front of the cadets."

"We have all experienced moments of panic today."

"This was more than that." She wrapped her arms around her middle as if creating a shield. "Every time I see anything that has to do with them." She jerked her head toward the enemy ship. "It makes me think of how Sasha died fighting them."

She'd never mentioned her sister's death to me, not even after I'd confronted her. "There is no shame in hating the Kronock."

"It's not only that. It's that I know I'm to blame for her death. I'm the one who challenged her to join the battle. I'm the reason she volunteered. I'm why she's dead."

I fought the urge to grab her shoulders and shake her, but she looked so fragile that I cupped her face in my palm and tipped her eyes to meet mine. "You did not attack Earth. You did not provoke a war. And I have a feeling that you could not have stopped your sister from joining the fight even if you'd tried."

She released a shuddering breath, her eyes glistening.

"If your sister was anything like you, she was *grekking* stubborn and a thorn in everyone's side. She went to battle because it was her choice."

Ariana's face twisted in outrage, then her lips quivered as she started to laugh. "She was even more *grekking* stubborn than me, and she was a massive pain in the ass." Her voice caught. "But I miss her."

My own throat tightened. Even though I'd grown up hating so many things about my father, and even after I'd learned that my father wasn't really my father, there was still a part of me that missed him. Memories of sitting on his lap as he laughed and told stories—always inappropriate ones, about things he'd done that were questionable at best—reminded me that he wasn't all bad. "You should miss her, but I think she would be proud of what you've done at the academy, of what you're doing now. It seems like the pilots in your family have a tradition of saving others."

She smiled. "I guess we do."

Another series of screams, these much closer, made us both jump. I dropped my hand as the warmth between us evaporated, and we both turned toward the opening to the other side of the maze.

"If some of the other cadets are being chased by the last monster..." Ariana let her words drift off, but we both knew the end to that possibility.

If they ran into the courtyard being chased by a deadly creature before we had the ships ready to fly, we'd all be dead.

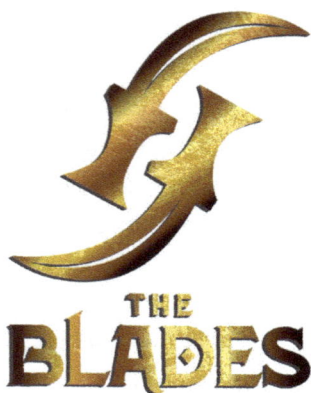

THE BLADES

CHAPTER 66

ARIANA

M Y CHEEK STILL BUZZED FROM VOLTEN'S TOUCH AS WE RAN to the next ship. Not only had his touch comforted and calmed me, but so had his words. He'd been right. My sister and I might have pushed each other, but neither of us did anything we didn't want to do. Sasha had been determined to defend Earth and proud to do it. Thinking otherwise was sullying her memory and her legacy.

I exhaled as my arms pumped by my side. Telling him my deepest fears and darkest guilt about Sasha's death had been like releasing a valve that had been overtightened, and I could finally breathe again. Talking about her death also freed me from the pain of it and made it possible for me to think about my sister without the memories being shrouded in guilt and shame.

"You know what?" I nudged Volten when we were standing at the next ship. "Sasha would have fucking loved this."

He lifted one dark brow as if he wasn't sure he'd understood me. "She would have loved being chased by monsters through a treacherous maze and having to climb over lava to reach freedom?"

A laugh burst from my mouth, a laugh that felt out of place in the deadly maze but also completely fitting. "Yeah, as crazy as it sounds, she would have. At least, she would have loved the camaraderie of it. And we loved playing The Floor Is Lava."

Volten paused after flipping open the panel. "Human children play games with lava floors?"

"We pretend that the floor is lava, and we have to jump on furniture to get anywhere."

"Strange," he said under his breath, and focused on reconnecting the thrusters of the enemy ship. "Drexians do not pretend, but our normal existence is probably more of an adventure than life on Earth."

I thought about some of the remote and environmentally harsh places I'd visited on Earth. "Don't count on it."

More screams made the hairs on the back of my neck stand at attention. The cadets were getting closer, which was both a good and a bad thing.

Torq and Jess ran up to us, and I had to work hard not to gape at the Drexian cadet's impressive chest muscles that were beaded with sweat. Now that I was thinking about it, Volten's bare chest looked even better with rivulets of sweat trickling down the taut muscle.

Not now, I told myself. Not now.

"Done." Torq shot a look behind him. "The women are finishing their last ship."

Now the screaming was accompanied by a monstrous howl, and the dusty ground rumbled beneath our boots.

"Time to leave." Volten waved for us to board the Kronock ship as Morgan and Britta joined us.

"Any trouble?" I asked the women.

Britta winked at me. "Trust the Irons." Then she leapt inside the ship.

Jess hesitated at the opening in the side of the scaly, gray ship. "Together?"

Volten swept an arm wide. "There were never enough vessels for every cadet to claim one. That's part of the challenge. *The Wings Go As One.* Can cadets work together to fly a ship from the maze? Pilots must be able to fly as a unit and work with a copilot. Being a Wing is about much more than personal glory."

"Since we don't know how many cadets remain in the maze, we should leave as many ships as possible," I added, even though I had an ominous feeling that not all the first-years had survived.

Everyone boarded the ship with Volten stepping inside last. Drexian ships were notable for their sleek design and an interior as black and polished as the hull. Similarly, the Kronock ships were as gray and reptilian inside as they were out. The metal floor panels looked like scales as did the walls, and the only light was from ambient strips that pulsed green on the high ceiling.

I pushed aside thoughts of the hulking aliens who were cruel and violent. If I dwelled on the fact that the same aliens who'd attacked Earth and so many other worlds had once been inside this ship, I wouldn't be able to pilot it.

Volten tugged the heavy door shut and strode through the cadets and toward the cockpit. "There aren't any seats on this thing except for the pilot and co-pilot, so hold onto something."

The center of the vessel wasn't huge, so there was barely enough room for the women to sit and link arms. Torq and I followed Volten, but I pushed past him when it came time to sit at the controls. "Sorry, Cadet. I'm pulling rank."

I paused before dropping into the copilot seat next to Volten, my feet not touching the floor. Even he looked slight in the oversized seat. I looked like I'd ended up on the wrong end of a shrink ray.

Volten didn't seem bothered by the huge interior. He flipped a few switches. "Powering up." He glanced at Torq who stood between us. "Time to grab a spot, Cadet, but it's not here."

The Drexian grunted and disappeared into the interior.

The ship roused noisily, the engines grumbling as the hull rattled. I wasn't much for deities, but I said a silent prayer that the thrusters were the only thing that had been sabotaged on the ship. I did not want to die in a Kronock vessel.

Then I peered out the glass of the cockpit as a cluster of cadets raced into the courtyard with a winged creature nipping at their heels. Literally nipping with extended fangs as it flapped black wings to move faster. Even more than not wanting to die on an enemy ship, I didn't want to die at the hands—or the beak—of that monster.

I didn't have time to wonder if the cadets were going to work together. They all ran onto the nearest ship before their pursuer could catch them. Now I had to hope that one of them would be able to fly the alien vessel.

A hand squeezed my leg, and I jerked my head to Volten.

"Ships aren't that different, remember?"

I finally allowed myself to focus on the controls of the Kronock ship. He was right. I didn't need to know the language—although the cadets would know more than I did—to know how to operate the thing. The controls were similarly placed, and the steering yoke was downright old school.

With a grin, Volten engaged the thrusters, which fired noisily and powered us off the ground. The second ship followed our lead a moment after us, and soon two ships were rising above the maze as the beast with wings I now saw were clipped lunged fruitlessly for us and shrieked in frustration.

I sank fully in the seat when Volten took us even higher, rising above the academy and through the clouds. Then he glanced over at me. "Can you forgive me?"

"Forgive you?" A sliver of panic danced in the back of my mind. "Why do you need my forgiveness?"

The ship hovered in the murky clouds as Volten turned to fully face me. "I never should have agreed to your foolish plan."

Now I was truly confused. "What foolish plan was that?"

"That we should only be colleagues. You were wrong about that, and you were wrong that we don't know and can't trust each other."

I tilted my head at him. "If this is your attempt at an apology for being a jerk to me, then it's seriously lacking."

"I was a—what do Earthlings say?—a fuckwit when I pushed you away."

"I mean, I guess some people from Earth say that," I mumbled.

"I never should have lashed out at you or accused you of keeping yourself from me. I regret my words and every moment I spent without you after that."

"Well, that's a little better," I admitted, the warm feeling returning to my chest.

"Do you forgive me?" Volten reached for my hands and held them in his. "And admit that you were wrong about all those other things?"

I fought an indignant smile that was teasing my mouth. "I might have been wrong, but you were wrong first."

He pulled me from the co-pilot's seat and onto his lap. "Agreed. I don't want you to ever think that I don't know you just because I don't know every detail about your past." He tangled a hand through my hair and dragged the pad of his thumb across my lips. "I know your heart, and that is all I need to know to love you."

My pulse spiked as I blinked at him and ran my hands down the hard, bare muscles of his chest. "Did you say you love me?"

"That's also something I need to apologize for." Volten pulled my face to within an inch of his. "I should have told you I loved you the moment I realized it."

My heart was hammering so loudly, I was sure the cadets behind us could hear it. "And when was that?"

"It might have been when you gave me a dressing down outside your classroom." He pulled me into a kiss so light that his lips

314

barely brushed mine. "Or it might have been when I had you pinned against the sparring cage."

I swatted his chest as he kissed me again then I pulled away and shot him a wicked grin. "I knew for sure when your foot slipped as you climbed over the lava. The thought of losing you made me realize that I couldn't. Not then and not ever."

"Then almost falling into lava was worth it, although I hope never to do it again." His voice became a rasp. "I would kill a legion of monsters for you, but I would also die a thousand deaths for you."

"Ditto," I said, my fingers caressing his slick skin. Volten tightened his hand in my hair and pulled my lips to his in a deep, claiming kiss that almost made me forget that we were still in an alien ship, and that there was much to do when we returned to the surface. But for the moment, I didn't care about anything but the Drexian I was kissing.

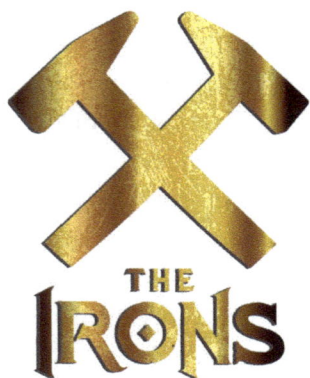

THE IRONS

CHAPTER 67

VOLTEN

"YOU SHOULDN'T BE NERVOUS." I ADJUSTED THE COLLAR OF Ariana's uniform as we stood in the center of the atrium in the School of Flight building.

"It's my first Wings initiation." She tipped her face to mine, her features illuminated in the flickering candlelight that surrounded us. "And the first initiation of a class that almost didn't make it."

I tried not to think about the chaos that had erupted when three Kronock ships had touched down in front of the visiting Drexian dignitaries, and we'd emerged alive. It hadn't taken Zoran more than a few snaps of his fingers to have the High Commanders surrounded by guards and taken away especially after Ariana had told him what she'd overheard and what we'd found in the maze. It helped that, despite being locked up when he'd threatened to reveal their plan and stop the trials, Vyk had escaped from the dungeons and spoken against the elite Drexians.

The treacherous plan hadn't been completely unsuccessful,

though. A handful of cadets had perished in the maze, but, in a shocking turn, none of them had been human. The High Commanders would now face their own trial for sending Drexian sons to their deaths and putting the treaty with Earth at risk. No matter what, they would be punished for everything they'd done.

I allowed myself to release a breath as I looked at Ariana. Even though she wore her Drexian Academy uniform, she'd donned the long, ceremonial jacket that almost reached her knees and was emblazoned on the chest with the wings crest stitched in gold. The pillar candles on stands around us caught the bronze highlights in her short, brown hair and the gold flecks in her eyes, which made her look even more breathtaking. "You look good in a Drexian dress uniform."

She pressed her hands to my chest. "So do you, although I prefer you wearing nothing."

My pulse quickened as I scanned the empty atrium that would soon be filled with the newest members of Flight. "Bold words, Lieutenant."

She lifted a brow in challenge. "What can I say, flyboy? After the maze, not much scares me."

"No?" I teased. "Not even the prospect of being caught with one of your fellow officers?"

She laughed. "I'm pretty sure everyone knows about us now, especially since we walked off the Kronock ship holding hands and have spent every moment since in your quarters."

I backed her up until I'd flattened her against one of the pillars surrounding the atrium. "I'm not proposing that we hold hands before the cadets arrive."

"What are you—?"

I silenced her question by crushing my lips to hers and her arms went around my neck. I opened her mouth to mine, our tongues tangling as she moaned into my mouth.

When I broke the kiss, her eyes were half-lidded and her lips puffy. I took her by the hand and pulled her farther from the illuminated atrium and down a darkened hallway with closed doors and empty classrooms. Then I pressed her up against the wall again and dropped to my knees, dipping below the belled hem of the long jacket, and tugging down her pants and panties in a single forceful motion until they were in a pile on the floor.

"Volt! What if someone sees—"

Her protests evaporated as she held my head through the fabric of the jacket and emitted a tortured sigh. There was little I loved more than hearing Ariana moan for me, her body twitching uncontrollably and her breath ragged. I didn't waste time as my tongue slicked through her, finding her bundle of nerves and sucking gently.

"Are you trying to get us both kicked out?" She managed to say between breathy sounds, even though I knew she loved the possibility of being caught.

Of course, she did. She was a Wing. She lived for thrills and danger, and there was nothing like the thrill of possibly being caught by the cadets and instructors who would be descending on the school for a ceremony.

She was panting as she held my head tighter. "You like being a bad boy, don't you?"

That didn't require an answer since we'd already determined that being with Ariana had made me break rules and defy regulations like I'd never even considered before. We'd also determined that I loved dancing on the edge of danger and risk, even if I'd fought it my entire life. Being with her had released my inhibitions, and now I was embracing life, not gritting my way through it. Starting with savoring every delicious, forbidden moment with Ariana.

Her thighs clenched, her body spasmed, and she let out a desperate gasp. I didn't hesitate to stand and jerk my own pants down to release my cock, holding my jacket up as I dragged my crown through her wetness. "Not as much as you love being bad for me and taking every bit of my cock."

"I don't know what you're talking about." Her eyes had a wicked glint. "You're a bad influence, and I'm a good girl."

"Yes, you are." I thrust into her, savoring the sharp intake of breath as she lifted one of her legs to hook it around my back. "A very good girl who takes me so well."

She groaned, her eyes half-lidded and heavy with desire. "And you love being the big, bad Drexian who ruined me for men."

I grabbed her by the ass and lifted her up so that both legs curled around my waist, then I flattened her back against the wall. "No more men for you—ever."

She scraped one hand through my hair and bit her bottom lip. "No?"

I jerked my head roughly from side to side as I drove deep. Even being inside her while thinking of her touching another man sent primal heat racing through me like wildfire. "You're mine, Ariana. Now and always."

A sound from the other side of the atrium made Arian's eyes flare wide, but I clamped a hand over her mouth and didn't stop thrusting into her. "Are you going to be nice and quiet while I fuck you, or do you want them to catch us with your legs spread for me?"

Her eyelids fluttered as she came again, her tight heat clenching me like a vise. I crushed my mouth to hers to keep from bellowing as I exploded inside her, holding myself until the tremors had stopped.

More sounds from behind us made me quickly drop her legs, readjust myself and my uniform, find her pants, and pull them up her legs. Ariana smoothed down the front of her dark jacket as I spotted her black lace panties still on the floor.

I snatched them up and shoved them in my pants pocket. "Ready for initiation?"

She gave me a sly wink and strode ahead of me. "That wasn't it?"

THE WINGS

CHAPTER 68

ARIANA

I CLAPPED AND CHEERED AFTER THE LAST WING WAS GIVEN HIS new insignia and welcomed into the school, meeting Volten's gaze and releasing a breath. It seemed impossible, but we'd done it. We'd made it through the first term and the trials. Even more impossible? The human cadets had made it through and were now moving to the next phase of becoming a Drexian warrior.

Only two humans had been chosen for Wings—one man and one woman—and neither were cadets who'd gone through the maze with us. I wondered where all those cadets had ended up, especially Torq, who'd been so sure he would be a Wing. I'd seen him earlier in his dress uniform, so I knew he'd been slotted into a school, but which one?

I pushed that thought aside as I congratulated the cadets before we all continued to the trial banquet.

When the crowd had thinned. Volten pulled me aside.

"You're insane if you think…"

His throaty laugh stopped me from telling him there was no way he could convince me to sneak off now, and he reached into his pocket. He held up a silver chain with a pendant of the academy's symbol for the Wings dangling from it. "I forgot to give you this earlier. You're a Wing now, so it needs to be official."

My throat closed, and my eyes burned with unexpected tears. "We'll match."

He grinned as he unhooked the necklace and reached behind my neck to close it, bringing him close enough to me that I could breathe in the warm, spicy scent of him that made my insides melt. "You'll match every Wing now."

I'd been initiated, inducted, invested before, but for some reason this intimate gesture of bringing me into the fold of the Wings felt more significant. Maybe because I'd almost died to get to this point, and I'd almost lost someone I couldn't imagine being without.

I touched the cool metal as it lay on the fabric of my dress jacket. "I love it."

Volten touched the pendent, letting his finger touch mine. "How does it feel to be one of us?"

"It feels like I was always supposed to be here and be a Wing." My voice cracked. "For the first time in my entire life, I feel like I'm part of a family. It's not a family by birth, but it's a family I've chosen."

"Chosen families are the ones that sustain us when the other fails." He reached for my free hand, entwining his fingers with mine. "No matter what happens, Ariana, I will always choose you."

I bobbed my head up and down, emotion making it impossible for the words to come out, but I squeezed his hand hard. For the first time since I'd lost my sister, I wasn't haunted by regret. For the first time in a long time, I belonged. For the first time in possibly my entire life, I felt truly loved.

Volten leaned down and kissed me, not a claiming kiss that stole my breath, but a gentle one that conveyed so much tenderness that my breath hitched in my chest. "Ready to celebrate?"

Before I could say yes, I sensed someone watching us. I turned to find Zoran's assistant Tivek. I scanned the straggling Wings in the atrium. "Are we late to the banquet?"

He gave a curt shake of his head. "The admiral wished to speak to you before the festivities started."

Volten was at my side. "Is this about what happened in the maze?"

Another shake of the head. "It is not."

I didn't know why the Academy Master would need to speak to me unless I was being called back to Earth or unless...I cut my gaze to the Drexian who'd had me pinned to the wall earlier. Was this about Volten?

"If you feel more comfortable with the lieutenant accompanying you, he may come."

I reached a hand for Volten as we followed Tivek from the atrium and School of Flight and up the sweeping stairs to the corridor that contained the school offices. The sound of the banquet was already drifting through the air as well as the savory scents of the food.

I waved at Reina as I spotted her in the doorway of the hall, and she gave me an enthusiastic wave back, her hair jiggling. I barely had a chance to debrief with her or Noora since the trials, but I knew they were as relieved as I was that we hadn't lost any of the human cadets we'd trained. I hoped whatever Zoran wanted wouldn't take long since I'd barely eaten since morning, and I was eager to catch up with Fiona and hear about the Assassin's initiation.

Tivek opened the tall door of the admiral's office, stepping aside once the door slid open. He didn't enter after us, instead letting the door close behind him.

Zoran was at his desk with his head down, but he jerked to attention once we were walking toward him. "You both came. Good."

My heart fluttered. If it was good that we'd both come, then this was definitely about our relationship. Before I could launch into a case for why two instructors could be involved without breaking any rules, he held up a hand.

"This is not about the two of you." He allowed a smile to cross his face as he locked eyes with Volten. "I am happy for you, brother. Human females are…quite the challenge."

Volten didn't look at me. "I will not argue with that."

I was on the verge of arguing when Zoran pivoted back to me. "This is about your sister."

My chest constricted. "Sasha?" As if I had another sister, but I couldn't think of anything else to say. What was there to say about a dead fighter pilot?

"I'm not sure if you know, but during the recent Kronock attack, several of their ships crashed on our planet. We were able to scour those ships' records and find some useful intelligence."

I still had no idea how this related to my sister.

Zoran walked from behind the desk as he spoke. "One of the ships in particular had been involved in the attack on Earth. Our experts have been studying the intelligence it provided."

My heart raced. Had they discovered the ship that had shot her down? Did the enemy have records of her fighter being destroyed? If they did, I wasn't sure if I wanted to know.

"We were able to download records about the attack and discover the number of ships that the Kronock vessel hit and how many it destroyed. We also discovered that the enemy took prisoners."

I wrinkled my nose. I hadn't heard about this. The enemy had never reached the surface. How had they taken prisoners? "Prisoners from Earth?"

"The records show that more than one pilot ejected before their ship was blown up, and the Kronock were able to snatch them before they could return to the surface. The fact that our enemy has the technology to do this is new information and relatively alarming, but that's not why you're here."

I shook my head, my ears starting to ring as Volten tightened his grip on my hand.

"Sasha was one of the pilots who was captured." Zoran's voice had become distorted, but I could still make out his words. "She's still alive and being held by the Kronock."

If the admiral continued talking, I didn't hear him. All sound morphed into a deafening roar in my head as I tried to make sense of his words.

My sister wasn't dead.

That was the last thought that echoed in my head before my knees buckled and everything went black.

EPILOGUE

JESS

MY STEPS WERE UNEVEN AS I MADE MY WAY THROUGH THE long tables toward the back of the hall. I'd had too much Drexian wine, and my vision was blurred as I made my way toward fresh air and quiet. More cheers went up around me as cadets celebrated making it through the maze or older cadets celebrated inducting new cadets into their school.

I didn't begrudge anyone their celebration. I was thrilled to have made it into the Assassins, which had been the school I'd always wanted. After the treacherous maze, I would have been happy with anything, although I didn't give myself great odds for lasting long in Blades.

Once I'd reached the end of the tables and emerged from the long hall and into the cooler and less raucous foyer, I took a greedy gulp of air. I walked to the stone banister and leaned against it as I focused on inhaling and exhaling until the dizziness—and urge to vomit all over my polished boots—passed.

"You okay, hon?"

I lifted my head to see long, skinny legs encased in shiny orange pants. Pushing myself up, I took in the rest of Reina's colorful outfit, a multicolored sequined tunic that would have looked at home in a nightclub. I managed to smile at her. "Just getting some fresh air."

"I don't blame you." She let out a high, chirpy laugh. "It's warm with all those celebrating Drexians." She glanced at the insignia on my uniform. "Congratulations on making it through, Cadet."

My weak smile broadened. "Thanks. I'm excited for what comes next, although I think what comes next for me might be bed."

Reina patted my arm. "Why don't I get you some cold water before you decide?" She backed away from me and toward the open doors. "I get the feeling that celebrations here are few and far between, so you might want to savor this one."

I watched her return to the hall, pivoting away and breathing in deeply. The Vexling might be right. The academy did seem heavy on the danger and light on the parties.

I took another few breaths and leaned against the banister again. I did feel better. Maybe I could return and raise a glass with my fellow female cadets one more time before turning in.

"Leaving so soon?"

I pivoted to the voice, startled that it didn't belong to Reina, but relaxing as Torq sauntered from the hall. "Not leaving. Taking a break."

He joined me at the banister, stretching his legs long in front of him and crossing one over the other. "Congratulations on becoming an Assassin."

"Thanks." Now that I wasn't surrounded by the heat of the candles and bodies and the swell of cheering and laughing, my head had cleared. I noticed the gold emblem on his dress jacket. "And to you for becoming a Blade."

He flinched, as if I'd struck him. "I'm the first one in my family to go through the academy and not be a Wing, but since my brother didn't even make it past the first term and some Drexians didn't make it out of the maze, I guess it isn't so bad."

"Are you kidding? I could never be a Blade. They're way too tough and scary."

He grinned. "Tough and scary isn't bad." He leaned closer to me. "You aren't scared of me, are you, Jess?"

His question surprised me, but it wasn't unwarranted. He was twice my size and had always struck me as a predator slowly stalking his prey. I remembered him cornering me at the bottom of the stairs the night before the trials but then I reminded myself of how he'd been in the maze. "Should I be?"

His smile was so silky that I almost didn't catch the narrowing of his eyes. "Not if you give me what I want."

My brain was sluggish, but it wasn't mush. "What?"

He moved quickly, his hands going to either side of me and pinning me in, although his smile hadn't faltered. "I heard what you said in the maze about coaching. I know that you and the other humans got extra help."

I opened my mouth to spin a lie, but he cut me off.

"I have no plans on telling anyone. Who knows? If you hadn't been coached, you all might not have gotten us through those challenges."

Despite what we'd been through together, I didn't believe that he was going to hold his tongue for nothing. Not the way he was eyeing me. "What do you want?"

He let his gaze roam lazily up and down my body before locking it onto my eyes. "Kronock lessons."

I gave my head a shake, not sure I'd heard him right. "You want—?"

"You said you're good at languages. I'm not, but even Blades must pass basic Kronock tests to advance to third year. You tutor me after class in Kronock, and I won't breathe a word of your other after-hours meetings."

My mind had come up with a heap of things he might demand me to do for him, so being asked to tutor the guy was a relief. "That's all?"

He leaned so close that his lips feathered my earlobe and sent a shiver of unwanted desire dancing down my spine. "For now." He took a deep breath as if he was memorizing my scent, before he pulled back, his gaze dark and dangerous. "Then we'll see what else."

THE BLADES

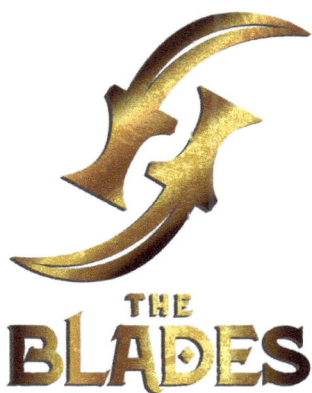

BONUS EPILOGUE

SHE SHOULD BE DEAD.

Some days she wished she was dead, wished she'd gone down with her ship, wished she hadn't been taken captive by the enemy she'd been fighting. But most days, Sasha spent her time planning how many of the hideous Kronock she would kill on her way out of her prison.

"Key guy will die first," she whispered to herself as she paced a circle in her compact cell, her frayed boots slapping the stone floor.

She hoped to strangle him, if for no other reason than to wipe the evil smirk from his elongated snout. Her fingers tingled as she imagined pulling tight enough to watch the life fade from his beady black eye and see the red of his cybernetic implant flicker out.

Once she'd dispatched the alien who held the key to her cell, she would go for the Kronock who stood guard outside the door at the end of the hall. Him she'd like to shoot, but since she didn't have a gun or blaster, she'd settle for cutting his throat.

She could almost smell the sour tang of his blood and feel the warmth of it pour over her hands, which helped her forget the cold of the subterranean prison and the foul, dank scent of rot and fetid water. For a highly sophisticated species with enough advanced tech to attack Earth and break through the Drexian blockade, they had crap prisons.

Sasha spun on one heel and scraped a hand through her long hair. Hair that hung limp and dirty down her back and served as a reminder of how long she'd gone without bathing. Not that it mattered. Not that there was anyone to see her or smell her in the Kronock cells except for the disgusting aliens who'd captured her.

"When I get out, I'm going to kill every fucking one of you." She didn't bother to whisper this since she was the only occupant of the cells and even key guy had gone on a break.

It felt good to think about what she would do when she escaped. It felt good to imagine killing her captors. It felt good to envision taking her revenge. Plotting her campaign of vengeance was the only way she'd been able to stay sane.

If Sasha allowed her mind to quiet, if she allowed herself to dwell on her situation and the chances of ever escaping, she'd go mad. Luckily, she'd been trained to plan and to plot and to never accept defeat. That was as much from her father as from her military training, but she also didn't want to think about her family too much.

Her throat tightened as an image of Ariana popped into her brain, the pain of regret and the ache of loneliness almost buckling her knees. What was her sister doing? Was she searching for her? Was she raising hell and raising an army to come after her?

Even though Ariana had always been chasing after her achievements and ignoring her advice, Sasha knew her sister wouldn't abandon her to the enemy. She wouldn't let her fester in captivity. *If* she knew that Sasha had survived.

Her heart hammered in her chest as she considered the very real possibility that no one knew that she'd survived her ship exploding, no one knew she'd been taken captive, no one knew where she was.

Sasha shook her head so hard her ears rang. She refused to believe that. She refused to give in to despair. She refused to accept that she'd live out her days in the rank darkness of a Kronock prison. She refused.

She took jerky steps to the long metal bench bolted into the wall and sank onto it. There wasn't much to be grateful for, but at least she was alive. She was alive, and she hadn't been tortured or experimented on or starved. And as long as she was alive, she had a chance.

"Come on, Sash." She could almost hear her sister's teasing voice in her head. "Don't give up now."

The challenge made her spine straighten and her resolve harden. This was not the end of her story. Not by a long shot. All she had to do was figure out how to kill a few Kronock.

"Strangle key guy, then cut door guy's throat." Returning to her plan gave her comfort. She stood and resumed her pacing. "Steal a blaster and take out the external guards…"

Her litany of murder was interrupted by the scraping of metal and the creaking of hinges as the door at the end of the cell block opened. Sasha stopped pacing and peered through the dim lighting , bracing herself for key guy's return. He rarely spoke, but just his presence made her shiver.

Instead of the hulking, scaly Kronock taking his post inside the door, a smaller figure was shoved through the opening. She squinted to make out the silhouette of a male. Then her shoulders sagged with relief when she realized that the guy was too big to be a human. At least the enemy hadn't snatched more of her fellow soldiers.

Sasha held her breath as the new prisoner was half pushed, half dragged down the hallway by key guy and door guy. Every struggle gained the captive a fresh blow from the Kronock, and by the time they opened a cell for him, he practically fell into it.

"Enjoy the company." Key guy directed this at her, his guttural language made intelligible by her universal translator implant.

Sasha didn't respond. She'd learned not to engage with her captors. She was saving all her clever quips for when she killed them.

The new prisoner didn't stir as the cell bars clanged shut behind him. He didn't move as the jailers stomped away, their long tails dragging on the stone. He didn't even flinch when the heavy door at the end of the hall slammed closed and the sound echoed off the low ceiling.

Sasha wondered if they'd hit him one too many times, and she took stealthy steps toward the bars between them. If he was dead, it was going to be very unpleasant to have him decay in the cell next to hers. "Please don't be dead."

A deep rumble made her jump. Had he laughed?

"It takes more than that to kill me, sweetheart."

Sasha bristled. Sweetheart? Who the hell was this guy? From the flickering light over the door at the end of the hall, she could make out dark hair cut close to his head and tattoos covering half of his bare back. Then she spotted the bumps running the length of his spine. "Are you Drexian?"

He stood to face her, revealing even more black ink covering his muscular chest and scruff dusting his cheeks. His eyes flashed an inhuman shade of gold that reminded her of a wild cat. "Even better, beautiful. I'm Inferno Force."

JOIN THE ACADEMY!

Want to take the quiz and find out if you're an Assassin, a Blade, an Iron, or a Wing (and get special initiation bonuses)?

Go to the quiz> www.tanastone.com/legacy-quiz

ALSO BY TANA STONE

The Barbarians of the Sand Planet Series:
BOUNTY (also available in AUDIO)
CAPTIVE (also available in AUDIO)
TORMENT (also available on AUDIO)
TRIBUTE (also available as AUDIO)
SAVAGE (also available in AUDIO)
CLAIM (also available on AUDIO)
CHERISH: A Holiday Baby Short (also available on AUDIO)
PRIZE (also available on AUDIO)
SECRET
RESCUE (appearing first in PETS IN SPACE #8)

ALIEN & MONSTER ONE-SHOTS:
ROGUE (also available in AUDIO)
VIXIN: STRANDED WITH AN ALIEN
SLIPPERY WHEN YETI
CHRISTMAS WITH AN ALIEN
YOOL

Raider Warlords of the Vandar Series:
POSSESSED (also available in AUDIO)
PLUNDERED (also available in AUDIO)
PILLAGED (also available in AUDIO)
PURSUED (also available in AUDIO)
PUNISHED (also available on AUDIO)
PROVOKED (also available in AUDIO)
PRODIGAL (also available in AUDIO)
PRISONER
PROTECTOR
PRINCE

THE SKY CLAN OF THE TAORI:
SUBMIT (also available in AUDIO)
STALK (also available on AUDIO)
SEDUCE (also available on AUDIO)
SUBDUE
STORM

All the TANA STONE books available as audiobooks!
INFERNO FORCE OF THE DREXIAN WARRIORS:
IGNITE on AUDIBLE
SCORCH on AUDIBLE
BURN on AUDIBLE
BLAZE on AUDIBLE
FLAME on AUDIBLE

RAIDER WARLORDS OF THE VANDAR:
POSSESSED on AUDIBLE
PLUNDERED on AUDIBLE
PILLAGED on AUDIBLE
PURSUED on AUDIBLE
PUNISHED on AUDIBLE
PROVOKED on AUDIBLE

BARBARIANS OF THE SAND PLANET
BOUNTY on AUDIBLE
CAPTIVE on AUDIBLE
TORMENT on AUDIBLE
TRIBUTE on AUDIBLE
SAVAGE on AUDIBLE
CLAIM on AUDIBLE
CHERISH on AUDIBLE

ABOUT THE AUTHOR

Tana Stone is a bestselling sci-fi romance author who loves sexy aliens and independent heroines. Her favorite superhero is Thor (with Aquaman a close second because, well, Jason Momoa), her favorite dessert is key lime pie (okay, fine, *all* pie), and she loves Star Wars and Star Trek equally. She still laments the loss of *Firefly*.

She has one husband, two teenagers, and two neurotic cats. She sometimes wishes she could teleport to a holographic space station like the one in her tribute brides series (or maybe vacation at the oasis with the sand planet barbarians). :-)

She loves hearing from readers! Email her any questions or comments at tana@tanastone.com.

Want to hang out with Tana in her private Facebook group? Join on all the fun at: www.facebook.com/groups/tanastonestributes.